Bernhard Tauchnitz

Chandos a Novel by Ouida

Bernhard Tauchnitz

Chandos a Novel by Ouida

ISBN/EAN: 9783741172533

Manufactured in Europe, USA, Canada, Australia, Japa

Cover: Foto ©Andreas Hilbeck / pixelio.de

Manufactured and distributed by brebook publishing software
(www.brebook.com)

Bernhard Tauchnitz

Chandos a Novel by Ouida

COLLECTION

OF

BRITISH AUTHORS

TAUCHNITZ EDITION.

VOL. 1156.

CHANDOS BY OUIDA

IN TWO VOLUMES.

VOL. 2.

LEIPZIG: BERNHARD TAUCHNITZ.

PARIS: C. REINWALD & Cⁱᵉ, 15, RUE DES SAINTS PÈRES.

COLLECTION

OF

BRITISH AUTHORS

TAUCHNITZ EDITION.

VOL. 1156.

CHANDOS BY OUIDA.

IN TWO VOLUMES.

VOL. II.

CHANDOS.

A NOVEL.

BY

OUIDA,

AUTHOR OF "IDALIA," "TRICOTRIN," "PUCK."

COPYRIGHT EDITION.

IN TWO VOLUMES.

VOL. II.

LEIPZIG

BERNHARD TAUCHNITZ

1871.

The Right of Translation is reserved.

CHANDOS.

BOOK THE FIFTH.

CHAPTER I.

In Exile.

IT was sunset in Venice,—that supreme moment when the magical flush of light transfigures all, and wanderers whose eyes have long ached with the greyness and the glare of northward cities gaze and think themselves in heaven. The still waters of the lagunes, the marbles and the porphyry and the jasper of the mighty palaces, the soft grey of the ruins all covered with clinging green and the glowing blossoms of creepers, the hidden antique nooks where some woman's head leaned out of an arched casement, like a dream of the Dandolo time when the Adriatic swarmed with the returning galleys laden with Byzantine spoil, the dim, mystic, majestic walls that towered above the gliding surface of the eternal water, once alive with flowers, and music, and the gleam of golden tresses, and the laughter of careless revellers in the Venice of Goldoni, in the Venice of the Past;—everywhere the sunset glowed with the marvel of its colour, with the wonder of its warmth.

Then a moment, and it was gone. Night fell with the hushed shadowy stillness that belongs to Venice alone; and in the place of the riot and luxuriance of colour there was the tremulous darkness of the young night, with the

beat of an oar on the water, the scent of unclosing carnation-buds, the white gleam of moonlight, and the odour
of lilies-of-the-valley blossoming in the dark archway of
some mosaic-lined window.

One massive and ancient house towered up amidst
many another palace,—a majestic, melancholy place, with
shafts of black marble and columns of porphyry, and deep
sea-piles that the canal bathed into a hundred umber
tints. Long ago some of the greatest of the oligarchy
had held there their highest state; now it was scarcely
habited, left to decay, and lost in gloom,—a sepulchre of
dead glories, while the insolence of foreign mirth and
the shame of foreign arms outraged the captive and
widowed beauty of the Adriatic spouse. It was lonely
and unspeakably desolate; with the gliding sheet of the
still water beneath its walls, and the long sombre lines of
forsaken palaces stretching beyond it on either side, and
facing it in the splendour of the early moon. Yet it was
infinitely impressive, infinitely grand, standing there with
its mediæval sculptures touched with rays of starlight,
and its costly marbles washed by the ebbing of the tide.

At one of its lofty, narrow casements a man leaned
out into the fragrant spring-tide air; he had risen from
close studies in the chamber within—vast in space as a
king's throne-room, barren in garniture as a contadina's
hut—to watch the fading of the sun, the sudden loss of
all the wealth of colour in the grey hues of evening; and
he lingered still, now that the night had wholly fallen.
In that stillness, in that soft lapping of the water, in that
glisten in the distance of the silvery lagune, in that
scarcely-stirring wind filled with the breath of opening
blossoms, there was a lulling charm,—there was the echo
of a long-lost youth.

His face was of a great beauty; though many years

had passed over it, time could touch and could dim it but
little; but in the eyes there was the exile's weariness and
the deep thought of the scholar; on the mouth there was
that look which comes of bitter pain borne, of strong victories wrung from calumny and poverty and hard defiance,—such a look as Dante might have worn, yet less
harsh, though not less mournful, than the Florentine's.
He looked down on the deep and sleeping shadows, on
the gliding darkness of the canal below; the sweetness of
the young night, the Adriatic fragrance of the sea-wafted
air, brought him a thousand memories across the desert
of long years.

Through his mind floated such thoughts as wearied
Cleon:—

> " Indeed, to know is something, and to prove
> How all this beauty might be enjoy'd is more ;
> But, knowing naught, to enjoy is something too.
> Yon rower with the moulded muscles there,
> Lowering the sail, is nearer it than I."

There had been a time when every breath of life
had been for him enjoyment, rich as the god's life of
Dionysus. In moments such as these he longed for that
dead time, as the poet Ovid, in the ice and winter storms
and snow-bound forests of his Danubian exile, longed for
the golden sunlight, for the purple pomp, for the glad
idolatry of the vine-crowned land that knew his place no
more.

"Am I any nearer the ambitions of my youth than I
was twenty years ago?—am I as near?" he thought. In
the voluptuous hush and fragrance of the Venetian night
his years seemed cold and fruitless and heavy-laden.

Where he stood, in the dark arch of the window, the
measured music of oars beat the water; beneath the walls
several gondolas glided; on the silence rose, chaunted by
the mellow voices of young Venetians, a hymn of liberty.

They might pay to their tyrants well-nigh with life for its singing; yet that knowledge gave no tremor to the cadence that rang so bold and so clear in the stillness. Passionate, yet unspeakably sad, rich as the world of colour that had just passed from the world, but melancholy as the breathless stillness of the calm lagunes, the ode of freedom was sung by the lips of those who knew themselves slaves,—young, fresh voices, the voices of youth and of vivid ambition, yet touched to a deeper meaning and vibrating with a hopeless desire; for they were the voices also of forbidden hope, and of thoughts held in bond and enchained. It was the "Io triumphe" of liberty,—

> "Thou huntress swifter than the Moon! thou terror
> Of the world's wolves! thou bearer of the quiver,
> Whose sun-like shafts pierce tempest-tossèd error
> As light may pierce the clouds:"

but also it was the lament of Leopardi,—the lament most weary, most utterly desolate, of all upon earth,—the lament of men whose hearts ache for lofty aims and noble fields, and whose lives are denied all purpose and all effort,— of men whose country is in thraldom.

The chaunt ceased; all the many and melodious tones which had risen on the night and swelled louder and sweeter down the canal, till the boatmen far off heard the echo and gave it back, were suddenly silenced, as a choir of song-birds will cease at noontide. In the prow of the foremost vessel a young Venetian rose, the gleam of his auburn hair and the kindling light on his face like some old painter's Gabriel or Michael yonder in the gloom of the ancient churches. He lifted his eyes to the arch of the casement where he stood up in the white, tremulous lustre of the moon.

"You have striven for the freedom of thought and for the liberty of judgment," he said, simply. "Venice, who has lost them both, loves you for that which you have loved, and gives you thus the only homage she now dares."

Without pause, without a word more, the rowers bent above their oars, the gondolas floated down the dark surface, the young impassioned faces of the singers turned backward with a fond and reverent farewell as their vessels swept into the shadows, so deep, so rayless, underneath the walls of the abandoned palaces: it was all they had to give, that song of freedom in a fettered land.

He to whom they gave it thought it more than the gift of crowns laid at his feet. It touched him strangely with its suddenness, with its meaning,—this gratitude rendered to him by the young, pure, patriot-voices of those who might pay the cost of that night's utterance with the pain of captive's bondage or of exile's banishment. It was more worth to him than any diadem with which the world could have anointed him,—this recognition of what he sought, this knowledge of why he laboured.

It came to him as answer and rebuke to the thoughts which had been with him as that unbidden music rose upon the night. To enjoy was much; but to seek truth and labour for freedom might be more.

"One fetter of tradition loosened, one web of superstition broken, one ray of light let in on darkness, one principle of liberty secured, are worth the living for," he mused. "Fame!—it is the flower of a day, that dies when the next sun rises. But to do something, however little, to free men from their chains, to aid something, however faintly, the rights of reason and of truth, to be unvanquished through all and against all, these may bring one nearer the pure ambitions of youth. Happiness dies as age comes to us; it sets for ever, with the suns of early years: yet perhaps we may keep a higher thing beside which it holds but a brief loyalty, if to ourselves we can rest true, if for the liberty of the world we can do anything."

For he was one of those who to the cause of freedom and of truth bring the wealth of their intellect and the years of their life, and receive but little requital save a sullen reverence wrung from an unwilling world, and the railing bitterness of the crowds who abhor light and hug error and tradition close. His words stirred with shame the hearts of nations steeped in lust and lethargy and the greed of gold; and they awoke to hoot and hiss the one who dared rouse them from their torpor or arrest them in their money-changing. His thoughts sank down into the unworn hearts of youth, and they shook themselves free from the ashes of superstition and the chains of creeds; and the priests of superstition cursed him. His utterance probed the surface of the world, and, piercing its panoply of wordy falsehood, brought to it the clear, keen light of scepticism and truth; and the world was weary of him, it slept so much more soundly beneath the veil and in the darkness. He loved men with a pity and a tolerance no trial could exhaust; he would have led them, if he could, to the search and to the knowledge of other things than their gold-thirst and their paradise of lies; and they turned back to their treasuries of money, to their granaries of hypocrisies, and would have none of him. Their ears were wilfully deaf, their eyes were wilfully blind, their feet loved the trodden paths, their hands were busy grasping their neighbours' goods; they wondered at and they reviled him; they would not follow to the mountain air he bade them breathe; they stayed in the mud, seeking a coin. He was alone. The world gave him fame grudgingly, reluctantly, because it could not withhold it longer; but it left him alone and condemned because he saw no holiness in the shrine of gold, and no right divine in the tyranny of tradition.

He was alone; eagles that love the high light-penetrated air, that has no mist and clog of earth-born dust, must ever dwell in solitude. Yet now and then there came to him, as there had come from the voices of fettered men to-night, an echo of his own thoughts, a recognition of his own labours, and these sufficed to him.

They who labour justly for the sheer sake of truth find no present reward: will they hereafter find it? A weary question;—one to which men never yet have gained an answer.

CHAPTER II.
In Triumph.

THE stars, as they shone on Venice, shone likewise farther northward on one of the mighty, labyrinthine, ink-black cities of labour. The heavy pall of smoke loomed over the forests of roof, of chimneys, of factories, of churches; the bells of the latter were chiming with incessant, joyous, pealing clangour, bells that rung a chime called of God every seventh day in the midst of the worship of Mammon, bells put up in many a steeple, iron offerings to Deity by iron hands that wrung the last bitter drop out of poverty, and clammed the last starveling of labour, and bought redemption cheaply by a sop to a parish priest.

The bells were rhyming wildly, with no pretence, happily, that it was in the honour of Godhead now,— tossing upward through the weight of murky air wave on wave of changing sound, of riotous triumph, of passionate, mirthful, random, uncouth music like the harmony of Thor's great hammers. Under the sea of iron-echoing noise vast crowds pressed tumultuous, in a grim triumph

like that of the metal melodies. Their hard, keen, indomitable faces were sharp-set as the knives they made,
were massive as the iron they worked; and on them was
the flush and the pride of victory. It was on the night
of a great election, an election that had followed in
Lenten time on a sudden and unlooked-for dissolution,—
an appeal to the country as agitating as it had been un-
foreseen; and they had brought to the fore their champion,
their idol, the most famous of all his party. In this vast
city of Darshampton there was but one name and but one
sovereignty,—his. The people had crowned him; and
who should dare to discrown?

In one of the chambers of a magnificent hotel, he
stood in the dusky red glow of the sunset that burned
through the smoke-laden atmosphere and fell about his
feet as though it too were eager to seek him out and
smile on him,—this man, omnipotent in all he undertook.
A crowd of friends were about him, breathless in con-
gratulation on what was but a repeated triumph, waiting
in delighted warmth of welcome on one in whom they
saw a deity more potent than all the gods of Semitic or
Achæan creeds,—the deity of a supreme Success. Throngs
had been about him from earliest days,—throngs of friends,
of flatterers, of men who believed in him honestly and
would have fought for him to the death had need been,
—of men who believed in nothing except the divinity of
success, and followed that idolatrously in him because
they saw his acumen never fail, his fortune never change.
The city would give him its banquet to-night; his party
brought him devoted gratitude and ecstatic pride, the
country bestowed on him scarce less admiration; young
men looked to him as their leader, elder looked to him to
reap the harvest of the seed they had sown in the future; the
aristocracy dreaded, the plutocracy bribed, the multitude

adored him. He was a great man already; later on he would be a greater,—popular beyond all conception, triumphant in whatever he essayed.

The shouts and the cheers of the populace swelled louder and louder; the clamour was hoarse, Titanic, almost terrible in its imperative power, as the voice of the People always is when once it thunders through the land, —imperative for murder as imperative for bread, mighty and resistless alike in both. Here it rose with one accord, with one word,—his own name. *They* had brought him in,—those men with their horny, supple hands, and their blackened, resolute brows, and their limbs like the limbs of the old Bersærkers, those men of the Black Country, who grasped so doggedly at truths sharp as steel, yet grasped but at half-truths, and, so blinded, reached but hatred of an Order when they thought they grasped at liberty for Mankind. The shouts swelled louder and louder, more and more full of peremptory demand; they had brought him through, or thought they had, and clamoured for their idol.

He humoured them ever, as a lion-tamer humours his cubs, that he may cut the claws and grind smooth the teeth and make the brave beast lie down passive as a spaniel at his beck, and turn to profit the world's terror when he shows how docilely he guides the wild, tawny, desert-king, that at his bidding would leap forth and tear and slay.

He went out on the balcony, and the din of the acclamations rolled up to the red evening skies like thunder. In the large square before the building, and in the transverse streets that crossed and met, the dense multitudes were gathered, wave on wave of human life, surging in in swift succession, and stretching far and wide away beyond the sight, like a stormy and restless sea. Their dark faces, swarthy and begrimed, shrewd and stern, were turned upward to the balcony with an eager pride and pleasure, while from the brawny chests of the iron-workers that tremendous welcome rang. The sun shone more burnished red in the crimson, heavy west, and, slanting in broad, glowing, dusky streams of light athwart the misty gloom, fell on that ocean of upraised faces, and across the eyes of the man they honoured,—eyes so keen, so mirthful, so unerring, so full of sagacious life, of triumphant victory.

"He is the man for the Future," said one stalwart worker, with the breath of the furnace-blasts and the blackness of the iron-foundry upon him, yet who read Bentham, and Fourier, and Mill.

One, less book-wise and more world-wise, pierced nearer to the secret of success, to the root of popularity, as he answered,

"He's more: he's the man for the Present."

"And the man for the People!" shouted a third, behind them. The words were caught up and echoed on all sides, till they ran through the packed thousands like electric fluid, till from the whole of the swaying gigantic mass the words broke unanimously, rising high above the pealing of the bells and the strife of the streets, hurling his name out in that grim, passionate, furious love of a multitude which has ever in it something, and wellnigh as much, of menace as of caress.

He nodded to them with a pleasant, familiar smile, —such a smile as a boy gives to his favourite and unruly dogs; then he stood more forward against the iron scrollwork of the balcony, looking down on that movement beneath him, and spoke.

Not for the first time here, in Darshampton, by many, the ringing, metallic, clarion-roll of the voice they knew so well stilled them like magic, thrilled them as hounds thrill at the notes of a horn, and held them in check as the horn holds the pack. He spoke as only those can speak who have been long trained to the public arena, who have studied every technicality of their science and every weakness of their audience, who have brought to it not only the talent of native skill, but the polish of long usage, the power of assured practice. He spoke well,—keen, trenchant, vigorous, humorous oratory, English to the backbone, coarse in its pungency, withal, here, as it could be scholarly elsewhere, striking to the heart of its subject as surely and as straightly as the arrow of Tell to the core of the apple. There was a breathless silence while he spoke, the trumpet-like tones of his ringing voice penetrating without effort to the farthermost of the listening throngs, the Swift-like humour and wit shaking sardonic laughter from the brawny chests of his hearers, the biting and incisive reasoning drawn in by them as eagerly as town-dusted lungs draw in the salt, fresh breezes of the sea. He was their master, though they thought themselves his electors and creators; and he played at will on them, as a strong, skilled hand plays on a stringed instrument, moving it to what cadence he chooses. They listened in devoted silence, only broken by tumultuous cheering, or by the hoarse, gaunt laughter that was ominous as any curses raised against what they hated. He spoke long, though so succinctly, so pungently, that the minutes of his speech seemed moments; then ceased, while the red sun-glow still strayed to his feet, and the chimes of the bells swung wild delight, and the shouts of the populace teeming below deafened the air with his name.

He laughed to himself as he bowed many times his thanks and his farewell, then sauntered from the balcony into the lighted and crowded room, glancing back at that shifting sea of upraised, earnest, hard-lined faces in the dusky heat of the fading sun.

"D—d rascals, every one of you, my friends," he thought, "or out-and-out-fools; God knows which. Rave about oppression and the wrongs of Capital to Labour, while you send your children to sweat, at five years old, in furnaces, and threaten to kill your brother if he don't join your trade-union and strike when he's told; clamour for the rights of man, and worry your brains after political economics, while you think all the 'rights' centre in scribbling your name in a poll-book and talking mild sedition in a tap-room! Oh, you precious fools! how we use you, and how we laugh at you!"

For he was not even wholly true to those who were so true to him; and he had no belief even in their thorough, heartfelt earnestness, erring from imperfect vision, and distorted from imperfect education, but sincere and true in its widest errors.

They thought they had made him what he was; he knew that they were his tools, his wax, his weapons.

He glanced back once on to the vast, oscillating crowd in the reddening angry sunset mist, and the laugh of a consummated victory, the insolence of a secure triumph, were in the backward flash of his eyes, mingled, too, with a certain proud power, a certain exultation of self-achieved distinction. His name was still echoing to the skies from the lungs of the close-packed throngs.

"Who dare sneer at that name now!" he thought; and there was in that thought the glow which Themistocles felt when they who had exiled him as a nameless thing of the people, to wrestle with the base-born in the Ring of Cynosarges, welcomed him in the city of the Violet Crown as the victor of Salamis, the slayer of Persia.

Then he went within from the stormy clangour and the scarlet flush of evening, and was feasted through that night by the men of the mighty town, nobles who hated him bearing their part in his honour, rivers of wine flowing to his toast, the crowds of the streets knowing no theme but his present and his future, the nation on the morrow saying, as the city said to-night, "He is a great man; he will be a still greater."

BOOK THE SIXTH.

CHAPTER I.

"Primavera! Gioventu dell' Anno!"

Down at the foot of the mountain-slopes reaching to Vallombrosa, hidden away in the deep belt of the chestnut-forests, was a little Tuscan village. Sheltered high above by the pines of the hills, and veiled from every glance by the thick masses of the chestnut-leaves, no strange foot ever scarcely wandered to it. It was out of the route of travellers; it had slumbered here for ages: it had been here when Milton looked on the Val d'Arno; it had been here when Totila thundered at the gates of Rome; it had been here when Plautus caught in the colour of his words the laughter, the mirth, the tavern-wit, the girls *à libre allure*, the wine-brawls, and the Bacchan feasts of the Latin life; it had been here through all changes, but it had never changed. Belike, it had been sacked by Cæsar, razed by Theodoric, visited by Stilicho, plundered by the Franks of Carl; but it was still the same, surviving all ruin, and covered in the spring-time with so dense a leafy shade that the grey tint of its stone, the red brown of its few roofs, showed no more than the oriole's nest through the boughs. The purple plums of the olives ripened and were gathered, the red osiers changed to tender green, the grapes were garnered with the vintage-tide, the cattle came down the hill-sides when the sun sank low, the chestnuts turned to ruddy brown and broke their husks and fell upon the moss; a few lives were born, a few lives were buried. These were all the changes known there, the changes of the night and day, of the seasons of the year, and of the coming of life and of death. The light of the after-glow shone on it, the scorch of the later summer parched its fields and woods, the snows of winter lay upon its hilltop and gleamed between the darkness of its pines, the breath of the spring breathed the flower-glory over its land, and uncurled the white spiral blossom of its arums in the water-bed; but through wars and rumours of wars, through the Campaign of Italy as through the wars of the Great Captain, through the ravages of the Cinque Cento as through the raids of the Goths and the Gauls, the little woodland nook of Fontane Amorose remained unaltered, as though the foot of Dionysus when it had pressed its sward had bidden its blossoms keep an eternal bloom, and the Dryads and the Satyrs, driven from every other ancient haunt, still lived beneath the green fronds of its trailing plants, and laughed amidst the bronzed gold of its autumn vines.

It was in the "mezza notte d'Aprile," beloved of painters, hymned of poets, which makes of all the Southern land one fresh and laughing garden. Upward yonder, higher still on the hills, there was some little chillness lingering still, and the air blew keener through the aisles of pines; but here, midway in the sloping of rich mossy greensward, deeply sheltered by its beeches and chestnuts and by the slopes of its fir-woods, the delicious spring of Italy was

in its fairest, with the purple orchid glowing in the noon,
and the delicate wind-flower fanned by the breeze, and
the young buds of the vine opening in the clear and
perfect light. A few miles from the clustering dwellings
of Fontane was a grove of beech-trees, always, save at
the height of noon, dark as twilight; for the branches
were dense, and the trees towered massive and many.
Yet in the heart of them was a nook fit for the couch
of a Naiad,—fit to have had laid down in it the fair lifeless limbs of Adonis. In the shade of the leaves the moss
and grass were ever fresh; the sun-tan of midsummer
never brought drought there; anemones and violets, and
all wild flowers that bloom in Tuscan woods, filled it
with odour and colour, and through it welled the bright
clear water of a broken fountain, so old that underneath
its moss might still be traced the half-effaced Latin in-
scription. By it perhaps Virgil once had learned, or Claudian rhymed his epic; at its spring the beautiful evil lips
of Antonina might have drunk, or, lying beside them,
Lucretius might have thought of the Etrurian shades,
looking far down into those deep, rayless aisles of beech,
sublime and sad as his own genius. Where the water
rippled, losing itself among the mosses and the orchids,
a glory of sunlight came, touching to silver the wing of
a wood-pigeon poised to drink, lending a warmer blush
to the white wild rose as the rifling bee hummed far
down in its violated chalice, and shedding its ripe gold
on the hair of a young girl leaning motionless there.

The birds, fearless of her presence, paused in their
flight to glance at her; the nightingales, thinking it night
in the beech-shadows yonder, sung her their softest songs;
the butterflies alighted on the flowers her hands held;
they knew her well, they loved her; they were her only
playmates in the long Italian day. Arum lilies, and the

pale-green blossoms of the ivy, and anemones glowing crimson, and the emerald coils of moss, were in a loose sheaf on her lap; she sat in a day-dream, watching the mystical flow of the water as though its patient music could sing her the hymn of her future.

She was very young, but on her beauty was the Tuscan glow; and she had already the tall, slender, yielding, voluptuous form of the South. In the hair, like a chestnut that has the fleck of the sunlight upon it, in the deep eyes with their blue-black lustre and their dreamy passionate lids, in the lips so soft, so proud, so mournful, in the brow, broad and thoughtful like an antique, in the brilliance and the light upon the face, were all the Southern types: it was only in the fairness of the skin that something more Northern might have been fancied; in all else it was the rich and sunlit loveliness of Italy.

Her hand rested on the stone that bore the Latin words, all covered now with the wild growth of ivy; her gaze rested on the water sparkling so bright in sunshine here, flowing so dark beneath the grasses there; the sheaf of woodland wealth rested listlessly on her lap. She leaned there, in her childhood's carelessness, in the classic solitude, against the black shades of the beech-woods that closed her in as in a temple, and only let the flood of sun pour down across the ruined Roman fountain and the countless flowers at her feet.

She was fair as Sappho while yet love was unknown and a child's laughter amidst the roses of Ionia was only hushed now and then by vague and prescient dreams; she was fair as Héloïse while yet only the grand serenity of the Greek scroll lay opened before her eyes and no voice beside her had taught a lore more fatal and a mystery more mournful than the wise words of Hellas.

She was very lovely, motionless here where no sound

came except the lulling of the water and the gliding
noise of a bird's wing, where the tender green blossoming vines hung coiled above her head, and where the
deep bronze of the beech-belt drew round her the gloom
of the night.

Where she leaned thus, one passing through the
denseness of that gloom saw her, unseen himself, and
paused; he thought of Proserpine among the flowers ere
the cruelty of fate fell on her. The young life and the
grass-grown ruin, the aisle of colour and sunlight, and
the mass of enclosing shade, were a picture and a poem
in one,—the gladness of a Greek idyl, with the mystic
darkness of a Northern Saga.

Once he would have lingered there, drawn the ivy-
wreaths from the hands, wooed the eyes from their musing gaze, paused beside her in the leafy peace—once, in
the days of his youth. Now he looked an instant, thought
how fair she was, and passed onward down his lonely
path far into the beechen shadows.

CHAPTER II.
Castalia.

SUDDENLY, without a warning, the radiance of the
late day clouded. Before the mules could patter along
the stony roads, before the contadine could reach homeward as they came from antique Pelago, before the workers
could leave the olive-fields and vineyards, before the mild-
eyed oxen of the Apennine could be driven through the
rank hill-grass, without warning, the mighty clouds gathered, the night fell, the fires ran down the heavens, the
storm broke.

Through it, as best he might, he who had an hour or
two before passed through the moss-grown path of the
beech-woods, made his backward way. It was now peril

to life and limb to be out in its fury; the melon-plants
were torn up by their roots, the twisted olives writhed
into tenfold contortion, the peaceful bubbling waters
turned into angry torrents, the young trees were uprooted
and hurled down the steep descents; the darkness was
impenetrable, except when the lightning lit the whole
land in its glare, and the rushing of stones and of boughs
and of saplings, as the winds tore them up and whirled
them on its blast, roared with a thunder only drowned
in the peals that shook from hill to hill and echoed
through the solitudes of the forest.

He could not even tell his road; he had lost its certainty in the blackness around. Unknown to himself, he
had wandered back once more into the beech-glades, and
was lost in their impenetrable shades, instead of holding
on his upward road along the hill-side through the pines.
As he went, feeling his way slowly through the dense hot
gloom, he trod on some fallen thing that his foot crushed
ere he felt it. He stopped and stooped to it; he thought
it might be some frightened hare or some large bird struck
in the storm and entangled in the yielding, clinging moss.
The darkness was dark as that of a moonless midnight;
he had no sense to guide him but the sense of touch.
The grasses and the flowers, all bruised and beaten, met
his hand; then, as it moved farther, it wandered to the
loose trail of some floating hair, and passed over the
warmth of human lips and the outline of a woman's cheek
and bosom. He thought of the Tuscan child whom he
had seen in the sunset light.

The heavy tresses lay in his hand; he could not tell
whether she were living or dead, she was so still in the
darkness. He passed his hand gently over her brow, she
did not move; he spoke, she did not hear; he drew her
loosened dress over her uncovered chest, she did not feel

his touch. There was warmth from the lips on his palm, there was a faint pulsation in the heart as he sought for its throb; that was all. Else she lay, as one dead, at his feet in the blackness of the driving storm, in the din of the echoing thunder.

The fire flashed from the cleft skies; the blaze of an intolerable light poured down. In it he saw her, and the broken stone of the Latin ruins, with the water gliding into its deep, still pool. He paused a moment, leaning over her with the thick wealth of the hair lying in his hand; he could not leave her, and succour there was none. With little thought, save such an impulse of pity as that in which a man might raise a fawn his shot had struck, or a song-bird his foot had trodden on, he stooped and raised her in his arms. Her head fell back, her limbs were powerless, she lay passive and unconscious in his hold; forsaken here, she must perish; death was abroad in every blast, in every flash. He hesitated no more, but leaned her brow against his breast, and, thus weighted, went on his toilsome and perilous way through the beech-glades. He knew his road now; that was much: and he was not very far from his own home. He forced his passage slowly and with difficulty through the denseness of the woods. It was a tedious and dangerous toil. But still as he went he sheltered her, and he pierced his road at length through the aisles of the beech-wilderness till he came into the broken arches of what had once been stately Roman courts. So far near his refuge, he paused a second to take rest; the vivid lightnings filled the arcade with their glow, the peal of the storm rolled above; he leaned against a marble shaft and looked down on his burden. Her head rested on his breast as peacefully as though she slept upon her mother's heart; the long dark lashes swept her cheek; her lips were slightly parted with a warmer breath. There was a touching sanctity in the unconscious rest, a plaintive appeal in the extreme youth and in its death-like calm.

"Poor child!" he thought, "she may live to wish she had been abandoned there to die in the peace of her childhood."

In other years his lips would have called back the sleeping life with a caress; now he looked on her with a passionless pity, gentle because profoundly sad, sad because she had so much youth, and that youth was a woman's.

Then he went onward through the shattered arches that were canopied and covered with impenetrable ivy and feathery grasses tinted to every hue in the flashings of the light, and entered by a low side-door the first court of a Latin villa half in ruins, crossed the court, and passed into the first chamber. It was long and lofty, and had in it the decay of greatness; fragments of a perfect sculpture were upon the walls, a fresco in hues fair as though painted but yesterday covered the ceiling, the pavement was of mosaic marbles; these were all of its old classic glories that time had left untouched: for the rest, it was an artist's studio, a student's library, strewn with papers and with books, with here and there a cast or bronze, at the far end a lectern with a vellum manuscript open upon its wings, and in the midst an Etruscan lamp swinging from on high and shedding a subdued silvery light and a soft perfume on the gloom. Here he brought her, and laid her gently down upon the cushions of a couch. She knew nothing of what was done with her. He went to a flask of Montepulciano standing near, poured some of the wine out, and touched her lips with it. She drank a little, by mere instinct; the warmth revived her; her lids trembled, then unclosed, and her eyes looked out with a dreamy, bewildered sightlessness.

"What is it? Where am I?"

"Have no fear, my child; you are safe now. I found you in the storm, and brought you here."

Her glance met his; consciousness came to her.

"You saved my life, eccellenza! How can I thank you?"

"By telling me you are unhurt."

She looked at him with that awed wistfulness, that earnest wondering gratitude, of a child.

He touched the bright masses of her hair, moving them back from her brow—she was so young; he caressed her with his hand as he would a wounded bird.

"I fear you are in pain? There is a bruise on your temple; and you were senseless when I found you. Do you suffer now?"

"Oh, no! not much. You brought me from the forest? How good! how merciful!"

She stooped her head with the supple grace of the South, and kissed his hand with the reverent supplication and thanksgiving of a young slave to her owner. He drew it from her quickly.

"My child, do not pay me such homage for a mere common charity. What creature with the heart of a man could have left you to perish alone? The blow must have struck you down senseless. Was it from a bough do you think?"

She shuddered with the memory.

"I cannot recollect. The storm came up from the back of the woods before I saw or thought of it; it burst suddenly, and as I went something struck me down; whether it was the flash or a fallen branch, I can remember nothing since, till I awoke—here."

She lifted herself a little, and glanced round the chamber with the startled wonder still in her eyes, as of one who wakes from a deep sleep in a strange scene; her glance came back to him, and dwelt on him with a venerating marvel and admiration: she knew his face well, though until that day he had never seen hers. Her sweeping lashes were weighted and glistening with tears as she looked—sweet, sudden tears of an infinite gratitude for her rescue, and to him by whom she had been saved. She was very fair in that moment.

Her hair, all loosened by the wind, fell backward and over her shoulders, like a shower of molten gold; the warmth of the chamber, and the surprise of her waking thoughts, gave a glow like a wild rose to her cheeks. Some of the ivy-coils that she had dropped in her haste to rise and flee from the storm had caught in the gay colour and the white broideries of her simple picturesque dress: an artist would have given a year of his life to have painted her as she was then, in the shadowy chiar'-oscuro of the lamplight, in the marble waste of the far-stretching, half-ruined chamber.

A dim fugitive memory wandered before him with the glance of her eyes,—a likeness that he could not trace, yet that pursued him, rose before him with the earnest, haunting beauty of her face. Far down in his past it lay; he could not disinter it,—he could not give it name or substance,—but its shadow flickered before him. She was like something remembered, like something recovered.

"You are tired and exhausted: lie still," he said, as she strove to rise. "They shall bring you food; I need some myself; and in an hour the storm may lull, perhaps. May I ask who it is that my roof has the honour to shelter?"

She looked at him still with that wistful wondering homage; she was shy with him, and the language of

courtesy was unfamiliar to her; it was very new to her
to be addressed so.

"What is your name, *poverina?*" he asked her.

"They call me Castalia."

"Castalia!—a fair and classic name! And what else?"

"Nothing else, eccellenza."

Her voice was very low; her head sank, the tears
glittered thickly on the length of her lashes. In the
answer she had told him all the history she had.

He was silent a moment, regretful that he had pained
her; his voice was very tender as he spoke again.

"And your mother—is she living?"

She shook her head.

He looked at her with a deep pity, this child with
the brilliance of Southern suns about her, and a fate so
lonely and so blighted at the outset.

He asked her no more; but, as a Tuscan woman answered his summons and brought into the chamber a tray
of fruits, and macaroni, and truffles, with some flasks of
Italian and Rhine wines, he served her with his own
hands as assiduously, as reverently, as any would serve
a queen. And as the rest and the food revived her more
and more, and more and more restored the animation to
her lips, the lustre to her eyes, she seemed, in the antique
classic Doric charm of the silent chamber, like some gem
of the old Venetian masters set in the white coldness of
the marble walls—like some lustrous, gold-leaved, Italian
flower, sprung in its bud from the grey solemnity, the
sublime decay, of Roman ruins.

He wondered whence she came and what she was—
this Tuscan child with the grace of a daughter of the
Antonines, who was without a name; and once more the
memory which had haunted him rose again, not to be
grasped, but lost in the mazy shades of a far-distant past.

The storm was at its height, there seemed little chance of its abatement; the mighty din of its thunder rolled like the roar of a hundred battles, and the moaning and trembling of all the beech and chestnut woods were heard on the stillness. She shuddered as she listened.

"Ah! I should have been lying dead in all that terror now, but for your pity!"

"Do not think of it," he answered soothingly. "Let the storm rage as it will, you are safe here with me. Tell me, where is it you live?"

She looked at him with an intense sadness, very strange upon the glow and glory of her youth; and, though the flush grew hotter in her face, it was proud and still in its pain.

"Illustrissimo," she said, softly, for there was a breathless awe of him upon her, mingled touchingly with a spaniel-like trust, "you ought to know whom your house shelters; it is only just. I have no name; I have no history. My mother died when I was a few months old; she came a stranger, and the village knew nothing of her, only this—she was not wedded. The Padre Giulio and his mother adopted me; they have been very good. The name they found on me was Castalia. I have nothing more to tell."

The simplicity of the words lent them but the deeper sadness; the restrained pain, the half-haughty, half-appealing shame, with which she spoke them, gave them but the stronger pathos. They touched her listener greatly.

"Thank you for your confidence, my fair child," he answered her, with a pitying tenderness in his voice—she was so young to be already touched with life's suffering and the world's reproach. "You do not know your history; there is room, then, to hope it a bright one."

She shook her head.

"Illustrissimo, how! It began in shame; it will end in a convent."

"A convent! Better the tomb!"

He spoke on an impulse. To cage her to that living death of the veil seemed barbarous as to shut away in darkness, till it died, one of the golden-winged orioles that fluttered through the length of a spring day below the slopes of Vallombrosa.

"Yes! better a thousand times! In the grave one sleeps unconscious! But, forgive me, eccellenza; I weary you. Let me go."

"Go! with the storm at that height! You would go to your destruction. No living thing could pass from here to Fontane in such a night. Wait a while; it may lull presently. And give me no titles of deference; I can claim none."

"You must be a great lord!" she said, softly and hesitatingly.

He smiled wearily.

"My greatness—if I ever truly had any—departed from me long ago. I am no noble. I am little richer than your peasants of Fontane."

She glanced round the chamber. To her, after the bare simplicity of the Fontane hamlet, the frescoes, the sculpture, the mosaics, though they were but the relics of Latin ruins, made it seem a palace; then her glistening meditative eyes dwelt on him.

"You are lord of yourself, at least!" she said, lingeringly, with the *naïf* expression of a child.

"I have but a rebellious subject, then," he answered, with a tinge of sadness that did not escape her. "But, *poverina*, you look feverish and tired. I have been thoughtless for you. Are you in pain!"

She smiled at him—a smile of infinite patience and

sweetness, that brought back in his thoughts once more a memory he could not follow.

"Not much: it is nothing."

She would not confess that, in truth, an intolerable pain ached through her bruised temples, and that an utter exhaustion was stealing fast upon her.

"Lie still, then," he said, bending over her; "the tempest is at its worst now. Take no heed of me, but sleep, if you can."

She thanked him, and obeyed him; she watched him with a reverent, wondering homage; she revered him already like a king, like a deity.

She had passed all her young years in the chestnut-shadows beneath Vallombrosa, and she had far too much innocence, far too much faith, to think of harm that could be done her in this solitude, to feel anything but a sublime, devoted trust in the stranger who had saved her life. Moreover, the weariness that was growing on her, the sleep that weighed down her eyelids, the reaction from the shock and peril of the night, left her little sense save of a lulling peace that surrounded her, of a voice that soothed her like music, of a wish to be silent and still, and keep unbroken this soft charm.

He left her, and went to the lectern at the farther end of the room, where the vellum scroll lay, a disputed manuscript of Boethius. On the wide stone hearth some pine-logs were burning, for the evenings were chilly, though the days were so warm; the aromatic odour of the lamp filled the room with a sweet, faint incense; the shadows were deep in all the farther parts of the hall, only about the hearth was the ruddy, flickering glow of the pines; all else was in gloom.

The hours passed uncounted; the thunder had some-what lulled, but the winds were a hurricane, and the drenching downpour of rain scoured the land and howled through the pine and the beech woods. It was a night which broke the mountain firs like saplings, and wrenched up the grey writhing olives by the roots, and laid the young birds stone dead by the score. No human thing could venture out in it and be sure of life. The twelfth hour struck from the campanile as the lull of a moment succeeded to the roar of the storm; he lifted his head from where he bent over the lectern, and looked at the young companion chance had so strangely brought there. In the glow of the embers she lay, in her delicate, richly-hued beauty, a child in her innocence and her tranquil rest, far more than a child in her grace and her charm,—a thing of light, and life, and colour, and youth, in the cold, classic solitude of the lonely and half-ruined hall, whose cracked mosaic had been worn by the passing of so many banished feet that had trodden through their brief day, and had glided onward down into their tombs. He watched her with an indefinable pity, with a fugitive, intangible remembrance pursuing him; her brief story was so mournful, and the memory that pursued him was so strong, though he could find it no clue, and would give it no substance. As a chord of music, as a flower blooming in a desert place, as a sound of harvest-chant or spring-bird's singing, will bear us back to long-gone hours, so the sight of her bore his thoughts backward to years that were sealed for ever,—thoughts that thronged on him, many, and embittered by their own dead sweetness, as the thought of all that he will never again see comes on the exile with the mere scent of faded leaves brought to him from the summer woodlands that hear his step no more.

In them he was lost, as he leaned against the broad bronze wings of the lectern-eagle, with his eyes on the

ring of ruddy colour that circled her like a halo. The
storm shook above the low, flat roof of the Latin villa,
breaking on it as with the force of a waterspout. He
roused himself and went near her.

"She cannot go out in such a night as this," he
thought.

She slept still, softly as a child, a proud, resigned
sadness, like the memory of her stained birth and lonely
fate, on her face. He was loath to break her rest, yet
he knew that to let her sleep on here would be to let the
coarse tongues of the mountain peasants touch even her
defenceless childhood. He stooped and passed his hand
lightly over her brow. At the touch, slight as it was, she
wakened instantly; the blue-black lustre of her eyes
startled into consciousness, the flush on her cheek bright
as the scarlet japonica blossoms. She started up, ashamed.

"Oh, eccellenza, forgive me! I have been asleep!"

"Naturally, after your danger and your fatigue. It
was the best restorative you could have. It is midnight
now, and the storm is scarce lessened——"

"Midnight? The Padre will be so wretched! What
will he think! Let me go; pray let me go."

"Impossible; you would go to your certain death. I
could not venture myself in such a night; you hear the
hurricane? You must remain with me."

"With you?"

"Surely: I would not let a dog leave my roof in such
weather as this is. Besides, you are miles higher on the
slope here than Fontane; the return to the village would
be impossible for those far hardier than you."

She looked at him with a wondering awe; he seemed
to her such an emperor as Marcus Antoninus, who had
laid down his pomp and come to dwell a while like other
men. The deep-blue, weary, brilliant eyes that gazed

on her made her think of the serene, imperial eyes of Augustus.

"I am a total stranger to you, it is true," he said, gently, misinterpreting her silence; "but you are not afraid to remain in my house? I am only here for a *villeggiatura*, and the place is desolate enough, but it will at least give you shelter."

"Afraid? Afraid of *you?* What could I fear? You saved my life; it is yours to command. All is—I cannot thank you enough."

The words were very touching in their liquid Tuscan, in their complete innocence, and in their perfect trust.

"You have nothing to thank me for; a mule-driver or a charcoal-burner must have done for you what I did," he answered her, his voice unconsciously softening. "And now go to rest; you want it. I will send the women to you, and they shall remain in your chamber; for you are not well enough to be left alone."

"Ah, eccellenza, how good you are!" she murmured. A few years older, and she would have been grateful to him in silence, better knowing the motive of his words. "But indeed I am strong now; we, below Vallombrosa, have the strength of the mountain air; and—shall I not trouble you with staying here?"

"Far from it; you bring your own welcome, like the birds that come and sing under our windows. Goodnight, and sleep well."

He held his hand out to her; she was but a child to him, and a child who had been sheltered on his breast through the driving of the storm. She stooped with the exquisite softness of movement of Southern women, and touched the hand he gave her, lightly and reverently, with her lips.

"I would thank you, eccellenza, but I cannot."

She did thank him, however, better than by all words,
with that hesitating touch of her young lips, with that upward glance of her eyes, languid with sleep and fatigue,
yet lustrous as the Tuscan skies by night,—eyes that
seemed to him to have some story of his past in their depths.

Then he summoned the women to her, peasants who
dwelt in the villa, and she left him.

He, having surrendered to her, though she knew nothing of it, the only habitable chamber that the half-ruined
villa afforded, stretched himself in the warmth of the pine
logs on the wolf-skins strewn before it. She had brought
back to him, why or whence he could not tell, memories
that he would willingly let die,—memories that, through
the length of weary years, burned still into his heart
with unutterable longing, with intolerable pain.

In the loneliness of the old classic hall, in the leaping
light of the pine flames, throngs of shadowy shapes arose
around him,—the shapes of his past, summoned by the
light of a child's smile.

She, meanwhile, lay wakeful, yet dreamy, gazing out
at the unfamiliar chamber and the swaying figure of the
peasant woman keeping watch over her, and nodding in
her sleep. Her thoughts were steeped in all the wonders
of legendary lore, and she fancied some enchantment had
been wrought in her since, out of that awful forest darkness, she had been brought to this charmed stillness, in
which only one remembrance was with her, the remembrance of the musing, lustrous, weary eyes that had looked
so gently on her, of the voice that had soothed her terror
and her pain with an accent softer than she had ever
heard. She thought of him, and thought, as one other had
once done before, that he was like the Poet-king of Israel,
but having known the bitterness of abdication, having
known the ingratitude of the people. Then her musing

became a dream, and, with a smile upon her lips, she slept under a stranger's roof till the tempest had passed away and the dawn was bright.

As she awoke, the morning had risen. The sun broke in full glory over a splendid mass of purple cloud and tumbled storm-mist that glowed in magnificent colour beneath the newly-risen rays. The earth laughed again even amidst her ruin,—her ruin of crushed olive-buds, and uprooted saplings, and trees rent asunder, and nests flung down, with the young birds killed, and the mothers flying with piteous cries over the wreck; but the wheat-sprouts were too low to be harmed; the vines, though they trailed and hung helplessly under the dead weight of rain-drops, were still only in blossom; the watercourses made the wilder, merrier music, filled to overflowing, and laying in swathes the rank grasses of their beds; the mules began to patter over the broken paths, picking their careful way over the dislodged bolders of rocks and the deep channels of brimming brooks. Beneath Vallombrosa the morning was fair and sun-lightened again, deadly though the tempest had been over-night, and rough work of destruction though it had wrought. With the sun she rose; her youth, like the youth of the spring and the earth, the brighter for the storm and the danger gone by. There was the flush of waking childhood and of past sleep upon her cheeks, and her eyes had the gladness of a wondering dream in them, as she found her way, marvelling if she dreamed a fairy-tale, down some broken marble steps and out into the air.

CHAPTER III.

"Gioventù! Primavera della Vita!"

THE full light poured into the open *loggia* before the half-ruined courts and halls of the Latin villa. Within, the one spacious chamber, with its frescoes and the mosaics, its books and scrolls, was bare enough. But the world of blossoming spring, of morning mists, of lavish foliage that opened out before it, made ample amends for any poverty and decay of the interior; and it was perfect for a *villeggiatura*, this deserted place that Roman pomp had once filled in Augustan days.

In this loggia, reading, her host sat,—a man no longer young, though as yet there was no silver amidst the fair and golden length of his hair; a man of a grave grace, of a serene, meditative dignity of look and of movement that had in it something that was very weary, yet something not less grand, not less royal: he might have been a king in purples rather than what he was,—an exile, and poor.

The book was open upon his knee, but his eyes were not upon it for the moment; they were resting on the gardens without,—gardens wild, forsaken, uncultured, but only the more beautiful for that. What he watched in them was the passage of the young Tuscan flitting through them with the freedom of a chamois in her step, and all the languor of a dew-laden flower in her loveliness.

Sixteen years beyond the Appenines bring womanhood; they had brought it to her in the loveliness nature had dowered her with, but in all else she was young as a child, —she had never wandered from the chestnut shadows of her village, had but dimly heard of another vast world beyond the beech-woods, had known no friends but the birds who sang to her, no pleasures but to watch a blue-warbler shake his bright wings in the myrtles, or to look deep down into the heart of a passion-flower and build a thousand fancies from its mystic burning hues. She was a child with the beauty of a woman; there could be no greater peril for her.

He thought so as he saw her in this deserted garden,

Art had no handling with her; the pure hill-air had made her all she was; and she had the unconsciousness of some rich-plumaged bird, now floating softly through the sunlight, now pausing on the wing, now alighting to drop down in happy rest in a couch of feathery grasses.

He gazed at her as she wandered through them, that exquisite ease in her step which many a royal woman has not, which a contadina may have balancing on her dark imperial head a pannier of water-melons. The lizards did not hurry from her, but watched her with curious eyes; the timid hares let her stoop and stroke them; the old owls blinking in the ivy let her lift her hand and touch their crests; the wood-doves flew about her and pecked the buds from the boughs she held up to them. She bent over the black swollen water, and saw her own reflection laurel-crowned as the branches met above her head; she gathered the lilies of the valley, the buds of Banksia roses, and the young green ivy-blossoms, and crowned herself with them till the wreath was too heavy and shook all her glistening hair downward in a shower of gold, like a picture of Flora. Then, lastly, she sank to rest on a grey rock of fallen sculpture, the crown of flowers still above her brow; and after the glad, thoughtless pastime of a child, the proud and profound sadness that usually in repose was on her face, succeeded it with a charm not the less great because so sudden.

It was like the sudden fall of evening over the brilliance and the glow of her own Tuscan landscape.

As he saw it, he left the loggia and went towards her. She did not hear his step till he had approached her close; then she sprang up with the swiftness of a fawn, and with words of gratitude made only softer by the awe of him which lent her its delicate coyness.

"I have been watching you for the last half-hour, Castalia," he said, gently. "I am glad you could find such companions in my flowers and my birds; there is little else here fit for your bright youth."

She put her hands up hurriedly to remove the dew-laden wreath of bud and blossom; she had forgotten it till his speech brought it back to her thoughts. He put out his own hand and stayed her.

"Not for worlds! I wished a Titian lived to paint you! you look like a young priestess of Flora. But, tell me, what spell have you that tames the lizards, and stills the hares, and brings all the birds to your hand?"

She lifted to him her musing eloquent eyes, grave as a child's when he pauses to think.

"I do not know, eccellenza, unless—it may be because I love them so well."

His face grew a shade darker and yet softer; her words recalled the fond belief of his own youth.

"You think love begets and secures love? I thought so once."

"And was it not so?"

"No; but—that knowledge should not kill love in us; there is much that is worth it, if there be much that is not. Because a viper turns and stings you, it would be wild vengeance to wring the wood-pigeon's neck."

He spoke half to his own thoughts, half to her; she regarded him with a reverent, grateful, wondering gaze; in her little beech-forest nest of Fontane she had never seen anything like him. She who had known but one bent old priest, and brown, brawny muleteers and vintagers from whom she shrank as the white sea-swallow shrinks from the hard beak and cruel pursuit of the kestrel, thought almost he must be more than mortal.

"I ought to leave you, 'lustrissimo?" she said, hesitatingly. "I have troubled you so long."

"Do you wish to leave me?"

"Wish? oh no!"

"Well, do not leave me yet, then. Come within, and let me see, though no Titian, if I can paint you with your crown of flowers. Your Padre Curato will feel no anxiety; I sent a messenger to him to say you were here."

The gravest contrition stole over her face; she looked penitent as a chidden child.

"Oh, 'lustrissimo! I had forgotten him. How ungrateful, when he is so good! How selfish one grows when one is happy!"

"Then are you happy with me?"

"Eccellenza," she said, under her breath, "it seems to me that I have been happier than in all the years of my life."

The reply pleased him. He had always loved to see happiness about him.

"I am glad it should be so. And do not believe that happiness makes us selfish; it is a treason to the sweetest gift of life. It is when it has deserted us that it grows hard to keep all the better things in us from dying in the blight. Men shut out happiness from their schemes for the world's virtue; they might as well seek to bring flowers to bloom without the sun."

He spoke again rather to his own thoughts than to her; but she understood him. This young Tuscan, lost amidst the chestnuts beneath Vallombrosa, had in her the heart of a Héloïse, the mind of a Hypatia, though both were in their childhood yet.

"Eccellenza," she said, hesitatingly, "that is true. If we keep light from a plant, it will grow up warped. When they condemn, do they ever ask if what they condemn had a chance to behold the light? Perhaps—perhaps if my mother had been happy she would not have been evil, as they call her?"

The colour burned hotly in her face, but her eyes were raised in wistful entreaty to him; it was but very vaguely that she understood the shame that she was made to feel was on her birth, but very dimly that she comprehended some vast indistinct error with which her dead mother was charged.

The question touched him with great pity.

"*Poverina*," he said, caressingly, "do not weary your young life with those subtleties. You do not know that error lies at all upon your mother's history; who can, since you say that history is wholly unknown,—even to her very name? It may be that the thing the world—your little woodland world, at least—blames in her, was some unrecognised martyrdom, some untold unselfishness. At all events, be she what she will, *you* are stainless and blameless; all you need seek is to be so for ever."

She looked at him with passionate feeling.

"I thank you, eccellenza, more for those noble words than for the life that you saved me."

The brief answer was very eloquent,—eloquent of her nature and of her gratitude. He said no more, but led her within to the old hall, only fit for a summer residence for an artist, or a scholar sufficiently content with its classic charm and forest wildness to bear its scant accommodation. An easel stood before the open colonnade facing the gardens; he paused before it, and glanced at her. A lovelier theme never lured any painter's brush, with the fresh crown of lilies and rose-buds and light-green blossoms of ivy shaking their dew upon the gold-flaked shower of her hair. He looked at her, then he threw aside the colours he had taken up.

"Twenty years ago I could have given your picture there," he said, half wearily. "Now I have not the heart

to paint you, my fair child. I have not the great inspira-
tion,—youth."

Twenty years ago he would have found no hour more
beguiling than that spring morning with the young
Tuscan, bringing the bloom of her beauty and of her
crown of flowers out on the canvas; now it only recalled
to him all he had lost.

A shadow stole over her eyes; he saw it, and turned
back to the easel.

"Are you disappointed?"

She looked beseechingly in his face.

"I never saw any paintings except those in our little
chapel."

"No! Well, then, I will try and give you your desire."

He took the brushes up again, and, standing before
the easel, sketched her as she leaned against one of the
pillars of the colonnade, the rich glow and warmth of her
young face but the brighter for the whiteness of the lilies
and the deep green of the leaves that circled her hair.
He had both the skill and the habit of Art; and the impassioned brilliance of her beauty, with the coronal of
blossoms weighting her forehead with the weight of all
diadems, rose gradually under his hand out of the sea of
brown opaque gloom on which it was painted. The hours
passed, and the picture grew; it beguiled him for the time
of heavier cares, and won him out of deeper thoughts;
yet ever and again, as he lifted his eyes and glanced at
her, the weariness which had made him turn from the
task came over him again. He thought of so many golden
hours, when faces as fair had bloomed to fresh life thus
on his canvas, and the glory of his youth had been with
him to lend its sweetness to the eyes, and teach the language of love to the lips, of those he painted. The soft
labour only recalled to him so many days that were dead.

The noontide was intensely still, the heat of the sun quivered down through the open arches of the colonnade, the picture grew clearer and richer beneath his hand, and the blossoms faded where they crowned her hair. She untwined them, and touched them mournfully.

"Ah, eccellenza, they are all dying!"

He smiled, not without sadness, too, though it was for deeper things than the flowers.

"Never mind; you have had their sweetness. Be content with that. Nothing endures."

"But it is better never to have had them than to see them withered!"

"I doubt that. If we should have been spared much pain, we should also have missed much joy."

His thoughts were with other things, though he spoke still in the figure of the flowers. He had seen his own crowns wither and fall and be trodden under foot, yet it was better to have worn them. She looked at him in silence, reverently, wonderingly; she mused on what his history could be; she thought him a king in exile. So, in a sense, he was.

There was an infinite shyness of him in her that gave her tenfold more charm, it was so innocent and so full of religious veneration. He seemed to her like the archangels of her Church, so full of majesty, so full of pity. She thought with him of all the grand, serene, lonely lives that she had read of in the Latin legends.

He rose, and turned the easel to her.

"Castalia, do what even wise men never do; see yourself as you are."

She came forward, and looked, as the sun fell full on the work of a few hours, and her countenance changed as by magic; a breathless surprise was on her lips, a scarlet flush upon her cheeks, the light of an immeasurable ad-

miration and amaze beamed in her eyes. She stood
entranced at the likeness of herself, as, with its diadem
of blossoms, it gazed out at her from the brown shadows
of the background.

"Well?" he asked her, smiling.

She turned to him bewildered and beseeching.

"Oh! 'lustrissimo, can it be? Am I as beautiful as *that?*"

"Did the river and the fountain never tell you so
before?"

Her head drooped, the colour in her cheek deepened;
her innocent delight had had no thought of vanity, but at
his words she remembered what she looked on was—herself.

"And yet it *is* beautiful!" she murmured, very low,
as though in apology. "And if I be really like it——"

"What then?"

A prouder glory flashed into her face; she lifted her
head with the royalty of a daughter of emperors, mingled
with a great softness of regard.

"Then, I think, if I could once see the great world I
might reign there, and I might win some love, and not
be scorned as peasants scorn me here."

He paused a moment; the words touched him to compassion.

"Would it not be so, eccellenza?"

"Yes," he answered, slowly; "doubtless it would. But do
not wish it, if you be wise. Your diadems would not be
so pure as the one that lies withered there; your brows
would soon ache under them, and for the love——"

"Ah!" she said, softly, whilst the glow faded, and her
eyes filled with tears as she spoke with the pathos and
the guilelessness of a child, "I long to be loved! All the
children of Fontane have their mothers, who look brighter
when they see them near; but I am all alone. I have been
alone so long!"

The words had an intense and touching piteousness in them; a harder nature than her listener's was would have been moved by them. How could he find the cruelty to tell her that the chances were as a million to one that the only love she would ever meet in this world beyond the pine woods to which she vaguely looked as the redresser of her wrongs, would be one less merciful to her even than the bitterness and loneliness which now visited on her innocence and her youth the unproven error of her dead mother?   Twenty years before he would have heard her with little thought, save to let his lips linger on the brow whence the faded ivy-buds had fallen, and murmur to her the tenderness which her unawakened heart longed for, as an imprisoned bird longs for the shelter of summer leaves and the whispers of summer rivers; now such a thought as this was distant from him as the wide unknown world was far from her.

But pity her he did, profoundly. This nameless, motherless child, with her radiant grace and her proud instincts, was as desolate as any chamois-fawn lost on the hills and driven as an alien from every herd with which it seeks a refuge.

"You will have love, some day, *poverina*," he said, gently, "and as much as you will; you will hardly lift such eyes as those to ask for it in vain."

She sighed, and her head sank lower, while she looked still at the painted likeness of herself. She was unaware of any tribute to her beauty in his words; she thought he meant that some, one day, would pity her.

"Ah," she answered, wearily, "where is the worth of love, if with it is scorn?"

The thoughtless taunts and the careless jests which among the peasantry had been cast at her from her birth up as a foundling—rather in the mothers' jealousy of her face and the children's resentment of her love of solitude, than from any cruelty or any real contempt—had sunk deeply into her nature, rousing rebellion and disdain well-nigh as much as they caused sorrow and a vague sense of shame.

He saw how great a shipwreck might be made of her opening life, even from the very purest and loftiest things in her, if this outlawry banned her long—if this passion of mingled defiance and humiliation were fostered by neglect. He spoke on that.

"Scorn! Why dwell on scorn? It is unworthy of you. It is a word that may bring a pang to those who merit it by their own ill deeds; it need have no sting for any other. Keep your life high and blameless, and you will afford to treat scorn with scorn."

She did not reply to him with words, but she flashed on him with an answering glance the night-like lustre of her eyes, in an eloquence, in a comprehension, in a promise, that accepted his meaning far more deeply and more vividly than by speech. He saw that she might be led by a cord of silk—that she would not be driven by a scourge.

He stood a few moments in the shadow of the colonnade, later, when she had left him, looking at the painting that had grown out of the deep, sombre backwork by the work of his own hand, the head alone luminous, from the veil of gloom around it, with its spiritual radiance, crowned by that wealth of flowers; he looked, then turned it aside towards the wall, so that the richness of colour no longer smiled out of the opaque shadows, and went within to his solitude. That face, gazing out from the darkness under the diadem of woven blossoms, seemed like the phantom of his own dead youth.

CHAPTER IV.

"Seigneur! ayez Pitié."

NEVER in the rich days of the Cinque Cento, or the
Dandolo age, when the cities of Italy were filled with
pomp and mirth and music, when the mighty palaces
were wreathed with flowers that lent their bright blush to
the white stone and glowed over the black marbles, when
the dark arches framed hair, like the gold arras that
draped the balconies, and lips ripe as the scarlet heart
of the rose that glowed in their bosom, was any beauty
rarer or more lustrous than that of the young Tuscan
who had grown up under the forest-shadows below Vallombrosa, scarce more tended, not more heeded, than one
of the passion-flowers that bursts into its glorious bud unseen by any eyes above the broken stone of some ruined
altar of Pan. Though her years were so few that the fulness of her beauty might yet be scarcely reached, she had
already the splendour of a Titian picture on her, the superb
grace, wild as a deer, proud as the daughter of Cæsars, that
here and there still lingers, as though to verify tradition,
in the women of Campagna or of Apennine.

The loneliness of her childhood, the consciousness of
a ban placed on her, the haughty instincts which had
wakened in self-defence against the shafts of scorn, the
solitary and meditative life which she had led, had lent
her a certain patrician pride, a certain thoughtful shadow;
a wistful pain sometimes gazed out of her eyes; a lofty
rebellion sometimes broke through the dreaming gladness
of her smile. She was happy, because she was young,
because she was sinless, because she had the innocence
which finds its joy in the caress of a bird, in the radiance
of a sunset, in the mere breath and consciousness of existence; but she had the pang of wounded pride, the burden

of a scarce-comprehended shame, and the vague, bitter, impassioned longing of a mind too ardent and too daring for its sphere; and these gave their character to her face, their hues to her youth; these made her far more than a mere child, however lovely, can be. She was like Héloïse ere her master had become her lover, and while her eyes, as they gazed on the Greek scroll or the vellum Evangeliarium, were brilliant with the light of aspiration and dark with the thoughts of a poet, but had never yet drooped, heavy with the languor and burning with the knowledge of love.

From the aged priest she had learned all his scholarly lore that plunged deep into the life of the past, and drank deep of Latin and Hellenic culture; he had loved the rugged roads of wisdom, the unfathomed sea-depths of knowledge, the buried treasures of cloister folios and of crabbed *copia*—she had loved them too. With no other in the obscure hill-side, to which fate had condemned him, to give him sympathy or understanding in these things, the stern old man had taken eager pleasure in steeping with them the virgin soil of a young and thirsty mind. In the bare, grey, narrow chamber of his dwelling, with its single lancet window through which crept the mellow sunlight from the cloudless skies, the fair head of the child Castalia, with its weight of burnished tresses, had bent above the huge tomes and the century-worn manuscriptum for hour on hour, like Héloïse in the cell of the canonry. She had a passionate love of those studies: and, whilst they filled her mind with great and impersonal thoughts, they did much to console her for her fate, and much to enrich her intelligence far beyond her years and her sex. They, and the beauties of the earth and the seasons, were her sole pleasures. The priest's mother, under whose roof she lived, was nearly ninety years, decrepit and harsh, who, well as she loved her foundling in her heart, could be no aid or associate to her. With the peasantry, the people who maligned her unknown parent, she would have no converse in their flower-feasts and their vintage celebrations. She lived alone with the learning of dead ages and the fragrance of a forest-world.

Some, such an isolation would have maddened or ruined; Castalia, with a singular vividness of imagination, and a proud patience beneath the passionate warmth of her nature, had received through it a higher character than any other and happier life could have developed.

She was a poem, with her slight, sad, all-eloquent story, that needed no detail to fill it up; with her touching desolation of circumstance and of destiny, and her brilliant youth that in its elasticity and its enthusiasm broke aside all barriers of doom and pain and found its careless joy God-given from a song-bird's carol, from a cloister-scribe's story, from the tossing of a sea of green rushes in the wind, from the dreams of an outer world, unknown and glorified in fancy into paradise. She was a poem in the spring-time of her life and in the spring-time of the year.

The smile of women's eyes had no beckoning light for him, the whisper of women's allurement no sorcery for his ear; he had been a voluptuary in an earlier time, but he had passed through bitterness and poverty, and sensuous charms had ceased to hold him. Yet there was enough of the poet lingering in him to make him vaguely feel some memories of youth and some tenderness of pity arise as he looked on the bright head that he had painted with its diadem of flowers, on the opening life that he had found in this beech-wood nest. Had chance not thrown her on him, he would never have sought her; brought to his protection, to his compassion, she won her way to him as some forest-fawn whom he should have found wounded

and beaten in the storm might have come to his hand
in after-days, and been caressed for the sake of its past
peril and its present gratitude.

He had sought the seclusion of the old Latin villa for
the isolation which he, a writer and a thinker of whom
the world spoke, often preferred to the life of cities, under
grey Alpine shadows, in still Danubian woods, by olive-
crested Southern seas, or amidst the Moorish ruins of a
Granadine landscape. Wealth he had none; but as each
young year awoke in its renaissance, he liked to have
around him the richness of colour and fragrance, the
beauty of the earth's dower, that needed no purchase, but
could be made his own by each who loved it well enough
to understand its meaning.

In the monastic twilight and silence of the old classic
hall, the painting with the crown of flowers glowed brightly
and vividly like a living thing from out the gloom; and
with the deep studies and the solitary thoughts which had
heretofore usurped him, the memory and the presence of
this fair child mingled, not without a charm,—a charm
which had in it something of recollection. The remembrance was fugitive, and he could never bring it clearly
before his knowledge; but it was there, and strong enough
to make him seek more of her history. The search was
futile: there was no more to know; her mother had died,
mute and nameless, and whence she came there was no
record—there was not even a suggestion—to show or to
hint. One thing alone was certain; her mother had worn
no marriage-ring, and the only word marked on the
child's linen was the single one Castalia.

The woman had been of great beauty, the peasants
said, though worn and haggard, with eyes that burned
like flame, and a terrible wandering look; but she had
been utterly exhausted when she had reached Fontane,

and had lain almost speechless until in the middle of the hot, heavy, tempestuous night she had looked with a glance that all could read from the face of the priest to the sleeping form of the child, and then had sighed wearily and restlessly, and died.

The blank in the history made it but the more mournful, the more suggestive. An exceeding pity moved in him, as he heard, for the life ushered in in such abandoned desolation, and for which there seemed no haven open save the cloister,—a fate as barbarous for her radiant and impassioned loveliness, which not even the melancholy of her fate could dim, as to wring the glad throat of a song-bird in the full rush of its forest melody. With him at least she was happy,—she who had never known what happiness was, except such forms of it as the sweet, irrepressible intoxication of the mere sense of existence which youth gives, and the joys that a vivid imagination and a passionate, poetic temperament confer. In his presence she was happy, and he could not refuse it to her. Few days passed without his seeing her, in the beech-grove where he had first glanced at her by the broken fountain, in the pine-woods sloping up toward Vallombrosa, in the deserted gardens or in the ruined hall of his own Latin villa. He had no thought in it save that of compassion, even whilst her lustrous eyes vaguely recalled him his past; and in the untutored thoughts that had fed in these hill-solitudes on the legacies of the Hellenic schools and the literature of the Renaissance, he found the wakening intellect of a Corinna. Love had long been killed in him; it was a thing of his youth, never, he believed, like that youth, to revive, and no touch of passion mingled with the pity she aroused in him; but that pity was infinitely gentle, and to her the most precious mercy that her life had known.

In her home, silence and austerity reigned with the stern simplicity of the primitive Church. From the peasants she met with at best a good-natured insolence that was to her instinctively imperial nature worse than all neglect; from him alone she met with what ennobled her in her own sight, and filled her towards him with a passionate gratitude and veneration that was only not love because no knowledge of love had dawned on her, and because an absolute submission and awe were mingled with it. To her he was the incarnation of all sublime lives that she had dreamed of over the histories of Plutarch, and Tacitus, and Claudian, of Augustin, and Hildebrand, and Basil; to her he was as an emperor to his lieges, as an archangel to his devotees; all grand and gracious things to her seemed blended in him, and all lofty and royal lives of poet, saint, or king with which her memory was stored seemed to her met in his. It was not love that she bore him; it was something infinitely more unconscious and more idealized: it was an absolute adoration.

She did not know why the hours were a dead worthless space unless they brought her to his presence, why the mere distant sound of his voice filled her heart with a joy intense as pain, why any suffering he had bidden her would have been sweeter than any gladness, why the forest-world about her wore a light it had never had before:—she did not know; she only knew that all the earth seemed changed and transfigured. He was not blind to it; it touched him, it beguiled him, it pleased him; it was very long since any thing had loved him and been the happier for his smile; it was very long since these softer, slighter things had come into his life, and they had a certain charm for him.

There had been a time when all women's eyes had gained a brighter light at his approach, though that time lay far away in a deserted land; yet in some faint measure it revived for him, as he saw the silent welcome, more eloquent than all words, of this young Tuscan's glance; and to him she was but a beautiful child, to be caressed, without deeper thought.

"Eccellenza!" she said, hesitatingly, one day that he had paused by her beside her favourite haunt by the Roman fountain in the black belt of the beech-woods, "you tell me that I have talent; you say that my voice, when I sing the Latin chants that you love best, is music the world would love too. Would they do nothing for me *in* the world?"

That "world" was so vague, so far off, so dim, so glorious to her! She could not have told what she thought lay beyond those chestnut-belts that she had never passed; but her ideal of the unknown land was divine as Dante's of the City of God.

He answered her slowly: he knew the fate to which her defenceless and nameless beauty would there be doomed; but he could not find the heart to break her fair illusion.

"They might,—they would; but you are better and safer here in your mountain shelter."

A quick sigh escaped her.

"Oh, no!"

"No? How can you tell that? You do not know what would await you. Be happy while you may, Castalia; the world would crush you!"

She looked at him wistfully, while a grander power and aspiration than the mere longing of a child for "fresh fields and pastures new" gleamed in eyes that in a little while would burn with passion as they now glanced with light.

"It is only the weak who are crushed. They could not scorn me for my birth and loneliness if I forced them to say, 'See! fate was harsh to her; but God gave her genius and endurance, and she conquered!'"

The words and the tone moved him deeply: the fearless youth, with its faith, its fervour, its courage, its sublime blindness of belief, recalled to him his own.

"Ah, Castalia!" he answered gently, "but the world loves best to dwarf God and to deny genius. And genius in a woman! Cyril's envy stones Hypatia, and casts her beauty to the howling crowds."

Her head drooped, but the look of resolve, though shadowed, did not pass off her face.

"Perhaps! Yet better Hypatia's glory won with her death, than a long, obscure, ignoble, useless life! You say, be happy here, 'lustrissimo: happy! when all my future is the convent?"

It was a great terror to her, that monastic doom to which the priest inexorably condemned her future;—other provision he could make none for her. She was so full of vivid, luxuriant, abundant, glowing life. Life was to her an unread poem of such magical enchantment, an ungathered flower of such sorceress-charm;—and nothing opened to her except that living tomb!

He gave an involuntary gesture of pain.

"God forbid! Some fairer fate will come to you than that. To condemn *you* to a convent-cell! it would be as brutal as the captivity of Héloïse."

A brooding weariness passed over the beauty of her face.

"But Héloïse was happier than I should be. She had been loved once!"

There was no thought in her as she spoke, save the longing for tenderness ever denied her, and an instinctive comprehension of the passion and the sacrifice of Paraclète.

Where he leaned against a beech-stem above her, his hand touched her hair lingeringly and tenderly, as it had done when he had brought her through the storm,—like a touch to a fluttering bird.

"You would love like Héloïse!"

She drew a deep, soft breath; she was always awed with the despair and the beauty, half mystic, wholly sublimated to her, of that eternal tale.

"Ah, who would not! That alone is love! 'Quand l'empereur eût voulu m'honorer du nom de son épouse, j'aurais mieux aimer être appelée ta maîtresse!'"

The words of Héloïse on her innocent lips, which uttered them with no thought save of their devotion and their fidelity,—their choice of slavery to her lover rather than of imperial pomp with any other,—had an eloquence and a temptation greater than she knew.

He sighed almost unconsciously; it was the love of which he had dreamt in his youth,—dreamt, and never found.

"Castalia! you make me wish we had met earlier!"

"Earlier! Why!"

"No matter! What is it you are reading there!"

She lifted him the book; an Italian translation of an English romance,—"Lucrèce."

A shadow, weary and heavy, came on his face as he glanced through the pages.

"You know it!" she asked him.

"Yes, I know it."

"I love it so well! It was left here by chance years ago, by some travellers going through to Vallombrosa. It is beautiful! It moves me as the winds do when they make their music through the woods, and seem as though they called on men to cease from evil and remember God."

The words, fantastic, yet very eloquent, while her eyes grew humid, and the colour on her cheek grew warm as the scarlet heart of a pomegranate, were perhaps the truest homage the work had ever known.

He closed the book and gave it back.

"Since you feel it so, you give the author his best reward."

"But you must think it great, too?"

"No; it is very imperfect. No one knew that better than he who wrote it."

"It is perfect to *me*. And who was he,—its writer!"

"You see his name there."

"Yes, his name; but his fate——"

"Was, they say, a very common one. It was the fate of Icarus, who thought himself a winged god, and fell broken to earth."

"He never fell ignobly," she said, below her breath. "He strove to rise too high, perhaps, and those who were earth-bound envied him, and shot him down as hunters shoot an eagle; but whoever wrote that book would only gather strength from any fall."

He answered her nothing.

The spring deepened into early summer; he had been seven weeks in the Latin villa since the day he had found her in the storm, and he saw her often. He was beguiled with her, and the thoughts of her cultured fancy, all untinged by the world's taint as they were, had a certain charm for the scholar, not less than her personal loveliness had a charm for one who had been, as the world held, a libertine. But either passion was dead in him, or her defencelessness lent her sanctity in his sight; for no warmer word or glance than that of a pitying and pure tenderness ever came from him to teach her either his power or hers.

She knew nothing of his history, not even his name; to the peasantry he was simply "the stranger." He was sojourning here for the *villeggiatura*, and into his solitude none had ventured until she had been taken there by the hazards of the mountain weather. Muse on what could be his history she often did, but to question him on it she would no more have thought of than, in the old legends of her Church, those whom angels visited thought of pressing curiously upon their reverenced guest. She followed other words of Héloïse, "En toi je ne cherchai que toi, rien de toi que toi-même." It was he who was the idol of her thoughts; what he was, whence he came, she never sought to know. The kingship of the earth would not have seemed to her an empire too superb for him to have forsaken. She would have believed whatever he should have told her of himself—save evil. As it was, he told her nothing; and he spoke her language and the dead Latin, which was equally familiar to her, so that he might have been a Tuscan by birth, or, as her fancy— imaginative to extravagance—sometimes could have al- most conceived, have lived in those ages of Augustan Rome or Gracchan Revolution of which he loved best to converse.

Utterly at his mercy she was; of peril to her from him she had no conception,—what he had commanded she would have obeyed implicitly; of her own danger she was profoundly ignorant; and that he could have erred she would have no more believed than the simple fanatics of her native beech-woods would have believed in the error of the saints and seraphs to whom they prayed. The very difference in their years, wide as it was, lent an additional charm to their intercourse, and even an additional danger, since it lent it also an apparent and fallacious security.

Later on that same day, returning through the forest above Fontane to the ruined villa, where he lived in the ascetic simplicity of a man whose only riches lie in his own intellect and in the books that he can gather round him, he saw her again, as the sudden break in the wall of leaves and the sudden descent of the rocky pathway brought him to a grey antique broken bridge that spanned what was now little save a dry water-course, orchid-filled, with a narrow, glimmering, brown brook under the flowers. She was leaning over the parapet, resting her arm on a basket of fruit. There was the indolent, reposeful grace of her southern blood in the attitude, but there was also something of depression; and while a joyous light flashed into her eyes, he saw that they had been dim with tears. He paused beside her.

"Castalia! what has vexed you?"

"An idle thing, eccellenza."

"Nothing is idle if it have power to wound you. Tell me."

A proud pain, that was half of it scorn for itself and half the impatience to repay scorn, was on her face as she raised it.

"It is my folly to *be* wounded! But as two contadine passed me a while ago, they thrust out their lips with a smile that was wicked, and looked at me. 'Like mother, like child!' And I knew that they meant disdain at me and at her; and my heart ached because I could not *revenge*. Revenge is guilt, the Padre Giulio says; it may be, but when they mock at her, it would be very sweet to me."

The strength of vengeance gleamed for a moment over the softness of her youth; he saw how easily the noble nature here might be driven to desperation and to guilt. If the lash of scorn fell on her, it would never chasten, but it would goad and madden into rebellion, perhaps into recklessness.

"*Poverina!*" he said, caressingly, "evil be to those who cause you one moment's pain. Does so much coarseness and cruelty exist even in your primitive valley? But do not heed them, Castalia; these women are beneath your regret; and, remember, calumny can only lower us when it has power to make us what it calls us."

Her glance gave him eloquent and grateful comprehension.

"Oh, 'lustrissimo! it is not *their* scorn that I heed; it is only—I am afraid that it may bring me yours. And death would be more merciful to me!"

The words touched him deeply,—more deeply than he showed; for he sought to turn her thoughts from herself, as he took her hands in his own, and looked down into the splendour of her eyes.

"Castalia, never fear that. I honour you for what you are, my child. Your mother's error—if error it were —can never rest upon you; and the world is often sorely at fault in its judgments. It condones its thieves, and condemns its martyrs. But you are rash to attach so much value to my opinion. You do not know who I am, —whence I come,—what my history may be."

"But I know *you*. Had I sought to know more, would you not have thought me unworthy of so much? The fable of Psyche is so true; where doubt has once come, faith is dishonoured."

He smiled at the fable she chose, and her insight into human nature.

"Right. I think Eros was justified in taking wing and in never returning; but still there is such a thing as prudence. How can you tell that some guilt does not rest on me?—that I come here because I am a marked and disgraced man? — that I may be utterly unlike all you believe me?"

She looked at him proudly and yet sadly.

"Eccellenza, those who bear guilt do not look as you look; and, whatever you be, you are *great.*"

"No! I told you I am a fallen Cæsar, and dropped my purples long ago."

"But his purples are the least part of Cæsar's greatness."

"Not in the world's estimate. Come, let me see you homeward."

He raised the load of yellow gourds and luscious summer fruits, glowing amidst leaves and wild flowers, as he spoke; she tried to take it from him.

"Oh, illustrissimo! do not do that! *You* must not carry a burden."

"I have carried many," he said, half with a smile. She looked at him still, with that reverent, wistful look; she wondered what he had been.

"You have! But they must have been the weight of royalties, then. Give me the fruit! Pray do not take it for me!"

"Castalia, an emperor is bound to serve a woman. We have that lingering chivalry among us, at least."

The rocky road wound down under beech-boughs, and over green turf, and into the twilight of dense woods, till the aerial campanile of Fontane rose in its delicate height like a frozen fountain out of the nest of leaves. The Tuscan sunset, in all its glow, was just on earth and sky as they entered the valley where the white spire and the masses of chestnut-wood stood out against the intense blue of the early summer heavens.

"Coleridge cried, 'O God, how glorious it is to live!'" he said, rather to himself than to her, as they came into the roseate radiance. "Renan asks, 'O God, when will it be worth while to live!' In nature we echo the poet; in the world we echo the thinker."

The light was gone, the twilight fallen, as he left her at the little châlet where the charity of the Church sheltered her. He drew her to him with an involuntary action of tenderness.

"Castalia, good-night!"

Her eyes looked up to his in the shadows heavily flung around them by the bending boughs. The infinite beauty of her face had never been more fair; almost unconsciously, something of the softness of dead years revived in him; he stooped his head, and his lips touched the flushed warmth of her cheek in farewell. The kiss startled her childhood from its rest for ever; with it the knowledge of love came to her.

A sudden consciousness, a sudden alarm, quivered through her; her heart beat like a caught bird, in a sweetness and joy that made her afraid at their terrible strength and made her tremble before him as though criminal with some great guilt; she stood like an antelope that in its wild, shy grace only tempts the hunter the more: what she felt had a strange awe for her, and as strange a rapture. Though given only in a compassionate tenderness, the caress had taught the meaning of passion; her colour burned, her eyes sank under his.

At that instant the tread of a heavy step was heard on the silence: she fled instinctively, fleet as a fawn, into the deepening shadow of the arched and open door; he turned away and went back up the woodland road to his own dwelling. Fronting him, in a faint ray of dying light that slanted through the wall of chestnut and of cypress, the old priest stood, his grave, austere features rugged as the riven rock.

"Give me a word with you," he said, simply.

He whom he checked in his path looked up and paused; he had scarcely seen, and as scarcely thought of, the self-appointed guardian of Castalia.

"A word with me? Assuredly."

The priest looked at him with searching eyes, in which there was still a great sadness and a great appeal.

"Whoever you be," he said, briefly, "whether great, as I deem by your bearing, or no, I speak to you not as to one owning authority, nor as one holding myself God's command, but simply as man speaks to man."

"Say on."

"Then I say, have you thought what it is you do now?"

"Do? I fail to understand you."

"I will make my meaning plainer, then. Do you mean to ruin that young life?"

"God forbid!"

"Then do you know that they speak evil of her on your score? Do you know that, through you, they say the shame of her mother is hers?"

"They lie, then—utterly! Teach your flock more charity to youth and innocence, holy father. And let me pass; I cannot wait for this catechism."

"I thank you for that denial; *I* did not need it; her eyes are too clear beneath mine. Yet allow me a few words more. You give her no love, probably; but you are already far more her religion than the creed I have taught her from infancy. How will you use your power over her?"

He was silent; his thoughts were little with the speaker; he was thinking of the lips that had trembled beneath his own.

"You may lead her where you will; I confess it you!

You, a stranger, who saw her first but a few weeks ago, have a force to mould and sway her that I never won— I who have reared her and succoured her well-nigh from her birth," said the Italian, with a bitterness in which was a yearning pain. "It may be that I have seemed harsh to her; it may be that I have missed my way— that, while I strove overmuch to shield her from her mother's error, I forgot to woo her trust and her heart— I forgot that a child, and a woman-child above all, needs love and needs indulgence. It may be that I erred. Be it so or not, you can command her; and I can no more stay her from your sorcery than I can check the winds. Yet you say you would not blight her life; you speak as though you had pity on her. You say you leave her innocence sacred; but will you, then, rob her of peace? You say you will not lead her to dishonour: will you not spare her also the bitterness of a knowledge that must destroy the virginity of the heart? You say the slanderers lie: will you not, then, be wholly merciful, and leave her ere she learns to love you too well? You can make her the plaything of an hour; but it will only be at the price of her whole future."

He stood silent still while the old priest spoke. He had not thought of cost to her.

"Your lips touched hers to-night," pursued the Tuscan. "The woman who has once felt shame under a caress has already lost half her purity. You gave her in that a memory which will burn into her heart with humiliation every time that she thinks of you. You may mean her no injury now; but you are one who has lived long, doubtless, in the pleasures of the world: how will it end if you remain near her?"

He raised his eyes, where they stood in the early

evening light falling so faintly through the parting in
the barrier of cypress, and looked full at the Italian.

"You plead with *me* for her; to what fate do you condemn her yourself? The cloister? Have you ever thought
what it is to bury her in that tomb which cannot claim
even the repose of the graves of the dead?—to bar her
out from light and laughter and melody and joy?—to
chain her loveliness where no kiss shall ever meet her
own, no heart beat on hers, no eyes see her smile, no
lover seek her embrace? Have you ever thought what
you will do when you seal down such luxuriant life as
hers to beat, and struggle, and desire, and pine, and wither,
and perish alone? Yours is the cruelty—not mine!"

The Tuscan's furrowed cheek grew paler; he was too
deep a scholar to be a fanatical churchman, and in his
close, stern, rugged soul he cherished Castalia tenderly.

"I mean no cruelty,—Christ knows. But I have no
other shelter for her, and there at least she would have
innocence."

"Innocence forced and untempted! what is it better
than sin? Let her take her chance in the width of the
world, let her even know trial and poverty and temptation,
let her be a wanderer and a beggar, if she must; but leave
her the free air, and the forest liberty, and the human
love that is her right, and the possibility at least of joy!"

The Italian sighed wearily.

"I strive for the best; and my cruelty is not as yours.
I would save her at least from actual pain; you—if you
do her no worse thing—will bind on her a passion and a
regret that will consume her to her grave. I know her
nature; and though she has the innocence, she has not the
inconstancy, of a child: she will not *forget*. There is but
one way to spare her: leave her."

He was silent a while longer, as the priest's words

ceased, and there was no sound save the falling of a water-course rushing downward through the gloom and through the leaves.

"I will leave her," he said, at last, "if you in turn give me your word never to force her life into a convent."

"I promise."

"So be it. I will make her no farewell; let her think me heartless of her, if she will; so she will best forget."

Then he went upward alone through the evening shadows, along the slope of the hills, to the loneliness of the Latin villa. In the gloom of the deserted hall the picture of the diadem of flowers alone gleamed radiant as a ray of the moonlight fell across it. He paused before the painting, and a sudden pity stole on him.

The promise that he had given had a certain pain for him. It was not love that he felt for her. There had been too great a darkness on his life for the softness of that passion easily to revive; but he had found a pleasure in once more, after lengthened solitude, being the subject of that sweet, reverent adoration; and she had inspired him with an unspeakable compassion for her fate, which could not let him muse without anxiety upon that fate's inevitable future. There had been a time when the lavishness of his gifts and the influence of his word could have lifted her into happiness as easily as a flower is transplanted into sunlight from the shade; but that time was far away. He felt the hardest pang of poverty to those of generous nature: he had *nothing to give.*

He had offered the promise, and he would redeem it because she was motherless and defenceless, and therefore sacred to him; but he stood and looked at the flower-crowned painting with a pang of regret.

"It is a harsh mercy that he asks of me," he thought; "and yet what else should be the end? Love is no toy for me now; and she is worthier of a happier fate than to be the passing fancy, the consolation of an hour, to a worn and wearied life."

On the morrow, ere the sun was high, he was far from Vallombrosa.

BOOK THE SEVENTH.

CHAPTER I.

"Do well unto thyself, and Men will speak good of Thee."

THE Member for Darshampton sat at breakfast in his house in town,—a fine mansion, whose rental was two thousand a year, yet in whose unostentatious and solid comfort there was the impress of sterling wealth, but not a trace of parvenu arrogance or ill taste.

He sat at breakfast in his dining-room; a long, low room, hung with crimson and with a few fine pictures; at the farther end was a white bust on a pillar of jaspar: it was the bust of a long-dead statesman, Philip Chandos. The Member for Darshampton was taking his breakfast, surrounded with a sea of morning papers; he had already done two hours' hard work with his secretary, dictating, annotating, reading reports, computing statistics, conning over *précis*. Leisure, indeed, was a thing he never knew; untiring, elastic, indefatigable, unsparing, he was an admirable man of business, and every moment of his day was consumed in a labour seemingly borne as lightly as it was in reality thoroughly done, whatever its nature.

Public life was his natural sphere; to it he brought a brain ever vigilant, an energy ever unconquerable, a facility that might have been almost too facile had it not been corrected by a keen and vigorous patience that

would never slur over anything, and that searched out
the minutest points of every subject. Yet the enormous
variety, and the intensity of application that characterised
his work, told in no sort of way on his health: he felt
well, looked well, slept well; he never found any tax on
his strength touch him, more than if he had been made
of oak or granite; he never knew what pain or what
weariness was. He reaped now the recompense of the
training, the temperance, and the entire freedom from
all license in vice that he had imposed on himself so
severely throughout his early manhood. His eyes were
as bright, his skin as clear, his teeth as white, his smile
as merry, as twenty years before; John Trevenna was
unchanged,—unchanged in form and feature, in manner
and in mind. In the first, the man was too healthily
framed to alter much with time; in the latter, he was
too integrally original, and bore too thorough and
marked an idiosyncrasy to alter while he had life. He
cut his impress on the world about him, he did not
take his mould from it: men of this type change little.
Moreover, Trevenna had Success: it is a finer tonic than
any the Pharmacopœia holds, specially for those who,
like him, are too wise to let it be also a stimulant that
intoxicates or an opiate that drugs them.

He had success of the richest and the fullest. Slowly
won, but surely, he had mounted his cautious and victorious
way to those heights that long ago had been a goal of
which men would have called him a madman ever to
dream, and had netted together the innumerable threads
of his policies and his efforts, till he had woven them into
a rope-ladder strong enough and long enough to reach
the power he had coveted from earliest boyhood. His
rise had, in appearance, been gradual, yet it had been
rapid in fruits and in attainment; and there were few men

living of whom so much was thought in the present, from whom so much was expected in the future. The sedulous training he had pursued so patiently had brought its own reward: none went to the political arena more finely prepared for it: none had more completely gained a footing and a power there.

The first words he had uttered in the House had told them his quality, had told them that no ordinary man had come among them to represent that little borough of the south-western sea-board; but he had been careful, and he had been wise. He had not alarmed them with a sudden burst of talent; he had been content to run a waiting race for the first, and to bide his time. He had let his influence *grow;* he had been noted earliest rather for his admirable common sense and his practical working powers, than for anything more brilliant; and gradually as his critical audience, who regarded him as an outsider and an adventurer, became cognizant of his value, he allowed the true resources and the real capabilities of his mind to be discovered. *Festina lente* was his motto, and he had followed it with a patience the more marvellous in one whose quick, energetic, prompt, caustic temper always urged him to instant action and ironic retort.

Now he had his reward; his weight was immense, his popularity with the large and wealthy and liberal mass of the country, extreme. Ministers dreaded him, chiefs of his own party recognised in him the first of all their auxiliaries; Government would have bought his silence with any place; the benches never were so crowded as on a night when one of his watched-for and trenchant speeches rang through the drowsy air of the Lower Chamber like the clear stirring notes of a trumpet. He was rich; his commercial speculations, made with that unerring acumen which distinguished him, had prospered

and multiplied a thousandfold; all he undertook succeeded. Those who had sneered him down had become
compelled to court and conciliate him; great orders who
had dubbed him nobody, and shut him with scorn outside their pale, now learned to dread him as their direst
opponent. Houses where he had used to enter on sufferance now received him as an honoured guest; statesmen who had once blackballed him at clubs now would
have given any splendid bribe he would have taken to
still his defiance or to secure his alliance. Against
prestige, prejudice, poverty, the sneer of the world, the
antagonism of the nobility, the uttermost disadvantages
and difficulties of position, Trevenna had fought his way
into a foremost rank, and compelled his foes to acknowledge
and to dread the man whom they had laughed down as
an insignificant *farceur*, a nameless club-lounger.

His conquest was grand; the indomitable courage that
he had brought to it, the exhaustless endurance with
which he had sustained defeat and humiliation, the untiring resolve with which he had kept one aim in view
so long, and beaten down the barriers of class and custom, are the most magnificent qualities of human life.
The work was great, and greatly done. The man who
vanquishes the opprobrium of adverse orders and the opposition of adverse circumstances, is a soldier as staunch
as the Barca brood of Carthage; but—the weapons with
which the fight had been fought here were foul as an assassin's, and the root, like the goal of the struggle, was
envy. A man may rise with an admirable perseverance
and dauntlessness; but the hatchets with which he carves
his way up the steep shelving ice-slope may nevertheless
be blood-stained steel and stolen goods. We are too
apt, in our wonder and our applause at the height to
which he has attained against all odds, to forget to note

whether his steps up the incline have been clean and justly taken.

Trevenna's frankness, his *bonhomie*, his logical brain, his racy eloquence, his practical working powers, his taking candour, with which he avowed himself of the middle classes, claiming no rights of birth, his cheerful and unerring good sense, with which he would alike treat a political question by examining its business utility, and disarm a social sneer by disclaiming all pretensions to rank or to dignity, charmed the world in general, paralyzed his aristocratic foes, and pioneered his way wherever he would, giving him a wide and sure hold on the classes to whose sympathies he made his direct appeal. The fine intrigues by which power had been secretly won to him; the merciless knowledge with which he coerced those whose histories he held in a tyranny none the less irresistible because tacit; the paths in which his finesses had wandered to gather his hold on so many; the sinks out of which his wealth had been taken, as gold is found in the sewers; the manifold infamies into which his bright skill had dived, to issue from them with a terrible omnipotence; the network of inimitable chicaneries, ever wisely to windward of the law, with which he had overspread the world he had vanquished; the commercial gambling in which he had filled his treasuries by a fluke, and doubled and quadrupled gains gotten by lies; the hearty, ironic, good-humoured, rascally contempt in which he held all mankind, and disbelieved in all honesty,—these were unknown, unguessed, alike by the people who believed in him, by the aristocracies who hated him, by the party who adored him, and by the world on which he had, against odds so vast, graven the impress of his daring and splendid talent.

When the white block of marble shines so solid and

so costly, who remembers that it was once made up of decaying shells and rotting bones and millions of dying insect-lives, pressed to ashes ere the rare stone was?

Trevenna's success was, like the bricks of the ancient temples, cemented with the blood of quivering hearts; but it was all the firmer for that, and none the less victorious. Now, where he sat in his dining-room, he glanced down the leaders of his own especial organ, a journal that ever sounded "Io triumphe" before him,—glanced amusedly over the closing words of the column devoted to the praise of "the most promising statesman we possess,—the assured chief of the future,—the great orator by whom Darshampton is so nobly represented."

"Of unflagging energy," pursued his *claqueur* of the *Communist*, "of the highest political probity, of a fixity of principle never to be turned from its goal by the gilded bait of office, of talents most versatile, yet which never interfere with his devotion to the smallest business detail or mercantile interest, essentially English in creed, bias, and temper, preferring solid excellence to the flashy fascination of superficial attainment, and signalized by cordial and earnest sympathies with the wishes and the rights of the masses, it is to Mr. Trevenna that all thoughtful and advanced minds must inevitably look for progress and assistance in the future of our nation. The laws, the liberties, the domestic virtues of the hearth and home, the independence abroad, and the prosperity of internal interests, the maintenance of religion and morality, the security of the birthright of freedom to the poorest life that breathes,—all that are so notably dear to every Englishman are equally precious to him; and their preservation from all foreign taint and alien tyranny is the object alike of his public and private career. Conquest does not recommend itself to him as peace and charity do; and the clash of arms is jarring on his ear when heard instead of the whirr of a myriad looms, bread-winning and bread-giving. The welfare of the vast industrial classes of Great Britain is at his heart before all else; and to the sway which he exerts over the Senate, even when its members be most strongly adverse to him, we may apply the trite lines of the 'Æneid' 'Hoc tibi erunt artes,' &c. &c."

So the *Communist*. Trevenna laughed : the lion had too much racy humour in him not to enjoy the ridicule of his jackal's fine peroration.

"Very well, my good fellow," he thought, condescendingly. "Laid on a trifle too thick, perhaps; and you *will* call the Commons a 'Senate,' and nothing will cure you of trotting out your bit of school Latin, whether it quite fits or not: still, it does very welL 'Virtues of the hearth and home'; ah! nothing brings down the House like that. We're as blackguard a nation as any going in vice; but we do love to amble out with a period about domestic bosh. My puffs were neater when I wrote 'em myself; no gale blows you so bravely along as the breeze you prick yourself out of the wind-bag. Who should know so well as yourself all your most telling hits, your titbits of excellence, your charming niceties of virtue? The puff perfect is the puff personal—adroitly masked. Mercy on us! I do believe Hudibras is right, and the cheated enjoy being cheated. If I told my dearly beloved masses, now, 'You're a lot of uneducated donkeys,—but you're my best stepping-stones, and so I make you lie down and I get into your saddles,' they'd be disgusted to-morrow. I talk liberties, moderated Socialism, philanthropy, and moralities; I wear the Bonnet Rouge discreetly weighted down with a fine tassel of British prudence, and they believe in me! Can't, either, quite, surely?

And yet I don't know; there isn't anything so easily taken in as a whole country. Nine-tenths of a nation are such fools,—that's where it is; of course the other tenth part do what they like with them."

With which reflection on the aggregate of whom he was an honored representative, Trevenna ate a *rognon au vin de Madère.* His delight in the infinite jest of the world was unchanged; he enjoyed with an unction never sated the whole of the vast burlesque to which he played the triumphant part of Arlecchino: his heart was as light as a boy's, and his humour as savory as Falstaff's. Having worn the robes of respectability of a grave and reverend signior, all day long before the people, he would come home and toss them off with as mischievous a glee at the perfection with which he had played his part, as in earlier days he had tossed aside his domino and mask after teasing the life out of everybody at a masquerade.

He ate his kidney, glancing over some other journals that echoed the *Communist* with a more or less different wording, and some Opposition ones that flattered him equally well by damning him so very strongly that nothing but an acute dread of him could make them so bitter. Of the two, perhaps these pleased him the best. Intense abuse may be, on the whole, a surer testimony to your power than intense praise; and, moreover, he was of that nature which is never so vigorously happy as when it has something to combat. He was made of splendidly tough stuff, this man who had been so long looked down upon as a mere town-chatterbox and diner-out; and he throve on every added effort which endeavoured to displace him, and only grew the more firmly rooted for it. Breakfast done, and a first-rate cigar or two smoked, he rose, nodded to the white bust at the end of the chamber with mischief in his eyes, as though it were a living thing (he liked to see that bit of statuary there, as soldiers like to see their enemy's standards droop on their mess-room walls, in witness of hard-fought and successful war), and went out to his busy day. He toiled none the less than he had done when self-educating himself for the tribuneship he now filled; he was not a whit less punctual, arduous, and methodical than he had been when he had ground logic and finance and laws of exchange, while the world thought him an idle *flâneur;* every thing he undertook was done with a conscientious thoroughness, none the less complete because its far-sighted motive was ultimate aggrandizement. Let him have risen as high as he would, he would never have spared himself: he loved work for its own pleasure, as a man loves swimming.

His party was out of office at this time,—had been so for some two or three years; whenever they should come in again, he knew they could not help but offer him a seat in the Cabinet; well as many of them detested him, they dared not risk his enmity or his opposition. To get them into office once more, therefore, and write himself the Right Hon. John Trevenna, he laboured assiduously, and for the opposite faction with a terrible ability. He had so weakened, undermined, countermined, impugned, ridiculed, arraigned, and stripped bare their policies, that it was generally believed they would be compelled before long to try an appeal to the country. They had no one strong enough in debate, though they had several brilliant speakers, to oppose the sledge-hammer force of his close arguments and the weight of his keen logic, that felled their defences with its sharp pole-axe.

He accorded now two hours after breakfast to correspondence and such matters; then he gave audience to a Darshampton deputation, who came in sturdily sullen,

but were received with such chatty familiarity, such
pleasant good nature, that they went out again docile
and enchanted, and never had time to remember till
they were half-way home that they had extracted no
pledge from him and received not one single definite
answer; then he saw some score or more of different
visitors, breathless with political anxiety or brimming
with political rumours; a private interview with a foreign
ambassador, and a confidential *tête-à-tête* with a great
lord of his party, followed; then he sauntered into one
or two of the Pall-Mall clubs, as full of news, wit, and
good humour as when he had made his repartees to get
his dinners; then he drove down to show at a couple of
garden-parties at a French prince's and a Scotch
duchess's, vivacious, full of fun, charming the ladies as
"so droll, so original!" and playing lawn-billiards as if
he had not another stake in the world; then he went to
the House for a couple of hours and launched a short
speech that told like a rifle-shot; then he went to a din-
ner-party at a great chief's of his party; and thence to
an Embassy-ball.

There were wars and rumours of war political pend-
ing; there was agitation in the great aristocratic ranks of
opposition; there were excitement and intrigue in the
whole of the world of state-craft. It was a crisis, as the
grandes dames murmured with emphasis, and he liked to
show these nobles, these hereditary statesmen, these
women who had once scarcely bowed to him as a "rank
outsider," that he could take the emergency with all the
sang-froid imaginable, gossip as pleasantly as though no
import hung on the night, and chatter with a duchess
about Tuileries tittle-tattle till he was called away and
carried forcibly off by a whip who was in the height of
haste and trepidation.

"He will cut some work out for you," had the old duke once said of him; and Trevenna made good his words. His party hated alliance with him, but they no more dared alienate him than they dared have called him in Darshampton what they called him in secret,—a demagogue. Of a truth he was no demagogue; he was far too wise and far too cultured. He was simply a sagacious, audacious, astute, and unerring politician, willing to lead the people as far as it was his interest to do so, but not one step farther, if they starved by the thousand.

Many lords had come down to hear the Debate; the Ladies' and Strangers' Galleries were full, the crowds outside the House packed close in expectation; it was known that the fate of parties hinged chiefly on this night's issue. With a grey paletot over his evening dress, he sauntered to his place, imperturbable, nonchalant, looking as bright and as keen as though he were just going up to the wickets at cricket. All eyes were on him; he was used to that by this time, and liked nothing better. He loved to know that his brisk, elastic step, and his good-humoured, easy bearing, were as well known here as the haughty grace of Philip Chandos once had been. The ambition of his life centred in the turn of the night; the hopes of his party centred in himself. It was his to attack, and, if possible, to defeat, the Government, and all the resources of his intellect had been brought to meet the need; yet, as he took his seat, he was as genial, as bright, as light-hearted, as though he were a school-boy, and was so without a shade of affectation in it. He had the qualities of a very great man in him, and he loved the atmosphere of conflict.

His famous rival's speech closed: it had been brilliant, persuasive, subtle, launching an unpopular measure with consummate skill, and fascinating, if it failed to convince,

all auditors. It was no facile task to reply to and refute
him.   Trevenna rose, one hand lightly laid on the rail,
the other in the breast of his coat; on his lips was his
pleasant, frank smile: the Opposition had learned to dread
its meaning.   The House was profoundly hushed as his
voice, perfectly moderated, but resonant, telling and
clarion-like, pierced the silence.   He knew well how to
hold its ear.

He was a master of the great art of banter.   It is a
marvellous force: it kills sanctity, unveils sophistry, traves-
ties wisdom, cuts through the finest shield, and turns the
noblest impulses to hopeless ridicule.   He was a master
of it; with it he rent his antagonist's arguments like
gauze, stripped his metaphors naked, pilloried his logic
and his rhetoric, his finance and his economics, and left
the residue of his ornate eloquence a skeleton and a
laughing-stock. He did this matchlessly, and did not do
it too much: he knew the temper of his audience, and
never transgressed its laws of courtesy.   He carried it
with him as by magic, and from his lighter weapons he
passed on, and took up the terseness of reasoning, the
closeness of logic, the mathematical exactitude, the shrewd,
practical common sense, without which no speaker will
ever thoroughly gain the confidence and homage of the
English Commons.   It might not be the silver eloquence
of a Demosthenes, but it was the oratory suited above all
to his theme and to his place,—classic, moreover, even
whilst it was business-like and restrained, as befitting a
gathering of gentlemen, even whilst most audacious,
most pungent, most merciless in raillery and attack.

The House cheered him in riotous excitement as he
sat down, and the supreme triumph of a triumphant life
was given him.   His speech did a rare thing in St.
Stephen's: it influenced the votes: the Government was

defeated hopelessly on a great issue, and could have no choice but to resign.

There was the grandeur, if there were the insolence, of supreme success, self-won, in Trevenna's eyes and in his thoughts, as he went out in the lateness of the night with the cheers which had ratified his victory still seeming to echo in his ear. He looked, as his carriage rolled through the gaslights, down the darkling streets of Westminster, and thought of the night he had stood there as a boy and trodden out the luscious Paris bonbons of a young child's gift. What he had done since then!

"Beaux seigneurs! what of the outsider *now?*" he mused, with his victorious smile on his mouth. "In a week's time I shall be called the RIGHT HON. JOHN TREVENNA: and they dread me so bitterly they will dare to refuse me no place in the Cabinet that I choose to command."

"The ministry will go out. Sit down, and don't yawn: there is no end to do," he said, curtly, to his secretary, as he threw off his paletot and entered his library. It was nigh four in the morning; but his indefatigable elasticity and energy knew no fatigue. As though just fresh to the work, he plunged into correspondence that no précis-writing could have made terser and no diplomatist have surpassed for masterly surface-honesty and secret reticence. A splendid campaign had been finished; a splendid campaign was to be commenced. The army of attack had been led triumphant; the army of occupation was to be headed in the future. There would be others higher than he in the titular dignities of office, but there would be none higher in virtual power.

"Do well unto thyself, and the world will speak well of thee." It was rare indeed that ever now there was found one bold enough to murmur against the wealthy speculator, the popular favourite, the astute politician, the audacious and sagacious winner of all life's choicest prizes, the bitter word that had long ago been cast at him,—"adventurer."

Others forgot that old time; he did not. He loved to remember every jot of it. He loved to remember the vow he had sworn in the midnight streets in his childhood. He loved to remember every privation endured, every smart felt, every insolence taken in silence, every long lonely night spent in hard toil and pitiless study, while the merry world laughed around in its pleasures and vices. He loved to count up how much he had conquered, and to pay back jibes of twenty years ago, treasured up and waiting their vengeance; he loved to make men who had turned their backs on him then bow before him now, and to glance downward on the vast decline up which he had mounted, and to think how the sureness of his foot and the keenness of his eye had brought him against all difficulty to the table-lands where he now stood secure. All he forgot were—benefits.

With these triumphal thoughts did remorse ever mingle? Did he ever remember the cost to other lives at which so much of his victory had been gained? Did he ever give a flush of shame when he recollected how he had rewarded evil for good, and bitten through with tiger-fangs the hand which had loaded him with gifts, and betrayed and robbed and driven down to ruin the most loyal friend that ever gave him fearless faith? Never once! Amidst the pæans of success conscience has small chance to be heard, and the temper of Trevenna was proof against all such weakness. He would have said that he knew neither form of ill-digestion,—neither dyspepsia nor repentance.

———

CHAPTER IL
The Throne of the Exile.

IT was in the boudoir of the great house of Lilliesford, where a political coterie wove its silken meshes for
men's souls and official places. Very beautiful women
were seen in it sometimes, but they were rarely the gay
young sovereigns; they were rather the older and more
stately leaders of the world political. For of these latter
was the Countess of Clydesmore.

She sat there now, in the darkest depths of the shadow,
her head slightly bent, no light on the rich brown wealth
of her hair or the sculpture-like perfection of her features.
She was a woman whom her own great world revered:
no levity ever touched her name, no coquetry ever lowered
her dignity. Ambitious she was, though she scarce knew
what for,—rather for the simple sake and sweetness of
power and of prerogative than anything else. If her
heart remained cold as ice to the man whose name she
graced and whose children she had borne,—if her young
sons never saw any smile in her eyes, but shrank from
her in their infancy, chilled and afraid,—her world did
not know this, and, had it known, would have thought it
no breach of the social code. We lay blame to society
because it judges from the surface:—idle blame: how
else can it judge?

She was a stainless wife, of a lofty purity of life; if
in her soul she hated with a hate intense as passion the
man to whom she had bound captive her beauty,—if
when she looked on the children she had brought him
she pressed her lips tight to hold back a curse on them
because he was their father,—who could tell this? None,
—save the husband who had heard another name than
his own murmured wearily in the dreams of her bridal

sleep,—save the young boys who glanced at her with timid, troubled eyes, and wondered why, when, for duty or for appearance, she had touched their cheeks with a kiss, she thrust them away with an involuntary revulsion as they saw her thrust a tiresome dog.

Now Lady Clydesmore leaned back, musing of the prospects of her party. She reigned for reigning's sake; she wove for weaving's sake; she was ambitious because her nature could not choose but be so; she intrigued because she was weary of her life and forgot herself a little the quickest in these cabals. It was neither for her husband nor her sons that she laboured; if the raising of her hand could have made the one a king, she would not for his sake have raised it; if by lifting it the others could have died out of her sight and out of her memory and sunk into their graves, it would have been lifted as eagerly, as pitilessly, as ever Roman matrons gave the sign for the slaughter in the arena. But the acquisition of privilege and the vanity of her own splendid dominion were the passions of her character: she had sickened long ago of the reign of her beauty; the domain of intellectual and political pre-eminence remained to her, and she had occupied it and usurped it.

The three ladies with her were talking now of one who had also won his way to that closely-fenced and closely-crowded table-rock of political strife.

"It could not have been formed without him," said one fair politician.

"Oh, no," assented a yet warmer partisan. "He could make his own terms."

"He was moderate to be content with the Colonial," murmured the Lady of Lilliesford.

"The Board of Trade might have done?" suggested the first.

"Certainly not; he would not have taken it," nega-tived the second, Lady Dorénavant, with a certain con-tempt. "The Foreign seals now——"

"Oh, no," dissented her adversary; "we should have twenty wars on our hands in as many weeks with his brusque, brief despatches. They would be very Napo-leonic; but he would say to the Pope, 'You belong to the past: off with you!' and would write to France, 'We hate you, and you hate us: why mince the matter?' He would not be conducive to European harmony."

Lady Dorénavant gave a lazy gesture of dissent.

"Is that all you know of him? In the Foreign Office, or anywhere else, he would always do just the thing that needed to be done, and no more. He can keep Dars-hampton in good humour; it is more unmanageable, on the whole, than Europe."

"I agree with you," murmured a third fair Chevreuse of politics. "I believe he would hold the Foreign port-folio and hold it well. He would keep peace; but there would be no fog in his correspondence, and no beating about the bush. What he had to say would be said briefly, firmly, and with infinite tact. The only pity is—he was nobody."

"Every one has forgotten that by now," said Lady Clydesmore, with a curl of disdain on her thoughtful lips, that was followed by a darker and more bitter shadow where she sat in the shelter of the curled tropic leaves.

"No: it is never forgotten and never forgiven," said the last speaker, with delicate disdain; for she was a very keen wit, a very truthful temper, and despised her own party now and then not a little. "But, you know as well as I, we can't afford to appear to remember it. He is so much to us."

"I do not see there is anything to be forgotten," said

Lady Dorénavant, who piqued herself on being positively
"Red" in her political tastes in theory, but who would
nevertheless never have set foot again in any house in
which the order of precedence had been violated in going down to dinner and the heraldic dignities of her
house been offended in any iota of ceremonial. "That
is such a miserable monopoly, such an old-world opti-
cism, to adhere so much to lineage. For my own part, I
never forget that the greatest men of all nations have
sprung from the people. Life is too earnest, truth too
broad, for these insignificant class-distinctions."

"Quite so, dear," yawned her pretty, inconsequent
antagonist. "We all say that nowadays. But why aren't
you true to your theory? Why don't you let Adine
marry poor Langdon?"

"That is absurd!" said the socialist peeress—a little
nettled; for no one likes to be twitted with turning theories into action. "Nobody is talking of marriage: we are
speaking of men who attain power without the hereditary
right to it. I confess, I admire self-made men; there is
such a rugged grandeur about the mere idea of all they
have contested with and conquered."

Which was a beautiful absence of all prejudice on her
ladyship's part, slightly nullified in its weight by the fact
that she had a month before half broken her daughter's
heart, and spent all her most bitter and deadly court-
liness of insolence and opprobrium on that daughter's
lover—a great artist, who had had the presumption to
think that his fine celebrity and his gallant love might
mate him with the young azure-eyed aristocrat, and in
return had been stoned and pierced with a great lady's
polished insults.

"Besides," she pursued, now on her favourite theme,
"you cannot call *him* a self-made man: he was always

among us, always at the best houses, entered Parliament at a very good age, has always known everybody and been seen everywhere. I remember his first speech so well! It was short—he had too much tact to detain the benches long—but so pithy, so trenchant, so precise to the purpose, so admirably uttered! I remember saying to poor Sir James that very night, 'See if I am not right; we shall have a recruit well worth studying and retaining there.' And he *did* see I was right."

She nestled herself among her soft cushions with complacent remembrance; she had been the first to discern the faint beams of the rising sun.

"What that man has done since then!" murmured the Countess of Clydesmore, rather to herself unconsciously than to her companions.

At that instant a hand thrust aside the sacred velvet curtain before the open folding-doors, that rarely was drawn aside save by the few privileged comers who were made free of the guild: the subject of their words and thoughts entered the boudoir. He was just then a guest for an autumnal week at Lilliesford.

Lady Clydesmore did not look up; a slight gloom came over her face, and the abrupt rapidity of entrance jarred her nerves. Lady Dorénavant smiled a bland welcome.

"Ah, Mr. Trevenna, you come to enliven us!"

"You have faith in my powers of enlivening? Well, so have I, I think. I actually once contrived to make a royal dinner only half as dull as a sermon!"

"What specific have you against dulness?"

"Don't know," answered the popular politician, shrugging his shoulders and hitting, as he usually did, the truth, —"except it may be that I never feel a dull dog myself."

"But then that's just it: how is it you *don't?*"

"Ah! that *is* just it. Can't say. Natural constitution, I suppose, and a good digestion; good conscience, if you like it better—that sounds more pretty and poetic. Though really, as a practical fact, I believe it's a good deal easier to carry a murder comfortably on one's soul than a Lord Mayor's dinner comfortably on one's chest."

"You speak as if you have tried both," said the languid, disdainful voice of his hostess from the shadow.

"So I have. I've eaten Corporation turtle, and I've murdered many a little Bill—hopeless little Bills that scarcely saw the light before I strangled them. But I can't say their slaughter was heavy to bear, whatever the debate upon them might be. Lady Dorénavant, what are you reading? Anything good?"

"An old acquaintance of yours," she said, handing him the book.

He had read it, but he turned the leaves over as though he had not, lifting his eyebrows where he lay back luxuriously coiled in the depths of a couch.

"Ah! Chandos! Frightens people dreadfully, doesn't it? Sort of Buddhism—eh? sublimated Cartesianism, intended for the thirtieth century or thereabouts? Makes a science of history, and gives a sinecure to Deity! Believes in other worlds, but smashes Providence as a used-up *Deus ex machinâ;* utterly contemns the body, and isn't very clear about the soul. That's the style, isn't it?"

The grand dark eyes of Lady Clydesmore loomed on him from her corner in the shadow.

"You travesty what you have not read," she said, slowly and curtly. "The book is a great book."

"Sorry to hear it! It won't bring him a shilling, then. As for writing all those heterodox before-your-time speculations and philosophies, it's the sheerest madness, if you want to live by what you write, as of course he does.

If you're an unfrocked priest, now, or a curate without
a chance of promotion, it's all very well to do it: you
have a piquance about you from having stoned your own
gods; and if you can't be a success, it's just as well to
go in for the other side *toto corde*, and come out in full
bloom a martyrdom. But just to write a 'great book,'
and look to posterity to reward you—mercy alive! I'd
as soon sow corn in the sea, or try to get a ladder to the
stars!"

"I can believe you," said the voice of his hostess,
with that veiled bitterness still in it; "no one would accuse you of doing anything without the certainty of present reward."

He laughed with the charming good humour with
which he always won over the most sullen and angry
mob, sooner or later, to his side.

"No: I don't 'go in for the angels.' Too unsubstan-
tial and too solemn for me. Where's the use of working
for posterity! A comet may have sent the earth fizzing
into space before it's fifty years older. Besides, I've an
English prejudice that real, sensible, practical work deserves its reward and gets it. I think in the long run all
things bring in their net value. It's only the mortified
vanity of those who carry bad goods to market that
makes them start the hypothesis that they're unsaleable
because they are too superior."

"They may be right sometimes, if they say—because
they are too true to be welcome," said the Countess of
Clydesmore, in that slow, languid, yet almost acrid tone
with which she had spoken throughout from her distant
nook of shadow.

"Oh, yes," he laughed, carelessly toying with the
book he still held. "Chandos, here, tells a good deal too
much truth: they'd forgive him his unorthodoxy sooner

than they'd forgive him his accuracy. All men are candid
when they're *in extremis* and have nothing left to lose,—
bankrupts, beggars, moribunds, authors in the Index, and
thieves in the Old Bailey!"

"You are complimentary to authors."

"Never liked them," returned the successful politician.
"They *are* so unpractical. If they write fiction, it's puppets; if history, it's prejudice; if philosophy, it's cobwebs;
if science, it's mares' nests: let them take what they will,
it must be more or less moonshine. Now, if I ever wrote
a book——"

"What should it be?" asked his fair partisan.

"Well, it should be what everybody should like,—a
true contemporary *Chronique Scandaleuse*, such as his secret
police summed up to Louis Quinze, every day, of the
doings of Paris. How it would sell!—specially with a
tag of religion to finish, and a fine blue-light of repentance burning for the British public at the end of every
wickedness! It would sell by millions where this book,
that my Lady Clydesmore says is a 'great book,' sells
by tens."

The languid *grandes dames* laughed softly; it was the
fashion to admire and to quote all he said as "so infinitely humorous," "so admirably original!" Yet beneath
the art-bloom on her cheek Lady Dorénavant felt herself
turn pale. There was a family secret of a terrible shame
to her house, that had been buried, as they had thought,
five fathoms deep, where none could disinter it; and John
Trevenna had found it out, and had let them learn that
he had done so. All the weight of her vast influence, of
her political favour, had been thrown into the scale many
years gone by to purchase silence: yet she had never felt
secure that her bribe, magnificent and mighty in profit
though it was, had availed. There is no sign and seal to

those bargains, and the tacit bond may any day be broken by the stronger side.

"A religious 'tag!' What a word!" smiled a radiant blonde. "I thought you were never irreverent now!"

"Never," he responded, promptly. "It never does to be unorthodox in a country where the Church is a popular prejudice——I beg pardon; I meant bulwark. I had my unregenerated days, I know, when I didn't go to church; but I hadn't heard grace said before dinner by an arch-bishop then; that does more than anything, I think, to-wards correcting one's soul, if it's a little adverse tendency towards cooling the soup. You don't talk Pantheism or Positivism when you've once stayed with a Primate. But I didn't come to chatter: I ventured into this *sanctum sanctorum* to show you these."

With which he unfolded some afternoon letters he had in his hand, and, lounging comfortably in that velvet nest, by the side of the priestess of his own especial party, went deep with her into their various contents and their news political,—as deep, at least, as he chose to go. He always satisfied his confidantes that they knew as much as he did; but he always spread the surface: he never showed the whole. There is not an art so delicate and so full of use as that art of apparent frankness: it con-ciliated the very women who had been his deadliest foes, and, while they imagined themselves his allies, they be-came at his fancy his dupes. They were his scouts, his sharpshooters, his skirmishers, his spies, those dainty, haughty, high-bred patrician châtelaines; they fetched and carried, they parried and bribed, for him; they played into his hands, and they worked out his will; and they never knew it, but all the while thought themselves con-descending with a superb grace and tact to secure a ser-viceable recruit, and guessed no more the remorseless and

vulgar uses to which he turned them than the sun guesses
the use that photography makes of his glory when it
turns his rays into detectives and brings them as witness
in law-courts.

He stayed there some twenty minutes; the boudoir
was not seldom a cabinet council-room in the recesses,
and all the ladies in it now were for him and were with
him.   He never sought women,—not a whit; they must
come to him, must need him, and must serve him; but he
knew how to turn to account better than any man living
all their armoury of slender, invincible, damascened
weapons,—the better because no glance of lustrous eyes
ever had power to quicken his pulse one beat, because
the softest voice that ever wooed his ear never had charm
to lull his wisdom for a second.   Love was a trumpery
nonsense that never could enter the virile sagacity of
Trevenna's mind.   And now, when he had done with the
ladies, he went to play rackets with the young Lord Lilliesford, the eldest son of the house.

He knew how to do this sort of thing,—how to enter
with infinite glee into a boy's sports, yet how never to
risk losing the faith he had impressed men with in his
unerring acumen and practical talents. Every one felt the
contagion of the bright, vivacious, untiring good humour
which could make a leading politician love a lark like
an Etonian, and it was not assumed with him.   He was
essentially full of animal spirits, and never had to simu-
late them by any hazard. It was one of the chief secrets
of his social success: men who might have feared him or
mistrusted him whilst they were with him in the political
field lost their awe or their distrust, and could not choose
but warm to him, when they saw him taking a blind fence
"like a good 'un," telling mischievous stories in a smoking-

room, or heartily snowballing public-school lads on the terraces of some famous house.

"Look at him playing with that boy! What a capital fellow he is! Goes in for it, by George, as if he hadn't anything else to live for!" said a peer, Lord Dallerstone, as he watched the science with which Trevenna caught the ball on his racket. He had ceased to be "Charlie," and had left far behind him the troubles of his F. O. days of dandyism and "dead money;" but he had never forgotten Trevenna's aid, and did him in repayment many a public service with most loyal gratitude. The popular favourite had always had the knack of so throwing his crumbs upon the waters that they returned to him in whole quarterns of wheaten bread.

Lady Clydesmore gave a careless glance at the game, then turned away with an imperceptible shudder. The haughty grace of her young son, so like her own, had caught her eyes, and she held him in a bitter aversion for his father's sake.

She would have condemned with all the icy severity of a patrician matron the errors of a too ardent passion, the devoted self-abandonment of an uncalculating love; but she placed no check on the silent, unseen indulgence of an intense abhorrence, that made her husband feel like a whipped hound under the lash of her unuttered scorn, and her children shrink from the frozen apathy of her fair face.

"There are serious complications," said the Earl, musingly, after a lengthened conversation with his guest, in a ride which had succeeded to the rackets. His party did not altogether relish union with the Darshampton representative, but they were glad of his alliance and dared not brook his opposition.

"I don't see anything that need disturb us," said

Trevenna, carelessly. He made no solemn mysteries of *his* political views: he always showed his cards frankly,—as frankly as the Greek shows them to the watching *galérie* when he knows the marks upon the backs of them are only to be traced by his own eye. "On the contrary, when the House meets, we shall have a good working majority that, well handled, should keep us in for years. If there be no internal dissensions among us, there can be positively nothing that can unseat us for sessions, unless very unlooked-for contingencies arise. You know we've such a good cry:—we're all for the people!"

He laughed a little as he said it. To Trevenna's acute mind, there was always a good bit of absurdity in the political dance of his *burattini*, and while he used his marionettes with all the gravity needful, he could not help being tickled at the gaping national audience which believed in them and never spied out the strings.

"Their interests, indeed, are always first at my heart," said the Earl, who was in the ministry himself, was a strict Churchman, and was considered a great philanthropist. "The country trusts no one better than yourself: in real truth, there are few, if any, to whom it owes more."

"You do me much honour by such an opinion," bowed Trevenna, who managed the noble lord as he liked. "It is my highest ambition to serve the nation to the best of my insignificant powers; but meanwhile I am quite content to yield the *pas* to men of your rank and weight."

"Sensible fellow," thought the lord; "so moderate! Who can be so blind as to accuse him of Socialism?"

"*Pro me* is more my cry than *pro patriâ*. I'm a selfish man," laughed Trevenna, with that confession of egotism which sounded so charmingly frank. "I don't pretend to be among the 'idealists.' Apropos, have you read that new book by Chandos? The Countess thinks very highly of it"

The Earl reddened: he had never ceased to be jealous of the man he had supplanted,—of the man he knew his wife still loved.

"I never read his books," he said, frigidly. "His influence is widely fatal. I am happy to think your acquaintance with him has been long at an end."

"Oh, we were old comrades in my wild and unconverted days. *I* should never have dropped him, indeed, for old acquaintance' sake; but years ago—time of his crash—he behaved ungratefully to me, very badly, on my word!—after I'd been slaving my life out for him, too. I'm not a sensitive man,—never was; but that cut me up a good deal."

"Ah! I am not surprised to hear it. It is singular that great genius is almost always companioned with so much depravity!"

Trevenna laughed.

"Thank God, he didn't give me genius,—only talent. Talent wears well, genius wears itself out; talent drives a snug brougham in fact, genius drives a sun-chariot in fancy; talent keeps to earth and fattens there, genius soars to the empyrean to get picked by every kite that flies. Talent's the port and the venison, genius the seltzer and soufflés, of life. The man who has talent sails successfully on the top of the wave; the man with genius beats himself to pieces, fifty to one, on the first rock ahead. Ah! there's our very man of genius's lost Clarencieux. Just see the tops of the towers. Would you mind riding over?"

The Earl gave a hurried though bland dissent.

"Pardon me: pray 'ide there if you wish; but I have promised to visit a tenant who is, I sadly fear, dying. We are close to his farm now. Call for me as you come back. The poor man begged to see me; and there are

high and holy duties which one must not neglect, even
when they are irksome."

"High and holy fiddlesticks, my friend! You're a very
poor hypocrite, but you're a very good card," thought
Trevenna, as they parted. Lord Clydesmore, with his
irreproachable moral character, great wealth, and solid
standing in public life, was one of his prize puppets in
the ballet that he made all his fantoccini dance, while he
turned the handle of the barrel-organ to what tune he
would.

Trevenna's hatred was class-hatred. Could he have
followed the bent of his mind, he would have had as little
scruple and as much zest in the sweeping away of the
Optimates as Marius had in their slaughter. He would
have held back his hand from their extermination as little
as did the ruthless old plebeian, hating them as Marius
hated the men who had worn the golden amulet and the
purple robe whilst he was following the ploughshare over
the heavy clods of the tillage. This animosity was strong
in Trevenna; nothing could cool it, nothing soften it;
success in no way changed it, for in success he saw that
these, his born foes as he thought them, dreaded him, but
detested him. The bitterness was oddly woven in with
the brightness and the vigour of his nature, otherwise too
healthy and too well balanced to cherish passion; but it
was deathless with him.

Still, he was too acute a man to let this appear in his
public or private life: he appreciated too ably the temper
of his times and his country to allow this wholesale enmity to be betrayed. Trevenna would have enjoyed to
be the leader of a great revolution; but he had no ambition to remain a popular demagogue in an anti-revo-
lutionary nation. He considered it very unpractical and
unprofitable, and, while he cared not one whit for all the

creeds and principles in the world, he cared very heartily
for the solid advantages and the real power that he set himself to win. The pure impersonal longing of a Vergniaud
or a Buzot, the sublime devotion of a Washington or a
Hampden, were utterly incomprehensible to him. Trevenna was too thoroughly English to have a touch of
"idealism," and not to measure all things, principles in-
cluded, by the pocket. Had he flung himself headlong
into the cause of the people, and into the service of a re-
publican code, he would have been a far better and more
honest man than he was; but he would not have been so
clever, and he would not, assuredly, have been so successful. He knew what he was about too well to tie himself
to a principle; the only principle he ever consistently
followed was his own interest. He was a man who could
tell the temper of the hour he lived in to a miracle, and
adapt himself to it with a marvellous tact and advantage.
They who do this are not the highest order of public men,
but they are invariably the most successful and most
popular. If a genuine loyalty to any creed could once have
fairly taken hold on him, it would have gone far to redeem him; but it could not. His hate was strong against
an order, certainly; but his solitary creed was a very
simple one,—his own self-advancement.

He rode now by himself, on a ride that he usually
took whenever he was staying at Lilliesford: he rode towards Clarencieux. A few miles of fair speed brought
him within sight of the magnificence of the building, with
the glow of the sun on its innumerable windows, and the
upward-stretching masses of the rising woods at its back.
It was grand, historic, inexpressibly beautiful in the decline of the day, with the golden haze over its dark sweep
of endless woodland, and the rush of water beneath the
twilight of the boughs, the only sound on the air. A

stranger coming thus upon it would have paused involuntarily at the solemnity of its splendour of sea and land, of hill and vale: Trevenna checked his horse, and gazed at it with a smile.

"'The glory has departed, and his place shall know him no more,'" he muttered. "How scriptural I grow! Ah! he's gone for ever! And *I* could buy that now; I will buy it, too, just to cut the forests down, and turn the pictures to the wall, and send the last marquis's coronet to the smelting-shop. He is gone for ever, and I come here as a Cabinet minister. Vengeance is a good Madeira: it gets mellower by keeping. There is nothing on earth so sweet, except its twin—Success!"

Seventeen years had gone by since he had first taken his vengeance; but whenever, in the full and rapid whirl of his busy life, he had time to remember and to look back, it was sweeter than of old, even to him,—deeper, richer, fuller of flavour, as it were, like the wine with which he compared it.

A labourer near him was working at a sunken fence in the deer-forest. The man looked at him, knowing his face.

Trevenna, always communicative and always good-naturedly familiar with the working-classes,—it was a part of his stock-in-trade,—nodded to him.

"Fine day, my good fellow. Have you an easy time of it on these lands?"

"Main and easy, sir," answered the man, thrusting his spade into the soil with his heel, and standing at leisure for a talk. "There's naught to complain of hereabouts."

"Glad to hear it," said Trevenna; though he thought to himself, "If everybody gave your answer, where the deuce would all politics and *our* trade be?" "So you're all content, are you, under the French Duc?"

The hedger and ditcher took his spade up with some clods of earth on it, turned them thoughtfully, as though there were consolation in the act, patted them, and looked up again. "The duke's a good master, and a free giver, —I ain't a-saying a word agen him; but——"

"But what? What else the dickens can you want, my man?"

The labourer lowered his voice, and uncovered· his head. "Sir, we want *him*."

"Him? Whom?"

"Him as we have lost this many year, sir," said the man, gravely and gently, leaning his arms on his spade. "We ha'n't a-forgot him,—we ha'n't. Not none on us."

"Indeed, my good fellow," laughed Trevenna, with a petulant anger in him that the exiled man should be remembered even by this labourer in the deer-forest, "you are uncommonly loyal for nothing. He thought deuced little about you."

"That's as may be, sir. He was a gay gentleman, and had many things to please him, and that like; but he was a good master to the poor, and we was proud on him, we was; that's just it—proud on him," continued the hedger and ditcher, with a steady resolve and a wistful regret commingled. "We won't see his like again; and the country-side ha'n't been the same since he was took from us. Old Harold Gelart, he died ten year and more ago; but his death-word was for him as we lost. 'Bring him back!' he cries; 'bring him back!' and he looks wild-like as he says it, and dies."

The speaker stooped and thrust his spade afresh into the rich, ·damp earth; he felt a choking in his throat. Trevenna dug the spur into his horse's flank, and urged him forward. It incensed him that he could not hurl down Chandos from this last throne left him,—the hearts and the memories of his people.

The labourer looked up once more, touching his hat with an eager anxiety: "I beg pardon, sir, but—you was his friend, you were: can't you tell me? A'n't there *no* hope we'll ever have him back?"

Trevenna laughed, and threw him down a half-crown.

"Not the faintest, my man. When you see those towers walk out and sit in the sea!—not till then. Beggared gentlemen don't get out of beggary quite so easily."

And he rode on at a hand-gallop.

"Mercy! what fools these clods are!" he thought. "How they remember! Seventeen years! Why, in the world, there, it's time enough for us to recast Europe, and knock down kings, and pull up old religions, and plant new ones, and bury whole generations and forget 'em again, and cry, 'Le Roi est mort! Vive le Roi!' fifty times over; and here are these dolts under their forests sleep the years away in idiocy, and dream of a prodigal and a bankrupt whom they haven't seen for half a lifetime!"

It incensed him that there should remain to the disinherited even such shadowy remnant of his forfeited royalty as lingered in the remembrance of these peasantry. He could not forgive the throne that the exile still held in the hearts of his lost people.

One other, as well as he, thought of Chandos in that moment. The mistress of Lilliesford sat alone in her writing-cabinet, and on the chillness of her face there was the mournful agitation which trembles on the cold surface of waters when the dead float below them. The dead were rising now beneath her icy calm,—dead words, dead days, dead love. In her hand, just taken out of a secret drawer, were some faded letters,—tender notes, short and graceful, such as are written by those who love, in days when they meet wellnigh every hour.

The wife whom the world quoted for her haughty honour, her unblemished name, the chaste purity of her proud life, looked on them till her head drooped, and her eyes grew dim with a thirsty pain, and her lips quivered as she gazed. She had forsaken him; but she knew now that she had erred to him. She would have given her life now to have felt his kiss once more upon her lips.

Though the traffic had been sanctioned by the Church, she had been in no sense superior to any courtesan who sells her beauty for men's gold, when she had sold her own in barter for the rank she held, for the things of wealth that were about her, for the possessions of a husband she scorned and hated. And in that moment of weakness she would have given them all back for one hour of the love that she had lost.

CHAPTER III.

"He who endures conquers."

UNDER the deep leaves of Fontainebleau, in the heart of the forest, in the golden pomp of early autumn, when only a few trees were bronzed with the reddening flush of the waning summer, there stood an antique wooden building, half lodge, half châlet, all covered with the quaint floral and faun carvings of the Moyen Age, and buried away beneath dense oak-boughs and the dark spreading fans of sea-pines. It was old, dark, fantastic, lonely; yet from under its low-peaked roof music was floating out like a Mass of Palestrina's from within a chamber dark and tranquil as an oratory.

The musicians were seated in the glow of a western afternoon sun, that shone all amber and crimson and mellow through the open, painted panes. They were strangely dissimilar, yet bound together by one love,— their Art. The first was a grand old Roman, like a picture of Bassano; the second a South German, with a fair, delicate head, spiritualized and attenuated as Schiller's; a third was a little, nut-brown, withered, silent creature, ugly and uncouth as Caliban; the leader was a cripple, with whose name the world had come to associate the most poetic and ethereal harmonies that ever rebuked the lusts and the greed of its passions and cares. They were often together, these four brothers in art, and no jealousies ever stirred amidst them, though they all served the same mistress; three of them implicitly loved and implicitly followed the fourth, though he never asked or thought of mastery, but was still humble in his great powers as a child, still thought the best that he could reach so poor beside his dreams of excellence. The world treasured his works, and paid lavishly with its gold for the smallest fragment of his creations, the slightest and briefest of his poems of sound; but this brought him no vanity, no self-adoration. He worshipped his art too patiently, too perfectly, ever to think himself more than a poor interpreter, at his uttermost, of all the beauty that he knew was in her. Success makes many men drunk as with eating of the lotus-lily; success only made Guido Lulli scorn himself that he could not tell men better all the sublime things his art taught him.

Their music filled the chamber with its glory, and that glory flushed his face and lit his eyes as it had always power to do, as the world had now seen it in the moments of his triumphs, until it had learned to know that the feeble visionary whom it called a fool was higher and holier than it in all its stirring strength and wealth. He roused to life the beating of its purer heart; he led it towards God better than any priest or creed. But he held himself throughout but an unworthy priest of the mighty hierarchy of melody; he held himself but a feeble exponent of all the glory, unseen of men, that with his dreams was opened to him. They thought and called him great; he knew himself unwise and faint of utterance as a young child.

Against the casement leaned one whom the Hebrew lad Agostino had likened in his youth to David of Israel in the fulness of royalty, when the smile of women and the sun of Palestine had their fairest light for the golden-haired, golden-crowned king; whom the young Tuscan Castalia had likened now to David when his royalty still was with him, but when the treachery of men had eaten into his soul, and the heat and burden of battle darkened his sight, and the shadows of night lengthened long in his path.

Chandos came here as men in the old monastic days came, war-worn and combat-wearied, into the hush, and the majesty, and the subdued colour-glow of the abbey sanctuaries, to leave their arms and their foes without for a while and forgotten, and to lie down to rest for a brief hour on the peaceful altars where in the silence they remembered God.

He was changed,—utterly changed; not so much in his face or his form; the beauty with which nature had dowered him so lavishly could not perish, except with death itself; and though the brilliance, the carelessness, the gay and cloudless light which had made painters paint him as the Sun-god were gone, the grave and serene mel-ancholy, the deep and weary thought, which were upon his features now shadowed them indeed, but gave them a yet higher, a yet grander cast: it had the power of Lucretius; it had the weariness of Milton. Dead in him for

ever, lost never again to be recovered, were the brightness, the splendour, the radiant and fearless lustre, of his
early years: they had been killed,—killed by a merciless
hand,—and could no more revive than the slaughtered
can revive in their tombs. Yet not wholly had calamity
conquered him; and from the black depths into which
misery had thrust him to die like a drowned dog, he had
risen with a force of resistance that in some sense had
wrung a victory from the fate that sought to crush him.

In the old court of the Rue du Temple he had accepted adversity, and lived for the sake of the honour of
his fathers, of the dignity of his manhood, of the heritage
of his genius. From that hour, though he had longed as
the tortured long for death many a time, he had never
swerved from the path he had taken; in the arid, lifeless,
burning desert-waste around him he had gone on, resolute
and unbeaten, wresting from its very loneliness and
barrenness the desert-gifts of strength and silence. His
nature was one to loathe the burden of existence unless
existence were with every breath enjoyment; yet when
every breath was pain he bore with it as men whose
tempers were far stronger and more braced by training
might never have found ability to do,—bore with it for
the sake of the loftier things, the prouder powers, that
would not die in him, and that naught except dishonour
or his own will could slay.

The little gold given for the silver collar had sufficed
to keep life in him a few days; when those were ended,
he had gone to the house at which the French editions
of his works had been produced, and asked the chiefs of
it simply for work. The heads of the firm touched to
more pity than they dared express, gave what he sought,
—classical work, which, though but the labours of routine
and of compilation, still brought his thoughts back per-

force to the Greek studies that had ever been his best-beloved treasuries of meditation and of knowledge. He laboured for his bare subsistence,—for his day's maintenance; but the exertion brought its reward. It gave him time to breathe, to think, to collect his efforts and his energies; for his intellect seemed dead, and his thoughts numb. He wondered if it were true that the world had told him so brief a time ago that he had genius. Genius! —his very brain seemed dull as lead, hot as flame. Yet he took the sheer laborious, mechanical work, and he bent himself to it; he bound his mind to the hard mental. labour as a galley-slave is chained to his oar; and he who had never known an hour's toil, spent day after day, month after month, in the thankless, unremitting mental travail. It brought its recompense: his mind through it regained its balance, his reason its tone; the compulsory exertion did for him what nothing else could. It took him by degrees back into that impersonal life which is the surest consolation the world holds; it revived the lost tastes, it reopened the deep scholarship, that even in his gayest years had been one of his best-loved pursuits; it led him to take refuge in those vast questions beside which the griefs and joys of life alike are dwarfed,—those resources of the intellect which are the best companion and the truest friend of one who has once known them and loved them. In his past career he had never exerted all the powers that nature had gifted him with; the very facility of his talents had prevented it, and brilliant trifles had rather been their fruit than anything wider or weightier. Now in the treasuries of study and ih the solace of composition he alike found a career and a hope, an ambition and a consolation.

The ruin that had stripped him of all else taught him to fathom the depths of his own attainments. He had in

him the gifts of a Goethe; but it was only under adversity
that these reached their stature and bore their fruit.

When the world had forgotten for some years, or, if
it ever remembered him, thought he had killed himself,
it learned this suddenly and with amazement. His name
once more became public,—never popular, but something
much higher. He was condemned, reviled, wondered at,
called many bitter names; but his thoughts were heard,
and had their harvest. Aristocratic as his tastes were,
and proud though he had been termed, he had always
had much that was democratic in his opinions; for he had
ever measured men by their minds, not their stations;
such freedom was in his works, and they had done that
for which the song of the Venetian youths had thanked
him. Against much antagonism, and slowly in the course
of time, he won fame. Riches he never made; he was
poor still; but he was nearer the fulfilment of the promise
of his childhood now, when the chief sum of the world
was against him, than in the days of his prosperity, when
the whole world lay at his feet. Happiness he had not;
it could be with no man who had such losses ever in his
memory as his; but some peace came to him; a great
and a pure ambition was his companion and his consoler,
and a grander element was woven in his character than
fair fortune would have ever brought to light. England
he never saw. The intercession of his relations or his
acquaintance might with ease have procured him affluent
sinecures; but he would have held it degradation deep
as shame to have taken them. By his own folly his ruin
had been wrought; by his own labour alone would he
repel it and endeavour to repair it. He accepted poverty,
and lived in exile, associating with many of the greatest
thinkers of Europe; but into the pale of the fashionable
world he had once led he never wandered, and in the

palaces in which he had once been the idol of all eyes he was never seen. The friends of that past time knew of him indeed by the intellectual renown that he had won, but it was very rarely that they looked upon his face. Cynic he could not grow; he did not curse the world because to him it had been base; he believed in noble lives and staunch fidelities though treachery had trepanned and love abandoned him. The bitterness of Timon could have no lodging with him; but an unspeakable weariness often came on him.

He had lost so much; and one loss—that of Clarencieux—gnawed ever at his heart with an unceasing pang. There were times when he longed for his perished happiness with the passion with which an exile longs for the light of his native sun.

He listened now to the melodies that filled the chamber. Lulli's was the sole life which had been faithful to him, save that of the dog, buried now under Sicilian orange-boughs, in the grave to which old age had banished it, but lamented and remembered with more justice than many a human friend is regretted and mourned. The music, a new opera-overture of the Provençal's, closed with its noblest harmonies, reeling through the air like a young Bacchus ivy-crowned. Then it stayed suddenly, the hands that drew out its charmed sounds pausing as moved by one impulse; three of them bowed their heads.

"It will be great," they said, reverently, adding no other word, and went their way silently and left the chamber. Guido Lulli was alone with his guest. The victorious radiance, the sovereignty in his own realms, that had been on him as he called out to existence the supremacy of his own creations, faded into the hesitating, doubting hope of a child who seeks the praise of a voice he loves.

"And you, Monseigneur?" he said, appealingly. "Can you say, too, it will be great?"

"You ask *me*, Lulli? The world has long told you, and truly, that you can give it nothing that is not so. You surpass yourself here; it will be noble music,—nobler even than anything of yours."

The eyes of the cripple beamed. The world had long crowned him with the *Delphica laurus*, yet he still came with the humility of a child to receive the laurel he loved best in the words of his old master.

"The world may have told me, monseigneur, but that were nothing unless you spoke also. What would the world have ever known or heeded of me without your aid? Known of *me*, do I say? It is not that I heed; it is my works. I shall pass away, but they will endure; my body will go to corruption, but they will have immortality. I thank God and you, not the world, that what is great in me will not perish with what is weak and vile."

"I understand you; others might not," answered Chandos, as he looked at the delicate kindling face of the only man who had given him back fidelity and gratitude,—a face that time had changed in so little, save in the white threads that gleamed among the dark masses of hair. "Men prostitute their genius now, as the courtesan her beauty; they think little—think nothing—of impersonal things. Hypocrisy pays; they supply it. Were blasphemy the better investment, they would trade in it. You are fortunate in one thing; you speak in a language that cannot be cavilled at or misunderstood."

"But deaf ears were turned to it till, through you, the disbelievers listened."

"Hush! Let the dead bury their dead. I do not look back; I wish that no one should."

"But I cannot forget! Such debts as mine are not scored out."

"In *your* nature. Yet I served many more than I served you. You are the only one who remembers it."

He spoke without bitterness; but the words were the more profoundly sad because there was no taint of acrid feeling in them. Lulli glanced at him with an anxious reverence.

"You served so many! yes; and they were curs who tore down one by whom they had been fed,—one whom they had fawned on for a word of notice! The vilest of them all, what is he now? High in honour among men."

A darkness passed over his listener's face, a gloom like night, yet a disdain as strong as it was silent,—such a look as might come upon the face of a man who saw one whom he knew assassin and traitor courted and adored by the peoples.

"Ah! give him your scorn now. One day you shall give him your vengeance!" cried the musician, with that passionate desire of revenge which he could never, under any wrongs, have known on his own behalf, but which he had felt for Valéria, and which he felt for Chandos.

Chandos' head drooped slightly where he sat, and into his eyes came the shadows of a thousand bitter memories.

"Perhaps," he said, under his breath.

The evil tempted him; if ever it passed into his hands, its widest exercise could be no more than justice. In his dark hours there were times when no other thing looked worth the living for, or worth the seeking, except this,— vengeance upon his traitor.

Lulli gazed at him regretfully and with self-reproach; he had not meant to stir these deep-closed poisonous pools of deadly recollection; he had not meant to recall a past that was, by a command he obeyed with the docile obedience of a dog, never named between them. His music was, to the man he honoured, as the music of the young Israelite was to the soul of the great stricken king whom men forsook and God abandoned. His conscience and his love alike smote him for having jarred on these forbidden chords, and wrought harm instead of bringing consolation.

He leaned forward, and his voice was infinitely sweet.

"Forgive me. You have loved truth, and served men through all, despite all; it is not to you that I should talk of such a tiger's lust as vengeance, though vengeance *there* were righteous. If they had not driven you from your paradise, would you ever have been your greatest? If you had not been forced from your rose-gardens out into the waste of the desert, would you ever have known your strength? Till you ceased to enjoy, you were ignorant how to endure."

The words were true. The bread of bitterness is the food on which men grow to their fullest stature; the waters of bitterness are the debatable ford through which they reach the shores of wisdom; the ashes boldly grasped and eaten without faltering are the price that must be paid for the golden fruit of knowledge. The swimmer cannot tell his strength till he has gone through the wild force of opposing waves; the great man cannot tell the might of his hand and the power of his resistance till he has wrestled with the angel of adversity, and held it close till it has blessed him.

Still, the thought will arise. Is the knowledge worth its purchase? Is it not better to lie softly in the light of laughing suns than to pass through the blackness of the salt sea-storm out of pity for men who will revile the pursuit of a phantom goal, that may be but a mirage when all is over?

This thought was with him now.

"God knows!" he said. "Do not speak against my golden days; they were very dear to me. I think I was a better man in them than I have ever been in my exile. A happy life—a life that knows and gives happiness as the sunlight; it cannot last on earth, maybe, but it is *life* as no other is, while it does."

Lulli was silent. The yearning regret that unconsciously escaped in the reply pierced him to the heart, even though he, to whom existence had been one long spell of physical pain, and to whom all strength and joy were unknown, could but dimly feel all that the man who spoke to him looked back to with so passionate a longing.

"The revellers in Florence," he murmured, softly, "had delight and gladness, and made of life an unbroken festa, while Dante was in exile. Who thinks of them now?—even of their names? But on *his* door is written, 'Qui nacqui il divino Poeta.'"

Chandos rose with a smile—a smile in which there was a weariness beyond words.

"A tardy and an empty recompense! While they write on his door to-day, reviling those who were blind in his generation, they repeat in their own times the blindness, and the persecution to free thought, by which the poet and the thinker suffered then and suffer still."

Throughout the years which had gone by since the fall of his high estate, no lamentation, no recrimination, had ever been heard to pass his lips. When the tidings floated to him of success piled on success that his enemy and his traitor achieved, he listened in silence, too proud to condemn what was beneath envy and beyond vengeance. Men sought oftentimes to make him speak of the past and speak of Trevenna; they never succeeded. He held his peace, keeping patience with a force of control which

amazed and bewildered those who had known him as an
effeminate, self-indulged voluptuary, and had looked from
him for a suicide's story, or, at best, for a bitter upbraiding of the curse of fate. They never heard a word from
him either of regret at his own ruin or of anger at his
debtor's success. He endured in as absolute a silence as
ever an Indian endured when bound to the' pyre. To
two only, two who alone remained to him out of the
throngs who had once thought no honour higher than to
claim his friendship, did he ever speak either of his fate
or of his foe; and to them he spoke but reluctantly.
They were Lulli and Philippe d'Orvâle.

The lustre of the descending sun was bright through
all the forest-glades as he left the musician's house now,
and went alone through the great aisles of oak and elm.
The love of the earth's freshness and fragrance and
beauty would never die in him; he had too much of
Shelley's nature. The bleakness of poverty, the narrow
rigidity of want, the colourlessness of life without the
glow of passion, the warmth of pleasure, the vividness of
sensuous charms and sensuous delights, the richness of
luxury, and the power of possession, all these, which he
had known in their deprivation and their misery, had
not altered this in him; and the chief solace of his life
had been the consolation that he had been able by his
temperament to find in the antique tranquillity of the
cities of Italy, in the solemn repose of mighty Alps, in
the intense splendour of Oriental landscape. The artist
and the poet were too closely blent in him for him ever
to cease to heed these things; and yet there were times
when there was in them for him an anguish that seemed
to pass his strength. He had once looked on them with
such careless eyes of sunlit joy, with the warmth of their
suns on woman's cheeks, and the laughter of idle sum-

mer-day love on their air! There are many natures, steel-knit, Puritan, austere, narrow in limit and in sight, which never know what it is to enjoy, and never are conscious of their loss; but to his, and to characters like his, life without this divine power of enjoyment differs in little—differs in nothing of value—from death.

Now, as he went through the woodland shades, with the checkered light across the moss of the paths, his heart went back to the time of his youth, the time when no other doubt had rested on him in such forest-luxuriance than to ask,—

"Oh, which were best, to roam or rest?
The land's lap or the water's breast?
To sleep on yellow millet-sheaves,
Or swim in lucid shadows just
Eluding water-lily leaves?
Which life were best on summer eves?"

It might be true, as the French cripple had said, that he was greater now than he had been then—that in conflict he had gained, and had become that which he would never have done or been in the abundance, the indolence, the shadowless content, and the royal dominion of his epicurean years. But for himself—in many moments, at the least—the vanity in all things, in wisdom as in riches, that Ecclesiastes laments, smote him hard; and he would have given the fame of a Plato, of an Antoninus, of a Dante, of a Shakspeare, to have back one day of that glorious and golden time!

The sun had wellnigh set; here, in the darkness of the oak-glades, there was little but a dusky, ruddy glow, fitful and flame-like. He passed slowly onward; his head was uncovered, for the air was sultry, and such breeze as arose was welcome; here and there a stray lingering sunbeam touched the fairness of his hair; otherwise the depth of the forest-shadow was on his face, that wore ever now, though it was serene in repose and its smile was infinitely sweet, the weariness and the dignity of pain silently borne, which long ago had hushed with their royalty of resolve and of suffering the hungry crowd gathered in the porphyry chamber. An artist, hidden among the thickness of the leaves, sketching, looked up as his step crushed the grasses—a swift, slight, breathless look; then, as though he saw some ghost of a dead age, the painter shivered, and let fall his brushes, and cowered down into the gloom of the tall·ferns with the shrinking horror of a frightened hare.

"Ah, Christ!" he murmured, in Spanish, "how weary he looks of his exile! Misery has not embittered him. He must have a rare nature. If I had found strength to tell him all that night in the street, how would it have been now? It could not have been worse with *us;* and it was an Iscariot's sin only to know,—to share!"

Chandos passed onward, not seeing him there beneath the shelter of the spreading ferns; his thoughts were sunk far in the past. He had met his fate with a tranquil endurance, with the proud and uncomplaining temper of his race, which had in all centuries risen out of the soft-ness of voluptuous indulgence to encounter misfortune grandly; but not the less was life very joyless to him, and the bitterness of its vain toil oftentimes pursued and mocked him. As he went, on the silence rang the clear mellow notes of a hunting-horn, and the echo of a horse's feet; into the open green plateau immediately below the rising ground on which he was, a horseman dashed rapidly, and reined up, looking about him,—a court guest, by the court hunting-dress he wore, with its scarlet and green and gold, and its gold-handled forest-knife.

"Holà! has the Palace party passed?"

As he glanced up, the words died on the speaker's

lips; for the first time their eyes met since the night in the Rue du Temple. In the red, faint, lowering light, under the dense shade of the oak-boughs, with the twilight of the autumn-bronzed leaves flung heavily down between them, Trevenna saw him where he stood on the slope, with the black wall of foliage behind him, and a single faint ray of the declining sun shed full across his eyes, that were filling dark as night with the sudden upleaping of silent passions, of thronging memories, of unavenged and unextinguished wrongs.

When they had last met, the murderous hand of his traitor had flung him down on the blood-stained stones of the old monastic court, and had left him to perish as he might in the heart of the sleeping city, in the cold of the winter's night. When they had last met, John Trevenna had cursed him where he lay senseless, and had wished his father's soul could know his ruin, and had believed no more that the life he had destroyed would ever again be raised among living men, and gather strength to vanquish and endure, than if he had struck to its heart with a knife and flung the corpse out to the river.

For the first moment there was no memory on either save that memory, and Trevenna's face paled and lost its healthful glow. He had known that his prey had survived to bear calamity and exile and follow the guidance of a pure and impersonal ambition; the world had often spoken each other's names on their ears; but they had never met until now—now when the form of Chandos rose before him in the reddened sullen glow of the dim forest-aisles, like a resurrection from the grave. And, in the first moment, all his intensity of hate revived in its ancient lust, burning in him none the less, but the more, because it had wreaked its worst to satiety. He hated to think

Chandos lived; he hated to know he had not sunk, body and mind, into debauchery and insanity; he hated the very beauty that he knew so well of old, because years and pain would not destroy it!

Then the insolence, the mockery the audacious greedy exultation of his triumph governed him alone; the pride of success and supremacy made him feel drunk with the joy of his victory. He bowed to his saddle with a contemptuous reverence.

"Ah, *beau sire!* it is many years since *we* met. We said once we'd see which made the best thing of life, you, the visionary, or I, the materialist. I think I've won, far and away, eh? The fable says iron pots and china pots can't swim down the stream together; your dainty patrician king's-pattern Sèvres soon smashed and swamped among the bulrushes; my nameless, ugly, battered two-penny tin pipkin got clear of all shoals, and came safe into port, you see. I was your palace jester once: what do you think of my success now?"

Chandos, raised above him by the rocky slope on which he stood, looked down and gazed at him full in the eyes: for the instant, Trevenna would have quailed less if a dagger had been at his throat. Neither shame nor conscience smote him; but for the instant some touch of dread, some throb of what was wellnigh fear, came to him, as the voice that had used to be so familiar on his ear, and that had been unheard through so many years of silence, fell on his ear in the hush of the forest, clear, low, cold as ice, with the quiver of a mighty passion in it.

"I think it great as your infamy, great as your treachery; greater it cannot be."

Trevenna laughed: his savage mirth, his taunting buffoonery, his unreined, exulting malice of triumph, were all let loose by the scorn that cut him like a scourge, and which he hated because he knew that, however high he rose, however proud his rank, however unassailable his station, this one man knew all that he had once been, knew whose hand had first raised him, knew that he was the vilest ingrate that ever sold his friend.

"Whew!" he cried; "you are as haughty as ever. How do they stand that, now you're only a heterodox author with a dubious reputation? You are bitter on me: well, I can forgive that. 'Tisn't pleasant, I dare say, to have sparkled like a firework and then gone out into darkness,—a failure! But you'd ten years of it, you know; and it's my turn now. I'm a Right Hon. and a millionnaire; I'm a Cabinet minister, and I'm staying at court. I mean to die in the Lords, if I don't die in the Lord; and I'm only waiting for the 'mad duke's' death to go and buy Clarencieux. When I retire into the Peers' Paradise, I'll take my title after it—John Trevenna, Baron Clarencieux! Won't it sound well, eh?"

With a single leap, light, resistless, unerring as in his earliest years, Chandos leaped down the slope on which he stood, his face darkly flushed, his lips set straight and stern in the shadowy fiery autumn light; with the swiftness and force of a panther's spring he threw himself on Trevenna, swaying him back off his saddle and out of his stirrups to the ground, while the horse, let loose from the weight of its rider, tossed its head impatient in the air and galloped alone down the glade.

"You make me vile as yourself! Dare to own or to taint Clarencieux, and—as we both live—I will kill you!"

The words were low breathed in his foe's ear as he bore him backwards, but the more deadly in meaning

and in menace for that; then he shook Trevenna from
him and left him, and plunged down into the dark thick
depths of the leaves. He knew if he stayed to look on
at his debtor the mere brute instincts, the sheer Cain-like
passions, which slumber in all, would conquer him and
force him on to some madness or some crime. The voice
of his tempter and betrayer had come back on him across
the wide waste of spent and desert years, and had brought
the passions and the shame and the despair of his conquered ruin fresh on him, as though known but yesterday.

"Oh, God!" he thought, "what have I vanquished,
what have I learned? This man makes me a brute like
himself; one trial, and my creeds and my patience and
my strength break like reeds!"

For Trevenna had been the bane, the temptation, the
tyrant, the poisoner, of all his life, and was so still.
Through his foe even the pure and lofty hopes which
had alone sustained him were broken and polluted. This
man had fame and success in a world that applauded
him! What was renown worth, since it went to such as
this mocker?—a crown of rotten rushes, an empty bladder
blown by lying lips, a meed to the one who dupes a
blind world best, a prize that goes to the stump-orator,
to the spangled mountebank, to the blatant charlatan, to
the trained posture-maker of political and intellectual
life! What avail was it to labour for mankind, when
this ingrate was their elected leader, their accepted representative? What worth to toil for liberty and tolerance, when the one whom humanity crowned was the
ablest trickster, the adroitest mime, the cheat who could
best hide the false ace in his sleeve by a face of laughing candour and a fraud of forged honesty?

Trevenna had robbed him of all; Trevenna had well-
nigh robbed him now of the only solace that his life

had left. The success of his traitor made him doubt truth itself.

CHAPTER IV.
"Qui a offensé ne pardonne jamais."

"CURSE him! When he lay in that garret dying, who could dream he would ever rise again, unless it were to go to a madhouse?" mused Trevenna before the fire in his dressing-room in the palace. He had been slightly bruised, but not hurt; and he had told the court party, whom he had found and rejoined as soon as he had called his horse to him, that an oak-bough had struck and blinded him, so that he had fallen out of his saddle. As he sat now, smoking, with his costly velvets wrapped around him, with all the elegance and luxury of a palace in the suite of chambers allotted him as an English minister and a guest of the first circle of autumn visitors, there were something of irritation and impatience even amidst his triumphant reflections. He could not resent the force used to him, for he was too wise to let the world know of that forest-meeting; and he hated to think that his intricate nets had had a single loose mesh, by which his prey had escaped the ruin of mind and body that he had made sure would accompany the ruin of peace and pride and fair fortune; he hated to think that while Chandos lived there would live one who knew him as he was, knew what he had been, knew the treacheries by which his rise had been consummated, knew the stains that darkened the gloss and the symmetry of the splendid superstructure of his success.

They had never met until now; and he hated to feel that the sting of his victim's scorn had power to pierce him; he hated to feel that a ruined exile could quote against him the time when he—the millionnaire, the minister, the court guest, the national favourite—had been a debtor in gaming-prisons, an adventurer without a sou.

"And yet I don't know," he mused on, while a smile came about his mouth, and he gave a kick to the ruddy embers of the fire. "I'm not sorry he lives, either: if he were dead he wouldn't suffer, and if he were dead he wouldn't see *me* rise! No! I like him to live. He'd have missed all the bitterness of it if he'd gone in his grave then. How I sting him with every step I get! How his heart burns when he reads my name in the Cabinet! How it must wring and goad and taunt and madden him when he knows I'm in his palaces, and have got his prosperity, and have won my way to the proudest position a man can hold in England. No! I'm glad he lives. Gad! I'll ask him to Clarencieux, one day."

And he laughed to himself. This was part and parcel of the man's jovial malicious, farcical, racy temper; and the sweetest morsel in all his triumphs was that each step and each crown of them was—a revenge.

"Mercy! what a fool he's been!" he thought. "Cared for nothing, while he had the power, but pleasure and revelry, and making love to women, and playing Lorenzo the Magnificent, and now solaces himself in his poverty with turning metaphysical questions inside out, and *brodant sur la toile d'araignée*, as they say here, and caring for the future of the world, and working out the scientific laws of history! Mercy! as if it mattered to *us* whether the world goes smash when we've no more to do with it! However, I don't understand him; never did. A man who could care so little for money as he did never could be quite sane. Even now he's such a fool; he's never said to me the one thing he might say,—that I was his debtor."

To dream that there might be a generosity too proud

to quote past services against a present traitor utterly escaped Trevenna: he was far too practical to have glimpse of such a temper; he only thought the man a fool, a wonderful fool, who forbore to taunt him, with the stone that lay so ready to his hand, in the reproach, "I served you."

"No; I'm glad he lives. It would be Hamlet with the part of Hamlet left out, if he didn't exist to watch *my* triumph!" he mused, clenching the matter in his own mind, and getting up to summon his valet and dress for dinner. His momentary bitterness was all gone. Here he was, the guest of a sovereign, with a name that had fame in the Old and New Worlds, riches as much as he needed them, a future brilliant as his present, an ambition without limit, and a station that enemies and friends alike must envy. He was content, very richly content, as he sauntered down to join the Palace circle, distinguished as the most eloquent, the most penetrating, the most liberal, and the most promising statesman of the English Cabinet, his opinion sought by princes and diplomatists, his words heard as words of gold breathed from the lips of one who would probably govern in the highest rank of all in the future, his views studied with interest, as those of the favourite of a great people, even his mere badinage graciously sought by *grandes dames* who once denied him cards to their receptions. The high orders detested him still, it is true; but they feared him, and they courted him. They thought they propitiated him by such concessions. Never was error wider. He used them, and— despised them.

"M. Trevenna, permit me congratulations on your late magnificent coup d'état," smiled the Comtesse de la Vivarol, who, under a new dynasty, reigned in the court, a power now, as she had earlier been a beauty.

He bowed his thanks.

"You do me much honour, madame. I trust we have the aid of your favouring sympathies?"

"Personally, yes; scarcely your party. You are all so decorous and so dull in your Parliament. Whoever turns the handle, the organ plays the same tunes."

"And you would like an infusion of the *ça ira?* Well, I should not object to it myself; but I shouldn't dare to introduce it. I'm very prudent!"

"Indeed! You go rather far, too, at Darshampton—" Trevenna shook his head.

"Darshampton! They will tell you there that I am devoted to the civil and religious institutions of the nation. Why, I have built a church! It cost me a deal in painted windows; but you don't know what it has done for me in reputation. It's made two spiritual lords believe in me, and given me *postiche* as a 'safe man' in perpetuity. Really, for a good public effect, I think nothing is better than a church. Men think you have such a thorough conviction of orthodox truth, if you adore the Lord in stucco and oak-carving!"

La Vivarol laughed.

"You were not so orthodox once?"

"No; but I am now. I go to church every Sunday, —specially when I'm down at Darshampton. To be un-orthodox is like walking out on a midsummer day in your shirt-sleeves. It's refreshing to take your coat off, and it's very silly to carry a lot of sheep's wool that you pant under; but all the same, no man who cares what his neighbours say walks abroad in his waistcoat. Orthodoxy and broadcloth are fallacies *à la mode:* if you air yourself in heresy and a blouse, the parsons and tailors, who see their trades in danger, will get a writ of lunacy out against you."

"You are a clever man, M. Trevenna! You know

how to manage your world.   But does it *never* tire you,
that incessant promenade in such unimpeachable broadcloth?"

Trevenna met her eyes with a gleaming mischief in
his own.   He attempted no concealment with her; the
keen wit of the aristocratic politician would, he knew,
have pierced it in an instant; and she, who had once
bidden him *apprendre à s'effacer*, alone never let him
forget that she had known him when he was on sufferance
and obscure.

"Tire?" he said now; "no, never!   Who tires on the
stage, so long as they clap him, and so long as it pays?
It is your dissatisfied, unappreciated men that may tire
of their *soupe maigre;* nobody tires of the turtle-soup of
success."

"Then you don't believe in surfeits?"

"Not for strong digestions."

"Perhaps you are right; and there is no absinthe that
produces incessant appetite so well as intense self-love."

Trevenna laughed good-humouredly; he acknow-
ledged the implication.

"Ah, madame, you know I never denied that I was
selfish.   Why should I?   If one don't love one's self, who
will?   And, I confess, I like present success.   Immortality
is terribly dull work; a hideous statue, that gets black as
soot in no time; funeral sermons that make you out a
Vial of Revelation, and discuss the probabilities of your
being in the regions of Satan; a bust that slants you off
at the shoulders, trims you round with a stone scallop,
and sticks you up on a bracket; a tombstone for the canes
of the curious to poke at; an occasional attention in the
way of withered immortelles or biographical Billingsgate,
and a partial preservation shared in common with mum-
mies, auks' eggs, snakes in bottles, and deformities in

spirits of wine—*that's* posthumous fame. I must say I don't see much fun in it."

The Comtesse smiled a gracious amusement over her fan.

"You have different views from your old friend."

"Who? Chandos! Poor fellow! he was always eccentric; lived in the empyrean, and had ideas that may be practicable in the millennium, but certainly won't be so before. 'Great wits to madness,' &c. After having squandered all that made life endurable, he consoles himself, I believe, with the belief that people will read him when he's dead. What a queer consolation! Stendahl thought the same thing: who opens his books now?"

"Though you despise immortality, M. Trevenna, it seems you can still grudge it," said La Vivarol, with that quick, penetrative wit which could be barbed as an arrow.

Trevenna felt angry with himself for having been trapped into the words.

"I grudge him nothing, madame," he laughed, good-humouredly, "least of all a mummy-like embalming by posterity's bibliomaniacs. Indeed, now I am come in office, I shall try and induce him to accept something more substantial. I believe he's as poor as Job, though he's still as proud as Lucifer."

"He had somewhat of Job's fortune in his friends," said the Comtesse, with a smile, as she turned to others.

"What does she still feel for him?—love, or hate? I can understand most things," thought Trevenna, "but hang me if I can ever understand love,—past or present. It's a Jack-in-the-box, always jumping up when you think it's screwed down. It's like dandelion-seeds for lightness, blowing away with a breath, and yet it's like nettles for obstinacy; there's no knowing when it's plucked up. A confounded thing, certainly."

Like a wise man, he had taken care to have nothing to do with the confounded thing, and, in consequence, digested all his dinners, and never muddled any of his affairs.

CHAPTER V.
"Ne chercher qu'un regard, qu'une fleur, qu'un soleil."

In the deep gloom of an antique, forsaken, world-forgotten town of Italy, silent, grass-grown, unspeakably desolate, with the brown shadows of its ancient houses, and here and there the noiseless gliding form of monk or nun flitting across the deserted spaces, a head, like a Guido Aurora in its youth, like a Guido Magdalen in its sadness, leaned out from the archway of a bridge-parapet, with the fair warmth of the cheek and the chestnut light of the hair lying wearily on the pillow of the rough-hewn stone. Fallen so, half unconsciously, to rest, the girl's form leaned against the buttress of the old river-way that spanned tawny shallow waters only traversed by some olive-laden canal-boat, whose striped sails flapped lazily in the sun; her brow was sunk on her hand; her eyes, full of a passionate pain, watched the monotonous ebb and flow of the stream; her whole figure expressed an intense fatigue; but on her face, with all its brooding, tired suffering, there was a look of patient and unalterable resolve.

"So endless!—so endless!" she murmured to the silence of the waters. "Surely God will have pity soon!"

There was only, in answer, the changeless, sullen ripple of the river far below,—the silence that seems so bitter to those who suffer in their youth, and who think some Divine voice will surely whisper consolation,—the silence eternal, in which later they find man must live and must die.

A bent, browned, weather-worn fruit-seller, with a

burden of melons and gourds and figs fresh from the tree, traversing the steep incline of the bridge, paused and looked at her. She was very poor, and she was old; but she had a tender soul under a rough rind. She touched the girl's fever-flushed cheek with the cool fragrance of a bough of syringa, and spoke very gently in her broad, mellow peasant-dialect:—

"*Poverina*, thou art tired. Take some fruit."

She started, and looked up; but there was almost apathy in the smile with which she shook her head,—it was so listless in its melancholy.

"You are very kind; but I want nothing."

"That is not true," said the old contadina. "Thou art in want of much; thou art too weary for thy youth. Where are thy friends?"

"I have none!"

"None! Mother of God! and so young! Thou art seeking some one?"

A deep flush passed over her face; she bent her head in assent.

"Ah! thou seekest those who love thee?"

"No," she said, simply. "I only seek to find one; and when I have found him, and heard his voice once more—to die."

She spoke rather to her own thoughts than to the peasant. The old woman's deep-set eyes grew very gentle, and her lips muttered, in wrath,

"Che—e—e! Is it so with thee? and so young! The Madonna's vengeance fall on him, then, whoever he be, for having caused thee such early shame!"

The words acted like a spell; she lifted herself from the drooping languor of her rest, and flashed on the peasant from the superb darkness of her eyes an imperious challenge of rebuke and amaze. Who the speaker was she forgot; she only remembered the sense that had been spoken.

"Shame? *I* have no shame! My only glory is to have seen and known the noblest life on earth. The only hope I live for is that I may be worthy to hear his words once more. Vengeance on *him?* God's love be with him always!"

She passed onward with a sovereign's grace, moving like one in a dream; though the passion of her words had risen to so sudden and vivid a defence, she seemed to have little consciousness of what she did, whither she went. Then, as though a pang of self-reproach moved her, she turned swiftly and came back, and stooped over the aged contadina, raising the fallen fruit with a self-accusative gentleness, beseeching even while it still was so proud.

"Forgive me! You meant kindness; and you did not know. I was ungrateful and ungentle; but I am very tired."

Her lashes were heavy with tears, and a sigh of intense exhaustion escaped her. The peasant, touched to the quick, forced the freshest fruits into her hands.

"I thought nothing of it. I only pitied thee."

"Pity is for those who ask alms, or stoop to shame: do not give it to me."

"But art thou all alone?"

"Yes; all alone."

"Christ! and with thy beauty! Ah! insult will come to thee, though thou art like a princess in exile; insult will come, if thou art alone in the wide world with such a face and such a form as thine."

On her face arose a look of endurance and of resistance far beyond her years.

"Insult never comes except to those who welcome it. Farewell! and believe me from my heart grateful, if I have seemed not to be so enough."

And she went on her way, with the mellow light of
a setting sun on her meditative brow, and the shadow of
the grey parapet cast forward on her path. The fruit-
seller looked after her wistfully, perplexed and regretful.

"The saints keep her!" she muttered over her tawny
gourds and luscious figs. "She will need their care bad
enough before she has found out what the world is for
such as she. Holy Mary! whoever left her alone like that
must have had a heart of stone."

The girl passed onward over the rise and descent of
the old pointed bridge; there was the flush of fever on
her cheek, the exhaustion of bodily fatigue in her step;
but her eyes looked far forward with a brave light, resolute while it was so visionary, and her lips had as much
of resolve as of pain on them. In one hand swung a
pannier full of late summer flowers, woven with coils of
scarlet creepers, and with the broad bronzed leaves of
vine, in such taste as only the love and the fancy of an
artist-mind could weave them; in the other she held,
closely clasped, the bough of blossoming syringa and a
book well worn, that she pressed against her bosom as
she went, as though it were some living and beloved thing.
There was an extreme pathos, such as had touched
the peasant woman, in the union of her excessive youth
and her perfect loneliness; there was something yet higher
and yet more pathetic in the blending in her of the faith
and ignorance of childhood that wanders out into the
width of the world as into some wonder-land of Faëry, and
the unwearying, undaunted resolution of a pilgrim who
goes forth as the pilgrims of Christendom went eastward
to look on their Jerusalem once, and die content.

The bridge led down across the river into a wide
square, so still, so deserted, so mediæval, with its vast,
abandoned palaces, and its marvellous church beauty,

with only some friar's shadow or some heavily-weighted
mule crossing it in the light of the Italian sunset. In
the low loggia of one of the palaces, altered to a post-
ing-house, a group was standing, idly looking at the
grass-grown waste, whilst their horses were changing.
They were a gay, rich, titled set of indolent voyagers
who were travelling to Rome from Paris. They saw her
as she came beneath the balcony, with the book against
her bosom, and the abundance of the flowers drooping
downward in rings and wreaths of colour as she bore
them. Murmurs of admiration at her loveliness broke
irresistibly even from the world-sated men and women
who leaned there, tired and impatient of even a few
minutes' dulness.

"The old traditions of Italia, the ideal of Titian himself!" said one of them. "*Bellissima*, will you not spare
us one of your lilies?"

She paused, and glanced at the women of the group.

"Those ladies can have them, if they wish."

"But must not I, my exquisite young flower-priestess?"
laughed her first questioner.

She let her grave luminous eyes dwell calmly on him.

"No, signore."

One of the women leaned down, amused at her companion's rebuff and mortification; the loggia was so low
that she could touch the flowers, and she drew out one
of the clusters of late lilies.

"My fair child, do you sell these?"

"I have done, signora."

"Then you will sell them to me," said the other, as
she dropped into the basket a little gold piece and took
up the blossoms. A hand as soft as her own put back
the money into her palm.

"I have sold them for what they are worth—a few

scudi; I give them to you gladly, and I do not take alms from any."

They looked at her in wonder; the dignity of her utterance, the purity of her accent, the royal ease in her attitude, amazed them. An Italian child, selling flowers for her bread, spoke with the decision and the serenity of a princess.

"But you will let me offer it you as a gift, will you not?"

She shook her head.

"Would you take gold as a gift yourself, signora?"

The great lady reddened ever so slightly; the words spoken in all simplicity pricked her. It was rumoured by her world that empires and governments had on occasion bought her silence or her alliance by magnificent bribes.

"*Pardieu*, my loveliest living Titian!" laughed the French Marquis who had first addressed her, "Madame la Comtesse does not sell flowers in the street, I fancy."

Her eyes swept over him with a tranquil, meditative disdain.

"There is but one rule for honour," she said, briefly; "and rank gives no title for insolence."

"Fairly hit!" laughed the great lady, who had recovered her momentary irritation. "My beautiful child, will you tell me your name, at the least?"

"It is Castalia."

Where she stood before the loggia, with a troubled seriousness in the gaze of her brilliant eyes (for the tone of the Marquis had roused more anger than his mere words), her hand moved the book against her heart. "If I were to ask these?" she mused. "It is only the nobles who will ever tell me; it is only they who can be his friends. I have never found courage to speak of him yet; but, until I do, I cannot know."

“Castalia!” echoed the aristocrat. “A fair name, indeed,—as fair as you and your flowers. You will not let me repay you for your lilies; is there nothing you can let me do for you?”

Castalia looked at her musingly; the words were gentle, but there was something that failed to reassure her. She stood before the half-insolent admiration of the men, the supercilious admiration of the women, of this titled and aristocratic group, with as complete a dignity and indifference as though she were a young patrician who received them; but she felt no instinct of regard or of trust to any one of them. Still she drew nearer the loggia, and held out the book reluctantly to her questioner; her eyes filled with an earnest, terrible, longing wistfulness; the words were only wrenched out with a great pang.

“Signora, yes: can you tell me where *he* is?”

Her hand pointed to the name on the title-page, and her voice shook with the intensity of anxious entreaty over the last two words.

The Countess glanced at the volume, then let it fall with amaze, as she gazed at the pleading, aching eyes that looked up to hers.

“Chandos! *Mon Dieu!* what is it to you?”

“You know him?” There was the tremulous thirstiness of long-deferred, long-despairing hope in the question, but there was also something of the passionate jealousy of love.

The aristocrat looked at her with searching, surprised, insolent eyes, in which some anger and more irony glittered, while she turned over the leaves of the book.

“It is ‘Lucrèce!’” she murmured,—“‘Lucrèce!’” In the moment her thoughts went backward over so many years to so many buried hours, to so many forgotten things, to so many bygone scenes. The book came to her like a voice of the past.

"You know him!"

"What interest has he for you?"

The lady had recovered her momentary amazement, and the smile with which she spoke thrilled with fire and struck like ice the heart of Castalia, though that heart was too guileless to know all the smile meant. But the anguish of a hopeless and endless search was stronger on her than the sense of insult; her eyes filled with a beseeching misery, like a wounded animal's, and her hands, as she drew back the volume, were crushed on it in a gesture of agonised supplication.

"You know his name, at least? Ah! tell me, for the love of pity, where he is gone!"

The aristocrat turned away with a negligent cold contempt.

"Your friend wanders all over the world; if you want to discover him, you have a very poor chance, and one I am scarcely disposed to aid."

"Chandos, now he has turned philosopher, retains pretty much the same tastes he had as a poet, I suppose?" she murmured, with a smile, to one of her female friends. "The girl is very beautiful, certainly; but how shameless to ask *us!* It is scarcely creditable to an author who writes such eloquent periods on Humanity to leave her to starve by selling lilies!"

The slight, scornful laugh caught Castalia's ear, as the cold words of the first phrases had stung all her pride and killed all hope within her; a great darkness had come over her face; but her face was white and set, and her lips were pressed together to hold in the words that rose to them. She turned away without another entreaty; not even to learn of him would she supplicate there. The Marquis, with a light leap, cleared the loggia and gained her side. He was young, handsome; and his voice, when he would, was sweet as music.

·   "You seek the writer of that book?"

The look she turned on him might have touched the sternest to pity.

"Ah, signore,—yes!"

The answer broke from her with a sigh that was beyond repression. Her eyes grew dim with tears. The world held but one idea, one thought, one existence, for her, and her love was at once too utter an absorption and too absolute an adoration to be conscious of anything except its one search.

"Come with me, then, and I will tell you what you wish."

A radiance of joy and hope flashed over the sadness of her face. She did not know how dangerous an intensity that sudden light of rapture lent her beauty; she only thought that she should hear of him.

"I will come," she said softly, while her hand still held the book to her bosom; and she went, unresisting, beside him to the place to which he turned,—a solitary, darkened terrace, heavily overhung by the stones of an unused palazzo, with the river flowing sluggishly below.

"Why do you want to seek him?" her companion asked.

In his heart he thought he knew well enough. Her lover had abandoned her, and she was following him to obtain redress or maintenance.

Her eyes dwelt on the water with the earnest, lustrous, dreamy gaze that had used to recall so vague a memory to Chandos.

"Signore, only to see him once more."

"To see him! To stir him to pity, I suppose,—to make some claim on him?"

She did not comprehend his meaning; but she lifted her head quickly with the imperial pride that mingled in so witching a contrast with her guileless and childlike simplicity.

"Signore, I would die sooner than ask his pity; it would be to ask and to merit his scorn. Claim, too! What claim? Have subjects a claim on their king, because he has once been gentle enough to smile on them? When I find him, I will not weary him; I will not let him even know that I am near; but I will search the world through till I look on his face once more, and then—the joy of it will kill me, and I shall be at rest with my mother for ever."

He looked at her, mute with surprise. If she had been attractive in his sight before, she was tenfold more so now, as she spoke with the exaltation of a love that absorbed her whole life, making her unconscious of all save itself, and the mournful simplicity of the last words uttered with a resignation that was content, in the dawn of her youth, to receive no other mercy than death. He was amazed, he was bewildered, he was entranced; he felt an envious passion in an instant against the one for whom she could speak thus; but comprehend her he could not. He was shallow, selfish, a cold libertine, and at once too young and too worldly to even faintly understand the mingling in her nature of transparency and depth, of tropical fervour and of utter innocence, of fearless pride against all insult, and of absolute abandonment to one idolatry. He spoke in the irritation of wonder and annoyance.

"The author of 'Lucrèce' is much flattered to be the inspirer of so tender a love! I am afraid he has been but negligent of the gift."

The words were coarser than he would have used

save on the spur of such irritation; their effect was like a
spell. The flush that was like the scarlet depth of a
crimson camellia covered her face in an instant, her eyes
darkened with a tremulous emotion that swiftly altered
to the blaze of wrath, her lips trembled, her whole form
changed under the sudden change of thought; the shame
of love came to her for the first moment, as the lips of
another man spoke it; she had been wholly unconscious
of it before. She was seeking him as devotees sought
the Holy Grail, as a stray bird seeks the only hand that
has ever caressed and sheltered it. The word or the
meaning of passion had never been uttered to her till
now. An intense horror consumed her,—horror of herself, horror of her companion; she shuddered where she
stood in the hot air, but the proud instinct of her nature
rose to sustain herself, to defend Chandos.

"You mistake, signore," she said, with a calm that
for the moment awed him. "He whom I seek, I seek
because he is my only friend,—my only sovereign lord;
because my debt to him is a debt so vast, a debt of life
itself that life can never pay. He was never negligent
of me,—never; he was but too good, too generous, too
gentle."

He looked at her, perplexed and incensed. He vaguely
felt that he was in error; but he was distant as ever from
the truth. All he knew was that he had never, in the
whole range of courts, seen loveliness that could compete
with the face and form of this young seller of the Tuscan
lilies.

"Forgive me," he murmured, eagerly; "I meant no
offence. Only to look on you is sufficient to——"

"You said you would tell me where he is." She
spoke very low, but her lips were set. She began to mistrust him.

"I will; but hear me first. He whom you talk of is very poor; he is no longer young; he is a madman who spent all his millions in a day, and who always played at his fancy with women, and left them. He is not worthy a thought of yours."

The glorious darkness of her eyes grew like fire; but she held her passion in rein.

"Keep the promise you made me," she said, in her teeth. "Tell me of him."

"I will. One moment more. He cannot care whether you live or die, or would he have left you thus?"

It was a random blow, essayed at hazard, but it struck home. She grew very pale, and her lips shook; yet she was resolute,—resolute in her proud defence and self-restraint.

"Signore, there was no cause why he should care. I was but as a broken bird that he was gentle to; he had a right to leave me,—no right to think of me one hour."

He repressed an impatient oath. He could not understand her, yet he felt he made no head against this resignation of herself to neglect and to oblivion; and the splendour of her face seemed a hundred times greater because of this impotence to make any impress on her thoughts.

"At least, if he had had the heart of a man, he could never have forsaken or forgotten you," he urged, tenderly. "Listen. I, who have seen you but a moment ago, give you too true a homage to be able to quit your side until you deal me my fiat of exile. In the world there—the world of which perhaps you know nothing—I have riches and honours, and pleasures and palaces, that shall all be yours if you will have them. Come with me, and no queen shall equal your sway. Come with me, and for all those lilies I will give you as many pearls. Come with me; you shall have diamonds in your hair, and slaves for your every wish, and I the chiefest yet the humblest of them all; you shall have kings at your feet, and make the whole world mad with one glance of those divine eyes. Come with me. *He* never offered you what I offer you now, if you will only trust to my truth and my love."

He spoke with all the hyperbole that he thought would best dazzle and entrance one to whom the beauties and the wealth of the world alike were unknown,—one in whom he saw blent the pride of patricians with the poverty of peasants,—spoke with his eyes looking eloquent tenderness, with the sun on his handsome head, with the mellow, beguiling music in his voice. For all answer where she stood, her eyes dilated with abhorrent scorn and slumbering fire; she shuddered from him as from some asp. She did not comprehend all to which he wooed her, all that he meant to convey; but she comprehended enough to know that he sought to bribe her with costly promises, and outraged her with a familiarity offensive beyond endurance.

"No!" she said, passionately, while the liquid melody of her voice rang clear and imperious,—"no! he never offered me what you offer me,—insult. Neither was he ever what you are,—a traitor to his word!"

She turned from him with that single answer, the blood hot as flame in her cheek, her head borne with careless, haughty dignity. She would not show him all she felt; she would not show him that her heart seemed breaking,—breaking with the bitterness of disappointment, with the sudden vivid sense of ineradicable shame, with the absolute desolation that came on her with the first faint sickening perception of the meaning and the tempting of evil.

Mortified, irritated, incensed at defeat where he had looked for easy victory and grateful welcome, the young noble caught her as she turned, flung his arms about her ere she could stir, and stooped his lips to hers.

"*Bellissima!* do you think I shall lose you like that?"

Before his kiss could touch her, she had wrenched herself free, flung him off, and struck him across the mouth with the bough of syringa. The blow of the fragrant white blossoms stamped him coward more utterly than a weightier stigma could have stamped it.

Then she broke the branch in two, threw it at his feet as a young empress might break the sword of a traitor, and, leaving all her lilies and wealth of leafage scattered there, she quitted him without a word.

Bold though he was, her pursuer dared not follow her. She looked down at the water, as she went along its sullen course, with a smile, and leaned her lips on the book's worn page.

"*He* touched them once," she thought; "no other ever should while that river could give me death!"

A deadly horror, a tumult of dread and of loathing, were on her. She never rested, all tired though she was, till she was far out of the town, and amidst the vine-fields, whose leaves were bronzed, and whose purple and amber clusters were swelling with their richest bloom, near the vintage. The shadows and the stone wilderness, and the contracted air and space of cities, were terrible to her; mountain-winds and forest-fragrance and the free stretch of limitless vision had been as the very breath of life to her from her infancy; caged in the darkness and the heat of cities, she would have died as surely as a caged mocking-bird dies of longing for the south. She dropped to rest, still by the side of the water under the shade of the vines, while the buildings and bridges of the town sank down behind a cypress-crowned crest of hills, grey with olives, or bare where the maize had been reaped. The browned leaves and the reddened fruit hung over her; the water-flags and the purling stream, narrowed and shallow here, were at her feet; alone, the great tears rushed into her eyes, and her scarce-flown childhood conquered.

"Oh, God! the width of the world!" she murmured, while one sob rose in her throat,—it seemed so vast, so endless, so naked, and so pathless a desert. This was the world to which she had used to look as the redresser of her wrongs, the battle-field of her victories, the fairy-realm of every beauty, the giver of such golden crowns, such hours of paradise!—this world that seemed so full of lives rushing to their tombs, wherein no man cared for his brother,—where all was hard, and heated, and choked, and pitiless, and none paused to think of God!—this world in which there was but one life for her, and that one lost,—perhaps lost for ever.

This boundless width of the world!—to wander through it, ever seeking, never finding, wearing the years away in fruitless search, pursuing what, like the mountain-heights, receded farther with every nearer step, looking in all the multitudes of earth for one face, one regard, one smile! The burden lay heavy on her young heart, and the heart-sickness of toil without end was on her to despair. But the nature in her was brave unto death, and the veneration she bore her one idol enchained and possessed her whole existence. She had a child's faith, a woman's passion, a martyr's heroism.

She looked up at the sunlight through the mist of her tears; and trust was strong in her, strong as the anguish that made her fair lips white and hot in its pain and her brief life seem near its ending.

"He is poor,—he has suffered," she mused, recalling the words that had been spoken against him. "He is so great; but he has lost his kingdom. When I find him, then, there may be some way I may serve him,—some way as slaves serve."

To hear that he had want and sorrow had seemed to bring him nearer to her, had bound her heart closer yet to one who was not less a sovereign to her because a sovereign discrowned. She marvelled what his history could be. All of glory, of dignity, of sacrifice, of desolation, that wronged greatness bears, thronged to her thoughts as the story of his life. She knew him now as the unknown man of whom she had said, on the faith of his written words, that he would have gathered strength from any fall; and she knew no more than this. It was enough; it spoke more to her than if she had been told of empires that he owned. She knew the kingdom of his thoughts, the treasuries of his mind; through his words he had spoken to her long ere her eyes had rested on him, and she had revered him as her master ere ever she had heard his voice, as Héloïse had revered the genius which roused the nations and shook the churches, ere ever Abelard had stood before her.

It bound her to him in a submission absolute and proud in its own bondage as was ever that of Héloïse.

It mattered nothing to her what his life had been,—a reign or a martyrdom, a victory or a travail; what *he* was was known to her, and she asked no more. Yet, where she leaned alone, the colour glowed into her face; she shrank and trembled in the solitude as though a thousand eyes were on her; for the first time the sense of shame had touched her, for the first time the vileness of evil had approached her, and both left her afraid and startled.

"They spoke as though it were sin to seek him," she

thought. "Will he be angered if I ever find him? I will
never go near him, never ask his pity, never let him know
that I am by; I will only look on him from some distance,
only stay where I can hear his voice afar off—if I live.
But whenever I see him the joy will kill me; and better
so,—better far than to risk one cold word from him, one
look of scorn. He said the world would crush me, and
stone me like Hypatia. The world shall not; but one
glance of his would, if it ever rebuked me!"

A shiver ran through her as she mused.

She had cast herself on the desert of the world in
darkness, as the lamps of sacrifice are cast on the stream
by Indian women at night. All was strange to her, all
cold, all arid, all without track or knowledge or light.
The beauty of her voice in choral service and the flowers
that she gathered from forest or river were all her riches,
and hand to guide her she had none. But all fear for
herself, all thought for herself, were banished in the domination of one supreme grief, one supreme hope. The
world was so wide! When would she find him?

Her tears fell heavy and fast, down into the white
cups of the faded lilies at her feet. The world was so
wide, and she was so lonely,—she whose heart ached for
love, whose eyes ached for beauty, whose youth longed
for happiness, as the hart for the water-springs.

CHAPTER VI.
"Nihil humani a me alienum puto."

"If you would but come back to us!" Philippe d'Orvâle spoke softly, as a woman speaks in tenderness. He
stood on the hearth of his great banqueting-room, rich and
dark in its burnished lustre of gold and scarlet, like an
old palace-chamber of Venice; his hair, that silky lion's
mane, was white, but under it his brown eyes flashed, full

of untamed fire, and from the depths of the luxuriant snowy beard laughter fit for Olympus would still shake the silence with the ringing, riotous mirth of yore. Now those eyes were grave with a wistful shadow, and the voice of the reckless Prince Bohemian had a silver gentleness. "If you would but come back to us!" he said, again, as he had said it many times through the length of weary years. "The people hunger for you. They bear patiently with me, but it is in bitterness; they have never been reconciled to my rule, though its yoke is light. Come back! It is unchanged; it will be as your own: it *should* be your own at one word, if you would but let me!"

Where Chandos stood, in the shadow of the jutting angle of the alabaster sculpture above the hearth, a shiver shook him that he could not restrain, like that which strong limbs give irrepressibly when a bared nerve is cut and wrung. His own voice was very low, as he answered,—

"To thank you were impossible; I have found no words for it through seventeen years. Your friendship may well avail to outweigh a whole world's faithlessness. But to accept were to sink myself lower in my own sight than my worst ruin ever sank me. *Were* I to go back on another's bounty, I would give the men who still remember me leave to stone me as I went, and curse me in my father's name."

Philippe d'Orvâle's superb head drooped in silence: the proud noble knew the temper that denied him, and honoured it, and could not dare to press it to surrender, —knew that denial to him was right and just, even whilst his heart longed most to wring assent. That denial had been given him steadily through the long course of seventeen years,—given by one who had once never known what it was to forbid a desire or control a wish,—by one to whom exile was the ceaseless and deadly bitterness that it was to Dante,—by one who longed for the mere sight of the forest-lands, the mere breath of the forest-winds, of the birthright he had lost, as the weary eyes of the Syrian Chief longed for a sight of the Promised Land, that he had to lie down and die without entering, banned out to the last hour.

Chandos saw the pain on him, and stretched out his hand.

"My best friend, if I could take such charity from any, it should be from you. But you must feel with me that to give consent to what you wish were to lose the one relic of my race I have striven to keep,—its barren honour."

"I know! I know! Yet all I ask is leave to give a sovereign back his throne. No more than my house did to my cousin of Bourbon."

"And the sovereign who bartered his kingdom for ten years' mad delight had but justice done him when it was swept away for ever. But speak no more of it for God's sake! I am weak as water, *here!*"

"Weak! and yet you refuse?"

"I refuse, because to accept were disgrace; but there are times when I could wish still that—bearing me the love you did—you had shot me like a dog, while I could have died in my youth!"

The words were hushed to a scarce-heard whisper, as they escaped through his set teeth; they were a truth rarely wrung from him,—the truth that through the patience and the peace and the strength he had forced from calamity, through the silence in which he had borne his doom and the high ambition which guided and sustained him, the old passionate agony, the old loathing of life that was pain, would break with a resistless force, and make him long to have died in that golden and cloudless light of his lost years,—died ere its suns had set for ever.

"Weak!   That is rather strength, since, wishing this thus, you still have borne against it, and lived on, and conquered!"

"I have no strength! A foe's taunt can make a brute of me, a friend's tenderness unnerve me like a woman. Sometimes I think I have learned nothing; sometimes I think that no reed was ever frailer than I.   A while ago a young girl showed me 'Lucrèce:' I knew, as I saw the book, what Swift felt when he shed those passionate tears for the genius he had in his youth!"

"Yours is greater than in your youth."

"Ah! I doubt it.   Youth is genius; it makes every dawn a new world, every woman's beauty a love-ode, every breath a delight. We weave philosophies as life slips from us; but when we were young our mere life was a poem."

Dark hours came on him oftentimes; the Hellenic nature in him, that loved beauty and harmony and the soft lulling of the senses, could not perish, and, imprisoned in the loneliness and colourless asceticism of need and of exile, ached in him and beat the bars of its prison-house in many a moment. He had subdued his neck to the yoke, and he had found his redemption in sublimer things and loftier freedoms, as Boethius under the chains of the Goth found his in the golden pages of the "Consolations;" but there were times when the Greek-like temper in him still turned from life without enjoyment, as from life without value.

The heart of Philippe d'Orvâle went with him. The careless, royal, headlong levity of the princely Bohemian had made of life one long unthinking revel. Dynasties and creeds and nations and thrones might rock and fall, might rise and totter, round him; he heeded them never, but drank the purple wine of his life brimming and rose-crowned, and learned his science from women's eyes, and sung a Bacchic chaunt while others grew grey in the gall of state harness, and shook the grand, mellow, rolling laughter from his colossal chest at the vain toil of the heart-burning world around him while he held on his gay, endless, Viking-like wassaiL Of a truth there are creeds far less frank and less wise than his; and of a truth there are souls far less honest and bold and bright. He would have lost life rather than have broken his word; and no lie had ever stained his fearless, careless, laughter-warmed lips. Of a truth the mad Duke had virtues the world has not.

His eyes dwelt now with a great unspoken tenderness on Chandos.

"Yet you are greater than you were then," he said, slowly. "I know it,—I who am but a wine-cup rioter and love nothing but my summer-day fooling. You are greater; but the harvest you sow will only be reaped over your grave."

"I should be content could I believe it would be reaped then."

"Be content, then. You may be so."

"God knows! Do you not think Marsy and Delisle de Sales and Linguet believed, as they suffered in their dungeons for mere truth of speech, that the remembrance of future generations would solace them? Bichât gave himself to premature death for science' sake: does the world once in a year speak his name? Yet how near those men are to us, to be forgotten! A century, and history will scarce chronicle them."

"Then why give the wealth of your intellect to men?"

"Are there not higher things than present reward and the mere talk of tongues? The *monstrari digito* were scarce a lofty goal. We may love Truth and strive to serve her, disregarding what she brings us. Those who need a bribe from her are not her true believers."

Philippe d'Orvâle tossed his silvery hair from his eyes,—eyes of such sunny lustre still.

"Ay! And those who held that sublime code of yours, that cleaving to truth for truth's sake, where are they? How have they fared in every climate and in every age? Stoned, crucified, burned, fettered, broken on the vast black granite mass of the blind multitude's brutality, of the priesthood's curse and craft!"

"True! Yet if through us, ever so slightly, the bondage of the creeds' traditions be loosened from the lives they stifle, and those multitudes—so weary, so feverish, so much more to be pitied than condemned—become less blind, less brute, the sacrifice is not in vain."

"In your sense, no. But the world reels back again into darkness as soon as a hand has lifted it for a while into light. Men hold themselves purified, civilised; a year of war,—and lust and bloodthirst rage untamed in all their barbarism; a taste of slaughter,—and they are wolves again! There was truth in the old feudal saying, 'Oignez vilain, il vous poindra; poignez vilain, il vous oindra.' Beat the multitudes you talk of with a despot's sword, and they will lick your feet; touch them with a Christ-like pity, and they will nail you to the cross."

There was terrible truth in the words: this man of princely blood, who disdained all sceptres and wanted nothing of the world, could look through and through it with his bold sunlit eyes, and see its rottenness to the core.

Chandos sighed as he heard.

"You are right,—only too right. Yet even while they crouch to the tyrant's sabre, how bitterly they need release! even while they crucify their teachers and their saviours, how little they know what they do! They may forsake themselves; but they should not be forsaken."

Philippe d'Orvâle looked on him with a light soft as

women's tears in his eyes, and dashed his hand down on
the alabaster.

"Chandos, you live twenty centuries too late. You
would have been crowned in Athens, and throned in Asia.
But here, as a saving grace, they will call you—'mad!'"

"Well, if they do? The title has its honours. It was
hooted against Solon and Socrates."

At that moment they were no longer alone; a foreign
minister entered the reception-room. Only at Philippe
d'Orvâle's house in Paris was Chandos ever seen by
any members of the circles which long ago had followed
him as their leader. With the statesmen, the thinkers,
the scholars of Europe he had association: but with the
extravagant and aristocratic worlds where he had once
reigned he had no fellowship; and the younger generation, who chiefly ruled them, had no remembrance and
but little knowledge of what his career once had been in
those splendid butterfly-frivolities, those Tyrian purples
of a glittering reign. A Turkish lily, when all its pomp
of colour and of blossom has been shaken down in the
wind and withered, is not more rapidly forgotten than
the royalty of a fashionable fame when once reverse has
overtaken it.

But his name had power, though of a widely different
sort; and its influence was great. Science saw in him
its co-revolutionist against tradition; weary and isolated
thinkers battling with the apathy or the antagonism of
men found in him their companion and their chief; young
and ardent minds came in eager gratitude to his leader-
ship; the churches stoned, the scholars reverenced him;
the peoples vaguely wondered at him, and told from
mouth to mouth the strange vicissitudes of his life. From
the deep, silent heart of old Italian cities, where many of
his years were passed, his words came to the nations,

and pierced ears most dead and closed to him, and carried far their seed of freedom, which would sink in the
soil of public thought, and bear full harvest only, as
Philippe d'Orvâle had said, above his grave. Men knew
that there was might in this man, who had risen from a
voluptuary's delight to face destruction, and had forced
out of adversity the gold of strength and of wisdom. They
listened,—even those who cursed him because he spoke
too widely truth. They listened, and they found that an
infinite patience, an exhaustless toleration, a deep and
passionless calm, had become the temper of his intellect
and of his teaching. It was too pure, too high, too profound for them, and too wide in grasp; but they listened,
and vaguely caught a loftier tincture, a more serene justice, from him.

The career which his youth had projected, in the
splendid ideals of its faith and its desire, could have
been possible only in the ages when the world was young,
and the sceptre of a king could gather the countless
hosts as with a shepherd's love into one fold, under the
great Syrian stars,—when the life of a man could be as
one long magnificence of Oriental day, with death itself
but the setting of a cloudless sun, and the after-glow of
fame a trail of light to nations East and West. The
dreams of his youth had been impossible: yet one thing
remained to him of them,—their loyalty to men and their
forbearance with them. In one sense he was greater than
his father had been: statesmen mould the actions of the
Present, but thinkers form the minds of the Future. It is
the vaster power of the two.

It was late when he left the Hôtel d'Orvâle. He had
spent the hours with some of the most eminent statesmen
of the continent. All men of mark heard his opinions
with eagerness and with deference. When he had had

the opportunity, he had never sought either rank or state power; now that his intellect was his only treasury, he never sought to purchase with it either riches or the revival of his lost dignities. They did not comprehend him; but the absolute absence of all personal ambition impressed them in one who, when his word was omnipotent, had never exercised it to obtain the place and the power which made up their own aims, and who now gave his years and his thoughts to the search of truth, unheeding what it brought him. They wondered that, with his fame, he endeavoured to attain no material rewards, no political influence: in that wonder they missed the whole key of his character. He had been too proud ever to be attracted by the vulgarities of social distinctions in the years when any could have been his for the asking; now the same temper remained with him. Then, as a careless voluptuary, he had smiled at and pitied those who wasted the golden days in the feverish pursuit of ephemeral renowns; now, as a great writer, he had the same marvel, the same contempt, for the minds which could stoop their mighty strength to seek a monarch's favour or a court's caprice, to gain a ribbon or to form a six-months' ministry. The strife and fret of party had little more dignity in his eyes than the buzzing and pushing of bees to enter a honey-clogged hive. The hero of public life is a slave, and a slave who must wear the livery of conventional forms and expedient fallacies. Chandos loved freedom, absolute freedom: he could no more have lived without it than he could have lived without air.

He knew that it was well that there should be men who would harness themselves to the car of the nations, and think that they led history, while they were in truth only the driven pack-horses of human development or national decadence; but he would no more have gone in their shafts than an eagle will wind a windlass.

As he went now, through the lateness of the night, with the fragrance of the Luxembourg gardens on the air, his thoughts were grave and far away.

The stillness of the night—so late that the crowds had thinned, and there were but little noise and movement even in the greatest thoroughfares—brought back on his memory the nights in which he had lain dying for a draught of cold water in the dens of this brilliant city,—of the nights when, in infamy, and shame, and misery, he had sought to kill remembrance and existence in joyless vice and opiate slumbers, in orgies that he loathed, in drugged sleep that lulled his mind into an idiot's vacancy. That time was vague and unreal to him as the phantasms of fever to the man who awakes from them; but he never looked back to it without a shudder. His fall had been so vast, and the plank so frail that alone had arrested his headlong reel into a suicide's grave or a madman's darkness! All men had forsaken him then, save one,— his enemy,—forsaken him, though their hands were full of his gifts,—forsaken him, leaving him to die like a dog. But he had not in return or in revenge abandoned them: he knew the terrible truth of the "Qui vitia odit, homines odit," and he would not let hatred of their ingratitude dwell with him and turn him cynic, for he cleaved to them in tenderness still. Perhaps in this yet more than in all other efforts of his later life he kept true to the dreams of his youth,—this patience with which he loved men and believed in their redeeming excellence, even through all which might have bidden him, as his foe had once bidden him, "curse God and die!"

As he passed now through the richer and finer quarters towards a retired and little-frequented street where he had his temporary dwelling in the centre of Paris, he passed close by the gates of a ducal mansion. Before them stood, among a long line, a carriage handsomely appointed, with powdered servants and laced liveries; the gates were open, and the court was in a blaze from a hundred lamps, with lackeys in their laced liveries moving to and fro. An English minister was coming out to the equipage, with some light, costly furs thrown loosely over his full dress. They looked at each other in the gas-light: a moment was enough for recognition.

Trevenna waved his hand towards his carriage with a laughing smile.

"Ah, mon prince! *you* on foot? How times are changed! Get in; pray do. I'm very forgiving, and I'll give you a lift for auld lang syne."

Chandos passed on,—without a word, without a sign, —as though he had not heard. Yet men have slain their foes, in hot blood and cold, for less than this mocker's baseness and outrage.

The petty jeer of the indignity was fouler than a wrong worthier of resentment. When the soldier of the guard spat in Charles Stuart's face, the insult was the worse because too ignominious for scorn, too low for revenge.

He went onward down into the solitude of the tortuous winding,—one of those streets in which bric-à-brac, and priceless china, and old pictures, and old treasures of every sort are heaped together in little, dark, unguarded windows, and are only told from the shadows by the shine of a diamond or the shape of a quaint vase forcing itself up from the dimness and the dust. There came feebly towards him in the gloom, the tall, bowed form of an old man, with white hair floating on his shoulders, and his hands feebly stretched before him in the wavering, uncertain movement of the blind. The figure was inpressive, with its long, flowing, black garments, and its stern, antique, patriarch-like look so painfully in contrast with the extreme feebleness of excessive age and that plaintive, flickering movement of the hands.

"Oh, my God!" he was muttering, piteously, "where is he? where is he?"

The grief and appeal of the accent, the helplessness of the sightless action accompanying it, arrested Chandos. He paused, and touched the blind wanderer on the arm.

"Whom are you seeking? Can I help you?"

The old man stopped his slow swinging step, and caught the gentleness of the tone with the quickness to sound that compensates for the loss of sight in so many.

"I search for my dog, sir," he answered. "He is my only guide, and I have lost him."

"Lost him! How far from this?"

"Some way. He broke from me: children lured him, I think. He was very pretty, and the life he led with me was but dull. It is natural he should forsake me."

Chandos listened, struck by the accent: he had known what it was to have an animal the sole friend left.

"Dogs rarely forsake us. I should hope he will come back to you. You cannot find your way without him?"

The other shook his head silently,—a grand, majestic, saturnine old man, despite the decrepitude that had bowed his back, and the melancholy supplication in which his trembling hands were outstretched.

Chandos looked at him silently also; there was something in his look and in his manner which impressed him with their intense sadness. No memory revived in him, but compassion moved him.

"Tell me where you live: I will see you home," he said, presently. It was not in his nature to leave any one so aged to wander wretchedly and uncertainly in the darkness of the after-midnight. Trevenna would have enjoyed stealing the dog away, and leading the harassed creature round and round in a circle by a thousand mystifications; but to Chandos there was something of positive pain in the sight of any human being stranded in the midst of that peopled city for sheer need of a hand stretched out to him. Men had been false to him; but he remained loyally true to them.

The blind man turned with an involuntary start of wonder and of gratitude.

"You are very good, sir! Will it not trouble you?"

"Far from it. Men must be very heartless if they could all leave you to need such a trifle as that."

"Men owe me nothing," said the other, curtly, whilst he went on to tell his residence.

Chandos said no more, but went thither, slackening his pace to the halting step of the one he guided. It was some little time before he could find the place he was directed to; when he did so, it was a tall, frowning, ruined house, jammed amidst many others, with the shutters up against the lower windows, and poverty told by all its rambling timbers.

"Open, sir, since you are kind enough to take pity on me," said the blind man, as he gave him a key, to which the crazy door yielded easily. "My room, such as it is, is the first on the fifth story."

It was a miserable chamber enough, bare and desolate, with a rough pallet bed, and an unspeakable nakedness and want about it. A little lamp burned dully, and threw its yellow light on the peculiar and striking figure of the man he had guided; and he looked at him curiously,—a man of ninety winters, with the dark olive of his skin furrowed like oak-bark, and his sweeping, pointed beard snow-white,—a man who had suffered much, needed much, endured much, and possibly done much evil in his day, yet commanding and solemn in his excessive years as the figure of a Belisarius sightless and poverty-stricken and forsaken by those for whom he had given his life-blood. He turned to Chandos with a stately and touching action.

"Sir, who you are I cannot tell; but from my soul I thank you, from my heart I would bless you—if I dared."

Chandos lingered, leaning against the barren, unsightly wall. He might be in a den of thieves, for aught he knew; but there was that in the Israelite (as he justly deemed him) that moved him to interest. Since the glory of his summer-day world had closed on him, he had gone far down into the depths of human suffering and human sin; he had known life in its darkest and in its worst, and he evaded nothing to which he could bring either aid or consolation. The mingled infirmity and wisdom of his glorious manhood had been to abhor and shun every sight and shape of pain; since he had tasted the bitterness of ruin, he had passed by no pain that he could hope to succour.

"You should not be alone at your years," he said, gently. "Have you nothing but this lost dog to take heed of you?"

"Nothing, sir: *he* is gone now."

"I trust not. I will try and find him for you. Pardon me, but at your age it is rare to be wholly solitary."

"Is it?" said the blind man, with a sententious melancholy. "I thought the reverse. We have outlived our due time. We have seen all die around us; we ought to be dead ourselves."

Chandos was silent; he stood, thoughtful and almost saddened by the Israelite's words. He was alone himself, —he, for whom the world had once been one wide palace, filled with courtiers and friends; he looked to be so alone to his grave.

At that moment there came the rush of eager feet, the panting of eager breath; the unlatched door of the room was burst open. A little dog of the Maltese breed scoured across the floor, and leaped on the old man with frantic caresses; its desertion had been but for a moment, and its conscience and its love had soon brought it back. The Jew took it fondly in his arms, and murmured tender names over it; then he turned his blind eyes on Chandos.

"Sir, I thank my little truant that through his abandonment I learned that one man lived so merciful as you."

"There are many; do not doubt that. Forgive me if I seem to force your confidence, but I would gladly know if I can aid you. Rich I am not, but there might be ways in which I could assist you."

He spoke very gently; this old man, grand as any sculpture of Abraham or Agamemnon, in his extreme loneliness, in his extreme poverty, awoke his sympathy.

The Hebrew drew his bent form straight, with a certain unconscious majesty.

"Sir, my confidence you cannot have; but it is only meet that you should know I am one who often has worked much evil, and who has been once branded as a felon."

Chandos looked at him in silence a moment; he could believe that evil had left its trace among the dark furrows of the sombre and stern face he looked on, but criminal shame seemed to have no place with the Jew's patriarchal calm and dignity.

"If it be so, there may be but the more cause that you need aid. Speak frankly with me."

"There are those who say my people never speak except to lie," said the Hebrew briefly. "It is untrue.

But frank I cannot be with you,—with any. Could I have been so, I were not thus now."

"How? Did you refuse the truth, or was it denied you?"

"Both. I heard a story once,—whether fact or romance I cannot tell; it struck me. I will tell it you. There was an old soldier of the Grande Armée, who was bidden by his chief to execute some secret service and never speak of it. He did it; his absence on its errand was discovered; he was tried for desertion or disobedience, I forget which. Napoleon was present at the trial; the accused looked in the face of his master for permission to clear himself by revealing the truth; the face was chill as stone, mute as steel; there was *no consent* in it. The soldier bared his head, and held his peace; he underwent his chastisement in silence; he muttered only ever after, in insanity,'*Silence à la mort!*'"

Chandos heard, moved to more than surprise. He saw that this poverty-worn blind Hebrew was no common criminal, and had had no common fate. He leaned forward and looked at him more earnestly.

"And the soldier's doom,—was that yours?" he asked.

The Jew bent his snow-white head, pressing the little nestling dog closer to his bosom.

"Much such an one."

"You were of the army, then?"

"No; but I had a chief as pitiless as Napoleon. No matter! he had the right to be so. It is not for me to speak."

The words were spoken with the patience of his race; an infinite pain passed over the harsh, saturnine sternness of his face.

"But you would seem to say that by silence you were wronged. Tell me more plainly."

A sigh escaped the close-pressed lips of the aged man.

"Sir, you have been good to me; it is not for me to deny what I can justly tell. That is not much. I was in the employ of an Englishman; we drove an evil trade, —a trade in men's ruin, in men's necessities, in men's desperation. It is a common trade enough, and there are hundreds who drive in their carriages, and live amidst the great, who have gained their wealth by that trade and by no other. I was a hard man, a shrewd, a merciless; I asked my pound of flesh, and I cut it remorselessly. Life had been bitter with me; it had baffled me when I would have done righteousness; it had denied me when I would have sought justice; it had damned me because of my wandering race: with the book of my religion in their hands, Christians flouted me and scourged me,—a Jew dog, a Jew cheat, a Jew liar! If I said truth, none believed me; if I did honestly, all laughed, and thought that I had some deeper scheme of villany beneath. I would have acted well with men, but they mocked me; and then—I took my revenge. I do not say it was right; but it was human."

He paused; the died-out light began to gather in his sunken eyes, the memories of manhood to kindle on his brown and withered face; his voice grew stronger and deeper, as it thrilled with the remembrance of other days. Chandos stood silent, looking on him with a strange force of interest, while the dull feeble flickering of the oil-flame shed its faint illumination on the old man's Syrian-like form.

"I was sorely tossed, and beaten, and reviled; I became bitter, and keen, and cruel. I was like iron to those Gentiles who needed me and, when they needed, cringed. I said in my soul, 'You call me a Jew robber; well, you shall feel my knife.' And yet I declare that, till they

made me so, I had served men and striven to make them
love me,—hard as it is for a poor man, and a Jew, to gain a
friend among Christians! They have stolen our God; but
they only blaspheme in His name, and call the people
whose creed they borrow, by the vilest obscenities of their
streets! So I grew like a flint, and I checked not at cun-
ning. One innocent may be wrongly suspected until he is
made the thing that the libel has called him. I was a
usurer: you know what that is,—a man who makes his
gold out of tears of blood, and fills his caldron with
human flesh till its seething brings him wealth. I had
only one softness in me: it was my love for my wife."

His voice quivered slightly; even the memory of the
dead love that lay so far away in the grave of buried
days had power to shake him like a reed.

"She was as beautiful as the morning, twenty years
or more younger than I; but she loved me with a great
love, and while she was in my bosom she made me seek
to be as she was. Well, she died. My life was as dark
as midnight, and my heart was ice. For a while I was
mad; when my senses came to me, I set myself to the
lust of gold, to the grinding out of my deadly pain on
the lives that had mocked me. Thus I became evil, and
men cursed me,—justly then. I made much money, and,
years after, I lost it, in schemes in which it had been
risked. I fell in the straits of extreme poverty; in them
I met, in the dens of a great city, an Englishman who
was good to me and succoured me. Afterwards we
entered into negotiations together; he joined my old firm,
—it did not bear my name; he became *it:* in fact, I was
but his manager, clerk, subordinate; but the public still
thought me the principal. He was very clever, very able;
he knew the world widely, and he had fashionable
acquaintances by the hundred. Between us,—he secretly,

I openly,—we spread our nets very far; we drew many lives into the meshes; we made much money;—he did, at least: his was the capital, his the profit; I did but the work at a salary. We were always strictly to the letter of the law; but within the law we were very hard. Oh, God! now that I am blind and forsaken, I know it! Well, meanwhile my son had come home to me from Spain,—a beautiful, gracious child, who brought his mother's look in his eyes. In him I was almost happy; for him I worked unceasingly; thinking of him, I did my master's bidding with alacrity and with little heed for those who suffered. For seven years my boy grew up with me from a child to a youth; and when he smiled at me with his mother's smile, I would have coined my life, if I could have done so, to purchase him an hour's pleasure. And in those seven years the firm had prospered marvellously, and my master—so I call him—made much wealth from it in secret. At the time of the eighth or ninth year, when my son was eighteen——"

He paused; though his eyes had no sight in them, he veiled them, drooping his head in shame as his words were resumed.

"The lad erred,—erred terribly. I cannot speak it! Dishonesty, glossed over, had been round him so long,— it was not *his* crime. He saw *us* thieve: how could he learn to keep his young hands pure? He forged my master's name, in thoughtlessness, and thinking, I believe, that such money was our common due, since I worked for it. I knew then a worse anguish than when my darling had died. My master found it out,—he found everything out: the boy was in his power. He could have sent the young life to a felon's doom: he was merciful, and he spared him. For it let me ever hold his name in blessing."

He bent his head with a grave, reverential gesture,

and was silent many moments, his lips mutely moving, as
though in prayer for the benefactor of his only son.

"He spared the youth always: let it be ever remembered by me," he resumed, while his voice was broken
and very faint. "To purchase his redemption, to repay
his ransom, I gave my body and my mind, by night and
by day, to travail. I did iniquity to buy my son's peace:
that was my sin. My master was lenient, and spared him
from accusation: that was his clemency. By one and by
the other the child was saved. He was so gentle, so loving, so bright, so full of poetic thoughts and noble longing; it must have been a mortal fear that ever drove him
to that single crime! Or rather, I have thought later, it
was the thoughtless fault of a child who did not know
the error that he did. Well, my master had been pitiful
to the thing I loved. I owed him my life—more than
my life—for that. A few years, and the test came to me.
I have said inviolate secrecy was kept on his association
with the business that I conducted. No living creature
guessed it. His own friends by the score were among our
clients, among our victims; but none of them ever dreamt
that *he* had anything to do with the usury on which they
heaped their curses. One night he had visited the office
(a thing he rarely did), and had taken away with him
the title-deeds and family papers of one whose extremity
of need had forced him to lodge them with me as security
for an immediate loan. That very night their owner came
down in hot haste; he had obtained money by a sudden
and marvellous stroke of fortune, and was breathless to
recover his pawned papers and pay back the loan. The
deeds were not there! To say *where* they were would
have been to betray my master. I could not produce
them; I could not explain their absence. The gentleman
was very fiery and furious; he would not wait; he de-

manded his papers back. Give them I could not, and I had neither time nor means to communicate with my master. The gentleman, hot-blooded and young, gave me into arrest for their detention and disappearance. The trial ensued. Since my arrest I had watched and waited for some word, some sign, from my master which should tell me what I should do. I waited in vain: none came. I was placed in the dock, and tried for the theft of the deeds. My counsel were bitter towards me, because I would not be 'frank' with them and explain; I could only be silent unless my master gave me freedom to speak. *He* knew he could trust me. Besides, had he not the lad's fame and life in his power? He was there,—in court,—listening. I looked at him; he looked at me. I read 'silence' hidden on his face, as the soldier saw it on Napoleon's. It was enough. I was silent. It was his due, and my right of obedience. He had spared my son in his error; I had sworn to keep his secret till death. The trial took its course; they found me guilty. I was sentenced to ten years' penal servitude. It was a grave offence. The deeds were gone: they were never found: I suppose my master destroyed them. It was a fearful loss for their owner, and they could not choose but judge that I had held them back or burnt them, for theft or for the sake of extortion. I suffered the punishment; but I never broke my silence."

There was a sublime simplicity, an inexpressible grandeur, on the old man, as he spoke, bowing his head as though borne down by the weight of that enforced burden of silence, stretching out his trembling hands as though in supplication to God to witness how he had kept his oath.

Chandos, where he stood in the gloom of the poverty-stricken chamber, uncovered his head with a reverent action, before the sightless gaze of the blind man.

"Let the evil of your life be what it may, in that martyrdom you washed it out with a nobility men seldom reach."

His words were low and heartfelt: the unconscious dignity of the self-devotion and of the fidelity to a promised word was too lofty to his thought to be insulted with any offering of mere pity.

A warmth of surprise and of pleasure passed over the withered olive face of the Israelite,—though it faded almost instantly.

"It was duty," he said, simply,—"the duty of a debtor."

"Rather it was the sacrifice of a martyr. But he, this brutal taskmaster, who could condemn you to such a doom, who could stand by and see you suffer for his sake,—what of him?"

"I say nothing of him: he is sacred to me!"

"Sacred! though he cursed you thus?"

"Sacred, because he spared my son."

Chandos bent his head.

"I understand you; I honour you.   But it was a terrible ordeal.   Few construe duty so.   And your son,—what of him?"

"I am as one dead to him."

Ignatius Mathias said the words very softly, whilst over the bronzed, worn rigidity of his patient face. came the softer look which it only wore at the thought of Agostino.

"Dead to him?   Is he, then, so ungrateful?"

The Hebrew shook his head with a quick negative gesture of his hands.

"He is never ungrateful; he felt only too vividly, and he loved me well. But I had sent him out of the country before this happened—sent him, my master permitting, to people of mine in Mexico. It was bitter for me to sever from him. But the lad's spirit was broken; I knew nothing but change of scene could ever restore him. Journals did not reach him there in the western country. I learned that he was recovering health and courage, was prosecuting a career for which he had from childhood shown genius. I learned that he knew nothing of my arrest and of my trial: I thanked God; for I knew how it would have grieved him. He might have done something very rash, had he heard that I suffered or was accused. As it was, I bade them tell him I was dead. It would cause him pain, great pain,—for he loved me, strange as it may seem that he should,—but less pain than the shame that must have fallen on him with the other knowledge. It was weak in me, perhaps, but I could not bear that my only son should think, with the world, that I could be guilty of that crime. And if he had not thought it, it would have been worse; he would have been galled to some act of desperation. He heard, as I say, of my death; he suffered, but less than he would have suffered knowing the truth, knowing the punishment I underwent. Yet the deadliest thing in my chastisement was that I could never look on his face, never listen to his voice, never let him hear that I lived!"

The old man's voice faltered slightly; even his strength, that had been like wrought iron to endure, and that had held his soul in patience for so long, could not look back at that time of torture and keep its force unbroken.

"At the end of ten years I was liberated. They had not been cruel to me as a convict. They pitied my age, I think, though at first they had little mercy because they held me a Jew thief. I was free—a beggar, of course; and at eighty-four years one cannot begin the world again. Besides, I was as one branded: go where I would, the police followed me, and warned others of me: I was a leper and a pariah in the midst of men. I did not starve, for my people are good to the helpless; but all thought me guilty, and no creature trusted me. I heard of my darling, of my son: he was prosperous. He was achieving fame and success in the life he had chosen; he was, I hoped, happy. I could not be so brutal, so selfish, as to seek him out and say, 'Behold, your father lives!' when he must have found in his father a convicted felon just set free from his public punishment. I could not blight his youth and his peace by rising up, as it were, from the grave, and forcing in on him my age, my poverty, my disgrace, as the world held it. He had mourned for me, and ceased to mourn long before: I could not open his wounds afresh; I could not humiliate him with a criminal's claim on him. Not that I wronged him ever, not that I ever doubted him; let me have been what I should, I knew his heart would be tender to me, and his roof be offered me in shelter. But *because* I knew, I could not bring that wretchedness on him; I could not injure him in the world's sight by standing by him a liberated felon; I could not torture him by showing him my wrists, on which the chains of the convict gang had weighed, by bidding him look back with me upon my prison-cell, my prison-shame. I left him to believe me dead. I never looked upon his face except by stealth. I never listened to his voice except standing hidden in some dark archway to hear him speak as he passed by me in the streets. I have watched for hours under the shelter of green leaves to catch one glance of him as he came forth. I have waited for a whole night through, in storm or snow, to see him leave some house of pleasure or some labour of his art. It was my only thought, my only joy. I thanked God that I still lived in the days when I had looked a moment on his beauty. And now that too is gone. I am blind, and I have nothing left except to listen for the echo of his step!"

Silence followed his closing words; his head sank, his hands were pressed together like one who is tortured beyond his strength. All answer, all consolation, seemed mockery beside the supreme renunciation and desolation of this living sacrifice of an immeasurable love, that gave itself to martyrdom without a thought of its own devotion, without a memory of the vastness of its own unasked and unrewarded sacrifice.

Veneration, strong as his pity, moved the blind man's auditor as he heard; the heroism of the abnegation was noble in his sight, with a nobility that no words could dare taint or outrage with either compassion or homage, —a nobility that raised the Hebrew outcast to a loftier height than the great of the earth often reach, than the sunlight of a fair fate ever gives.

"Your Psalmist said that he had never beheld the righteous forsaken, nor the seed of the virtuous begging their bread," he said, slowly, at length. "How is it that *you*, then, are poor? You should be in the smile of your God."

The Israelite sighed wearily.

"It has ever seemed to me that David spoke in a bitter irony. Yonder in Syria, as here among us, sin throve, doubtless, and loyal faith passed unnoticed, unrecompensed by a crust. Yet I do not say this for myself. I merited all I suffered. I was merciless; I lived to want mercy. It was very just."

There was the inexorable meting out of the Mosaic code to his own past, and to his own errors, in the still, calm, iron resignation.

"Moreover," he added, with a certain light and hope

that kindled the faded fire of his sightless eyes, "if we follow duty because it brings us gold and peace and man's applause, where is there effort in the choice of it? It is only when it is hard that there can be any loyalty in its acceptance. Not that *I* should speak of this. I loved evil and avarice and cruelty too long, and followed them too fondly."

"At the least, your atonement might outweigh the crime of a Cain!"

The Hebrew sighed wearily again.

"Can evil ever be outweighed? I doubt it. We may strive to atone, but we can never efface. The past work spreads, and spreads, and spreads, like a river broken from its banks; and all the coffer-dams we raise in our atonement cannot stay the rushing of the waters we have once let loose. Ah! if when evil is begun we knew where it would stretch, men's hands would be kept pure from the very dread of their own awful omnipotence for ruin!"

The words died faintly away. Remorse had too wide a part in this man's memories for any thought that he redeemed his past crimes by his present sacrifice to have power to enter into him in any form of consolation.

He recovered himself with an effort, raising his blind eyes as though he could still read the face of the one who listened to him.

"Sir, you have heard me with a gentle patience. I thank you. I never spoke of these things until I spoke them now to you. Your voice is sweet and compassionate; it seems to me as though I had once heard it before now. Will you tell me your name among men?"

"Willingly; though I have no memory that we have ever met before. My name is Chandos."

A change, as intense as though some sudden pang of disease had seized him, convulsed the Israelite's whole frame; his thin withered lips closed tight, as though to hold in 'words that rushed to them; his hands clenched together. A revulsion passed over him, as if the whole dark, poisonous, pent tide of his past years swept in, killing with their return all the higher and better thoughts that but now had ruled him.

"Do you know me?" asked Chandos, in surprise.

The Spanish Jew answered with an effort, and his voice was harsh and jarring:—

"I know your name, sir; all the world does."

Chandos looked at him with awakened curiosity: the agitation which this old man showed at his recognition was scarcely compatible with the mere scant knowledge of his public reputation. Still, no remembrance of the solitary morning in the porphyry chamber, when he had seen the Castilian, came to him. In that terrible hour he had only been conscious of a sea of unfamiliar faces,—thirsty faces eager for his wealth, strange faces forcing themselves in to see the ruin of his race, and hungry, insolent faces gathered there to be the witnesses of his abdication and his fall. He remembered them distinctly no more than Scipio could have remembered the features of each unit of the libellous crowd that thronged about him to attaint his honour and discrown his dignity, until beneath the shadow of the Temple of Jupiter he rebuked them with one word,—"Zama."

"If you know my name, then," he said, after a slight pause, "I hope you will let it be a guarantee to you that I will do my utmost to serve you, if you will but show me the way. You interest me powerfully, and I honour you from my heart. Can I not help you?"

The old man turned away, and leaned over the lamp, so shading it that the light burned low: he had learned the marvellous self-guidance of the blind in those matters,

and knew by its warmth that the flame was high and fell
upon his face.

"No one can help me, sir. That I may be forgotten
is all I ask."

"Do·you mistrust my willingness, then? I hope not,"
said Chandos, gently. He noted the harsh, abrupt change
in the Jew's manner; but he thought it might be but the
weariness and waywardness of old age and long and bitter
endurance.

"I mistrust you in nothing," said the Hebrew, while
his voice was very low. "But I need no aid: my people
will not let me want. I thank you for your goodness;
and I bid you remember me no more."

There was a mingled austerity and appeal in the tone
that gave it a singular vibration of feeling; in it there
was something like the thrill of shame.

Chandos lingered a moment still; he was loath to leave
the old and sightless sufferer to his solitude, yet he saw
that his presence was unwelcome now, however gratitude
forbade the Israelite to say it.

"But your people forsake you," he persisted, gently;
"you have but a dog for your friend. I have known what
such solitude is; I would gladly aid you in yours. Will
you not trust me with your name, at the least?—or your
son's name?"

The Hebrew turned resolutely away, though his voice
trembled as he replied,—

"My son's will never pass my lips. Mine was buried
for ever in my felon's cell. I have told you—I am dead!
Leave me, sir; and believe me an ingrate, if you will. I
have been many things that are worse."

Chandos looked at him regretfully, wonderingly; he
was loath to quit the chamber in which so strange and so
nameless a tale had been unfolded to him.

"There is nothing worse; but I shall credit no evil of you," he answered; "and when you need friendship or assistance, think of my name, and send to me."

There was no reply: the face of the blind man was turned from him. He waited a moment longer, then went out, and closed the narrow door of the room, leaving the Hebrew to his loneliness.

He would willingly have done more here, but he knew not how.

The little dog, sole companion of the Castilian's solitude, nestling to him, as the door closed, with caressing fondness, felt great tears fall slowly one by one upon its pretty head, and lifted itself eagerly to fondle closer in the old man's bosom. But Ignatius Mathias paid it no heed; he had no answering word for it: his hands were wrung together in an agony.

"Oh, God!" he murmured, "and I lent my aid to rob, to ruin, to destroy him! Oh, God! why could I not die before he heaped the fire on my guilty head, with his gentle words, with his pitying mercy?"

CHAPTER VII.

"Pâle comme un beau soir d'automne."

As Chandos descended the staircase, he paused to ask a woman, who seemed mistress of the house, the Hebrew's name. She gave him the *alias* by which the old man was known there. It told him nothing: the real name would scarcely have told more. The whole time of his adversity was almost a blank in his memory, blotted out at the moment of his suffering by that suffering's sheer intensity, and effaced yet more utterly, later on, by the gambler's orgies into which for a year he had sunk without an effort at redemption. It seemed to him sometimes now that the cloudless life he had led ere then must have been the golden and lotus-steeped dream of some summer night: of the darkness which had followed on its ending he had barely more recollection than a man has of the phantasma of fever. Between the night when he had first learned his irreparable losses, and that on which he had been struck down by his foe in the court of the Temple, all was a blank to him, from which a few broken points of terrible remembrance alone stood out,—the sole measure-marks in that wide waste of desolation.

The stairs were narrow and crooked, ill lit by a dusky oil-lamp flickering low in its socket. Something in the house had seemed familiar to him, and as he passed downward he knew it again. It was the place in which he had laid dying and unconscious, with the winter stars looking down through the broken garret-roof, and the dog's fidelity alone watching beside him. He shuddered as he recalled it: for the moment the thought stole on him, would it not have been better that his life should have ended there? The richness and the frailty of his nature alike had needed light and colour, and the sweetness of delight, and the vivid hues of beauty and of pleasure. Now that, like Adam, he had long toiled alone in the bleak and barren earth of his exile, like Adam he might have gathered the bitter wisdom of far-reaching knowledge; but also, like Adam, the gates of Paradise had closed on him for ever. He was a wanderer, and without joy; there were times, as he had said that night, when he wished to God that it had been given him to die in his youth.

As he passed now down the stairs, the black, sweeping folds of a woman's dress touched him: he paused to give her space. In the gleam of the lamp-light a face, still beautiful, though haggard and darkened, was turned on him: it was the face of Beatrix Lennox.

She started, and a gentler, better look shadowed and
softened her features.

"*You!*"

She knew him,—knew him as soon as her eyes lighted
on him in that dusky yellow gloom,—this woman who, in
the midst of a reckless, sensuous, unscrupulous, world-
defiant life, had borne him a tenderness as silent as death,
pure as light. His face was graven on her heart,—that
face which she had first known in all the splendour and
all the radiance of its earliest manhood,—which she had
recognised once in the blackness of the stormy, snow-
veiled winter night,—which she knew now in the dignity
and the sadness of its later years.

He paused a moment, surprised and uncertain. All
that past time was so dim to him, all remembrance of
her had been so merged in the misery he had endured
on the night of their last parting, when he had learned
that the one he then loved had forsaken him, and had
been so swept away in the blank of starvation and of
bodily illness which had succeeded it, that he had little
memory of all he had owed her in that wintry midnight
when she had found him sinking into the sleep of death.
It was confused, and it made indistinct even his knowledge of her as she stood beside him now, after the
passage of so many years. Her eyes, once so victorious
in their empire, so unsparing in their sorcery, dwelt on
him with an extreme desolation.

"Ah! you have forgotten me? Well you may; even
Death forgets me, I think."

Her voice, so liquid and so silver-sweet, stirred his
memory as the features in their change could not do.
He took her hands in his.

"Forgotten! Never. Do not so wrong my gratitude.
Some part of my life seems a blank to me; but that life

lived in me at all was owing to you. And now that we meet, how can I thank you? There are no words for such a service."

She smiled, though her eyes still dwelt on him with that desolate and longing look.

"Is it so great a service to save life? Mercy were rather the other way. Yet perhaps not for you; you have made a noble use of adversity. But it was little enough *I* did. I would have served you, God knows; but the power was never mine."

He looked at her with a pang at his heart. All the companions of that joyous royalty, in which Fortune had seemed but the slave to obey his wish and to crown his desire, were dead or lost, forgotten or unknown to him, now; and her voice struck chords long unsounded and better left in peace,—awoke memories of a world abandoned for ever, of a youth for ever gone. Those long nights of pleasure, those dazzling eyes of women, those chimes of laughter without a care, those flower-smothered Cleopatran revels, those hours of careless joyance that had not a thought of the morrow,—how far away they seemed! He stood looking down on her in the sombre shadow of the wretched staircase, his thoughts rather in the past than with her. He did not know that she loved him,—he had never known it,—loved him so that she, the reckless and lawless Bohemian, would for his sake, had it been possible, have led the noblest life that ever woman led on earth, —loved him so that, through that purer love hating herself, she would no more, in the days of her beauty, have wooed him to her than she would have slain him, no more have offered him her tenderness than she would have offered him hemlock,—loved him too well ever to summon him amidst her lovers.

"How is it that we have never met?" he asked her,—

"never met until in such a place as this and at such an hour?"

She smiled. *She* had looked on his face many and many a time, unseen herself; she had suffered for him in his bitterness, she had gloried in his endurance, though she had never gone nigh him, but had rather withdrawn herself from every chance of recognition.

"You have never seen me? I have been long dead, you know. Women die when their beauty dies. Come within: I have one word to say to you."

She turned into a chamber somewhat lower on the staircase, poor, dark, chilly, in the feeble light of flickering candles.

"You live here?"

When he had known this woman, she had commanded what she would from peers and princes, who had been only too proud to be allowed the honour of ruin for her sake.

She flung off her the heavy folds of her cloak; and, as the richer hues of the dress beneath were dimly caught in the faint light, there was something still of the old regality which had made Beatrix Lennox the fairest name and the haughtiest queen in the whole of the dauntless army of the Free Companions.

"No; I am not quite so bad as that yet. I came here to-night to see one who is dying fast, with not a living soul to tend him."

"Ah! you belied the charity of your heart, then! at least you know the mercy of human pity still, as you knew it once for me."

"Hush! Charity! *Mine?* You do not know what you say. Is repenting of a millionth part of a torrent of evil—charity? The man who dies there was *my* victim. Years ago I drew him on till he fooled away everything

he owned for my sake. I cared no more for him than
for the sands of the sea; but it amused me to watch how
far his folly would go. He loved his wife; I made him
hate her. He had ambition; I made him scoff at it. He
had riches; I made him squander them for an hour's
caprice of mine. He had honours; I made him trail them
in the mud, like Raleigh's cloak, that I might set my
foot on them. Well, then I flung him away like a faded
flower, like a beryl out of fashion; and I find him, years
after, dying in want and shame. Call mine charity!
Call me a murderess, rather!"

There were no tears in her eyes; but there were more
intense misery and remorse in the calm words than ever
tears yet uttered.

He looked on her with infinite compassion.

"*I* call you nothing harsh: you were at least my
saviour."

Her beautiful, dark, wild eyes gazed at him with
gratitude, in which no acceptance of the forgiveness of
herself mingled.

"Ah, Chandos, I am heart-sick of the world's babble
about *your* sex's tempting. It is *we* who tempt you; it is
we who blindfold you,—*we* who are never satisfied till we
have won your lives to break them,—*we* who curse you
in sin and in pleasure, in license and in marriage,—*we*
who, if we see you at peace, think our vanity is at stake
till we drive peace away! The moralists rant of us as
martyrs! They little know that our mockery of love de-
stroys a thousand-fold more lives than it has ever blessed."

She spoke with passionate bitterness. He answered
nothing; he felt the truth of her words too well; and yet
with the thoughts of love there stole on him one fresh,
one soft memory,—that of the child Castalia.

Beatrix Lennox roused herself with the smile which

even in its sadness had something of the sorcery that nature had given her, and that death alone could take away.

"Forgive me! It was not to speak of these things that I brought you here. It was but to ask you, have you found yet who is your worst foe?"

"Yes; I was my own."

"Well, you were,—because you loved others better than you loved yourself. But that is not my meaning. Long ago, did you ever receive an anonymous letter that warned you against John Trevenna?"

His face darkened at the name. He paused, silent for a moment. She gave him no time to reply.

"If you did, I wrote it."

"You?"

"I! I dared not warn you more openly; I was in his power, as he had so many in his power. I knew that he hated you terribly, bitterly. There was something between you he never pardoned. Why was it? What wrong had you ever done him?"

"None: I only served him."

"Ah! then it was that he could not forgive! I knew it as women know many things men never dream that they even divine. I knew it by a thousand slight signs, a thousand half-betrayals, which escaped his caution and your notice, but which told his secret to me. As for its root, I knew nothing. It was jealousy; but whether simply of your social superiorities, or whether complicated by more personal antagonism, I cannot tell. I used to fancy that some woman might be the cause of the envy. Where tares grow to choke the wheat, it is always *our* hands that sow them!"

"A woman?" He thought of the words that, long years before, had been spoken by the old man whom his adversity had slain. "There was no love-feud between us; and I doubt if love ever touched him: he was not one to harbour it."

"An egotist can always love well enough to deny what he loves to another. Be the cause what it will, he hated you,—hates still, I have no doubt, though the world has found out an idol and a celebrity in him. Ah, Heaven! what a travesty of all justice is that man's success!"

"It is the due of his intellect."

It was not in him to disparage the merits or the attainments of his foe. She looked at him with a wonder in which mingled something of impatience, more of veneration.

"You speak well of your worst traitor!"

"I but give him the due of his abilities: you would not, surely, have me do less?"

"But you know he is your vilest enemy."

"Yes; he has declared himself so."

"And still you give him generous words!"

"Words! What are words! If it ever came to deeds, I might prove little better than he in brute vengeance."

The animal lust, the evil leaven, which lie in the loftiest and the purest forms of human nature, ready to rouse and steep themselves in Cain's revenge, were on him as he spoke. He knew how this man's outrage had power to move him; he knew how, if vengeance ever came into his hand, he would have passion in its using, beside which all the tolerance and self-knowledge gathered from suffering would break like reeds, would crumble as ashes.

She watched him still with that same blent wonder and reverence in her aching eyes.

"Chandos, for less than this Iscariot's crime men have cursed their foes living and dying; and you—you still are just to him!"

"Because the man is vile, would you have me sink so low myself as to deny him his meed of intellect, and decry his success, like a mortified woman who depreciates her rival? He is famous, and his intellect deserves his fame. But think me none the better that I say so. There are times when I could find it in me, if a reckoning came between us, to wring life out of him as I might wring it out of any snake that poisoned me."

There was the vibration of intense passion in the words, though they were low-spoken. As the evil influence of Trevenna had betrayed his youth and drawn his manhood to its ruin, so it entered him now and filled him with the virus of brute longing, and shook to their roots the proud patience and the pain-taught self-discipline which he had learned in the years of his exile. There were times when, remembering the friendship and the gifts he had lavished on this man, and remembering the taunts, the mockery, the hatred, the injury with which he had in turn been requited, he could have gone back to the old barbaric weapons, and dealt with the traitor hand to hand, blow for blow.

The venom of envy could never enter him; but he would have been more than human if, through these many years of loss, and weariness, and divorce from all he had once loved and owned, the triumphant passage of the man who would but for his aid have been obscured in a debtor's prison, the plaudits that the world bestowed on the man whom he knew base as any assassin who slew what had saved and succoured him, had not possessed an exceeding bitterness for him,—had not sickened him oftentimes of all hope or belief in justice, earthly or divine. Once Trevenna had hoped to wreck his genius as well as his peace, his intellect as well as his fortune, his soul as well as his beauty and his heritage. Once Trevenna had loved to think that his well-planned murder would kill in its victim all higher instincts, all likeness of honour, and all purity of conscience: it was possible that, even at the end, his wish might find fruition,—that, under the weight of accumulated wrongs, long-chained passions and long-stained endurance might give way and find their fall in dealing retribution, which, just in its chastisement, would still be the forbidden justice of some involuntary and avenging crime. Some thought of this passed over the mind of the world-worn and reckless Bohemian who gazed at him. She stooped forward eagerly, and, in the yellow shadows, the softened emotion that was upon it lent the fairness of other years to her face.

"Chandos, whatever he be, he is beneath you. An evil impulse wrung from you is more than all his baseness is worth. He has robbed you, I believe, of much; but his worst robbery will be if ever he wrench from you your better, your nobler nature."

An impatient sigh escaped him.

"That is to speak idly. I am no better than other men; and I am no demi-god, to rise above all natural passions and see evil triumph unmoved. It were a poor, paltry vanity to point at his successes and tell men they were unjust because the winner of them was my foe. He is famous; let them make him so. But not the less, if ever the power of chastisement come into my hands, shall I hold the widest as his due. Robbed me, you say? Yes, I believe now that half my ruin was robbery, or little better; but the theft was wisely to windward of the law. If he thieved from me, there was no proof of it."

She shook her head.

"He was too keen, too prudent, too wise. Devour your substance I know that he did; but he would have ever been mindful of Bible precedent, and would only

have taken your inheritance by persuading you to dis-
inherit yourself for some pottage of pleasure or of indolence. Men who break laws are, at their best, but half
knave, half fool: he is too able to be numbered among
them."

"Doubtless! the world's greatest criminals are those
who never stand in a dock," he answered her, as his mind
went back to the story of the blind Hebrew. "There is
a man here, a Jew, whose history tells that: he rejects all
assistance, almost all sympathy; but he merits both. Will
you see him, if it be possible?"

"Surely,—for you. A blind Jew! I have noticed him
as I passed; but I am no fit missionary of consolation to
any living thing! *I*, Beatrix Lennox!"

"Well, you," he said, gently,—"you are here on an
errand of mercy to-night."

She flashed on him a glance almost fierce, had it not
been so melancholy.

"*Grand' chose!* I am here because one whom I murdered lies dying, without a creature to tend his death-bed.
A noble mission, truly! Ah, Chandos, I am not one of
those miserable cravens who, having given all the flower
of their years to the working of evil, buy a cheap virtue
back by insulting a God they disbelieved in over their
revels, with the offer of the few tame, barren, untempted
years they have left them! That is a wretched travesty,
a terrible blasphemy: do not think I stoop to it And
yet *you*—you who know human nature so well, and are
so gentle to it, though it basely abandoned you—you,
who have the heart of a poet and the tolerance of a
philosopher—will believe me when I tell you that there
are times when I hate myself more utterly than any ever
hated me, justly though they had cause? You will know
that there may be so vast an evil in us, and yet that

there may linger some conscience!" Her words swept on, without waiting for answer. "You never knew my story. None will ever know it,—as it was. I was sold into marriage, almost in childhood, as slave-girls are sold to a harem. Well, if I hated my bondage as they hate theirs, where was the wonder? where was the sin? But that matters nothing. Those who err can always find apology of their error; I will be no such coward. Still, it was through this that John Trevenna had his hold on me. My husband"—her dark, imperial face still flushed and the long hazel eyes still flashed at the words—"held his wife's charms only as his property, to turn to such account as he would. He was very poor, very extravagant. He found that rich men, fashionable men, admiring me, gave horses and carriages, and venison, and game, and dinners, and invitations to great houses, and anything and everything, and would play on in our drawing-rooms at whist and billiards till the stakes and the bets rose to thousands and tens of thousands. You can guess the rest. I was his decoy-bird. What a school of shamelessness for a girl not twenty! How I loathed it! how I loathed it!—only the more because it was glossed over with fashion. Well, Trevenna had immense sway over Colonel Lennox; he had it over every one, when he cared to attain it. He saw my hatred of the part I was driven to play; he contrived to lighten it. He never hinted any love; it served to give me confidence in him; he was the only man who never spoke of it to me, never so much as whispered a thought of it. He earned my gratitude by freeing me from my husband's persecution; but he made me understand that, in return, I must serve him by acquainting him with all the embarrassments, all the weaknesses, of the innumerable men about me. I was glad to comply: the terms seemed light, and, mind you, they were only tacitly offered. I bought my freedom by being his tool. I did not know I did harm then: I have believed, since, that I did more than when I allured them by my coquetries that my husband might win their gold at pool or at cards. That was how I came into Trevenna's power; that was why I dared not write more openly to you of a hatred I had fathomed, though he had never uttered it. Forgive me, Chandos, if you can, for so much weakness, so much selfishness!"

He had listened, absorbed in the history she told, in the dark and cruel pressure which had been upon one whom the world had held so heartless, so reckless, so wayward, so dazzling: he started at the last words like one whose dream is broken.

"Forgive! I have nothing to forgive. I had no claim that you should care for my friends or my foes. And this was the way he gained his power! My God! is it possible——"

He did not end his words; the thought swept past him, extravagant and vague, were the taskmaster of Beatrix Lennox and the taskmaster of the Castilian Jew one and the same! She looked up; she saw his face darken; she heard his breath catch as, for the first time, the possibility that his enemy was the tyrant whose hand had lain so heavy on the Hebrew, flashed on him.

"What is it?"

"Your words have brought a strange fancy to me; that is all. A groundless one, perhaps, yet one I must follow."

She rose; and her deep, sad eyes dwelt on him with a love that she had never let him read,—she in whose hands love had been but a net and a snare.

"Follow it, then, and God speed you! It is of your enemy, of my bondmaster!"

He bent his head in silence. Thoughts had rushed in on him with so sudden and so passionate a force that to frame them to words was impossible; they were baseless and shapeless as a dream, but they came with an irresistible might of conviction. He waited a moment, with the mechanical instinct of courtesy.

"Can I not aid you? The dying man whom you spoke of, can I do nothing for him?"

She gave a gesture of dissent, almost savage,—if the softness of her inalienable grace could have ever let her be so.

"Why always think of others instead of yourself? You had never been ruined but for that sublime folly! No; you can do nothing for him. He will be dead by the dawn. I killed him. I never cared for him; but I do care that you should not look on my work. It has been thoroughly done: no woman ever wrecks by halves."

There was in the half-ironic, half-scornful calmness of the words a grief deeper than lies in any abandonment of sorrow. He stooped over her an instant, touched, and forgetting his own thoughts in hers.

"I do not say, Feel no remorse; for that were to say, Deny the truest of your instincts. But you were cruelly wronged, cruelly driven. There is much nobility still, where so much tenderness lingers. Farewell: we shall meet again?"

She looked at him with that long, lingering look that had so hopeless a melancholy.

"Ah! I do not know. Death will be here to-night; perhaps he will be gentle and generous for once, and take me with him,—at least, if his promised sleep have no awakening. There is the fear,—the old Hamlet-fear, never set at rest either way!"

He left her; and she leaned awhile against the bare

table, her hands clenched in the still rich masses of her hair, her lips pressed in a close weary line, her eyes filling slowly with tears.

"Ah!" she mused, in the aching of her heart, "have nine tenths of us ever any real chance to be the best we might! If I had lived for him, if he had ever loved me, or one like him, no woman would have been truer, gentler, purer, stronger to serve him, or more utterly under his law and at his feet, than I!"

He left her, and went again upward to the Hebrew's chamber. A strange instinct of vengeance, a sudden impulse of belief, urged him on. Though no hint had been dropped that the Jew's tyrant was the enemy of his own life, a conviction strong as knowledge had centred in him that the man spoken of was John Trevenna. He thrust the door open hurriedly, and entered; the little lamp still burned dully there, but the blind Israelite and the dog were both gone. Standing alone in the desolation of the narrow chamber, he could almost have believed that the tale he had heard had been a dream of the night, and the antique form of the old man but one of its sleep-born phantoms. There had passed but the space which he had spent with Beatrix Lennox since he had been told the recital: yet either answer was purposely denied to his questions, or the refuge the Jew had sought amidst the people of his nation was too secret to be unearthed, for no search and no inquiry brought a trace of him; he was lost, with the vague outline of his history left unfilled, lost in the wide wilderness of a large city's nameless poverty.

With its memory upon him, Chandos went out into the grey, subdued light of the now-breaking dawn; the thoughts which had moved him had stirred depths which time had long sealed. For many years he had striven to put from him the remembrance alike of his wrongs and of his losses; he had believed the first to be beyond avenging, as the latter were beyond redemption; he had striven to live only the impersonal life of the thinker, of the scholar, to leave behind him alike the unnerving weight of regret and the baneful indulgence of a vain suspicion. But here the things of those dead days had risen and forced themselves on him; to his mind came what until then had not touched him,—the belief that his foe had dealt him wider treachery than the mere treachery of friendship,—that Trevenna had done more than leave him unwarned in a dangerous downward course, but had robbed him and trepanned him under the smooth surface of fair and honest service. The utter extravagance and heedlessness of his joyous reign had left him no title to accuse another of causing any share of the destruction which followed on it; and the organisation of his mind was one to which such an accusation could but very slowly, and only on sheer certainty suggest itself. Yet now, looking backward to innumerable memories, he believed that, in the pale of the law, his traitor had been as guilty of embezzlement as any within the law's arraignment; he believed that his antagonist had tempted, blinded, robbed, and betrayed him on a set and merciless scheme.

Recalling the points of the Spanish Jew's relation, slight and nameless as the recital had been in much, something that was near the actual truth came before his thoughts. He remembered how heavily the claims of a money-lender's house had pressed on him for obligations in his own name, and for those where his name had been lent to others. If his foe and the Hebrew's tyrant were one, how vast a network of intrigue and fraud might there not have been wound about him! It was but imagination, it was but analogy and possibility, that suggested themselves vaguely to him: yet they fastened there, and an instinct for the "wild justice" of revenge woke with it, passionate and unsparing. To fling his foe down and hold him in a death-gripe, as the hound pulls down the boar, was a longing as intense upon him in its dominion as it was on David of Israel, when the treachery of men and the triumph of evil-doers broke asunder his faith and wrung the fire of imprecation from his lips.

As he looked back on all he had suffered, all he had lost, all he had seen die out from him for ever, and all that for ever had forsaken him, he felt the black blood of the old murderous instinct latent in all human hearts rise and burn in him: utterly foreign to his nature, once grafted, it took the deadlier hold.

"O God!" he said, half aloud, in his clenched teeth, as he passed the entrance of the miserable house, "shall his crimes *never* find him out?"

These crimes had given his betrayer a long immunity; they had given him a lifetime of success; they had given him riches and favour and the fruition of ripe ambitions; they had given him the desire of his heart and the laurels of the world:—would the time ever come when they should be quoted against him and strip him bare in the sight of the people? The bitterness of unbelief, the weariness of desolation, fell on Chandos as the doubt pursued him.   He had cleaved to honour for its own sake, and had loved and served men,· asking no recompense; and he remained without reward. Pursuing fraud, and tyranny, and the wisdom of self-love, and the tortuous routes of unscrupulous sagacity, his enemy prospered in the sight of the world, and put his hand to nothing that ever failed him. There was a pitiless, cold, mocking sarcasm in the contrast, which left the problem of human existence dark as night in its mystery, which shook and loosened the one sheet-anchor of his life,—his loyalty to truth for truth's own sake.

The heart-sickness of Pilate's doubt was on him; and he asked in his soul, "What *is* truth?"

As he passed out into the narrow-arched doorway, some young revellers reeled past him,—handsome, dissolute, titled youths, who had been flinging themselves in the air in the mad dances till the dawn, at a ball of the people, dressed as Pierrots and Arlequins. They were going now to their waiting carriages, talking and laughing while the sound of their voices echoed through the stillness of the breaking day in disjointed sentences.

"Castalia! *Beau nom!* Selling lilies with a face like a Titian:—how poetic!"

"Very. But somebody, apparently, had left her to the very dull prose of wanting her bread,—a common colophon to our idyls!"

"Wandering with a few flowers; and Villeroy could neither tempt her nor trap her! He must have been very *bête!* Or she——"

"A Pythoness. He is terribly sore on the subject. *Pardieu!* I wish we had her here! Women grow dreadfully ugly."

They had passed, almost ere the sense of the words had reached his ear and pierced the depths of his thoughts: involuntarily he paused where he stood in the entrance.

"Castalia!"

He murmured the name with a pang: the indefinite words he had heard suggested so terrible a fate for her; and his heart went out to her in an infinite tenderness, —that beautiful child, brilliant as any passion-flower, desolate as any stricken fawn!

“Who is she?”

Beatrix Lennox, standing unseen near him, heard alike the revellers’ words and his echo of the name.

He started and turned to her.

“She whom they spoke of? I do not know; at least, I hope to Heaven I do not!”

“But the one who is in your thoughts?”

She, who loved him, had caught the softness of his voice and its eager dread as he had repeated the name that had suddenly floated to his ear in the depths of Paris. He paused a moment; then he answered her:—

“You have a woman’s heart; if it can feel pity, know it for her. She is nameless, motherless, friendless; and I could only—as a harsh mercy, yet the best left to me— leave her.”

Her face grew paler; her lips set slightly.

“You loved her, Chandos?”

An impatient sigh escaped him.

“No! at least those follies are dead with my youth. If we had met earlier——”

“Love is not dead in you; it will revive,” she said, simply. “Tell me of her.”

“There is nothing to tell. Her parentage is unknown; she lives below Vallombrosa, and has but this one name, —Castalia. She will have the beauty and the genius of a Corinne; and she lies under the ban of illegitimacy, with no haven except a convent.”

“But if she be the one of whom those youths spoke? The name is rare.”

“Hush! do not hint it! If harm reach her, I shall feel myself guilty of her fate.”

“What, then? You only forsook her when you had wearied of her?”

“No: you mistake me. No man could weary of that

exquisite life; and it is as soilless as it is fair. I meant but this:—I believe her young heart was mine, though no love-words passed between us; and I have doubted sometimes if my tardy mercy were not a cold and brutal cruelty. Because passion has no place in my own life, I forgot that regret could have any place in hers."

He spoke gravely, and his memory wandered from his listener away to that summer eve when some touch of the old soft folly had come back on him as his lips had met Castalia's,—away to the hours when the lustrous eloquence of her beaming eyes had reflected his thoughts, almost ere they had been uttered, in that pure and perfect sympathy without which love is but a toy of the senses, a plaything of the passions.

Beatrix Lennox looked at him long in silence.

"She *is* dear to you?"

"If I let her be so, it would be the sure signal for her loss to me."

Then bending his head to her in farewell, he went out into the dawn alone.

Beatrix Lennox stood in the dark and narrow entrance, watching him as he passed away in the twilight of the dawn, through which the yellow flicker of the street-lights was burning dully. Her black robes fell about her like the laces of the Spanish women; her face was very pale, for there was no bloom of art on its cheeks to-night, and her large eyes were suffused with tears over the darkness of their hazel gleam. There was beauty still in her,— the beauty of an autumn evening, that has the faded sadness of dead hopes, and the tempest-clouds of past storms on its pale sunless skies and on the red fire of its fallen leaves.

"He loves her, or he will love," she murmured, in her solitude. "I will seek out this child, and see if she be worthy of him.   Ah! no woman will be that!   A great man's life lies higher than *our* love, loftier than *our* reach."

A few hours later, in the writing-cabinet of her Roman villa, a famous diplomatist sat,—one who wove her fine nets around all the body politic of the Continent, who schemed far away with Eastern questions and Western complications, who had her hand in Austria, her eyes on Syria, her whisper in the Vatican, her sceptre in the Tuileries, her allies among the Monsignori, her keys to all the *bureaux secrets*, her subtle, vivacious, deleterious, dangerous power everywhere.

She was a terrible power to her foes, a priceless power to her party.   Those brilliant falcon eyes would pierce what a phalanx of ministers could not overcome; that unrivalled silver wit could consummate what conferences and coalitions failed to compass; that magical feminine subtlety could dupe, and mask, and net, and seduce, and wind, and unravel, and give a poison-drop of treachery in a crystal-clear sweetmeat of frankness and compliment, and join with both sides at once, and glide unharmed away, compromised with neither, as no male state-craft ever yet could do.   The only mistake she made was that she thought the growth of the nations was to be pruned by an enamelled paper-knife, and the peoples that were struggling for liberty as drowning men for air, were to be bound helpless by the strings of Foreign Portfolios. But the error was not only hers; male state-craft has made it for ages.

Now it was of an idle thing she was speaking.   One of her attendants stood before her, a slight, pale, velvet-voiced Greek, long in her service, and skilled in many tongues and many ways. He was reciting with his finger

on a little note-book, the heads of some trifling researches,
—very trifling he thought them, he who was accustomed
to be a great lady's political *mouchard.*

"Still wandering; close on Venetia; will soon want
food; takes no alms; left Vallombrosa two months ago; is
known only by the name of Castalia; parentage unknown;
reared by the charity of the Church; supposed by the
peasants to have fled to a stranger who spent the spring
there in a villeggiatura. That is all, madame."

She listened, then beat her jewelled fingers a little
impatiently.

"That is not like your training,—to bring me an unfinished sketch."

"There is nothing to be learned, madame."

The amused scorn of his mistress's eyes flashed lightly
over him.

"If a thing is on the surface, a blind man can feel it.
Go; and tell me when you come back both the name of
this stranger and the name of her mother."

"It is impossible, madame."

She gave a sign of her hand in dismissal.

"You must make impossibilities possible if you remain
with me."

The voice was perfectly gentle, but inflexible. Her
servant bowed and withdrew.

"I *will* know what she is to him," murmured Héloïse
de la Vivarol.

The fair politician had not forgotten her oath.

Two weeks later, the Greek, who dared not reappear
with his mission unaccomplished, sent his mistress, with
profound apology for continued failure, a trifle that, by
infinite patience and much difficulty, had been procured,
with penitent confession of its theft, from a contadina of
Fontane Amorose,—a trifle that had been taken from the

dead, and secreted rather from superstitious belief in its holy power than from its value. It was a little, worn, thin, silver relic-case: on it was feebly scratched, by some unskilful hand, a name,—"Valeria Lulli."

CHAPTER VIII.
"Record one lost Soul more."

In his atelier, early in the next day, an artist stood painting. The garden was very tranquil below; and the light within shone on casts, antiques, bronzes, old armour, old cabinets, and half-completed sketches, all an artist's picturesque lumber. He had a fair fame, and, though not rich, could live in ease. He did not care for the gay Bohemianism of his brethren; he had never done so. A sensitive, imaginative man,—poet as well as painter,—of vivid feeling and secluded habits, he preferred solitude, and made companions of his own creations. He stood before one now, lovingly touching and retouching it,—a man with a rich Spanish beauty that would have been very noble, but for a look of wavering indecision and a startled, timorous, appealing glance too often in his eyes.

It was not there now; he was smiling down on his picture with a blissful content in its promise. It had the pure, clear, cool colour of the French school, with the luxuriance of an overflowing fancy less strictly educated, more abundantly loosened, than theirs; it was intensely idealic, far from all realism, withal voluptuous, yet never sensual. The type of his nature might be found in the picture; it was high, but it had scarcely strength enough in it to be the highest. Still, it was of a rare talent, a rare poetry, and he might well look on it contented; he only turned from it to smile more fondly even still in the face of a young girl who leaned her hands on his shoulder to look at it with him,—a girl with the glow in her laughing loveliness that was in the warm autumnal sun-light without, the loveliness rich and full of grace of a Spaniard of Mexico.

"You are happy, Agostino, with it and with me!"

"*Mi querida!* you and it give me all of happiness I ever know."

As he stood before his picture, in the peace of the early day, the door opened, a light quick step trod on the oak floor.

"Ah, *cher* Agostino! how go the world and the pictures? You and La Señora are a study for one!"

The painter started, with a sudden shiver that ran through all his limbs; a deadly pallor came under the warm olive tint of his cheek; he stood silent, like a stricken man. The Spanish girl, who had hurriedly moved from his embrace, with a blush over her face, did not see his agitation; she was looking shyly and in wonder at the stranger who entered so unceremoniously on their solitude.

"Haven't seen you for some time, my good Agostino," pursued Trevenna, walking straight up towards the easel, without taking the trouble to remove his hat from over his eyes or his cigar from between his lips. "What are you doing here?—anything pretty? Queer thing, Art, to be sure! Never did understand it,—never should. Let me see: a young lady without any drapery,—unless some ivy on her hair can be construed into a concession to society on that head,—and a general atmosphere about her of moist leaves and hazy uncomfortableness. Now you've 'idealised' her into something, I'll be bound, and will give her some sonorous Hellenic title, eh? That's always the way. An artist gives his porter's daughter five francs and a kiss to sit to him, dresses her up with some two-sous bunches of primroses from the Marché des Fleurs, paints her while they smoke bad tobacco and chatter *argot* together, and calls her the Genius of the Spring, or something as crack-jaw. Straightway the connoisseurs and critics go mad: it's an 'artistic foreshadowing of the divine in woman;' or it's an 'idealic representation of the morning of life and the budding renaissance of the earth;' or it's a 'fusion of many lights into one harmonious whole;' or it's some other art-jargon as nonsensical. And if you talk the trash, and stare at the nude 'Genius,' it's all right; but if you can't talk the trash, and like to look at the live grisette dancing a *rigolboche*, it's all wrong, and you're 'such a coarse fellow!' That's why I don't like Art; she's such a humbug. 'Idealism!' Why, it's only Realism washed out and vamped up with a little glossing, as the raw-boned, yellow-skinned ballet-hacks are dressed up in paint and spangles and gossamer petticoats and set floating about as fairies. 'Idealism!'— that's the science of seeing things as they aren't; that's all."

With which Trevenna, with his glass in his eye and his cigar in his teeth, completed his lecture on Art, hitting truth in the bull's eye, as he commonly did, refreshing the Hudibrastic vein in him for his compulsory hypocrisies by a sparring-match with other people's humbugs. He lied because everybody lied, because it was politic, because it was necessary, because it was one of the weapons that cut a way up the steep and solid granite of national vanity and social conventionalities; but the man himself was too jovially cynical (if such an antithesis may be used) not to be naturally candid. He would never have had for *his* crime the timorous conventional Ciceronian euphemism of *Vixerunt;* he would have come out from the Tullianum and told the people, with a laugh, that he'd killed Lentulus and the whole of that cursed set, because they were horribly in the way and were altogether a bad lot. He held his secret cards closer than any man living;

but all the same he never pandered with his actions under specious names to himself, and he had by nature the "cynical frankness" of Sulla. Indeed, this would sometimes break out of him, and cleave the dull air of English politics with a rush that made its solemn respectabilities aghast,—though the mischief happened seldom, as Trevenna, like Jove, held his lightning in sure command, and was, moreover, the last man in the universe to risk an Icarus flight.

Meanwhile, as the great popular leader uttered his diatribe against Art, the painter had remained silent and passive, like a slave before his taskmaster. The girl had left them at a murmured word in Spanish from him, and they stood alone. Trevenna dropped himself into the painting-chair with his easy familiarity.

"You are not lively company, *cher* Agostino, nor yet a welcoming host," he resumed. "Didn't expect to see me, I dare say? I haven't much time to run about ateliers; still, as I was staying at the Court, I thought I'd give you a look. So you've married, eh? Very pretty creature, too, I dare say, for men who understand that style of thing; myself, I'm a better judge of a *bouillabaisse* than of a mistress. Married, eh? You know what Bacon says about marriage and hostages to fortune, don't you?"

The artist's dry lips opened without words; his eyelids were raised for a moment, with a piteous, hunted misery beneath them; he knew the meaning of the question put to him.

"Don't know very well what Bacon meant, myself," pursued Trevenna, beating a careless tattoo with the mahl-stick. "Wives and brats are hostages most men would be uncommonly glad to leave unredeemed, I fancy, —goods they wouldn't want to take out of pawn in a hurry, if they once got rid of 'em. So you've married? Well, I've no objection to that, if *you* see any fun in it: *I* shouldn't. You've learned one piece of wisdom: you never try dodging now. Quite right. Wherever you might go, *I* should know it."

The man who stood before him, like a slave whom the blood-hounds have run down and brought back to their bondage, shuddered as he heard.

"Oh, God!" he murmured, "can you not spare me yet? I am so nameless a thing in the world's sight, beside you! You have such vast schemes, such vast ambitions, so wide a repute, so broad a field: can you *never* forget me, and let me go?"

"*Cher* Agostino," returned the Right Honourable Member, "you are illogical. A thing may be insignificant, but it may be wanted. A pawn may, before now, have turned the scale of a champion game of chess. Take care of the trifles, and the big events will take care of themselves. That's my motto; though, of course, *you* don't understand this, seeing that your trade in life is to scatter broad splashes of colour and leave fancy to fill 'em up,—to paint a beetle's back as if the universe hung in the pre-Raphaelism, and to trust to Providence that your daub of orange looks like a sunset,—to make believe, in a word, with a little pot of oil and a little heap of coloured earths, just for all the world as children play at sand-building, in the very oddest employment that ever a fantastic devil set the wits of a man after! You are unpractical, that's a matter of course; but you are more:—you are desperately ungrateful!"

A quiver of passion shook the artist's frame; the scarlet flood flushed the olive of his delicate cheek; he recoiled and rebelled against the tyranny that set its iron heel upon his neck, as years before the beautiful lad whom the old Hebrew loved, had done so in the gloomy city den.

"Ungratefull Are men grateful whose very life is not their own? Are men grateful who hourly draw their breath as a scourged dog's? Are men grateful who from their boyhood upward have had their whole future held in hostage as chastisement for one poverty-sown sin?— grateful for having their spirits broken, their souls accursed, their hearts fettered, their steps dogged, their sleep haunted, their manhood ruined?· If they are grateful, so am I; not else."

Trevenna laughed good-humouredly.

"My good fellow, I always told you you ought to go on the stage: you'd make your fortune there. Such a speech as that, now,—all *à l'improviste*, too,—would bring down any house. Decidedly you've histrionic talents, Agostino; you'd be a second Talma. All your raving set apart, however (and you're not good at elocution, *trèscher;* who can 'fetter' hearts? who can 'break' spirits? It sounds just like some doggerel for a valentine), you *are* ungrateful. I might have sent you to the hulks, and didn't. My young Jew, you ought to be immeasurably my debtor."

He spoke quite pleasantly, beating a rataplan with the mahl-stick, and sitting crosswise on the painting-chair. He was never out of temper, and some there were who learned to dread that bright, sunny, insolent, mirthful good humour as they never dreaded the most fiery or the most sullen furies of other men. Even in the political arena, opponents had been taught that there was a fatal power in that cloudless and racy good temper, which never opened the slightest aperture for attack, but yet caught them so often and so terribly on the hip.

"Very ungrateful you are, my would-be Rubens," resumed Trevenna. "Only think! Here is a man who committed a downright felony, whom I could have put in a convict's chains any day I liked, and I did nothing to him but let him grow up, and turn artist, and live in the pleasantest city in the world, and marry when he fancied the folly, and do all he liked in the way he liked best; and he can't see that he owes me anything! Oh, the corruption of the human heart!"

With which Trevenna, having addressed the exposition to the Dryad on the easel, dealt her a little blow with the mahl-stick, and made a long, cruel blur across the still moist paint of her beautiful, gravely-smiling mouth, that it had cost the painter so many hours, so many days, of loving labour to perfect.

Agostino gave an involuntary cry of anguish. He could have borne iron blows rained down on his own head like hail, better than he could bear that ruin of his work, that outrage to his darling.

"I do it in the interest of morality; she's too pretty and too sensual," laughed Trevenna, as he drew the instrument of torture down over the delicate brow and the long flowing tresses, making a blurred, blotted, beaten mass where the thing of beauty had glowed on the canvas. He would not have thought of it, but that the gleam of fear in his victim's eyes, as the stick had accidentally slanted towards the easel, had first told him the ruin he might make. To torment was a mischief and a merriment that he never could resist, strong as his self-control was in other things.

It was the one last straw that broke the long-suffering camel's back. With a cry as though some murderer's knife were at his own throat, the painter sprang forward and caught his tyrant's arm, wrenching the mahl-stick away, though not until it was too late to save his Dryad, not until the ruthless cruelty had done its pleasure of destruction.

"Merciful God!" he cried, passionately, "are you devil, not man? Sate yourself in my wretchedness; but, for pity's sake, spare my works, the only treasure and redemption of my weak, worthless, accursed life!"

Trevenna shrugged his shoulders, knocking his cigar-ash off against the marvellous clearness of limpid, bub-bling, prismatic, sunlit water at the Dryad's feet, that had made one of the chief beauties and wonders of the pic-ture.

"Agostino, *bon enfant*, you *should* go on the stage. You speak in strophes, and say 'good-day' to anybody like an Orestes seeing the Furies! It must be very ex-hausting to keep up that perpetual melo-dramatic height. Try life in shirt-sleeves and slippers; it's as pleasant again as life in the tragic toga. Be logical. What's to prevent my slashing that picture across, right and left, with my pen-knife, if I like? Not you. You think your life 'weak and worthless;' far be it from me to disagree with you; but what you think you 'redeem' it in by painting young ladies *au naturel* from immoral models, putting some weed on their head and a pond at their feet, and calling it 'idealism,' I can't see: that's beyond me. However, I'm not an idealist: perhaps that's why."

With which he swayed himself back in the painting-chair, and prodded the picture all over with his cigar, leaving little blots of ash and sparks of fire on each spot. Martin and Gustave Doré are mere novices in the art of inventing tortures, beside the ingenuity of Trevenna's laughing humour.

The man he lectured thus stood silent by, paralysed, and quivering with an anguish that trembled in him from head to foot. Agostino had not changed; the yielding, timorous, sensitive nature, blending a vivid imagination with a woman's susceptibility to fear, was unaltered in him, and laid him utterly at the mercy of every stronger temperament and sterner will, even when he was most roused to the evanescent fire of a futile rebellion.

"Oh, Heaven!" he moaned, passionately, "I thought you had forgotten me! I thought you had wearied of my misery, and would leave me in a little peace! You are so rich, so famous, so successful; you have had so many victims greater far than I; you stand so high in the world's sight. Can you *never* let one so poor and power-less as I go free?"

"Poor and powerless is a figure," said Trevenna, with a gesture of his cigar. "You *will* use such exaggerated language; your beggarly little nation always did, calling themselves the chosen of Heaven, when they were the dirtiest little lot of thieves going, and declaring now that they're waiting for their Messiah, while they're buying our old clothes, picking up our rags, and lying *au plaisir* in our police-courts! You aren't poor, *cher* Agostino, for a painter; and you're really doing well. Paris talks of your pictures, and the court likes your young ladies in ivy and nothing else. You're prosperous,—on my word, you are; but don't flatter yourself I shall ever forget you. I don't forget!"

He sent a puff of smoke into the air with those three words; in them he embodied the whole of his career, the key-note of his character, the pith and essence at once of his success and of his pitilessness.

A heavy, struggling sigh burst from his listener as he heard; it was the self-same contest that had taken place years previous in the lamp-lit den of the bill-discounting offices, the contest between weakness that suffered mor-tally, and power that unsparingly enjoyed. The terrible

13*

bondage had enclosed Agostino's whole life; he felt at times that it would pursue him even beyond the grave.

"Is there no price I can pay at once?" he said, huskily, his voice broken as with physical pain,—"no task I can work out at a blow?—no tribute-money I can toil for, that, gained, will buy me peace?"

"As if I ever touched a sou of his earnings, or set him to paint my walls for nothing! Mercy! the ingratitude of the Hebrew race!" cried Trevenna, amusedly, to his cigar.

The black, sad, lustrous eyes of the Spanish Jew flashed with a momentary fire that had the longing in them, for the instant, to strike his tyrant down stone-dead.

"Take my money? No! You do not seek that, because it is a drop in the ocean beside all that you possess, all that you have robbed other men of so long! I make too little to tempt you, or you would have wrung it out of me. But you have done a million times worse. You have taken my youth, my hope, my spirit, my liberty, and killed them all. You have made a mockery of mercy, that you might hold me in a captivity worse than any slave's. You have made me afraid to love, lest what I love should be dragged beneath my shame. You have made me dread that she should bear me children, lest they be born to their father's fate. You have ruined all manhood in me, and made me weak and base and terror-stricken as any cur that cringes before his master's whip. You have made me a poorer, lower, viler wretch than I could ever have been if the Law had taken its course on me, and beaten strength and endurance into me in my boyhood, by teaching me openly and unflinchingly the cost of crime, yet had left me some gate of freedom, some hope of redemption, some release to a liberated life when my term of chastisement should have been over,— left me all that *you* have denied me since the hour you first had me in your power, in a cruelty more horrible and more unending than the hardest punishment of justice ever could have been."

The torrent of words poured out in his rich and ringing voice, swifter and more eloquent the higher his revolt and the more vain his anguish grew. This was his nature to feel passionately, to rebel passionately, to lift up his appeal in just and glowing protestation, to recoil under his bondage suffering beyond all expression, but to do no more than this,—to be incapable of action, to be powerless for real and vital resistance, to spend all his strength in that agonised upbraiding, which he must have known to be as futile as for the breakers to fret themselves against the granite sea-wall.

Trevenna listened quietly, with a certain amusement. It was always uncommonly droll to him to see the struggles of weak natures; he knew they would recoil into his hand, passive and helpless agents, conquered by the sheer, unexpressed force of his own vigorous and practical temperament. Studies of character were always an amusement to him; he had a La-Bruyère-like taste for their analysis; the vastness of his knowledge of human nature did not prevent his relishing all its minutiæ. What the subjects of his study might suffer under it, was no more to him than what the frog suffers, when he pricks, flays, cuts, beheads, and lights a lucifer match under it, is to the man of science in his pursuit of anatomy and his refutation of Aristotle.

"Very well done! pity it's not at the Porte St. Martin. All bosh! Still, *that's* nothing against a bit of melodrama anywhere," he said, carelessly. "Shut up now, though, please. Let's go to business."

The artist seemed to shiver and collapse under the bright, brief words; the heart-sick passions, the flame of sudden rebellion, and the fire of vain recrimination faded off his face, his head sank, his lips trembled: just so, years before, had the vivid grace of his youth shrunk and withered under his taskmaster's eye.

"You paint the Princess Rossillio's portrait?" pursued his catechist.

Agostino bent his head.

"And go to her, of course, to take it?"

The Spanish Jew gave the same mute assent.

"Can't you speak? Don't keep on nodding there, like a mandarin in a tea-shop. You'd words enough just now. You paint it in her boudoir, don't you, because the light's best?"

Agostino lifted his heavy eyes.

"Since you know, why ask me?"

"Leave questions to me, and reply *tout bref*," said his interrogator, with a curt accent that bore abundant meaning. "You've seen a Russian cabinet that's on the right hand of the fire-place?"

"I have."

"Ah! you can answer sensibly at last! Well, that cabinet's madame's despatch-box. You know, or you may know, that she is the most meddlesome intriguer in Europe; but that's nothing to you. In the left-hand top drawer is her Austro-Venetian correspondence. Among it is a letter from the Vienna Nuncio. When you leave the boudoir to-day, you will know what that letter contains."

Agostino started; a dew broke out on his forehead, a flush stained his clear brown cheek with its burning shame; his eyes grew terribly piteous.

"More sin! more dishonour!" he muttered, in his throat. "Let me go and starve in the streets, rather than drive me to such deeds as these!"

Trevenna laughed, his pleasant *bonhomie* in no way

changed, though there was a dash more of authority in his tone.

“Quiet, you Jew dog! Really, you do get too melodramatic to be amusing. There’s no occasion for any heroics, but—you’ll be able to tell me this time to-morrow.”

The artist covered his face with his hands, and his form shook to and fro in an irrepressible agitation.

“Anything but this!—anything but this! Give me what labour you will, what poverty, what shame; but not this! I can never look in peace into my darling’s eyes, if I take this villany upon my life!”

“Nobody’s alluding to villany,” said Trevenna, with a tranquil brevity. “As to your darling’s eyes, they’re nothing to anybody except yourself. If the only men who ‘look into’ women’s eyes are the honest ones, the fair sex must get uncommon few lovers. You’ve heard what I said. Know what the letter’s about. I don’t tell you *how* you’re to know it. Get the princess to show it you. You’re a very handsome fellow,—black curls and all the rest of it,—and her Highness is a connoisseur in masculine charms.”

With which Trevenna laughed, and got up out of the depths of the painting-chair.

Agostino stood in his path, a deep-red flush on his forehead, the blaze of freshly-lightened rebellion in his eyes.

“You use your power over me to force me to such things in your service as this! What if they were spoken? what if they were cited against you? You, high as you are in your success and your wealth and your rank, would be thought lower yet than *I* have ever fallen. Do you not fear, even *you*, that one day you may sting and goad me too far, and I may give myself up to your worst work for the sake of obtaining my vengeance?”

Trevenna smiled, with a certain laughing good-tempered indulgence, such as a man may extend to a child who menaces him with its impotent fury.

"*Très-cher, who would believe you?* Say anything you like; it's nothing to me. I have a little bit of paper by me that, once upon a time, M. Agostino Mathias signed with a name not his own. I was very lenient to him; and if he doesn't appreciate the clemency the world will, and think him an ungrateful young Hebrew cur, who turns, like all curs, on his benefactor. Prosecute you now it wouldn't, perhaps, since the matter's been allowed to sleep: but criminate you and disgrace you it would most decidedly. You'd be hounded out all over Europe; and for your pretty Spaniard, I heard a Court Chamberlain admiring her yesterday, and saying she was too good for an atelier:—she'd soon be his mistress, when she knew you a felon. Ah, my poor Agostino, when you once broke the law, you put your head into a steel-trap you'll never draw it out of again. Only fools break the laws. Excuse the personality!"

Under the ruthless words of truth Agostino shrank and cowered again, like a beaten hound; he had no strength against his taskmaster,—he never could have had: he was hemmed in beyond escape. Moreover, now he had another and a yet more irresistible rein by which to be held in and coerced,—the love that he bore, and that he received from, his young wife.

"You'll do that, then!" said Trevenna, with the carelessness of a matter of course. "Bring some picture to show me to-morrow morning,—Darshampton likes pictures, because it couldn't tell a sixpenny daub from a Salvator Rosa,—and remember every line of the Nuncio's letter. You understand? I don't want to hear your means; I only want the results."

"I will try," muttered Agostino. He loathed crime and dishonour with an unutterable hatred of it; he longed, he strove, to keep the roads of right and justice; his nature was one that loved the peace of virtue and the daylight of fair dealing. Yet, by his unconquerable fear, by his wax-like mobility of temper, by his past sin, and by his future dread, he was forced into the very paths and made the very thing that he abhorred.

"People who 'try' aren't my people," said the member for Darshampton, curtly. "Those who *do* are the only ones that suit me."

Agostino shrank under his eye.

"I will come to you to-morrow," he murmured, faintly. He had no thought, not the slightest, of how he should be able to accomplish this sinister work that was set him; but he knew that he must do it, as surely as his countrymen of old must make their bricks without straw, for their conquerors and enslaveis.

Trevenna nodded, and threw down his mahl-stick with a final lunge at the Dryad.

"All right! of course you will. You ought to be very grateful to me that I let you off so easily. Some men would make you give up to them that charming Spanish Señora of yours, as Maurice de Saxe took Favart's wife *de la part du roi*. But that isn't my line. I've coveted a good many things in my day, but I never coveted a woman."

With which he threw his smoked-out cigar away, and went across the atelier and out at the door, with a careless nod to his victim. He had so much to fill up every moment of his time, that he could ill spare the ten minutes he had flung away in the amusement of racking and tormenting the helplessness of the man he tortured, and he knew that he would be obeyed as surely as though he spent the whole day in further threats.

Trevenna had two especial arts of governing at his fingers' ends: he never, by any chance, compromised himself, but also he never was, by any hazard, disobeyed. He had a large army of *employés* on more or less secret service about in the world; but as there was not one of them who held a single trifle that could damage him, so there was not one of them who ever ventured not to "come up to time" exactly to his bidding, or to fail to keep his counsel with *silence à la mort.*

The artist Agostino, left to his solitude, threw himself forward against the broad rest of the chair, his arms flung across it, his head bent down on them: he could not bear to look upon the defaced canvas of his treasured picture; he could not bear to see the light of the young day, while he knew himself a tool so worthless and so vile. He might have been so happy! and this chain was for ever weighting his limbs, eating into his flesh, dragging him back as he sought a purer life, waking him from his sleep with its chill touch, holding him ever to his master's will and to his master's work,—will and work that left him free and unnoticed perhaps for years, and then, when he had begun to breathe at liberty and to hope for peace, would find him out wherever he was, and force him to the path they pointed!

Agostino had hoped oftentimes that as his bond-ruler rose in the honour of men and the success of the world, he would forget so nameless and so powerless a life as his own: he had found his hope a piteous error. Trevenna had said truly he never forgot; the smallest weapon that might be ready to his hand some day he kept continually finely polished and within his reach. The painter knew that he must learn what was indicated to him,—by betrayal, or chicanery, or secret violence, or whatsoever means might open to him,—or be blasted for life by one

word of his tyrant.   He abhorred the dishonour, but he
had not courage to refuse it, knowing the cost of such
refusal. It was not the first time by many that such mis-
sions had been bound on him: yet every time they brought
fresh horror and fresh hatred with them.   But he was
hunted and helpless; he had no resistance; throughout his
life he had paid the price exacted, rather than meet the
fate that waited him if it were unpaid.   He clung to the
sweetness, the tranquillity, the growing renown, and the
newly-won love of his existence; he clung to them, even
embittered by the serpent's trail that was over them, with
a force that made him embrace any alternative rather
than see them perish, that laid him abjectly at the mercy
of the one who menaced them.

Lost in his thoughts, he did not hear the footfall of
the Spanish girl as she re-entered the atelier. She paused
a moment, amazed and terrified, as she saw his attitude
of prostrate grief and dejection, then threw herself beside
him with endearing words and tearful caresses, in wonder
at what ailed him.   He raised himself and unwound her
arms from about him, shunning the gaze of her eyes. She
thought him as true, as loyal-hearted, as great, as he knew
himself to be weak and criminal and hopelessly enslaved.

"What is it?   What has happened?" she asked him
eagerly, trying to draw down his face to hers.

He smiled, while the tears started woman-like beneath
his lashes. He led her gently towards the ruined canvas.

"Only that;—an accident, my love!"

The brightness of the Dryad all blurred and marred
by the ruthlessness of tyranny was a fit emblem of his life.

By noon that day, in the boudoir of the Italian princess, all glimmering with a soft glisten of azure and silver

through its rose-hued twilight, he chanced to be left for a few moments in solitude. Her Highness had not yet risen.

"O God!" he thought, "*do* devils rule the world? There are always doors opened so wide for any meditated sin!"

'Then, with a glance round him like a thief in the night, his hand was pressed on the spring of the Russian cabinet; the letter of the Nuncio lay uppermost, with its signature folded foremost; a moment, and its delicate feminine writing was scanned, and each line remembered with a hot and terrible eagerness that made it graven as though bitten in by aquafortis on his memory. The note was put back, the drawer closed; the artist stood bending over his palette, and pouring the oil on some fair carmine tints, when the Princess of Naples swept into the chamber.

She greeted him with a kindly, careless grace, with a pleasant smile in the brown radiance of her eyes; and she saw that his cheek turned pale, that his eyelids drooped, that his voice quivered, as he answered her.

"*Poverol com' è bello!*" thought Irene Rossillio; and she laughed a little, as she thought that even this Spanish Jew of a painter could not come into her presence without succumbing to its spell.

BOOK THE EIGHTH.

CHAPTER I.

The Claimant of the Porphyry Chamber.

BEFORE the door of an Italian albergo, some men had been drinking and laughing in the ruddy light of an autumn day, just upon the setting of the sun,—men of the mountains, shepherds, goatherds, and one or two of less peaceable and harmless callings,—rough comrades for a belated night on the hill-side, whose argument was powder and ball, and whose lair was made with the wolves and the hares. The house, low, lonely, poor, was overhung with the festoons of vines, and higher yet with the great shelf of roadside rock, from which there poured down, so close that the wooden loggia was often splashed with its spray, a tumbling, foaming, brown glory of water that rolled hissing into a pool dark as night, turning as it went the broad black wood of a mighty mill-wheel. The men had been carousing carelessly, and shouting over their wine and brandy snatches of muleteer and boat-song, or the wild ribaldry of some barcarolle, their host drinking and singing with them, for the vintage had been good, and things went well with him in his own way, here out of the track of cities, and in the solitude of great stretches of sear sunburnt grass, of dense chestnut-forest, of hills all purple and cloud-topped in the vast, clear, dream-like distance. Now, flushed with their drink and heedless in their revels, rough and tumultuous as wild boors at play, they were circled round the doorway in a ring that shut out alike all passage to the osteria and all passage to the road; and they were enjoying torture with that strange instinctive zest for it that underlies most human nature, and breaks out alike in the boor who has a badger at his mercy and the Cæsar who has a nation under his foot.

They had the power and they had the temptation to torment, and the animal natures in them, hot with wine and riotous with mirth rather than with any colder cruelty, urged them on in it; one or two of them, also, were of tempers as coarse and as savage as any of the brutes that they hunted, and peals of brutal laughter rang out from them on the sunny autumn air.

"Sing, my white-throated bird!" cried one. "Dance

a measure with me!" cried another. "Pour this down
your pretty lips, and kiss us for it!" "You'll be humble
enough before we've done with you, my proud beauty!"
"We'll tie you up by a rope of that handsome bright
hair!" "Come, now, laugh and take it easy, or, by Bacchus,
we'll smash those dainty limbs of yours like maize-stalks!"

The shouts echoed in tumult, ringing with laughter,
and broken with oaths, and larder with viler words of
mountain-slang, that had no sense to the ear on which
they were flung in their polluting mirth. In the centre
of the ferocious revelry, beneath the bronzed and crimson
canopy of the hanging porch-vine, and with the western
light shed full upon her, stood Castalia. The tall, lithe,
voluptuous grace of her form rose out against the darkness of the entrance-way like the slender, lofty height of
a young palm; the masses of her hair swept backward
from her forehead. Her face was white as death to the
lips; an unutterable horror was on it, but no yielding fear;
it was proud, dauntless, heroic with the spirit that rose
higher with every menace. Her eyes looked steadily at
the savage, flushed faces round her, so coarse, so loathsome in their mirth; her hands were folded on her bosom,
holding to it the book she carried. They might tear her
limb from limb, as they threatened, like the fibres of the
maize; but the royal courage in her would never bend
down to their will. They had hemmed her in by sheer
brute strength, and their clamour of hideous jest, their
riot of insolent admiration, were a torture to her, passing
all torture of steel or of flame; but they could not wring
one moan from her, much less could they wring one
supplication.

"*Altro!*" laughed the foremost, a sunburnt colossal
mountain-thief of the Appenine. "Waste no more parley
with her. If she will not smile for fair words, she shall

squeak for rough ones.   My pretty princess, give me the first kiss of those handsome lips of yours!"

He launched himself on her as he spoke, his hand on the gold of her hair and the linen broideries of her delicate vest; but her eyes had watched his movement: with a shudder like the antelope's under the tiger's claws, she wrenched herself from him, pierced the circle of her torturers before they could stay her, and, before they could note what she did, had sprung with the mountain swiftness of her childhood on to the rocks overhanging the water-wheel.   Another bound in mid-air, light and far-reaching as a chamois's, and she stood on the broad wooden ledge of the wheel itself, that was stopped from work and was motionless in the torrent, with the foam of the spray flung upward around her, and the black pool hissing below. A yell of baffled rage broke from her tormentors; yet they were checked and paralysed at the daring of the action and at the beauty of her posture, as she was poised there on the wet ledge of the wheel-timber, her hair floating backward, her eyes flashing down upon them, her hands still holding the book, the roar and the surge of the torrent beneath her moving her no more to fear than they move the chamois that spring from rock to rock.   They forgot their passions and their fury for the moment in amaze and in admiration, wrung out from them by a temper that awed them the more because they could comprehend it in nothing.

"Come down!" they shouted, with one voice; "come down! You have gone to your death!"

Where she stood on the wood-work, with the water splashing her feet and the boiling chasm yawning below, she glanced at them and smiled.

"Yes; I have that refuge from you."

"*Per fede!*" thundered the mountaineer who had first

menaced her, "there are two can play at that game, my young fawn!"

With a leap, quick and savage as his own rage, he sprang on to the shelf of rock. There was only the breadth of the falling water between them; she had cleared it, so could he. She looked at the pool, cavernous and deep, at her feet, then let her eyes rest on him calmly.

"Do it, if you dare!" she said, briefly; and her gaze went backward to the torrent with a dreaming, longing, wistful tenderness. "You will save me!" she murmured to the water. "There is only one pain in dying,—to leave the world that has *his* life."

She swayed herself lightly, balancing herself to spring with unerring measure where the eddy of the torrent was deepest. Arresting her in the leap, and startling her persecutors, a voice, deep and rich, though hollow with age, fell on the silence.

"Wait! Will you be murderers?"

Out of the darkness of the entrance issued the tall, bent, wasted form of the blind Hebrew, majestic as a statue of Moses, with his hands outstretched, and his sightless eyes seeking the sunlight.

"I am blind," he said, slowly; "but I know that wrong is being done. Maiden, whoever you be, do not fear; come to me; and the curse of the God of the guiltless fall on those who would seek to harm you!"

The men, stilled though sullen, riotous rather than coldly cruel, stood silent and wavering, glancing from her, where she was poised amidst the dusky mist of the foam-smoke, to the austere and solemn form of the old man suddenly confronting them: they were shamed by his rebuke; they were awed by her courage; they hung like sheep together.

"Take care!" murmured the host, who was alarmed,

and wished the scene ended. "Let her go. The Jew
has the evil eye."

A faint smile flitted over the withered, saturnine face
of the Israelite.

"Yes," he answered, with a bitterness that under the
turn of the words was acrid with remorse,—"yes, I have
the evil eye. Many souls have been cursed by me; many
men have wished that their mothers had never borne
them when once I have looked on their faces; many lives,
that were goodly as the young bay-tree ere I saw them,
withered and fell under my glance. Let the maiden come
in peace to me; and go, or worse will happen unto you."

The subtlety of the Hebrew turned to just account
the boorish and superstitious terrors of the men: they
slunk together in awe of him.

"It was only play," they muttered: "we meant no harm."

The blackness of the stern sightless eyes that were
turned on them filled them with terror; they crossed themselves, and wished the earth would hide them from his
poison-dealing glance. Castalia, where she stood, watched
him with that meditative, far-reaching gaze that had all
the grave innocence of a child, all the luminous insight
of a poet. She held her perilous station still high above
on the plank of the wet mill-wheel, with the white steam
of the torrent curling round.

With the instinct of the blind, Ignatius Mathias turned
towards her.

"Come down, my child: I will have care of you."

"I will come when they have left."

The Jew turned to them with a gesture majestic as
any prophet's command.

"You hear her; go!"

With sullen, muttered oaths, snarling like dogs baffled
of a bone, the mountaineers slunk from him into the

osteria, to drown their wrath and quench their superstitious fears in some fresh skins of wine. Then he lifted his eyes to the place where he knew that she was, and where the rushing of the torrent told him her danger.

"I cannot aid you; I have no sight; but you will trust me!"

She looked at him a moment longer, then, with the deer-like elasticity and surety of her mountain training, sprang once more across the width of the falling stream, and down the stone ledges, slippery with the moisture and holding scarce footing for a lizard, and came to him.

"Yes, I will trust you. I thank you very greatly."

He raised his hand, and touched her hair.

"I cannot see you. Your voice is sweet, and sounds very young; but it is proud. It is not the voice of a wanderer; it speaks as though it ought to command. What are you?"

"Very friendless."

"Truly. Are you far from your home?"

"Very far."

"And why have you left it?"

"Partly, because they said unjust evil."

"Of you?"

"Of me and of one other. I would not stay where the false speakers dwelt."

"You had better have sought the refuge beneath the water, then; you will find no footing to your taste on earth. Are you alone, wholly alone?"

"Yes."

"Ah! and are still but a child, by the clearness of your voice. To-day is but a sample of the dangers that lie in wait for you: the lions will not let such a fawn go by in peace."

"There is always death."

"Not always. And where is it you are bound now?"

"I want to go to large cities."

"To go to the lion's den at once, then. Large cities! And for you, who chose the risk of your grave rather than a rough caress from these men of the hills? Do you know what cities are?"

"No; but I must go to them." Her hands pressed the book closer; she thought that in cities alone could she see or hear what she sought.

The austere, worn, darkened face of the Hebrew grew gentler; she moved his pity, all pitiless though he had been; she recalled to him the youth of his dead darling, when, far away in the buried past, his heart had beat and his life had loved in the summer glories of the sierras. He was very old, but that memory lived still.

"And do you know the way to any cities?"

"Not at all."

"How do you guide yourself, then?"

"By chance."

"And chance plays you cruel caprices, my homeless bird! What chance was it led you to those men?"

She shuddered; but the passionate blood that ran in her, flushed her cheek and glowed imperially in her eyes.

"They were boors, and had boors' barbarity! I asked my way, and wanted a little bread, if they would sell it me at the osteria; and, before I could see them, those men were round me, bidding me laugh and dance and sing."

"Mayhap if you had done so you would have put them in good humour."

He was blind, and could not see the look that glanced on him from the dark shadows of her lashes.

"*I!*—beg their sufferance, by obeying their bidding, by amusing their idleness like any strolling tambourine-singer? They should have killed me first!"

14*

"Verily, you should have emperors' blood in you! You well-nigh killed yourself to escape them."

"Well, what else was there to do? Men can avenge themselves; women can only die."

He bent his eyes on her as though, sightless as they were, he would fain read her features.

"You have grand creeds. Who taught them?"

"They are not creeds, I think; they are instincts."

"Only in rare natures. But have you none in all the world to shield you from such risks?"

"None. But I can shield myself."

"How do you live, then?"

"I have sold the flowers, and sung an office here and there. God is always good."

The tears welled slowly into her eyes. She would not say what she had suffered.

"But why is it that you wander thus? You can come of no peasant blood?"

She was silent. She could not have spoken of the thoughts that lay at her heart,—of the goal that made her search for the sake of life itself. The words which had been said to her in the Italian town had wakened shame and frozen her to silence, though neither her purpose nor her will faltered.

"What has sent you out alone? Have any done you wrong?"

"Only they who spoke evil unjustly."

"If you hold *that* a wrong, do not come into cities. But you speak faintly. Have you broken your fast?"

"Not to-day."

She spoke very low; she could not lie, but she could not bear to say the truth,—that she had eaten but a little milk and millet-bread in the past twenty-four hours. She had intense strength to endure, and she had too much pride to complain, though a faint weakness was on her, and her limbs seemed weighted with lead in the aching exhaustion that comes from want of food. His sightless eyes sought her with a grave compassion; the self-restraint and force of endurance touched the iron mould of his nature as softer things might not have done.

"Well, see here. I am poor, but I am a little wealthier than you. I go to cities where my people are good. I am very aged; but still I can give you some guidance, some shield, at least from insult. Come with me."

"No. It is a gentle charity; but I cannot take charity."

"Whoever you are, you should be the daughter of kings! Listen. You are but a child, and I claim the title of age. I am blind, as you see; I am solitary, I have no companion save only my little dog; you can aid me in much. Lend me your sight, and I will lend you my counsel. It will be quittance of all debt between us. I go to Venice; come there, and from there you can do what you will."

"To Venice!"

Her eyes lightened; it was the city of which she had heard most from him whom she sought,—the city whence Chandos had come into the beech-woods below Vallombrosa

"Yes," answered the Jew. "One is gone thither whom I follow. Your eyes will be fair friends to me; let me have their companionship on the road, at least."

She wavered. The longing on her was great to reach Venice. She thought that there the silence that reigned between her and the life she had lost might be broken.

"Shall it be so?" he asked her.

"If it will not weary you."

"That is well! Who should serve each other, if not the desolate? And yet I spoke not altogether wrongly when I told those ruffians that I had the evil eye. Not in the sense of their fools' superstitions, but my eyes *have* been evil; sight has been blasted from them in a just judgment. My life has been long, and cruel, and darkly stained. You have no fear of me?"

She looked at him with a musing, lingering gaze. The face she saw was stern and harsh and ploughed with deep lines; but she read its true meaning aright.

"No," she said, simply; "I have no fear."

The brown, furrowed brow of the old man cleared. Because he had forfeited the right to trust, trust was the sweeter to him.

"So!—that is right. Youth without faith is a day without sun. Yours will not be wronged by me. Wait a while, then; I need food, and they shall bring you some grapes. Your hands are hot. When I have fairly rested, we will begin to travel onward. Guide me to the shade. Are there no trees? There; let us stay there. Have no fear; your persecutors will not return."

So they rested beneath the gold-flecked boughs of a broad sycamore that grew beside the pool of the water-mill, with the depth of shadow flung on the white Syrian head of the old man, and the deep space of the eddying stream, and the sun through the leaves lighting on the grace of her young limbs and the musing beauty of her eyes, as, where the book of "Lucrèce" lay open on the grass, they dwelt on the words that Castalia knew by heart as a child knows his earliest prayers,—that had never spoken to any as they spoke to her,—that were richer in her sight than all the gold of the world, and were to her as in Oriental ages the scroll that their prophets and kings had traced were in the sight of the people's awed love and listening reverence.

"It was not true to say I was alone," she mused; "not alone while his thoughts are with me."

And in them solitude, and danger, and the gnawing of famine, and the heart-sickness of her young life, cast adrift on the fever and the wilderness of the world, were alike forgotten where she leaned, in the autumn light, beside the only man among his creditors who had not uncovered his head before the dignity of calamity in the porphyry hall of Clarencieux.

CHAPTER II.
"Magister de Vivis Lapidibus."

UNDER the great smoke pall that overhung Darshampton there were riots,—riots of the eternal conflict which has been waged since the Gracchan Proletariate, and will be waged on, God knows how long, through the cycles of the future. Prices were high; trades were bad; political ignorance was run mad, catching half-truths and whole wrongs as it went, but braying of them so that the sane were fain to stop their ears, in the same blunder as the burrowing ostrich makes. Workers had struck almost to a man; masters would not or could not yield; there were misery, error, wild justice, blind injustice, crippled creeds groping in twilight, wrong codes hunger-sharpened, right premises and wrong deductions, the *ignoratio elenchi* of individual suffering, that thought itself an injured world, the passion of starving lives that persuaded themselves want of bread was resistless logic; all the eternal antagonisms of Labour and Capital were camped here as it were on one common battle-ground, with the angry smoke looming above their hostile battalions.

The mighty-sinewed iron-workers, like the Moyen-Age smiths of Antwerp and Bruges, the pale delicate artisans of the loom, wan and frail as the flax they wove, the gaunt giants of the blasting-furnaces, and the sickly weavers of fine linens, the men poisoned with stifling air,

the men scorched with foundry flames, the men dying of
steel-dust in their lungs, the men livid with phosphorus-
flames inhaled to get daily bread, the men who died like
so many shoals of netted herrings, that the Juggernaut
of trade might roll on,—all these were here, or their re-
presentatives, men who were told, and believed it, that it
was the Aristocratic Order which wronged them, never
thinking that it was the merciless Thor of Commercial
Cupidity which crushed them under its sledge-hammer,
beating gold out of their bruised flesh. All these were
here, filling the vast squares and the dark streets with
clamour and menace and sullen ominous murmur,—the
volcanic lava which runs beneath the fair surface of the
careless world, which soon or late will break from bondage and overflow it—to fertilize or to destroy?

To fertilize, if light be given them; to destroy, if
darkness be locked in on them.

The thirst for liberty was in them,—the liberty that
the sons of men knew while yet the earth was in her
youth,—the liberty of pathless woods, of trackless seas,
of wild fresh winds, of free unfettered life. They wanted
it, though they had never known it. These—who from
the birth to the grave were pent in factories, and sheds,
and garrets, in gas-glare, and crowded alleys, and dens
of squalid vice, with the whirr of machines ever on their
ear, and the dead weight of smoke ever in their breath,
wanted life,—wanted the sweet west winds they never
breathed, the strong ocean air they never tasted, the
waving seas of grass they never looked on, the unchained
liberty of boundless moorland they had never seen but in
their dreams, the human heritage of freedom that in all
ages through is taken from the poor in price for the scant
barren porridge of daily sustenance. Ah, God! it is a
bitter price to pay,—a whole life given up for food

enough to keep alive in knowledge that life is endless pain and endless deprivation!

They wanted this grand simple freedom that instinct made them pine for, though its knowledge had never been theirs or their sires'; and their teachers told them they needed the ballot-box and the game-laws' repeal!

It is many centuries since Caius Gracchus called the Mercantile Classes to aid the people against the Patricians, and found too late that they were deadlier oppressors than all the Optimates; but the error still goes on, and the Money-makers still churn it into gold, as they churned it then into the Asiatic revenues and the senatorial amulets.

The trades had struck. They were wrong, very wrong, in the application of theories and predicates which had their root in right. But it were hard not to be wrong in philosophies when the body starves on a pinch of oatmeal, with the whole width of the known world drawn in between the four pent walls of a factory-room or the red-hot stones of a smelting-house. It is the law of necessity, the balance of economy: human fuel must be used up, that the machine of the world may spin on; but it is not perhaps marvellous that the living fuel is sometimes un-reconciled to that symmetrical rule of waste and repair, of consumer and consumed.

They were sullenly angry, tempestuously bitter, these surging tumultuous masses, now raging like seas in a storm, now more ominously silent, with the yellow sickly gleam of the pale sun shining through the reeking fog on to their faces, here so white and eager and emaciated, there so black and dogged and bull-dog like, here so gaunt with old age of hungered patience, there so terrible with youth of vicious desperation. They were at war with all the world in the aching of their hearts, in the dimness of their insight; at war even with their darling whom they had so often crowned, their hero whom they had long been content to follow as hounds follow their feeder.

They were riotous and desperate. The furnaces had long been cold, the looms had long been idle, the wheels had long been silent throughout their country; their own Unions had been hard on them, and there were dark tales afoot of what had been done on renegades in the Unions' name. Their employers would not yield, and it was said that strange hands were pouring in and taking the work they had left,—taking it at peril of answering with life and limb for the temerity. They were very bitter, very savage, very maddened, in the nauseous fog-mist steaming round them, in the cold northerly cutting air, burdened black with smoke, though through them the chimneys had so long been without warmth. They were fierce in their wrath; their hearths were fireless, their children had no food, their women were dying of fever, their old people lay dead by the score of famine; their hand was against every man's, and they clamoured even against their Representative. He was faithless to them, he was untrue to his pledges; he feasted in foreign palaces, and forgot them; he sold them for the sake of office; he grew great himself, and let them perish; he joined the ministry, and denied all that he had said to them. Thus they murmured, and yelled, and hooted against him, in their restless misery. The love of a People is the most sublime crown that can rest on the brow of any man; but the love of a Mob is a mongrel that fawns and slavers one moment to rend and tear the next, sycophant whilst bones are tossed to it, savage when once not surfeited.

They loved him with a bold, rough love, that was a million-fold truer than his own heart ever had been; they were proud of him; they would have died for him; they believed in him; but, irritated against him they were capable of killing their god, and weeping over it, when shattered, like Africans. Imprecations even on him were hurled at intervals through the city, while the crash of falling slates, of shivered glass, of flung stones, of levelled bricks, was added to the hurricane of noise, where, clamorous for bread, or incensed at the stranger-hands hired by their employers, the mob wrecked a provision-shop or tore down a machine-house. It was a pandemonium under the dark murky atmosphere; in the dull glare cast from the westward flames, where some had fired a factory; in the midst of thousands let loose and made savage with hunger; in the storm of curses thundered out from the bared hollow chests gnawed with want, —curses that blasted even their idol's name. He had sold them for the bribe of office; he had betrayed them for the possession of power; he had gone over to their oppressors for the sake of his own aggrandizement!

Perhaps it was but a multitude's reaction and caprice; perhaps it was that the great, weary, fettered heart of the people, earnest with all its tyrannous error, and tossed by demagogues from lie to lie, vaguely felt that its own living, aching humanity was but used as a stepping-stone for ambition,—vaguely felt that what it trusted was not true! Be it which it would, they upbraided and menaced and cursed him. He was theirs, and he coalesced with the nobles; he was theirs, and he went to banquet in palaces; he was theirs, and he was betraying them to sit in the Cabinet Council and to wear the gewgaws of honours!

The murmur and the threat rose louder and louder, stretched wider and wider. When the tempest was at its height, into the surging waves of the stormy human sea Trevenna rode leisurely down.

Staying at the country-seat of a millionnaire some ten miles away, whither rumours came with every hour of

the Darshampton riots, he had heard how his subjects had
mutinied against him,—heard as he was shooting over a
pheasant-cover that had been specially reserved for him,
with sundry other good shots of the nobility of rank and
the princes of the plutocracy. He had given his gun to
a loader, without a second's hesitation, and ordered a
horse to be saddled. His friends had crowded round him,
and sought to dissuade him; he had shrugged his shoulders.
"They curse me behind my back; let's see what they'll
dare say to my face." There was no bravado in it; but
there was the cool audacity, the dauntless zest in peril,
which made him, despite all his self-love and caution,
bold in a fray as a mastiff; his teeth clenched, his hand
gripped a riding-switch with a meaning force: the lion-
tamer had no thought of leaving his lion-whelps to riot
unchecked; and he rode now into Darshampton, with the
gentlemen who were his hosts and fellow-guests, about
him like a *cohue* of courtiers round a king.

"It is very unwise to risk it," whispered one of them.
"They are at wild work, and your life is of national value."

Trevenna laughed, and bowed his thanks for the compliment.

"Nobody's life's of value, my dear lord: there are
always plenty to fill the vacancies. There aren't two
people whose death would lower the Consols for two days.
To affect the money-market is the acme of greatness: I'm
afraid the exchanges would scarce stay twelve hours below par for me yet."

And he rode leisurely down, as he would take his
morning canter along the park, into that sea of turbulent,
hooting, swaying, sullen, fog-soaked human life that, for
the first moment since his clarion-words had challenged
Darshampton, were angered against him and upbraiding
him as a renegade. There was laughter in his eyes as

they glanced over the heaving mass. To his worldly
wisdom and bright sagacity, there was an irresistible
comedy in this passionate, raving, undoubting sincerity
of a hungry multitude; there was an inexpressible ridicule
for him in these poor purblind tools that rushed with such
ardour to do his work for him, thinking all the while
they were doing their own,—never knowing that they but
tunnelled the way, or threw the bridge, by which he
would pass to his ambitions, while they would lie gasping,
kicked aside and unknown. To his shrewd common sense
there was something unutterably droll in the sight of men
in love with an idea, amorous of a principle, sincere in
anything except self-love; there was something unutterably ludicrous in the notion of men who starved for lack
of a crust crazing their heads about the world's government. Trevenna was a democrat, because he hated everything about him, delighted to lead, and held a bitter
grudge against the pestilential tyranny of class; but at
heart he cared not a button more for the people than
the most supercilious of aristocrats, and, had he been
given a supreme power, would have been as strong a
tyrant in his own way as ever made a nation the mill-
horse to grind for his treasuries and fill his granaries.
He had a thorough, manly, passionate contempt for the
differences of rank; but all the same his one motive was
simply to get rank for himself, and such a sentimentality
(as he would have called it) as pity for the suffering of
multitudes could never enter into the strong, practical
astuteness of his sagacious temper.

But bold he was, bold as a lion, and more politic even
than bold: so he rode now down into the close-wedged
ranks of the crowds, into the sulphurous heat from the
distant flames, into the clamour and the uproar and the
storm of rage, till his horse could push way no more, and

he faced the whole front of those who were clamorous against him, with the dull red light shining full on the keen brave blue of his eyes.

They were amazed to see his apparition rise there so suddenly out of the cloud of smoke and fog: he was their idol, moreover, though they had cursed him when they had no bread, as men beat the god Pan when he sent them no game for the hunting; and a silence fell for a moment on them: in it he spoke:—

"So, fellows, you are damning me, they say. Tell me my faults to my face, then!"

There was the familiar, half-brusque, half-bantering tone that was so popular with the throngs he challenged; but beneath that there was something of the grand insolence of Scipio Æmilianus:—"Surely you do not think I shall fear those free whom I sent in chains to the slave-market!"

"You sold us for office!" "You have broken your pledges!" "You have been false to your promises!" "You have abandoned Reform!" "You have been bribed by Courts!" "You have recanted your creeds!" "You have joined the aristocracy!" "You have feasted in palaces!" "You have turned traitor!" "You only seek your own dignities, and leave us to starve!" Sullen, hoarse, savage with uncouth oaths, yelled out in the northern accent, the charges were hurled against him. The multitude were waking, in their irritation, to the truth, and vaguely feeling their way to it,—vaguely feeling that they were only used by the idol whom they had hugged the belief they had created and could dethrone.

He heard them quite patiently, his bold frank eyes resting on them with a certain insolent amusement that lashed them like cords: it was the amusement of the lion-tamer who lets his mutinous cubs fret and fume beneath

his gaze, knowing that a crack of his whip will break
them into obedience.

He laughed a little.

"You rebuke me for taking office! Why did you re-
elect me after my acceptance of it, then?"

The mob, indignant to have their own inconsistency and
mutability brought in their teeth against them, broke out
into tenfold uproar; shrieks, curses, yells, hooting menaces,
crossed each other in horrible tumult; a shower of stones
was hurled through the darkened air, a thousand hands
struck out with massive iron weapons or cleft the mist
with flaming fire-brands. His horse reared and fretted,
while the masses of half-naked figures were jammed and
crushed against its flanks; a thousand arms were stretched
out, brawny and terrible in their threats, ten thousand
voices thundered imprecations, hungry savage eyes glared
on him like wild beasts', hot breath panted on him from
mouths foul with curses and livid with famine. Trevenna
sat firm as a rock, with the fresh sanguine colour in his
face unblenched, and his eyes watching the riot as though
it were an opera ballet. Had Trevenna been Napoleon,
he would have won at Waterloo ere Blucher could turn
the day, or else would have died with the Old Guard.

The missiles of iron, and stone, and lead, and wood,
and slate, flew about him, hissing and roaring through
the fog; his horse plunged nervously, but he never swerved
in his saddle, never moved his head to avoid the blows
that with every second rained at him, as the angered
worshippers pelted their god because their bodies were
fasting. At last, a flint, sharp, jagged, heavy, struck him,
cutting through his clothes and wounding him in the
shoulder; the blood poured out down his arm.

With a careless glance at it, he thrust his hand into
the breast of his coat, took out his cigar-case, struck a

fusee, and began to smoke,—smoke, as calmly and with as much indifference as if he were on the couch of a smoking-room.

The crowds fell back, the thirsty menacing eyes stared vacantly at him, the yells dropped down into a low, unwilling, sullen muttering of wonder and admiration; the cool bravery, the calm *sang-froid*, of the action struck a chord never dumb in the English heart; they had pelted their god, and, lo! he was but the greater for it. They loved him once more with all a people's swift, passionate, volatile repentance; they broke out into riotous cheering, they tossed his name upward to the murky skies, with all the old faith and honour. Without speaking a word, he had conquered.

"That was like the Clarencieux blood!" thought Trevenna of his own coolness, with a smile. Then, sitting there in his saddle, he spoke,—spoke with all his skill and all his eloquence, rating them soundly like a whipper-in rating his hounds, till the great masses hung their heads penitent and ashamed before him, yet speaking so that they loved him more furiously than they had ever done, and making them, to a man, believe that all he took, all he did, all he said, all he projected, were only with one view,—their service. And on the morrow the whole nation was full of adoring applause for the self-devotion and the courage and the serenity with which a Cabinet Minister had risked his life to quell the northern riots, and to lead the people back to conciliation and to quietness with the charm of his eloquence and the spell of his personal daring.

"Magister de Vivis Lapidibus" was the title given in the Gothic age to the sculptors of the Gothic fanes. Trevenna might have borne it: it was out of the living stones of other men's lives that he carved the superstructure of

his envied triumphs. It is only to those who have this
supreme art that success comes.

CHAPTER III.
"To tell of Spring-tide past."

IT was the blossoming-time of the early year in Venice,
with the glow on the variegated marbles, and the balmy
breezes stirring calm lagunes, and the scent of a myriad
of spring-born flowers filling the air with their fragrance
from the green-wreathed ruins of arches and the deep
embayments of pillared casements. The world was waking after winter, and the joy of its renewed life laughed
in every smile of colour, and crowned the earth with a
diadem of leaf and of bud like a young Bacchus rousing
from sleep to his revels.

"How its youth renews!" said Chandos to his own
thoughts; "and we only know the value of ours when its
beauty has faded for ever!"

"L'artiste est un dieu tombé qui se souvient du temps
où il créait un monde." The memories of his perished
world were with him,—the world in which his word had
been as the thyrsus of Dionysus, a wand beneath whose
touch all the earth laughed round him into fragrance. He
had resisted the mandragora-steeped despair in which the
great lives of Byron and De Quincey quenched their pain
and ebbed away; he had taken the broken wreck of his
peace boldly and calmly, and had sustained himself,
sustained his courage, by desires loftier than happiness, by
the treasuries of intellect, by the consolations of freedom.
He had borne with the desolation of life for the sake of
his manhood until it had ceased to be wholly desolate
because filled with the dignity of a high and a pure labour.
He had done this, and done it so that no Ciceronian
lament for exile ever was heard to pass his lips,—done it

so that through it there had come to him the power most
foreign to the careless sensuousness of his inborn nature,
—the power of serene and unswerving endurance. He had
suffered, but he had never lamented. He had known that
to yield to suffering was to debase manliness, and that
resistance and conflict are the only noble weapons with
which adversity can be worthily met. He had been stung,
and bruised, and cheated; he had been offered the bitterness of the hyssop and vinegar when his whole life was
athirst for the living waters of loyalty and joy. Men had
fooled him, betrayed him, forsaken him; but he had never
in turn abandoned them, never reviled the humanity with
which he had common bond, never abjured the faith and
the creeds of his youth. The love he had borne men
when they were at his feet, and the suns of a cloudless
day had been shed across his path, lived with him still,
now that he had been stabbed deep by their traitor-blades
and had passed through the starless night of bereavement
and of despair.

Yet at times the anguish of a great longing stole on
him; at times the lust of a great vengeance seized him.
At times he would wake from some dream of his youth,
some dream that had borne him, for its hour, back to the
home he had·lost,—borne him to the fresh shelter of its
forest leafage, to the sight of its beloved beauty, to the
lulling echo of its familiar waters; wake, and, seeing the
grey gleam of some foreign city in its wintry dawn or
the torrid, reddened sun-glow of some eastern sky around
him, clench his teeth like a man in torture to keep down
the great tearless sob that shook him as the wind shakes
reeds. At times he would break from the noble and tranquil repose of philosophy, from the treasuries of intellectual creation, from the calm of deep and scholarly ambition and meditation,—break from them as men break from

the stillness of monastic cloisters and the coldness of monastic vows, with an agony of desire for the vivid joys and the vivid hues that had died from his life,—with as passionate an agony for the mere bloodthirst of revenge, that, under the goad of a giant wrong, will change the purest nature to the sheer brute instinct of self-wrought amends, of Mosaic justice.

He drifted now through Venice, beneath the marble walls and the casements dark and narrow, out of whose twilight glowed the smile of the flowers' birth, with the water lazily parting under his boat's prow, and the green of spring-time foliage hanging over the jasper ledges. His heart was with spring-times that were past, when there had been no shadow on the earth for him, and the kiss of a woman's lips had made his idle golden paradise. "Love!" he thought, with a momentary regret that was in itself almost a passion. "It can live no more in my life; it is dead with all the rest." Yet now—for the instant at least—he would have given the kingship of half the world, had he owned it, to steep himself once more in the sweet, senseless delirium; he could have murmured, with Mirabeau when he looked back in his dungeons to the hours of his love, "Jouissance! jouissance! que de vies je donnerais pour toi!"

"If I returned to her?" he mused, in a doubt, in a desire, that had long haunted him, mingled with an anxiety that was almost remorse. "And yet—a child's love; it may be forgotten ere this. Besides, God knows her fate now; and, whatever it may be, I have no right to sacrifice her life to mine."

But there, in the sunset radiance, in the lulling of the water's murmur, in the heavy fragrance of the many blossoms, the thoughts of his youth were with him, and they wandered alone to Castalia. He had not known it whilst he had been with her, but in absence the desire of his heart had gone to her in what was scarce less than love. He had thrust it from him, because on her the world would have visited that love as dishonour.

As he passed through the charmed peace of the silent city in the first hour of his arrival there, all odorous and rich in the hues of the flowers' spring-tide luxuriance, the vessel floated down the noiseless highway into a sequestered, desolate street, whose dark walls faced each other with all life, all movement, banished, only with the intense glow of the sun on its many-coloured stones, and the wreathing of stone-clinging leafage filling the gaps of its broken sculptures. It was that in which, a few years before, the young patriots of Venice had given him the homage of their song of liberty. It was lonely, decayed, abandoned, with no sound in it but the endless lapping of the water on its sea-stairs; but it was grand, despite that, with its mute records of the glory that once had reigned there, its imperishable memories of things for ever perished.

The keel grated on the marble steps, worn and glistening with the splash of the water-spray; he landed, and passed up them to the place where he had once made his dwelling in Venice. The arc of a vast archway spanned the slope of the stairs, shutting out the light of the sun, and leaving only a flickering ray of the daylight's brilliance to lie across the interspaces of dense shadow that were cast downward from the mighty structure and the massive carvings, rich in jasper, and porphyry, and agate, which loomed in the height above. In the depth of the gloom, midway on the stone flight, a resting figure leaned in the passive, motionless repose of fatigue or of exhaustion,—a form that would have arrested an artist's glance in long-lingering admiration, that was Venetian in its perfect grace, Titian-like in its perfect colour, that was set as a brilliant painting in an ebony framework in that cavernous gloom of the arch, in exquisite harmony yet in exquisite contrast with the antique and melancholy majesty of the forsaken palace-way. The head was drooped forward; but there was no sleep in the eyes that gazed wearily down on the ebb and flow of the gliding canal; the lids were heavily weighted, but it was not with slumber, but with an unshed mist of tears; the lips were slightly parted, as with pain, but there was on them a proud fixity of resolve; the hands leaned on the twisted osier handle of a basket, from which spring flowers fell unheeded in coils and masses of blossom down about her on the worn stone. The single flash of sunlight that found entrance beneath the marbles fell, intense and concentred in its heat and its glow, alone on the scattered foliage and on the golden gleam of her uncovered hair. The attitude, the flower-fragrance, the languor of repose, were the same as they had been under the beech-shadows of Tuscany; but the dreaming peace of childhood was banished for ever.

He saw her as, coming out of the splendour of the day, he glanced, half blinded, up the twilight of the palace-steps; and her name left his lips with a cry,—"Castalia!" She looked up with a look in her eyes that smote him with a pang keen and heavy as a murderer's remorse, and, starting from her musing rest, sprang towards him with all the wealth of the spring buds and blossoms scattered into the gliding darkness of the water; then—like a shot fawn—she fell downward at his feet, the shower of her glistening tresses trailing on the sea-wet marbles of the stair.

If he had never loved her, he loved her then. He lifted her, senseless to his touch, into his arms, where she had rested through the tumult of the storm; he murmured to her a thousand names that had never been on his utterance since ·the days of his youth, when there was no toy so fair to him as the fairness of woman; he swept the burnished weight of her hair back from the face from which he had exiled the smile of its childhood, the light of its peace. For 'the moment he was once more young; for the moment time and calamity, and the bitterness of disillusion, and the coldness of dead hopes and dead desires, were as though they had never been; for the moment passion once again transfigured all existence, and blinded him with its warm golden glow, so sweet because so transient, so strong in power and so vain in reason. The cost of it is oftentimes deadly and far-reaching; but its lotus dream of forgetfulness is worth it while it lasts.

The shock of joy had stunned her; she lay unconscious in his embrace. No living thing was near them in the darkness of the old sea-palace; there was only the sound of the retreating oars beating out a soft, sad, distant music; there was only the one broad beam of vivid light that flushed the tint of the fallen carnation-buds to scarlet, and burned on the loosened splendour of her hair that swept across his breast. He stooped his head over her, gazing on her with a love that had silently grown, born in absence and from pity, and that sprang up like a tropic flower which springs to its height in one short Eastern night, with the sudden sight of her young beauty.

As though his kiss wakened her and called back the mind from its trance, her heart, where it beat on his own, throbbed faster; her eyes opened wide and startled, as they had opened when he had roused her from her sleep in the storm; for an instant she lay passive in his arms, gazing upward at him with the glory of a joy, bewildered as a dream, dawning, as the day dawns, on her face.

"O God, be pitiful!   Let me never wake."

Such dreams so often had mocked her.

"Castalia, look at me, hear me.   I am with you. Have you loved me so well, then?"

At the sound of his voice a flush like the scarlet heat of the fallen carnation-leaves glowed in her cheek; her eyes looked upward to him, but half conscious still.

"At last! at last!"

The murmur broke from her, stifled with the rush of tears; she quivered from his embrace, and crouched down at his feet, till her face was veiled from him.   The knowledge of love was on her, and it stilled and filled with the dread of his scorn the anguish of joy with which her heart seemed breaking as a nightingale's breaks with the rapture of song.

He stooped to her, and his hand touched her with a gentleness that thrilled her with its caress like fire.

"Castalia, have you loved me despite my desertion,— through all my cruelty?"

Her brow drooped still, till the bright masses of her hair bathed his feet.

"Eccellenza!   I have only prayed God to let me see your face, and die."

The words were so low they barely stirred the air, yet he heard them; and his eyes grew dim: it was long since any had given him love; it had an infinite sweet- ness for him.   He stood silent and motionless a moment, looking down on her where she knelt with the Venetian light shed like an aureole about her.   Then the old dominion, the reckless sovereignty, of passion vanquished him; he drew her once more into his arms, he lifted again her bowed head, that sunk downward like a broken

flower on the chill dark marble of the water-stairs; the
gaze that had never, sleeping or waking, been absent
from her memory, met hers with a look that made her
senses sick and faint with the paradise of joy that doubted
its own being.

"Castalia, we are both alone; let us be the world to
one another."

She lay passive in his hold; her face was turned upward to him with the radiance of the sun fallen across
her proud bright brow; her lips trembled; she heard him
with a breathless incredulity, a breathless ecstasy.

"Oh, my lord, you mock me! Love! *your* love!—
for *me!*"

It seemed to her the gift of so divine a world, the
treasury of so vast a sovereignty, the benediction of so
godlike a mercy! She could not think that it could be
her own. She could not hold a lifetime of service and
of sacrifice title sufficient for it.

He drew her closer and closer to his breast, and, for
all answer, spent his kisses on her lips.

"Do you doubt *now?*"

With the touch of his caresses the consciousness alike
of the passion she wakened and the passion she cherished
stole on her; the barrier between them, that her veneration for him had raised by the deep humility of its own
worship, seemed to fall as his eyes gazed down into hers;
for the first time the knowledge of what love he might
bear her, of what love she might render him, came to her
with the glow of its warmth, with the wonder of its deep
and hushed delight. The carnation flush of her face
burned deeper in its soft shame; a sigh trembled through
her, where she rested in his arms as a hunted bird rests
in its haven of shelter.

"For the pity of God—if I am dreaming, kill me while I dream!"

The words died in their prayer; her gaze met his, heavy with the voluptuous weight of new-born thoughts, the eyes of Sappho under the first breath of love. His hand wandered among the floating gold of her sun-lightened tresses; his lips sought ever and again the warmth of hers.

"Let me dream with you, if I can! Let me dream, too, once more,—dream that you give me back my youth!"

CHAPTER IV.
"To thine own Self be true."

HE gazed down on her, and wondered how he could ever have left her.

The flight of a few months had brought her loveliness to its perfection; and the silence of endurance, the passion of suffering, had left on it a heroism and a power that gave tenfold more beauty to the luxuriance of its youth, more intensity to the splendour of its hues. Young though she was, hers was already a life to be a poet's mistress, to comprehend and to inspire loftiest ambitions, highest efforts, noblest thoughts, to gain from the lips of a man the words of Dante,—

> "Quella che imparadisa la mia mente,
> Ogni basso pensier dal cor m'avulse."

As the full consciousness of his presence and of his love wakened in her, as the sense of his words and the truth of her dream dawned on her till her heart seemed breaking with its rapture, she drew herself from his embrace, and sank down beside him, her head bowed upon his hand.

"Ah! this is but your pity!"

The words were low-breathed as a sigh.

To her, he was so far above her, far as the stars in their divine majesty; to her it seemed that she could have nothing to raise her into fitness with his life. For all answer he lifted her head upward as he stooped over her.

"Only pity! Look in my eyes and see!"

Once before he had said the last words to one whom they had no power to stir, whose heart was chill as ice against his own. Now the whole fervour of a southern nature thrilled in answer to them. Castalia looked up, and met his gaze; then the burning colour flushed her cheek and her bosom, a light like a flash of sunlight trembled over her face, her lips parted with a deep broken breath. From his eyes she had learned what her reverence in its humility could not realise; she never asked, she never doubted, again whether he loved her.

And the weight and the wonder of its joy seemed to kill her with its glory.

> "What can I give thee back, O liberal
> And princely giver, who hast brought the gold
> And purple of thine heart?"

her own heart asked.

"Oh, my lord, my king!" she murmured, while her lips hesitatingly touched his hand in the kiss of a slave's veneration, "I am not worthy! A word from you, a smile from you such as you give the dogs, were all *I* prayed for! What can I render you? I am nameless and desolate!"

Of the gifts of her own loveliness she never thought; she had known them no more than the passion-flower knows its own hues.

"You will give me yourself, and you will give me youth,—gifts more precious than the treasures of a world, Castalia! My love!—all my youth through I sought your likeness, and never found you! You waited to be the

angel of consolation to the darkness of years, that were
without a joy in them until you brought one."

"Ah! you are not happy?"

He smiled, a smile in which the melancholy of his
fate was tinged with impassioned tenderness for her.

"When I look on you, I am."

"Oh, my lord! if I can make you so one hour, I shall
have lived enough."

He understood her. This vivid, intense, devotional
love was very precious to him; he had dreamed of it in
the ideals of his poetic fancies; and it was doubly sweet
now that it came to him after the desert waste of many
years, in which no smile had lightened for him, no lips
touched his own. Where he rested in the shadow and the
solitude of the old palace-entrance, the dead days revived
once more for him. Once more he lost himself in the
languor and the warmth and the oblivion of passion, as
he murmured to her a thousand caressing names, and
drew from her the story of her wanderings, touched beyond words by the pathetic simplicity of that search for
him through the vastness of an unknown world.

"I sought you, Eccellenza; yes," she murmured, while
she looked up at him with an appealing deprecating
prayer, "I could not stay when you were gone; my heart
was dead, my life was broken. And I heard them speak
evil against you, and the Padre Giulio lifted up his voice
with them; and I would not wait and eat the bread of
those who had once touched your name. For I heard
that name at the last, and I knew you then greater than
any kings; I knew the book that I loved as your book,
the thoughts I had treasured as your thoughts. But,
though I sought you, it was not to seek your pity, not to
ask your mercy. I never meant that you should know
that I was near:—if ever I met you, I only meant to

watch you from a distance, to hear your voice, to see your face, while you knew nothing. You believe me?— you believe it?"

The terror on her was great, lest he should think that she had followed him to appeal to his compassion, to force herself on his life. His eyes were dim, his voice quivered, as he answered her,—

"Believe it? Yes! each word that your lips say. My darling, my darling, what you have suffered! and suffered through and for me!"

"Eccellenza," she said, under her breath, "I would suffer a thousand years of *that* for this one hour."

"Hush! hush! or I shall love you too well; and all that *I* love I lose. Such courage, such patience, such fidelity; and you ask, what you have that you give me?"

"Those are nothing," she said, dreamily. "The mercy is—to let me render them. It has been so long, O God! so long! Here in Venice it was a little happier. The people speak of you; they love you, though they say it beneath their breath, because of the tyranny. They said you would come here with the spring; and so—I waited."

The words were simple, spoken with the tears of re-membered anguish heavy on her lashes; but all her story was told in them. "She had waited," with the faith of a child, the passion of a woman: it was the epitome of the intense volition and the silent power of sacrifice that met in her nature. It was the ideal of which he had once vainly dreamed; it moved him now to an emotion keen to pain.

"Castalia, in my youth I loved many, yet my youth never had such love as yours. What you have suffered while I knew nothing! And you never loathed me for my cruelty?"

"Cruelty? You were never cruel. You saved my

life; it was yours to take or to leave, to command or to neglect."

"But I left you to this loneliness, to this peril! How have you lived, fragile and friendless, and dowered with the danger of such beauty?"

Her face grew pale. The past was terrible to her,—a time never to be dwelt on without a horror of remembrance; and she would not wound him by confessing all she had endured.

"It is over," she said softly; "let it sleep."

"It will never sleep in *my* memory. And now, now that we have met, what does the thought of my love bring you?"

Her eyes dwelt on his, deep and dreamy as the night, with the fire of a tropic nature in their depths; her voice was hushed below her breath.

"How can I say? I know now how possible it is to die of joy; I feel as if I should die so to-night!"

He drew her nearer still into his embrace. The words sent a chill through him; all that his heart had clung to had been taken, soon or late.

"God forbid! Live to bless me, Castalia; live to be my love, my consoler, my mistress, my wife!"

The last word left his lips in unconsidered impulse. She was his so utterly, his to cherish or destroy, to honour or dishonour, to lead as he chose, to make what he would; the absolute defencelessness of her life, the absolute abandonment of her trust, forbade him to seek from her aught that others would have held her sacrifice.

Where she rested in his arms, she trembled from head to foot, the liquid darkness of her eyes grew burning with the bewildered vision of a future that passed all which her thought had ever reached; her senses seemed blind and faint; she felt as though angel hands had been laid

on her and had raised her upward into the light of eternal
suns.

"No, no!" she murmured, while her gaze dwelt on his
with all the humility and all the idolatry that were in
her; "I have no title! I was born of shame, they say;
I am without name, or kin, or worthiness. I am yours
to neglect, to smile upon, to forsake, to command,—as
you will! Let me be as your slave; let me follow and
serve and obey you as spaniels may; let me live in your
sight, and have honour enough in one word, in one touch:
—that is all that *I* am meet for from you!"

The words moved him as no words that had claimed
her justice or his tenderness would ever have done,—
words that had the sublime self-oblivion and self-devotion
of Héloïse.

"Not so! You were worth empires if I had them in
my gift. Castalia, there is but one passion possible between us now. The world, as its bigotry stands, would
call that passion your shame, unless my name were bestowed with it,—unless the marriage-benediction were on
you. I have little left to give; but such as I have shall
be yours."

The scarlet flush deepened over her bosom; her head
drooped till her. lips touched his hand again in their
reverent kiss; her voice was broken and lost in tears.

"Ah, God! what can I say to you? how can my life
repay you? You gave me all—gave me the world—when
you once gave me your love!"

Past the darkened arch of the entrance a gondola
floated slowly down the solitary and neglected street,—a
vessel richly arrayed, and piled in the prow with a
fragrant load of gathered violet and red carnation buds,

Lying back in it was a form, delicate and patrician, covered with costly laces and velvets; her cheek rested on her hand; her hand glittered with diamonds. She looked up languidly as the boat dropped past the high and massive sculpture of the mighty archway. The gloom was deep as twilight beneath its arc, yet her eyes pierced it and caught the hues of the fallen flowers, the gleam of the golden hair,—eyes falcon-bright, pitiless, and unerring,—the eyes of Héloïse de la Vivarol.

"She has found him!" she said, in her teeth. "And he loves her. So it comes round,—so it comes round!"

So her vengeance came round to her,—her vengeance vowed in the years that were gone. Women may forget their love, and change it; but there are few who ever forget the oath or the desire of jealousy.

The flitting by of that single gondola was unseen by them, the noise of its oars drowned in the ripple of the water beneath the wide slope of the stairs. He surrendered himself once more to the forgetfulness and the sweetness of passion; and her life seemed to rest in a trance divine as that which comes to the lotus-eaters. The darkness of the vast stone pile enclosed them in its shadow and its solitude; the red gold of the fast-declining sun only stole in a single ray across the lustre of her eyes as they looked up to his. The heavy fragrance of the fallen flowers weighted the air; the delicious monotone of the water's ebb and flow below against the marble alone stirred the stillness. Time passed on; neither counted its flight. The sun set, the odorous night fell; it seemed to her at once brief as a moment, long as a lifetime, since she had found him whom she had grown to hold her sovereign and her religion.

Through the gloom, as the depth of night fell, a voice came from above them.

"Castalia, art thou not home?"

"Who is that?" Chandos said, swiftly. "Who calls you by your name?"

"Ah! I had forgotten him!" she murmured, with that soft contrition with which she had once pleaded her forgetfulness of the Tuscan priest. "I was wrong to say I was wholly friendless. He has been very good. He is a Jew, old, and blind, and poor; but he led me here, and he brought me to some women of his nation, who have been gentle to me, because they knew me to be homeless and motherless."

As she spoke, the old man came slowly down the steps, feeling his way with that wavering uncertain movement of his hands that was in so pathetic a contrast with the dignity of his austere and venerable age. A gleam of the white luminous Venetian moon fell across the majesty of his bowed head and lofty form.

"Good God!—at last!"

The words escaped involuntarily as he rose to his feet, facing the figure of the Israelite. He had sought the old man far and diligently since the night when he had found him wandering in the streets,—sought him on the vague, baseless, shapeless thoughts and the unerring instinct of the desire for vengeance.

The Jew paused and listened; his quick ear apprised him of her presence, and of another beside hers.

"Castalia, who is with thee?"

"It is I!"

At the sound of his voice the Jew started, and over the brown worn sternness of his face, Chandos saw the look that had come there when he had spoken his name in the blind man's ear.

"It is I," he continued, as he passed up the sea-stairs, and stood beside the Israelite on the breadth of the marble landing-place. "You have been good and pitiful to a life that is very dear to me, I hear. Take my deepest gratitude for every tenderness you have shown her, every pang you have striven to spare her."

Over the old man's face swept the look of pain and of shame that had been there in the after-midnight in Paris, —a look that hardened instantly into a rugged iron calm.

"I have served her little," he said, briefly. "The maiden has gained her own bread by the choirs of her Church, and the sale of flowers while flowers bloomed. I owe her more than she owes me. And what is she to *you?*"

"The only thing I love."

A sigh rose to the Hebrew's lips. Castalia's life had been precious to him; he had grown to listen for her voice, and her step, and her presence, as the aged listen for the only thing that reminds them of the world in which they once had place: he knew that she would be lost to him now. But the rigid austerity of his face kept its reticence.

"Love! And you left her to wander and starve?"

"I had no knowledge of her fate. *Had* I left her as you think, I should merit now your worst reproach, your worst rebuke."

"Pardon me, sir. *I* should not have doubted your mercy. Yet, for the child's sake, I would hear more. Is she your daughter?"

"Mine! God forbid!"

The Hebrew turned his sightless eyes on Castalia.

"Wilt thou leave us?"

She passed from them into the darkness of the palace-entrance. The Hebrew bent his face so that the moon-light which he felt was on it, should not be shed there.

"Sir, I have no title to arraign you. Yet they tell me she has a marvellous loveliness. Will you make of her but your mistress?"

"No; she shall bear my name."

"Verily? And you were ever so proud!"

"I am too much so now, perhaps. Yet I may justly be too proud to mislead what trusts me."

"Ah! your creeds were never those of your fellow-men. They are not of the world, sir,—not of the world!"

There was an acrid bitterness in the Israelite's words, because he felt a poignant suffering; he moved to feel his feeble way down the steps, to escape the presence that was one continual rebuke to him. Chandos laid his hand on him and arrested him. Memories were rising from the vague chaos of far-off remembrance; knowledge was coming to him dimly and with difficulty.

"Wait! We have other words to speak. Who was your chief, your tyrant?"

For a moment the Hebrew's frame shook in every fibre; the next, the complete control, the steel-like power of endurance, in him returned,—immovable.

"That secret will be buried with me."

"Buried? It is not buried; it is clear to me. Answer me. Your bondmaster was my foe?"

His face grew eager, and quivered with swift-rising passion, in which all softer memories were lost. The Hebrew's features never changed; they were cast in bronze, when he would.

"It may be so. Perhaps your foes are many."

"You equivocate! Answer me,—yes or no. It was John Trevenna?"

"I equivocate in nothing; I simply keep silence. I shall keep it until death."

The answer was so unmoved in its iron serenity that

not even the man who watched and who heard him could gather one sign by which to know the truth.

"Keep it! And he tortured you, chained you, cursed you!"

There was a magnificent grandeur in the old man's attitude as he raised his head.

"What of that! I swore the oath to the God of Israel; I keep it because he spared the life of the youth. The Gentiles take oaths by our God, to break them; ours are redeemed, come what will."

Chandos stood silent a moment. On his nature, even in the first agony of the desire for vengeance, the appeal could not be lost. He recognised the greatness of the fidelity, even whilst it stood like a barrier of granite between him and the justice of retribution, the knowledge of his past. But, as he gazed on the Hebrew, the light of remembrance broke on him; the crowd of the porphyry chamber came back on his memory; a great cry broke from him.

"Wait! *I* swear that this darkness shall be made light. You were among the claimants on Clarencieux?"

The Jew turned his sightless eyes, his rugged face upon him, impassive as death.

"Say that I was; what does that prove! There were many claimants, and just ones."

"It proves enough to me! A Jew firm was the largest of my creditors: that firm was yours. Your tyrant ruled it: that tyrant was my traitor. My wealth went to him: he devoured it. The world called me mad: I was so, for I was his dupe! Answer me: your torturer and my enemy were one?"

The Hebrew's features were impenetrable as the night; he was stirred no more than were the marbles around him.

"You speak widely, sir, and without warrant. It is

16*

vain to appeal to me. I neither deny nor affirm; I keep
the silence for which I suffered."

"Suffered!—and for a fiend?"

"Suffered,—for my oath's sake."

The grandeur of the resistance to him wrung his
reverence from Chandos, even whilst the anguish, the fire,
the impotence of awakening wrath and awakening knowledge rose in tumult.

"Keep it!" he said, while his voice rang with the
might of his passions. "Kept or broken, it shall avail
nothing to guard him from my vengeance. I know
enough, without more knowledge, to stamp his infamy in
the sight of men. Those lost deeds, that hidden usury,
that trading in the trust and the necessities of his friends,
—it will blast his name through Europe!"

The Hebrew's harsh calm tones answered him with
judicial brevity.

"What do you know? Nothing! You suspect;—you
will speak on suspicion; baseless and unproved, the accusation will recoil harmless from the accused, to brand
the accuser as a libellist and a false witness."

Chandos quivered in every limb as he heard; the rage
of justice paralysed from its stroke, of truth impotent to
make manifest its truth, seized him with maddening misery.
He was once again in the coils of the net that had wound
itself so long about his life to fetter and destroy.

"Oh, God!" he said, "why will you shield your destroyer and mine? why will you shelter the iniquity you
have said you repent? Your own soul is noble: what
sympathy have you with the villany you have abjured?
Your own sacrifice has been grand: why will you have
so much tenderness of sins that are vile as murder?"

"I have none; but I am true to him by whom my
son was spared."

"What! are traitors, and tyrants, and criminals to find such loyalty, whilst honest men are betrayed and abjured by the score? Have you no pity, no remorse, for the wrongs of a life?"

"Sir, if I had ever known either pity or remorse, I had not been what I was."

Chandos' hand clenched on the old man's shoulder. Conviction, strong, unbearable, intense, was on him that this Hebrew held the secret of his enemy's hatred, and that John Trevenna was the curse of both their fates; yet he was as impotent to wring the truth as to force blood from the cold black marbles beneath their feet.

"Listen! I have pitied you from my heart, honoured your endurance from my soul; but I have the wrongs of a lifetime to avenge. I *know*, as though the proof were by me, that my foe is one with your master, that fraud and treachery and baseness had more share in my ruin than my own extravagance. Speak now, or—as we believe in one God—the law shall make you."

The Hebrew turned his blind eyes on him with the patience of his race.

"The law? It did its worst on me: had it power to make me speak?"

"Great Heaven! crime gets such loyalty as this, while I found love and friendship traitors!"

The Jew's bronzed face grew paler, his close-set lips shook slightly under the snowy whiteness of his beard; but he remained immovable. Chandos stood above him, his eyes black, his teeth set.

"Man—man! if you ever loved, if you ever hated, give me my vengeance!"

"Sir," said the Hebrew, with his grave and caustic speech, "beware! You lust for an evil thing."

"No! I claim a barren justice."

"Justice is not given on earth. Hear me. You urge
me to evil——"

"I urge you to the service of truth, to the chastisement of infamy——"

"It may be so; yet hear me. You tempt me to evil,
because you tempt me to forswear the sole fidelity in gratitude that redeems my baseness. I know your life; I
know your thoughts; I know that you have loved men
well, served them unweariedly, taught them high and
gracious things. When you heard my story, you called
it a martyrdom whose nobility men seldom reached: why
call it now a sheltering of evil, because your own wish
is to behold that evil unearthed? You told me then I had
atoned for my past: why tell me now I only stain it
further? This is unworthy you,—untrue to your creeds.
Were your passions now unloosened, your life now un-
biassed, you would be the first to say to me, 'Before all,
keep your oath sacred.'"

Chandos' hand fell, his breath came loud and quick;
he stood like one pierced to the heart with an exceeding
bitterness.

"Sir," went on the Hebrew's unbroken, impassive
voice, "it is true that you have a secret of mine that you
can torture me with, if you will; but I have read your
nature wrong if you will use against me the weapons that
I, unconscious, placed in your hold. You have passed
through vast calamities since the day that I stood amidst
your spoilers; they will have failed to teach you what I
believe they have taught you, if you tempt another to
dishonour because through that dishonour you believe
your own desires would be served, your own revenge
gained to you."

Chandos stood silent still; a mortal struggle shook him.

"I am no god. What you ask of me is a god's divine,

impartial justice! I claim a man's right, a man's weakness, a man's sin of vengeance."

"It may be so: yet, if you be true to yourself, it is that very impartiality of justice—all hard though ·it may be—that you will render."

There was a long silence, in which only the lapping of the water sounded. No demand that honour had ever made on him had been so merciless in cruelty as this, no contest that had wrung his life so hard to meet. His voice was very low as it fell at last on the stillness.

"You are right! I tempt you no more."

The Hebrew bowed his head.

"There a great life spoke."

Then, slowly, with his sightless, feeble movement, he passed down the water-stairs till the dignity of his dark, bent form, was lost in the breadth of the shadows. Chandos let him go, unarrested. He stood there, blind to all around him, dead to all memory save one. The blackness of night was on his soul, and the violence of baffled passion shook him as a storm-wind the strength of the cedars. There was but one terrible thirst upon him, — the thirst for his vengeance.

Where he stood, his arm dropped as though the nervous force of it were broken; his eyes gazed without sight down the shaft of the gloomy stairs, where the water glistened cold and gliding in the flicker of the moon. The conviction of his foe's guilt was scored on his mind as though he had beheld it written up through the length and breadth of the lands! the meshes of his own impotence for chastisement and retribution bound him helpless as one paralysed; the human lust of evil possessed him as his madness possessed Saul.

A while, — and in the soft Venetian darkness of the young night Castalia stole to him, she touched his hand with the suppliant kiss of her tender homage, she raised upward to his face the dreamy lustre of her eyes.

"My lord, is regret with you because you were too merciful to me? If it be, say it. My life is only lived for you."

His arms drew her to him in the vibration of the passions that beat in him.

"Regret!—when in you I find all the consolation I shall ever know? Castalia, dark hours come on me: you must not fear them. My heart is sick because of its own failure. Tempted, I am weak as water, I am cruel as murderers. I have lived, and striven, and suffered, and sought to serve men, only at the last to reel back into a barbarian's lust,—to be athirst with a Cain's desires!"

For the evil that his foe had wrought him had not yet reached its end, and it poisoned now the first sweet hours of reviving happiness.

It might go farther yet, and close his life in crime.

CHAPTER V.
The Codes of Arthur.

In the darkness of large, jutting marble blocks, in another quarter of Venice, Ignatius Mathias held his almost nightly vigil,—the vigil which had but one aim and but one reward,—to hear the passing footstep of his son. Agostino had come to Venice in the restlessness of one who has peace nowhere and vainly thinks with each new refuge to escape what haunts him. He lived the life that a hare leads in hunting seasons: the season may pass and leave the animal in safety, unmolested under the shade of fern and thyme, but none the less with every hour must its heart beat, and its sleep be broken, and its nerves tremble at every crack of the branches, every sough of the wind, lest its hunters be out on its scent. Years would

go, and his tyrant need nothing of him; but all the same
he was never sure but that some cruel task might any day
be required at his hands, and no alternative left him but
to do its work, however abhorrent, or to brave the shame
of public slander and public exposure, from which the
feminine terrors of his nature had so long shrunk as more
unendurable than death. But of this tyranny that ruled
his life his father knew nothing: he heard of the painter's
fame, of his talent, of his growing wealth, of his adoration, of his art, of his love for his Spanish wife, and he
believed Agostino happy with the happiness that he had
himself sacrificed all to purchase for "the lad." He was
ever but a youth in the old man's thoughts, a beautiful,
yielding, caressing, tender-natured boy, won by a smile,
crushed by a stern word, as he had been when the eyes
whose blindness now kept him ever young in their mé-
mory had last looked upon the graciousness of his early
years. That Agostino could grow older with the growth
of time never came to the remembrance of one who had
parted with him in his boyhood; he had eternal youth in
the love of the sightless man. There is thus far mercy
for the blind, that they know nothing of the stealing
change that robs the beauty which is cherished from the
eyes that cherish it, slowly and cruelly, until the last
change of all.

Ignatius Mathias stood now, so guiding himself by
the marvellous compensative instinct which his calamity
confers, that he was secured from all passers-by by the
jutting-out of the stone, and his long, black, floating
garments could scarce be told from the marble that
shrouded him. If by any chance a stray moonbeam
wandered through to the deep shelter of the statueless
niche, it would have seemed to any casual passer-by that
it was filled by some sculptured figure of prophet or of

priest which was in perfect keeping with the solemn and
melancholy grandeur round.　He was listening eagerly,
intently; but his hands were clenched on the marble
where he leaned, and his heart ached with the burden
of remorse, the dry, tearless, hopeless grief of age.

It had pierced him to the quick to remain steeled to
Chandos' prayer, as it had been bitter to him to show no
sign of respect in the porphyry hall at Clarencieux, when
all the heartless crowd about him had been moved and
awed by the dignity of adversity.　The keen Israelite
could reverence from his soul the man who in his deadliest passions was still obedient to the demand and the
duty of justice; and he felt that he too had sinned towards him.

"It was a villanous sin to rob him," he mused,—
"vilest treachery, vilest murder.　He heaped coals of fire
on my head with every one of his just words; and yet it
would bring him nothing even if he knew all.　*We* were
always within the law.　He would wreck all the nobility
of his nature in the blood-hound thirst of vengeance;
he would do what would belie his life.　Pshaw! why do I
deal with these sophistries?　If he slew his foe, and slew
me, it would be no more, as he said, than barren justice.
But give it him I never will.　Sin or martyrdom, whichever it be, added crime or atoning fidelity, I will die
silent; I will be true to him by whom my son was spared,
—true to the last."

His face set in stern, unflinching resolve, the firmness
of silence; the dignity of faithfulness, which would be
true to its bond, even if that bond were forged by crime,
lent it nobility; then the caustic and ironic bitterness in
which his temper had steeled itself long to all gentler
things passed over it.

"Why should I care for *one?*" he muttered.　"There

were thousands. If I ever spoke, I should unloose hell-dogs; if I ever made atonement by turning traitor, what lives I should have to summon out of their graves to hear my *mea culpa*, if I called all my auditors!"

The smile was evil on his face, though that evil was more sad than other men's sorrow. His hands had been as millstones, grinding all that went through them to powder, that the grist might feed the yawning sack of money-lust. If all his accusers would rise against him, the tomb must yield up its dead.

A slight sound caught his ear; he started, and listened as Indians listen. He had kept this vigil long and often, in divers scenes and divers hours,—under the cold shadow of green leaves, under the driving snow of winter nights, under the broad gables of antique houses, under the drenching rains of autumn skies, under the mild stars of vintage eves, moving unweariedly in the changing, restless track of an artist's wanderings, content if reward came in the echo of a laugh, in the distant murmur of a voice, in the passing of a far-off footfall. Unseen, unthanked, unrecompensed, save by such fleeting things as could be borne on summer air or heard through winter blasts, his great and silent love endured. A step passed by him; he held his breath as it went; he knew that his son was nigh. Then the faint sound died to silence, and the light died from his face; this was all, all that was left him,—one moment to be scored against a martyrdom; and his lips moved in voiceless prayer and thanksgiving. He breathed his blessing on the life that passed by him in the hush of the night; he was grateful even for so little. It sufficed; his son lived.

———

Where the silver lustre of the Venetian moon poured

down through lofty casements of a desolate palace-chamber, Chandos, as he looked into the eyes that once more spoke to him in the language of his youth, strove to put from him the remembrance of his traitor, the thirst for his vengeance; and he could not. The darkness of a violent and unsparing hatred had seized him. Hate was foreign to his nature, yet it had sprung in growth fast as poison-plants from poison-seeds in the rank soil of Africa. With his foe in his hands now, he could have stamped his life out with as little mercy as men show who crush a rattlesnake. The fangs of a snake had bitten him; the coils of a snake strangled him; the virus of a snake entered his whole life to change and wither and consume it. The snake was Treachery; and he could have killed the traitor with the fierce meed of such justice as men took when the sword made alike law and judge and avenger.

He strove to thrust it from him, and it would return, —return to darken and embitter the sweetness of a love long denied to him, vivid and voluptuous as any that had usurped him in the years when the fairness of woman had made his paradise. He had left her a child, to pity, to caress, to play with, without deeper thought; he found her in a few brief months, extreme as her youth still was, a woman in her superb beauty, her courage, her genius, her patrician grace, her far-reaching meditative thought, her endurance of suffering, her fearlessness through danger. With the simplicity of a child, she had left Vallombrosa on the sting of coarse jests of the peasantry, that she had resented without wholly comprehending, of imputed dishonour to her and to him which had roused her like a young lioness, though she had but dimly known their meaning,—left it, and flung herself on the unknown, untraversed world with the simplicity of a child. She was now abandoned to him, to his will, to his wish, to his power, asking him nothing of his life, yielding him an absolute submission, and seeking no more of him or of the world than the one joy of his presence. But the intense strength of a supreme passion vibrated through the unquestioning idolatry she rendered him. "*Poco spero, nulla chiedo*," had been the soul of the reverence she bore him, but with it ran the burning warmth of the suns that had shone on her from her birth.

It was the love of which he had dreamed,—the love which he had desired, and never found.

In those long hours of the spring night, while the lulling of the water sounded softly through the open casements, and no light was about them except the light of the great stars above Venice, he almost resigned himself to their enchantment, he almost cheated himself into the belief that the years of his youth had revived,—almost. The desire of vengeance, the baffled justice, the impotence to cast off one stone from the granite cairn that had been heaped to crush his peace beneath it, all these that were upon him forbade him the one lotus-draught he longed for,—forgetfulness.

Love itself is youth, and cannot revive without bringing some light of youth back with it.

With her, his life seemed once more what it had been when, in the languor of the East, and under the glow of Southern skies, he had loved and been loved in the careless vivid sweetness of a poet's passions, deep-hued and changing as a sapphire in the sun. But when later he left her for the few short hours remaining of the night, left her lest foul tongues should touch her defenceless innocence, the spell broke. His soul was set upon his vengeance,—set in the impotence of David's desperation: "How long, O Lord! how long!" It seemed to him as though no retribution could ever serve to wash out his wrongs, and stamp his traitor what he was in the sight of the people who followed and believed in him; it seemed to him as though no justice that could rend the living lie of this man's life asunder, and show its hidden vileness to the world he fooled, would ever cut deep enough, ever reach wide enough, ever avail enough to avenge the endless treachery with which his foe had taken food and raiment and wealth from him with one hand, to thieve and stab him with the other. "My God!" he thought, as he went alone through the stillness of the after-midnight, "what could vengeance do sufficient? None could give me back all the world I have lost, all the years I have consumed, all the joy he wrecked for ever, all the youth he slew in me at one blow. Vengeance! the worst would be as a drop beside an ocean."

If the means came to his hand to strike his enemy down from the eminence of station and the fruitage of achieved ambition, it could do at its best so little; if it could destroy the future, it could efface nothing of the past, it could change none of these years that had seemed so endless, through whose course he had dwelt in banishment and bitterness and seen his Iscariot caressed and crowned. Though his hand should ever dash down the brimming cup of Trevenna's success, the uneven balance between them could never be redressed; the world-wide wrong must ever remain unrequited, uneffaced. What could give him back all it had killed for ever in him? What could bring back to earth the gallant and beloved life of the old man whom it had slain? What could restore him to all he had forfeited through it? What could make him ever again as he had been when its ruin had blasted the glory from his years for ever?

Where he went in the silence of the late night, past

the great Austrian palaces, that were filled with revelry
and music, and the fragrance of flowers, and the masking
of Carnival balls, with the gay riots of the melodies echoing through the conquered city, and the wreathing of
gold and silk and many-coloured blossoms hanging all
alight with lamps over the melancholy and the dignity of
the time-honoured, sea-worn marbles, the rich, rolling,
silver cadence of a Bacchic chant, sung with careless
mirth and deep Olympian laughter, rang across the waters
and above the strains of the Austrian music. It was the
voice of Philippe d'Orvâle.

In his Carnival dress, with its scarlet-and-gold floating back, and the light of the stars and the crescents of
lamps glittering on its jewelled brilliance, he came down
a flight of stone stairs from some reckless revelry, the
song on his lips, the laughter still given back in answer
to a challenge from some fair maskers that leaned above,
the fragrance of wine only just dashed from the auburn
silver-flecked waves of his beard. "*Vivre selon son cœur!*"
was the epitome of "the Mad Duke's" life, as of Diderot's;
and, as in Diderot's, there was a grand, careless, Titan
majesty in this handsome head, tossed back in such fiery
defiance, such sunny laughter, against the laws of con-
ventionality and the snow barriers of prejudice. Life
was too rich with him to be stinted by a niggard measure;
its joys, its passions, its treasures, its scope, too wide, to
be meted out by the foot-rule of custom; and while men
of his own years grew grey about him, the prince-
Bohemian laughed at Time, and found the roses of his
wine-feasts' blossom never fading to his hand.

His Bacchan chaunt paused; a gentle, softened look
gleamed from the flash of his brown, fearless eyes, as in
the shadow of the street he saw Chandos.

"Ah! *c'est toi!*" And in the touch of his hand as it

fell on the shoulder of the man he loved best, there was the welcome of a friendship close as brotherhood.

Not a tree had ever been felled at Clarencieux, not a picture been stirred, not a horse, useless from age, been shot, not a trifle in the whole length of the chambers, not an unfinished sketch in the forsaken atelier, not a disordered manuscript in the solitude of the Greuze Cabinet, been touched, under Philippe d'Orvâle's reign. With him the exile was honoured; with him the memory of the disinherited was kept green and cherished and sacred in the hearts of the people. "I am but his viceroy: keep your homage for the absent," he had said once when the peasantry had addressed him as their lord.

"So! you are in Venice!" he said, softly, where he paused in the deeper shadow, with the festoons of light and the arabesques of flower-wreathed balcony far above, reflected in the black surface of the canal. "I half hoped to meet you here when I came for this riotous Carnival time with which our Austria Felix tries to drown the murmurs of her prey. You have not been long?"

"I came but to-day. Lulli needed me——"

"Lulli! what ails him?" This princely Bohemian, whose own strength was so superb and whose existence so joyous, had always had a singular compassion and tenderness for the cripple whose art was his only happiness: his home had always been open to him, his aid always ready for him. The strong hand of the aristocrat had often raised the fame of the musician above the envy or the rivalry that had tried to crush it, and not a little of the wealth given to Lulli for his music had gone in secret from D'Orvâle, unguessed by the recipient.

"Nothing ails him," Chandos answered, wearily; his thoughts were far in other things. "But a singer has been arrested here for giving some of his music in public,

—some song of freedom too free for Austria; and his heart is set on her liberation."

"Ah! I will see to that. They shall give her her liberty in twenty-four hours. The fools! Every weakness persecuted becomes strength against its persecutor when once hunted into martyrdom. And they will not know that!"

"When they do, human life will have entered on a very different phase from what we live in."

Philippe d'Orvâle flashed a quick glance on him. This wild, headlong, insouciant rioter could read men like a book.

"Tell me, tell me; you have had some fresh pain,— some new wrong?"

"Scarcely; but I have had fresh temptation, and I have little strength for it."

"You always underrate your strength!"

"Not I. Sometimes I think that were impossible. We flatter ourselves we have strength, we pride ourselves on our codes, on our philosophies, on our forbearance; and the moment a spark is dropped on our worst passions, they flare alight, and consume all else!"

"May-be! But the age rants too much against the passions. From them may spring things that are vile; but without them life were stagnant, and heroic action dead. Storms destroy; but storms purify."

"There is truth in that; but we are, at our best, half passion, half intelligence, and at a touch the brute will rise in us, and strangle all the rest. No man can wholly suppress the animal in him; and there are times when he will long to *kill* as animals long for it."

"Ay!" Philippe d'Orvâle's fair frank face flushed, and his right hand clenched; he had known that longing.

"Tell me—tell me whether to-night I was weak as a fool, or did but barren justice. I barely can tell myself,

John Trevenna has been the foe of my life; you know that——"

"Know it! Yes!—a hound who turned on his master! By my faith, when I see that man in honour and eminence, I know what Georges Cadoudal meant when he said, 'Que de fautes j'ai commis de ne pas étouffer cet homme-là dans mes bras!' If there be a regret in my life, it is that *I* did not kill him where he stood laughing and taunting on your hearth, while you went out to your exile!"

"You left it for me!" There was a terrible meaning in the brevity of the words. "Well, to-night I could have had my vengeance on him, to-night I could have unearthed his villany to hold it up before the nation that takes him as a chief; to-night I know as though I saw it written before me that he betrayed me, chicaned me, robbed me as usurers rob; and—I let justice go!"

"Let it go! Are you mad?"

"That is what I doubt! I would sell my own life for justice on him; I fear I could kill him with less thought than men kill adders!—and yet I let it go. I could not reach it without forcing another to break his oath, to forswear his conscience, to sin against the only redemption of his life: what could I do?"

"Do? I would have crushed ten thousand to have struck at *him!* Tell me more."

"I cannot. It is another's secret, not my own; were it mine, you should know it. All the laws of justice and humanity bound me powerless; I could not break through them. I had honoured this man's fidelity when I was in ignorance whom it was rendered to: I could not dishonour it because I learned that it was shown to my enemy."

"Few men would have stayed for that."

"May-be! It was hard for me to stay for it. It is hard as death now! It were surely small crime to tempt any one to betray a traitor; it were but to turn against him his own poisoned weapons. One oath broken more or less, what would it be in self-defence against one who has broken thousands, broken every tie and bond of gratitude, of honesty? And yet—right is right. I could not bid another turn betrayer because I had been betrayed. Look! to have my justice of vengeance, I must have done injustice to one placed, in his own unconsciousness and by his own trust, in my power. Which could I choose?—to forego it, or to wrong him?"

Philippe d'Orvâle lifted his lion's head with a toss of his lion's mane; his eyes rested on Chandos with a loyal, flashing, noble light.

"*Forego it!* Your vengeance were ill purchased by any falsehood to yourself."

Chandos stretched out his hand in silence; D'Orvâle's met it in a close firm grasp. They said no more; they understood each other without words: only, as they parted farther on in the lateness of the night, the prince-Bohemian's regard dwelt on him with something that was wistful for once almost to sadness,—a thing that had no place in the brilliant and heedless career of the "mad duke."

"Chandos, you were made for Arthur's days, not for ours. Those grand creeds avail nothing—except to ruin yourself. Yet you would rather have them? Well, so would I, though I am but a wine-cup roysterer."

As he spoke, the lights burning above among a sea of flowers and colours, in crescents and stars and bands of fire, shone on the leonine royalty of his head and the majesty of his height, all lustrous with the scarlet and the gold and the diamonds of his Carnival attire. There was an unusual softness in his brown, bold eyes, an unusual touch of melancholy in his voice:—that one memory of him was never to pass away from Chandos.

17*

CHAPTER VI.

Et tu, Brute!

THROUGH the brilliance of the earliest sun-dawn a gondola shot swiftly through the silent highways, with the light on the water breaking from under its prow in a shower of rippling gold, and the brown shadows lazily sleeping under the arches of bridges, and under the towering walls, as though they were loath to wake and flee before the rising of day. It was just morning; no more, but morning in all its radiance, with the scarlet heads of carnations unclosing, and the many-coloured hues warm over land and sea, with the darkness only left in the hushed aisles of churches, and the breath of the sea-wind blowing balmily from the Adriatic.

Guido Lulli, where he leaned in the vessel, saw it all with an artist's eye, felt it all with an artist's heart, and wove magical dreams of sound from the melody of the oars. Life had been but captious with him, giving him the head of a seraph and the limbs of a stricken child, the heart of a man and the frame of a paralytic, breaking his youth into weakness and torture and starvation and strengthlessness, calling his manhood into the fame of the world and crowning him with the great masters; it had been cruel and lavish at once, taking from him all happiness, all knowledge of happiness, all consciousness of what health could mean or freedom from pain be like, all sense of "the wild joys of living" and of the liberties and heritage of manhood, taking them from him, from the hour of his birth, and making every desire of his heart an unending pang; yet—giving him in one Art, giving him with the eye, and the ear, and the temperament of genius, a sovereignty wide as the world, and a treasury of beauty that could only be closed when the touch of

death should make his sight dark and his hands motionless. Others, beholding him, saw but a pale, shattered,
silent cripple, with great wistful eyes, ever seeming to
seek what they never found,—a man whom a child could
cheat, whom a buffoon could mock, whom a stare could
make nervously and unbearably wretched; but others had
come to know that this man had a kingdom of his own
in which he was supreme, had a power of his own in
which he was godlike, and lived as far above the fever
and the fret of their own lives as the stars move above
them in their courses. He heard what they never heard,
he saw what they never saw; and to Lulli's sublime
transcendentalism the whole universe was but as one
chaunt of God.

As his gondola glided now, he was looking dreamily
upward: he was in Venice because the young Venetian
had been arrested for singing a song of liberty from one
of his operas, might be imprisoned, might be scourged
perhaps, and he came to save her from chastisement, or
to insist that he had a right to share it. He knew nothing
of her except the fact that she had suffered through singing his music in defiance of the usurpers; but he had a
lion-boldness where wrong menaced weakness, and a pure
chivalrous instinct conquered, whenever it was needed,
the shrinking sensibilities and the physical feebleness of
this man, whom other men had called for three parts of
his life—a fool. The buzz and the fret and the money-
seeking crowds of the world passed by him unnoticed,
unheard; he took no more heed of the stir about him than
if he had been a palm-tree set in their midst, and they
thought him a fool accordingly; but let one spark from
the flame of wrong, one blow from the gauntlet of tyranny,
fall on anything near him, and the enthusiast, the dreamer,
the isolated visionary, became on the instant filled with

fire and with action.   And for this yet more they called him fool: the man who does not care for his own purse and his own palate, but only rouses for some alien injury, what is he but the Quixote of all ages?

As he went now, to welcome to Venice the one friend of his life, he looked up at that towering marble and the blue of the cloudless skies above.   Above a lofty archway, out of an oval casement, with her arms resting on the jasper ledge, and the umber darkness behind her, so that as the sun fell full upon her face and her hair she was like one of those old master-pictures where the golden head of a woman gazes out from a black unbroken surface of deepest shade, leaned Castalia.   Her eyes were glancing above, following a flight of white pigeons whose wings flashed silver in the light; and on her face was the look, more spiritualised than any smile, more intense than any radiance, more hushed and yet more passionate than any words can paint, of that happiness which is "the sweetest vintage of the vine of life."

Lulli glanced up and saw her there, leaning down over the dark mosaics; he strove to rise, ere the boat had swept past.

"Valeria!"

As the name left his lips, reason and memory and the space of years were all as naught; he was back in the days of his youth and his poverty; he believed that his lost one lived unchanged, unaged; with the warmth of southern suns upon it, and made richer and fairer yet by that higher and softer light it wore, the face of his lost darling looked on him once more from the jasper setting of the Venetian casement.   A gondola, that had followed him from his dwelling, glided up swiftly in his wake, and came side by side with his own; from the awning a woman's hand was stretched, and touched his arm.

"Signor Lulli, one word with you."

"With me1 Whom——1"

"A friend to you, and to one you lost1 Let us wait a moment, there in the shadow."

The speaker who had arrested him leaned from beneath her awning, her hand lying on the side of his gondola; he could not see her features, but her voice was very melodious and low.

"There was once a life that was very dear to you in the old days at Arles1"

He trembled violently. The thought of touching at last the secret buried so long overcame him, as when they come, at last, upon the gold vein, the toil-worn and heart-sickened gold-searchers are beaten with their joy.

"Dear to me1 Yes, God knows1 You bring tidings of Valeria1"

She whose form was lost in the shapeless folds of a Carmelite's habit, and whose face was obscured by the hood of the order, stooped from under the black shade of the gondola.

"Land; and I will tell you all I have to telL"

He obeyed her, his weakened limbs bearing him slowly and with labour up the water-stairs. Fronting them was the porch of a church,—a great, grey, dim, noble place, with marvellous carvings of time-browned stone, and feathery grasses floating from its colossal height, and Titan statues that looked blind and weary down from their niches on the water below, as though evil days had fallen on them and on their Venice.

The entrance was wide and of vast depth, a lofty cavern, roofed and walled with carvings on which countless hearts and hands had spent their lifetime's labour; and from it, in the body of the building, were seen by changing glimpses, as the air moved the vast moth-eaten fall of Genoese velvet to and fro, glimpses of twilight gloom with the ethereal tracery of the ivory pyx gleaming white from the shadow, and the marble limbs of a crucified Christ nailed against a dark pillar of Sienna marble. She motioned him to rest on the stone bench within the porch, and stood herself beside him. He never asked her who she was; he never thought of her save as one who knew Valeria; her religious habit made her sacred in his eyes, and his soul held but one thought,—the fate of the one lost to him. His eyes sought the Carmelite's with longing anxiety.

"Speak now! Valeria?"

"Is dead."

The word was spoken very gently, but it dealt him a keen blow; though he had long said that she was dead to him,—said it in the bitterness of his soul when he had first heard of her flight to dishonour,—he had unconsciously cherished hope that some day, ere it should be too late, he would find her.

"Dead? and without one word for me! But that face yonder?—it was hers!"

His heart was full, and he spoke on its impulse; he never remembered that he addressed a stranger; he only knew that he spoke to one who might give him some link with his long-broken past. His life had been entirely uneventful, and the few things that had marked it held him for ever, as they could never have held a life of action.

"She brings you some memory?" pursued his questioner. The voice was subdued, and yet had a certain imperious command in it that would not be resisted and was unaccustomed to delay as to disobedience. The eyes of the cripple turned with pathetic entreaty upon her.

"You must know that she does, or why speak to me

of her! Whoever you are, whoever she be, tell me, for
the love of mercy."

"She whom you now saw is her daughter."

The Provençal's face flushed scarlet, his eyes lighted
with an infinite tenderness, that flashed and darkened
into the fiery wrath that had used to arise in them against
the unknown lover of the last of his name.

His teeth set; his hands clenched.

"Her daughter? My God! And *he*——"

"He—led Valeria where dishonour was forgotten in
recklessness, and shame was lost in diamonds and wine
and evil laughter."

"His name?" It was but a whisper; yet a vibration
ran through it that told without words the strength which
this frail and suffering-worn cripple would find against
the spoiler and polluter of the only life round which his
memory, his imagination, and his heart had ever woven
the fair, if the vain, dreams of love.

"Can you bear its telling?"

"I will not bear its denial. His name? and may my
worst vengeance light——"

"Hush! You know not whom you curse."

"Nor care! If he live, my hate shall find him. His name?"

"Wait! Be calmer ere you hear it."

"Calmer! when her child lives there?"

"Her child knows nothing of her parentage! nor
what that parentage is can I well tell. Valeria's life grew
very evil."

The dark blood grew purple over Lulli's delicate features, his lips turned white as death; he suffered excru-
ciatingly; no noble was more tenacious of the honour of
his name than he.

"Speak! Who was her tempter? Who lured her first
to her sin?"

"Wait! Hear her history first. She was a beautiful, heartless, wayward, unscrupulous woman, to whom honour was nothing, to whom levity and shame were sweet."

"He made her that, if ever she became it. The greater, then, his crime. His name?"

"Patience: do not hasten your own bitterness."

"I hasten to end it. It can only be quenched in vengeance."

"She lived for a while in sinful magnificence; but she died in the utmost poverty, in a Tuscan village. It is a common fate."

He shook in his whole frame as he heard.

"And then you bid me withhold my curse? She died in want, after a short, shameful life of gilded vice? *No* curse is wide enough to reach him, if he drove her to that infamy."

"It was scarce his fault; she loved the fatal power of her beauty but too well. She died at Fontane Amorose: if you need a witness, it is here." She stretched out to him a small, silver, heart-shaped relic-box, worn and almost valueless, on which were rudely graven the words "Valeria Lulli." A moan broke from him as he saw it; his face grew white, his eyes filled with tears.

"Oh, God! I gave her this myself; she was a child then,—a child so beautiful, so innocent!" His voice sank, his head drooped; the sight, the touch, of the little relic struck him to the heart; the hour of its gift came back on him as though lived but yesterday,—the hour when, with many a denial of self, he had treasured up coins till he had bought the thing that had been the wish of her heart, and slung it, as his recompense, round the fair throat of the laughing child, who paid him with her kisses.

"She left it, on her death-bed, with a contadina for me. I had known her in days evil to us both. There

were a few feeble lines to me with it, unfinished. The
peasant kept it, telling no one of it, and thinking it of
value for its holiness, till a few months ago, when the
child Castalia was lost from Fontane, the woman's conscience woke, and she sent it to me. I have left the
world; I am in a religious order now: thus it was long
in finding me. Once received, and hearing also for the
only time of this young girl's life, my first wish was to
seek out you, and leave you to become, if you should
choose, the avenger of the dead, the protector of the
living."

The words had a pathetic and solemn earnestness.
Lulli bowed his head, and pressed his lips on the silver
heart.

"I swear to be both," he said, simply. "And *now*,
once more, his name?"

"Her lover was—Chandos!"

A cry, such as that which men give on a battle-field,
broke from him,—a cry of torture.

"It is false—false as hell!" he swore, in the agony of
his passion. "No lie ever touched his lips; no treachery
ever belonged to him."

"No," said the Carmelite, gently: "you are right.
But Valeria Lulli was only known to *him* as—Flora de
l'Orme."

The Provençal's attenuated form seemed suddenly to
shrink and wither and lose all life as he heard; the name
came back on his memory after long oblivion of it; he
had used to hear it in those days that were gone, the
name of the magnificent, reckless, extravagant adventuress
who had wasted her lover's gold right and left, and given
but a mocking laugh at his ruin.

"He met her in Arles," pursued the voice of his companion, with a gentle pity in its intonation. "She left

Arles with him. She was known to him only by her *nom de fantaisie.* What her life became you are aware."

He scarcely heard her; his hands had clenched on the stonework; he quivered from head to foot; the flame in his eyes had died in an anguish beside which the mere fury for vengeance was dwarfed and stilled as he gazed down on the silver relic.

"O Christ! have pity. I swore my oath against *him!*"

The words were inarticulate in his throat; every fibre in him thrilled with the fire of his rage against Valeria's tempter, and every debt his life had owned bound him in fealty to the man whom in his blind haste he had, unknowing, cursed. He loved with such loyalty, such faith, such honour, such self-oblivion, as those with which patriots love their country, the one in whom he had found the succour of his existence, the giver of every earthly gift that had redeemed him from the bondage of poverty and pain; and in him he must now for ever see the foe on whom he had sworn to wreak the wrongs and the shame of the dead.

The man to whom he had held his very life a debt to be yielded up if need arose, from whose lips alone he turned for the sole praise he heeded, whose liberal and royal charity had lifted him from a beggar's death-bed into the light of the world's renown, and to whom his heart had clung more tenderly and truly in the darkness of adversity than even in the splendour of fair fortune, was the injurer against whom through the long course of so many years he had cherished his silent and baffled hate!

The dead love and the living love, the bonds that bound him to her memory and the bonds that bound him to his gratitude, wrenched him asunder,—divided,—agonized. Choosing betwixt them, he must sin, whichever he cleaved to,—be faithless, whichever he elected.

He let his head fall on the cold stone arm of the
bench; he knew nothing, felt nothing, was conscious of
nothing; he only seemed numbed and killed with this
one thought,—the feud that rose to stand for ever between
him and the man he loved with the love of the son of
Saul for David.

"Oh, God!" he moaned; "and I ate of his bread, I
was saved by his mercy!"

The Carmelite looked at him, then gently glided away,
leaving the silver relic in his hand. He never heard her
or remembered her: he sat in the grey shadows of the
church-entrance as though he were turned to stone, silent
and senseless as the robed statues of the Hebrew kings
that had kept their motionless vigil above, while the centuries passed uncounted, and the glory of Venetia fell.

He could not have told how long or how brief a time
had swept by: he had sense and memory for nothing
save the one knowledge that had come to him. The street
and the church were alike deserted: nothing aroused him.
He sat there as in a stupor, his clasped hands clenched
above his head. The lapping of the water, the warmth
of the sun, the flight of time, were all lost to him; the
great pall of the velvet wavered with the wind, the
gleam of the white passion was seen from out the gloom
within; all was still, and he had no consciousness except
his misery.

A hand touched his shoulder; the only voice he
loved fell on his ear.

"Lulli! you here! What ails you?"

The Provençal started and shuddered under the
touch as at the touch of flame; he staggered to his feet, his
eyes looking at his solitary friend with the wild piteous-

ness of a dog that has been struck a death-blow by its master's hand. His lips parted, but no sound came from them; he gasped for breath, and could find no words; there, face to face with the saviour of his life, with the spoiler of the honour dearer than his own, the force of the old love borne so long, the force of the old vengeance so long sworn, rose in twin strength, wrestling with and strangling each other.

Chandos gazed, amazed and touched with a vague dread: he laid his hand on Lulli, and drew him gently within the hushed aisles of the church, where the still, brown, sleeping shadow slept so darkly, only broken by the pale gleam of some white carving or the glow of some blazoned hue.

"You are suffering greatly.   Tell me——"

"Tell you,—oh, Christ!   How can I tell you?"

"Why not?   Did I ever fail you?"

The words had the gentle compassion that he had first heard when he had lain dying among the bleak and rugged hills of Spain; the voice had ever been sweet to him as the echoes of music, welcomed as the weary drought-parched forests welcome the stealing breath of the west wind: it pierced him to the heart, it killed him with its very gentleness. He threw his arms upward, and his cry rang shrill and agonised as a woman's.

"Great God, have pity!   Let my curse light on my own head! I knew not what I did!"

Chandos laid his hands upon his shoulders and held him there, in the twilight of the lofty narrow aisle, with the Crucifixion looming cold and white out of the mist of shade.   His eyes looked down in Lulli's, where he stood above him, and stilled him as a dog is stilled by its master's gaze.

"You rave!   What grief has befallen you?"

A convulsion shook the Provençal's frail, yielding form: he loved so utterly the life he had voted to vengeance, the life on which in his sight rested the crime of Valeria's fall, of Valeria's shame, of Valeria's death.

"Grief! grief!" he muttered, in his throat; "it is *shame*, —black, burning, endless shame! I have broken your bread, while you wrought her dishonour; I have cursed you, when my whole life is but a bond to you for debts beyond life, above life! Which is the worst sin, the worst dishonour! *I* know not!"

"Sin! dishonour! And whose?"

"Hers, and mine, and yours."

The syllables left his lips stifled and slowly; the last two barely stirred the silence. He had honoured the man to whom he spoke then as though he were a deity; he had obeyed him as though he were a king.

"*Mine!* No other living should say that to me. Mine! And for what?"

Lulli lifted his head: his wasted, misshapen frame gathered suddenly vitality and vigour; there was the dignity of wrong and of manhood in the carriage of his head.

"For this:—you were the lover of Valeria."

"Of Valeria?"

He repeated the name mechanically: it had been unspoken between them for so long; it had scarce a meaning on his ear.

"You brought her to the pomp of vice; she died in the misery of vice. I, your debtor, lived on the alms of the destroyer of the last of my name. Valeria was your mistress,—Flora de l'Orme."

The words ran cold and clear; in the moment of their speech he had forgotten all save the disgrace that had made him the guest, the debtor, the alms-taker, of the one by whom she had been tempted into the ruin that had devoured her in her youth. Chandos stood silent, his eyes fixed on Lulli's face; back on his thoughts rushed a flood of forgotten memories,—memories of the splendid, vile, pampered beauty who had stooped her rich lips to his wine and wound the scarlet roses in his hair in many a careless, riotous hour,—memories of the night when, in the studio at Clarencieux, he had paused before the picture of Arles and been haunted for a moment with the doubt of that which he now heard.

"Valeria!" he echoed, slowly, an intense pity and contrition in the tone of his voice; "Valeria! Is it possible?"

"It is true." The musician's words had a fierce, dogged misery in them, and his hand clenched on the silver heart. "A Carmelite has given me her story. She died long ago; but her wrongs do not sleep with her."

Chandos looked at him a moment, and a great pain passed over his face. Had this man also forsaken him? He could have said that this woman had been shameless ere ever he saw her, that her heart was false as her form was perfect, that gold and luxury bought her love as it would, that she had been vain, merciless, evil, corrupt to the core; but he held his peace, since to speak in his own defence would have been to pierce and wound the cripple who still believed in her.

"If this *be* true," he said, simply, "you will not doubt my faith to you, at least? You will know that I was as ignorant as you? She came from Arles—it might have told me; but I never thought that she had other name than that by which she called herself. You know—you must know—that the vilest thing on earth should have been sacred to me had I been told you heeded it."

"I believe! Nothing but truth was ever on your lips. Yet none the less were you her lover, her tempter, her

destroyer; none the less does the curse of her shameless
life, of her bondage to evil, lie with you,—you alone."

He spoke hoarsely: his hand was clenched on the
relic, his head was lifted, his eyes flashed, and over the
spiritual fairness of his face the darkness of avenging
hatred gathered.

Chandos looked at him, and a slight, quick sigh
escaped him.

"You too!" he said, involuntarily. "Well, the wrong
I did you was in ignorance: if it must part us, let us
part in peace."

To the man who had loved him, as to the enemy who
had betrayed him, he alike never quoted the claim of the
past, never argued the one reproach, "I served you." But
in the words there was a weariness beyond all speech,
there was the *et tu, Brute*, which once had pierced even
the adamant of his traitor's hate; and it cut to the heart
of the hearer deep as a scourge cuts into the bared flesh;
its very gentleness rebuked him with the keenest reproach
that could have pierced him. His life-long debt, his subject reverence, his deathless gratitude, his loyal love for
the man by whose mercy he was still amidst the living,
and by whose aid the creations of his genius had been
given their place and their name among men, rushed
back on his memory in a tide that swept aside the passions of the hour and broke asunder the chains of his
oath. He seemed to himself vile as any ingrate that ever
stabbed the heart of his benefactor. The moment of supreme temptation had come to him, the test that should
prove whether he was as others were,—loyal only whilst
the gift of generous service bound him, faithless and without memory the instant that ordeal came. The hour was
here for which he had often longed, the hour that could try
the truth of his allegiance, and in it he had been wanting.

All the tenderness of his nature, all the remorse of his heart, went out in wretchedness to the man whom he had arraigned and upbraided and wounded as though no debt of life, no years of charity and pity and succour, had stood between them; he had no thought left except the sin of his own unworthiness. He bowed down at Chandos' feet, his face sunk on his hands, his supplication passionate with all the swift and mobile emotion of his nation and his temperament.

"Monseigneur, forgive me! I knew not what I said. I swore an oath before Heaven to avenge her, but I break it now and for ever, if it must light on you. Let my curse recoil on my head; let the weight of my forsworn words be on my life; let me forsake the dead and abjure my bond. Better any crime than one thought of bitterness to you! Forgive me, for the pity of God, what the vileness of my passion spoke. If you killed me now with your own hand, you would have right. *I* should be bound to let my last breath bless you!"

Wild, incoherent, senseless, the words might be, yet they were made rich and sweet as music by the faithful love that spoke in them; they gave full recompense to Chandos for many weary years of patient faith in human life and patient forbearance with its traitors and time-servers. Against all trial, and through all suffering, the heart of this cripple was true to him; in his creeds, the one fidelity sufficed to outweigh a thousand Iscariot kisses.

He stooped and raised him gently.

"Forgiveness! It is I who must ask it. Whatever debt you think you owed me in the past, you have paid and overpaid now."

Lulli stood before him, his head still sunk, his face very white in the grey hues of the darkened aisles.

"No: there are debts which we can never pay, which

we never wish to pay," he murmured, faintly. Though his fidelity had stood its trial, the trial was not less terrible to him: in the man he loved and honoured he still saw the destroyer of Valeria, the unknown foe on whom his hate so long had fastened.

"But her daughter?" he said, suddenly, as the remembrance flashed on him,—"that beautiful child,—here in Venice——"

"Here? Where?" His voice, hoarse and rapid, cut asunder the Provençal's words; his face grew livid, a hideous dread possessed him.

"The daughter she left in Tuscany, the young girl, —Castalia."

"Hold!—O Heaven!"

Chandos staggered forward, as he had done when the bolt of his ruin had struck him: the sweat of an unutterable terror was on his brow; the agony of an unutterable guilt devoured him.

"Her daughter—*her's!*"

The words were stifled in his teeth; he could not breathe his thought aloud; the fire of a love whose very wish was nameless sin consumed him; the blankness of an utter desolation fell on him, passing all that his life had known of misery.

The Provençal watched him, paralyzed, silenced with a great bewildered fear; he swayed heavily back; guilt seemed to thrill like poison in his blood; his face was dark with the flushing of the black, stagnant veins; he reeled blindly against the sculpture of the marble Christ.

"Love between *us!* Great God! what horror!"

With the mellow flood of artificial light that still shone there, instead of the glory of the risen day, shed

about her, Héloïse de la Vivarol stood before her mirror
in the dressing-chamber of the Venetian palace that was
honoured by her for a brief space: her haughty, delicate,
regal head was lifted; the grey, heavy serge of a religious
habit fell back from the brilliantly-tinted hue of her face
and the still exquisite grace of her form: it was the habit
she had worn at a prince's Carnival ball, shrouding her
beauty, for once, under an envious disguise and in a
whimsical caprice, that she might more surely be unknown by those titled maskers with whom she had played
the carte and tierce of her state-craft fence. By mere
hazard, the caprice had served her well; her subtle, unerring wit was ever served well, alike by the weapons
she forged and the accidents that favoured her.

Now, her glance flashed a cruel triumph at her own
reflection, that was given there with the glow from the
silver branches on its bright hawk eyes and on its arched,
smiling, mocking lips. She had waited nigh twenty years,
but she had her vengeance.

"*I* have divorced them!" she thought, "for ever,—
for ever! And none can trace my hand in it, suffer as
he may, search as he will."

And none ever did.

CHAPTER VII.

Liberd.

THERE was a great tumult rising through Venice.
Swelling at the first from a distant quarter, it had been
borne nearer and nearer through the silence of the city
of the waters, the tumult as of a surging sea, as of the
roar of sullen winds,—the tumult of a people, long suffering and launched at last against their oppressors. The
sound had not penetrated the depth of the church aisles;
only its low muffled echoes could reach there, and they

had been unheard by those who stood in its solitude, lost
in the misery of their own passions. In the clear golden
morning, in the luxuriance of colour and of beauty, in
the warmth of the fragrant air, in the hush of the tranquil
streets, revolt had risen as it had risen in the great
northern hive of labour; but here, in the "sun-girt South,"
it rose for liberty; there in the gaunt, smoke-stifled Black
Country it rose for wages. Venice was athirst for her
freedom; the north-men had been hungry for so many
more coins a week.

They were but the youths whose hearts were sick,
and whose lives were aimless, like the life of Leopardi,
the children of eighteen or twenty summers, whose blood
was kindled and whose souls were pure with patriot fire;
who would have flung themselves away like dross to cut
the fettering withes from their Venetia; whose ardour
thought the world a tournament, where it sufficed to name
"God and the Right" to conquer and to see the foe reel
down; who fed their eager fancies on the memory of
Harmodius and Aristogeiton, and who refused to see that
the nations of their own day adored the Greeks in story,
but called a living patriot an "agitator" if he failed, and
sent him to the cell, the scourge, the death of felons. It
was the boyhood of Venice that had risen. The past
day had been an Austrian festa for an Austrian chief,
and the music, the laughter, the glitter, the salvoes of
artillery, the wreaths of flowers, all the costly follies, had
driven the iron deeper into the souls of those who closed
their shutters to the sound of revelry, and mourned, re-
fusing to be comforted, desolate amidst the insolence of
the usurper's magnificence and mirth. The festa, following on the arrest of a songstress beloved of the city,
who had been seized for singing an ode of liberty, had
broken their patience down, had driven them mad, had

made them believe once more, in their old sublime fatal blindness, that a pure cause and a high devotion would prove stronger than the steel and the granite of mailed might. They expiated the error as it is ever expiated; they were made the burnt-sacrifice of their own creeds.

They met with little mercy: in the sight of their foes they were but seditious malcontents, to be shot down accordingly, or pinioned alive like young eaglets taken for a caravan cage. The soldiers of Austria made swift work with them,—so swift that the hundreds who had risen with the dawn with the shout of *"Libertà"* upon their lips as with one voice, and the noble insanity of the liberator's hope beating high in their fearless breasts, were, almost ere the first echo of the chaunt had rung through the silent highways to wake the slumbering spirit of a Free Republic, shot down, cut down, well-nigh as quickly as seeding-grasses fall beneath the scythes,—were driven as the deer are driven under the fire of the guns, yielding never, but overborne by the weight of numbers and the trained skill of veteran troops, never losing their courage and their resistance and their scorn, but losing order and adhesion, and seeing their young chiefs fall in the very moment of their first gathering, seeing their long-counted enterprise, their long-watched opportunity, their long-cherished hope of union and strength and victory, fade and wither and perish under the upward course of the bright morning sun.

The tumult had been brief; the chastisement would be life-long for such as lived under the heavy iron pressure of the battalions that forced them down, through the mitraille of the balls that hissed along the brown, still waters and shook the echoes of the mighty palaces. They were young, they were nobly trained; they chose death rather than life in a prison-cell with a convict gang, than the shame of the gyves and the scourge. One band of them, some hundred, fought inch by inch, step by step, their backward passage into the great porch of the church, into the dim and solemn loneliness of the aisles, gaining breath from their enemies for a while, holding aloft still their standard,—the colours of a free Italy.

Suddenly, and with the tempest of sound without as suddenly entering there with the forcing open of the large bronze doors, they fell backward, with their faces ever to the foe, into the darkness and the silence of the edifice. The burst of clamour rolled strangely through the stillness of the avenues of stone; the conflict of the world seemed to pour like hell let loose into the sacred hush and peace; the throng of hot, heroic, ·fever-flushed, tyranny-wrung life, with the vivid colours of the banner-folds flung high above their ardent, sun-warmed faces, filled as though they had sprung from the sealed tombs where the great of Venetia lay dead, the grey, cavernous gloom of the porch, the twilight of the stretching aisles, the marble space beneath the marble Christ. Crueller wrong had never sought the refuge of sanctuary, the shelter of the altar, the shadow of the Cross. But they did not come here to ask for peace, to demand protection: they came to die with their colours untouched, with their limbs unfettered.

The bronze gates of the larger entrance were forced open by their pressure in the very moment that a horror, beside which all Chandos had ever borne looked pale and painless, rose from the depths of his past to seize the one dream of revived happiness that had come to him. In the first instant that its blow fell on him, he had no sense but of unutterable loathing, of sickening despair, before the abyss of unconscious guilt that had yawned beneath him,—no consciousness but of the living love that burned in him passionate as the love of his earliest years, and the dead love that made it hopeless and forbidden and accursed, that made it a sin before which all his life shuddered and recoiled, that made each kiss of her lips poison, each word of his tenderness crime.

As the thunder from the streets smote his ear, and the flood of the daylight poured in, he was shaken from his trance of misery as men are started from a nightmare: his eyes were bloodshot, his face flushed red, his limbs shook; he was blind and deaf, he knew neither where he was nor who had spoken; but his hands fell heavily on the shoulders of Lulli, swaying him backward.

"It is false! Castalia—her child—mine! God! such horror could not be. Do you know what she was?—a shameless, loveless, profligate woman, a vampire, whose thirst was gold,—a Delilah, who stole her lover's strength to shear him of all value. Castalia sprung from *her?* It is a lie, I tell you, coined to pollute and to divorce from me the fairest thing that ever lived or loved me!"

Lulli stared fear-stricken in his face.

"Loved you!" he echoed; "loved *you?*"

"Ay, loved me as I was never loved. And you tell me a life so pure as that was born from a courtesan! You tell me that I—I——"

The words died in his throat; he could not shape in them the ghastly thought that he flung from him as men fling off an asp's coil about their limbs. He gasped for breath, where he stood there above the man who had brought this lemure from his past: there was the ferocity of a maddened beast in him.

The bronze doors were burst open; the shock of the firing without pealed through the stillness; the throng of the young soldiers poured in. They saw him,—him to whom they had rendered the homage of their song of liberty in the summer night of a few years past,—and the echoes of the vaulted roof rang again with one shout, one Viva to his name.

They knew his face well,— it had long been among them in Venice; they knew his words well, that in the poems of his early manhood and in the deeper thoughts of his later years had borne so far the seeds of freedom; they honoured him and loved him.

His eyes dwelt on them a while without light or sense; he felt drunk as with an opiate under the storm of disbelief and sickening terror that possessed him. They filled the space about him under the crucifix that hung aloft, with the sad, passionless, thorn-crowned face of the statue bending above from out the darkness, and the white limbs stretched in martyrdom. The folds of the standard streamed above the crowd of upturned faces with the glow of their earliest manhood and the resolve of their settled sacrifice set as with one seal upon all. They had fallen in close in their ranks, and stood so still in unbroken phalanx. Alone and foremost was the youth with the head like the head of a Gabriel, who had spoken in the summer eve the gratitude of Venice to the teacher and the lover of liberty. Their weapons were in their hands, and their blood poured from their wounds on the black mosaic pavement worn by priestly feet. Some had their death-wound, and knew it; but they only pressed their hand closer, to stay for a moment the stream that carried life with it, and they looked with a smile to his face.

One—a child in years, scarcely seventeen, with the flushed fair features of childhood still—stooped and touched his hand with a kiss of homage.

"Signore, wait and see how we can die; see we do not dishonour your teaching."

The simplicity of the words pierced his heart; through the wreck of his own misery, through the sirocco of his

own passions, they came to him with the weary, eternal
sigh of that humanity which, however it had deserted
him, he had never, in requital, forsaken. Death would
have laid its seal upon his lips, and chained his hand,
and veiled his sight, ere ever he would be cold to the suf-
ferings of his fellow-men, silent to the prayer of the peoples.

That love, unswerving and unchilled, for mankind,
which had given so noble a glow to the dreams of his
youth and filled with so gentle a patience the temper of
his later years, survived in him now amidst all the desolation of his fate, all the horror that glided from the
shadows of his past and seized the one hope left him.
As the heart of Vergniaud was, to the last on the scaffold,
with the human life in which he had placed too sublime
a faith, for which he had dreamed of too sublime a destiny,
so his heart was still, even in his own torture, with those
young lives self-given up to slaughter. The boy's touch
roused him; he looked at the heaving mass that pressed
about him, at the pale, brave faces that turned to him
with one accord in the gloom of the aisle. He saw at a
glance they were there as sheep are hemmed into the
shambles; he divined what folly had brought them,—folly
nobler, perhaps, than most prudential wisdom. He pressed
forward into their van on the simple instinct of their defence, while they fell back and made way for him, watching him reverently as he passed. He had loved Venetia,
he had served Liberty; he was sacred in their sight. In
the front the standard caught a beam from the golden
air without, and was wafted higher and higher by the
breath of a free sea-wind; behind, far in the gloom, the
altar-lights burned dully, rayless in the blackness of the
shadow shrouding them,—meet symbols of the clear noontide of freedom, of the midnight mists of creeds and churches.
He forced his passage to where that banner floated.

"Children, children! what are you doing? Why will you spend your lives like water?"

The youths of the front file, the first rank that would receive the shock of the bayonets or the fire of the musketry with which the soldiers would in another moment come to drive them down into obedience, lowered their arms as guards lower them to monarchs.

"Better to lose our lives than spend them in usurpers' prisons! Leave us while there is time, signore; you can trust us to die well."

They left the space free,—the space out into the glowing sunlight, into the fragrant air. He stood still, and motioned their weapons up.

"You know me better than that."

Their eyes filled; he had lived much amidst them, and his written words had sunk deep into their hearts. The young patriot who held the banner—held it with his left hand, because the right wrist had been broken by a spent ball—flashed back on him an answering comprehension.

"We know the greatness of your nature—yes; but the greater your life, the less should you expose it here. There will be slaughter; the world must not lose *you*."

He heard but vaguely, half without sense of what was spoken; his life seemed on fire with the torment that possessed him,—the hideous doom from which his whole soul shuddered. Instinctively his eyes sought the musician; the look that was in them was worse to Lulli than if he had seen them glazed and fixed in death.

"Go you," he said, briefly: "I wait with these."

The flush and light that only stole there when in music he lost the feebleness and the pain of his daily being, came on Lulli's face.

"I deserted you one moment," he murmured low; "not again,—never again!"

The tramp of the Austrian soldiery came nearer and nearer, ringing like iron on the stone pavements without; the flash of metal glanced in the sun beyond the great bronze doors of Cinque Cento arabesque; the arch of the entrance was filled with dark faces and the glitter of the levelled steel; behind were the dim, solemn, majestic aisles of the church, with the white Passion gleaming through the gloom, and the ethereal tracery of the pyx rising out of the sea of shadow; in front, hemming them in with a circle of bayonets, and blocking up the lofty space through which the blue sky and the sunlit air of the living day were seen, were the mercenaries of Austria.

Some touch of reverence for the sanctuary that their Church had made sacred from earliest time to all who sought the refuge of its altars, stilled their zest for slaughter and held back their weapons; there was a moment's pause and silence. The boy-patriots only gathered closer in their ranks, and looked out on the bristling line of rifles in the sunlight of the day. Chandos forced his way to the front, and stood between them and their foes.

"O children! why will you give the unripe corn of your young life to such reapers as these?" he said, passionately. "You serve Venice in nothing; you but drain her of all her youngest and purest blood! Why will you not learn that to contain your souls in patience for a while is to best perfect your strength for her? Why will you not believe that there is a world-wide love higher even than patriotism,—that while men suffer, and resist, anywhere upon earth, there we can find a country and a brotherhood?"

They heard in silence, their young faces flushing; they knew that he who spoke the rebuke to them spoke but what he had himself done,—that, under exile and wretchedness, he had not fled to the refuge of death, but had made of truth his kingdom, and of mankind his brethren.

"It is better to die than to live fettered!" they murmured, as they lifted their eyes to his.

"True! But when the freedom of a nation, the deliverance of a people, rest on our bearing with the chains a while, that we may strike them off with surety at the last, the higher duty is to endure in the present, that we may resist in the future. Malefactors have died nobly: it is the greater task to live so."

His voice, rich and clear with the music of the born orator, rang through the silence of the church, moving the hearts of the young Venetians like music, and stirring even the fierce and sullen souls of the German soldiery, though to them the language of its utterance was unknown. He had the power in him which leads men by the magic of an irresistible command,—the power that, in forms widely different, his enemy and he alike possessed. In the early ages of the world he would have been such a ruler as Solomon was in the sight of Israel, such a liberator and leader of a captive people as Arminius or Viriathus, when the life of a country hung on the life of one man, and fell when that life fell.

The Austrian in command, to whom his face was unknown, thought him the leader of the revolt, and wondered who this chief was that thus swayed even whilst he rebuked his followers. He lowered his sword courteously.

"Signore, surrender unconditionally, or we must fire."

Chandos stood between the ranks of the combatants, unarmed, his head uncovered,—behind him the dark hues of the paintings, within the whiteness of the sculpture and the shade of the vaulted aisles, a single breadth of light falling across his forehead and the fairness of his hair.

"I cannot dictate surrender to them, for they have

done no crime," he said briefly; "and to shoot them down you must fire first through me."

The Venetians nearest him pressed round him, shielding him with their weapons, and covering his hands, his dress, his feet, with their kisses.

"Signore!" they shouted with one breath, "we will surrender to save you. *You* shall not die for us. We can find some way to kill ourselves afterwards!"

He put them gently back; his eyes rested on them with a great tenderness.

"No: you shall not surrender. I know what surrender means. Besides, it is only cowards' resort. Do you think I am so in love with life that I fear to lose it? I could not die better than with you."

As the words left his lips, through the ranks of the soldiery, through the serried lines of steel, as the men in amaze fell back before her, and she thrust aside the opposing weapons as she would have thrust aside the stalks of a field of millet, through the radiance of the day, and the gloom of the ribbed stone arches, Castalia forced herself with the chamois-like swiftness of her mountain-training and the dauntless courage that ran in her blood. Before the Austrians could arrest her, she had pierced their phalanx, crossed the breadth of the marble pavement, and reached Chandos, where he stood beneath the sculpture of the crucifix. His face grew white as the face of the sculptured Christ above, as he saw her.

"Oh, God! what love!"

Involuntarily, with a great cry, he stretched his arms out to her. At that instant a large stone, cast over the heads of the soldiery from an unseen hand behind them, was hurled through the air, and struck the colours of a Free Italy from the grasp of the youth who held them: he reeled and dropped dead: the blow had fallen on his temple.

As the banner was shivered from his hold, the folds drooping earthward, Castalia caught it and lifted it in the front of the German troops. Her eyes flashed back on them with a daring challenge; her face was lighted with the glow that liberty and peril lend to brave natures as the sun lends warmth.

Then, with a smile that had the heroism of a royal fearlessness, with the fidelity of a spaniel that comes to die with its master, she came and stood by Chandos, her eyes looking upward to him, her hand leaning on the staff of the standard. Unconsciously, in the violence of the torture that consumed him at her sight, her touch, her presence, he drew her to his breast, crushing her beauty in an embrace in which all was for the moment forgotten, save the love he bore her, save the love that sought him even through the path of death.

Roused by the echo of that rallying-cry, infuriated by their comrade's fall, seeing her loveliness given into their defence, the Venetian youths sprang forward like young lions, their swords circling above their heads, their hearts resolute to pierce the net that held them, or to perish. The Austrian raised his sword:—

"Fire!"

Obedient to the command, the first file dropped on one knee, the second stood above them with their rifles levelled over the shoulders of the kneeling rank, the bayonets were drawn out with a sharp metallic clash, the double line of steel caught the morning rays upon the glitter of the tubes: every avenue of escape was closed.

Chandos stooped his head over her, where he held her folded in his arms, to shield her while life was in him.

"You do not fear?"

She smiled still up into his eyes; she saw in them an agony great as that which the sculptor had given to the marble agony upon the cross.

"I have no fear with you."

His embrace closed on her in the vibration of a dying man's farewell.

"Death will be mercy for *us!*"

With the sunlight of her hair floating across his breast, he stood looking straight at the levelled musketry; her eyes rested on his face alone, and never left their gaze. With his arms thus about her, with her head resting on his heart, she had no fear of this fate; he wished it, he resigned himself to it; she was content to die in the dawn of her life, with him, and at his will.

Guido Lulli stood near them. He was forgotten—he had no thought that it could be otherwise; but where he leaned his delicate withered limbs on the sculpture beside him, his eyes rested calmly on the circle of the soldiery, on the gleam of the rifle-barrels; weak as a woman in his frame, he had no woman's weakness in his soul. He had forsaken the man he loved for one moment in life; he would be faithful to him through the last pang of death.

The sudden crash of the volley rolled through the silence; the white thick clouds of smoke floated outward to the brightness of the day, and downward through the length of the violated church. Castalia never shrank as it pealed above her; she only looked up still to the face above her. There was not a sound, not a moan; when the smoke cleared slightly, they stood untouched, though shots had ploughed the stone above them and beneath them; but under the white sculpture of the Passion the young lives of Venice lay dying by the score, their lips set in a brave smile, their hands still clenched on their sword-hilts. A voice rang out like thunder on the stillness:

"Brutes!—do you murder in cold blood?"

Thrusting his way through the dense crowds of the entrance, as Castalia before him had thrust her's, Philippe d'Orvâle strode through the soldiery into the church, felling down with a blow of his mighty arm a rifle that was levelled at Chandos; with his hair dashed off his forehead, his glance flaming fire, he swung round and faced the German levies, grand in his wrath as a god of Homer.

"So! you turn the church to a slaughter-house? Not the first time by many. By my faith, a fine thing, to shoot down those brave children! Cowards, tigers, barbarians, fire again at your peril!"

The passion and the dignity of the reprimand stilled them for a moment by the force of surprise; but only for that, only to rouse their savage ruthlessness in tenfold violence. Dressed, in one of his Bohemian caprices, in the boat-dress of a *barcarolo*,—for he loved to mingle with the people in their own garb and in their own manner, —and but dimly seen in the midst of smoke and the twilight of the building, they failed to recognise him; they took him for a Venetian and a revolutionist. Infuriated by his words and by his forced entrance, the Austrian in command gave the word to fire again. The volley of the second line rolled out as he stood in the midst between the soldiery and the body of the church, as a lion stands at bay; he staggered slightly, and put his hand to his breast; but he stood erect still, his bold, brilliant eyes meeting the sun.

"You have killed me; that is little. But kill more of *them*, and, by the God above us, I will leave my vengeance in legacy to France, who never yet left debts like that unpaid!"

Then, as Chandos reached his side, he reeled and fell backwards; he had been shot through the lungs.

"If it stop the carnage, it was well done," he said, as the blood poured from his breast.

Awed at their work, recognising him too late, terror-stricken to have struck one for whose fall vengeance might

be demanded by a nation that never slurs its dishonour
or lets sleep its enemies, the Austrians in command,
motioning back their soldiery, pressed towards him, to
raise him, to succour him, to protest their lamentation,
their ignorance, their horror. Chandos shook them from
him, and swept them back.

"His blood is on your heads: you murdered him!
Stand off!"

Philippe d'Orvâle had known that his death-wound
had struck him in the instant that the ball had crushed
through the bone and bedded itself where every breath
of life was drawn; but the careless laughter of his wit,
the fine scorn of the old Noblesse, was on his face as
he looked at the Austrians.

"So! brave humanity, messieurs! You apologize for
shedding my blood, because my blood is called princely;
if I had been a gondolier, you would have kicked my
corpse aside! No, dear friend, let me lie. No good can
be done, and it will be but for a moment."

A voiceless sob shook Chandos as he hung over him;
he knew also that but for a moment this noble life would
be among the living.

The thoughts of Philippe d'Orvâle were not of himself; they were with those children of Venice, who were
perishing from too loyal and too rash a love for her.
His eyes gathered their lion fire as they rested on the
Austrians; his voice rang stern and imperious.

"If you regret my death, give me their lives."

The officers stood mute and irresolute: they dared
not refuse; they dared not comply.

"Give me their lives!" his voice rolled clearer and
louder, commanding as a monarch's, "without conditions,
free and untouched for ever. Give me them, or, by Heaven,
I will leave France to avenge me. Give me them, I say!"

There was no resistance possible, in such an hour, to such a demand, they submitted to him; they pledged their honour that the lives he asked for as his blood-money should be spared.

"That is well; that is well," he said, briefly, as the rush of the air through his wound checked his utterance, where he lay back in Chandos' arms just beneath the sculpture of the Passion. "All that youth saved! No shot ever told better. Ah, Chandos! do not suffer for me, *caro*. It is a fair fate,—a long life enjoyed, and a swift death by a bullet, with your eyes on mine to the last. Dieu de dieu! what room is there for regret? I am spared all the lingering tortures of age. That is much!"

"Oh, God!—to lose you!"

The cry broke from Chandos in an anguish mightier far than if his own life had been ebbing out with every wave of the blood that flowed out on the marble floor. He had lost all else,—and, at the last, this life he loved was taken!

Philippe d'Orvâle's eyes looked up at him, tender as a woman's.

"*Chut!* If *I* be content, what matter? 'The king will enjoy his own again.' You will take from your friend dead what you refused from him living. Make my grave in Clarencieux, Chandos,—under the forests somewhere, —that your step may pass over it now and then, and the deer come trooping above me."

"Hush! hush! You kill me."

Hot and bitter tears welled into Chandos' eyes, and fell on the brow that rested against his breast: he would have accepted exile and poverty for ever rather than have bought the joys and the wealth of a world at such a price as this.

Philippe d'Orvâle smiled,—the sun-lit, careless, shadowless smile that had always been on the lips of this bright, fearless reveller, though the blood was pouring faster and faster out as his chest heaved for breath, and the chillness and numbness of death were stealing over the colossal limbs that were stretched on the marble floor.

"Nay; I tell you I am fortunate. My roses have never lost their fragrance yet, and now—I shall not see them wither. Do not grieve for *me*, Ernest; it is well as it is, —very well! Ah, Lulli! is it you?"

He stretched out one hand to the Provençal, who bent over him convulsed with the unrestrained impassioned grief of his temperament; it seemed to him strange and terrible beyond compare, that this mighty magnificence of manhood should be laid low while death passed by his own strengthless, pain-racked frame and left unsevered his own frail bonds to earth.

An intense stillness had fallen over the scene of the carnage where the prince-Bohemian lay dying in the broad space of the arched aisle; the soldiers of Austria stood mute and motionless; the young Venetians gazed heart-broken at the man who had given his life for theirs. All those who were wounded lay as still as the stiffened dead beside them, letting existence ebb out of them with the same fortitude as his. The tumult had died; a stricken awe had come upon the multitude. Above, in the twilight of the dim vaulted vista of columns, the free colours of liberty still floated, catching a gleam of light still on their folds. Castalia held them where she stood looking down on the first death that her eyes had ever watched, as the purple stream of the blood flowed to her feet, and each breath, as it convulsed the vast, torn, heaving chest, dealt a separate pang to her as though her own life went with it.

The glance of Philippe d'Orvâle, growing more languid

now, and losing the fiery brilliance of its gaze, dwelt on her with a gleam of wonder and of light.

"Who is that?" he asked, as he raised himself slightly.

She knelt beside him, holding the standard still, while its bright hues drooped on the marble.

"They call me Castalia."

He looked at her dreamily.

"Castalia! Ah! you have eyes that are like some I loved once. I loved so many,—so many! Life has been sweet,—sweet as wine. Stoop down and touch me with your lips; it will be a better assoilzement than a priest's chrism."

She lifted her eyes to Chandos, where she knelt beside him; he bent his head in silence, then at the sign from him she stooped softly nearer and nearer, and let her lips rest on the French Prince's brow in the farewell he asked.

He smiled, and touched her hair with his hand.

"I thank you, *belle enfant*," he said gently; the light was fading fast out of his gaze, his senses were fast losing all their hold on earth, as wave on wave of his life-blood surged from the broken, shattered bones of his breast. He lifted himself slightly with a supreme effort, and the sunlit laughter·with which he had ever met existence was on his face as he met his last hour.

"Your foe waited for the 'Mad Duke's' death! Well, we have cheated him: he will see the rightful lord go back to his heritage. It irked me reigning there, Chandos, while *you* were exiled. No Austrian bullet ever did a better stroke. Nay! why mourn me? I have drunk the riches of life, and I am spared the gall of the lees. Your hand closer, dear friend. I do not suffer; it is nothing, nothing! Let me see your eyes to the end, Ernest. So!—that is well!"

And with these words his head fell back, and under the white sculpture of the Passion Philippe d'Orvâle lay dead.

While Venice was hushed in awe at the greatness of
the victim who had fallen, and the vengeance of tyranny
was stayed in obedience to his last wish, the Prince who
had died for the People was borne with reverent hands
into the gloom of a state-chamber of his own palace, and
laid reverently down, with the radiance of the morning
shut out, and the gleam of funeral lights burning round.
A pall of purple covered the limbs; fine linens veiled the
breadth of the chest, with its yawning, blood-filled cavity.
The face was still left unshrouded, with its fair, frank
brow pale in the pallor of the wax-light, the luxuriance
of the curling beard flecked with silver threads, the eyelids closed as in a peaceful slumber. There was but one
watcher with him. Beside the bier Chandos knelt, motionless as the dead, with his forehead resting on the hand
which in life had never clenched but in a righteous cause,
and which, once clasped in friendship or in pledge, would
have been cut off sooner than have let go its bond. That
hand, cold as ice, and lying open like the strengthless
palm of a child, had given him his home, given him more
than empires; that hand, by its last act and will, had
restored him the one longing of his life, had summoned
him from exile to the honour of his race once more; that
hand had swept aside a score of years, and brought him
back his birthright. This gift of a recovered joy such as
dreams sometimes had mocked him with, came to him in
the very hour that a horror worse than guilt laid his heart
desolate. One desire of his soul was bestowed on him in
the very moment that all others were laid waste and banned
as sin,—one resurrection of dead hopes granted him in the
very moment that all other hopes were blasted from his
hold. It was his once more, this land that he had never
forgotten, this thing that he had mourned as Adam mourned
the forfeited loveliness of paradise, this lost treasure to

which his memory had gone, waking or sleeping, with every flicker of green leaves in morning twilight, with every sough of summer winds through arching aisles of woodland, with every spring that bloomed on earth, with every night that fell;—and it was his only when the one friend that had cleaved to him loyally was stretched dead before his eyes, only when the poison of his past rose up and turned to incestuous shame the love which had seemed the purest and the fairest treasure that his life had ever known! He knelt there, where the daylight was shut out and the stillness was unstirred as in a vault. That he had regained his birthright by the seal of eternal silence laid for ever on those brave lips that no lie had ever tainted, could assuage in nothing the bitterness of his regret; to have summoned Philippe d'Orvâle back amidst the living, he would have taken up for ever a beggar's portion and a wanderer's doom.

Where he had sunk down, with his arms flung over the motionless limbs, and his frame shaken ever and again by a great tremor as the scorch of passions that he had been told were guilt thrilled through him, a woman's hand was laid upon his shoulder. As he started and raised his eyes, he saw, in the pale silvery shadows of the death-lights burning round, the gaze of Beatrix Lennox bent upon him.

"Ah! I am too late," she said wearily. "I am always too late for good: for evil one is sure to be ready."

Her voice was very low; she stood looking not at him, but at the noble head that had fallen never to rise again, at the mouth that still wore its last smile, from which no chaunt of laughter, no melody of welcome, would ever again ring out.

Chandos rose and stood in silence also. There was too great a wretchedness on him to leave him any wonder at her coming there, at her forcing her entrance into the

state-chamber where the guards without denied all comers.
He thought some tie might bind her to Philippe d'Orvâle's
memory: he had never known that it was himself she loved.

"He had a lion's heart, he was true as the sun, he
never lied, he never broke a bond, he never failed a friend;
no wonder the world had no name for him but 'Mad!'"
she said, as her voice fell on the stillness of the funeral
chamber. "He died but four hours ago, they say; and I
—was those four hours too late. It is always so with me!"

"He was dear to you?"

"No! If he had been, do you think I could stand
calmly here? But he was a superb gentleman: he died
superbly. The world has few grand natures; it can ill
spare them. Besides, I have much to say to you."

"Hush! not *here.*"

"Yes, here. What I shall say is no desecration to his presence. He would have been the first to be told it, had he lived."

She waited some moments; then, with her face turned
from him, she spoke:—

"Chandos, she whom you love——"

"Spare me *that!*"

"What! is she false to you?"

"Would to God she were, rather than——"

"Rather than what?"

He shuddered.

"I cannot tell you!"

"You must—if but for her sake. It is——?"

"That Valeria Lulli was her mother."

"That is the truth! What if she be?"

"*What?* She was my mistress!"

"It is false! It is basely, utterly false!"

He caught her hands in his.

"Prove it, prove it!—and no saint was ever merciful
as you——"

"I *can* prove it. Valeria Lulli gave her birth; but her father—lies there."

He drew a deep gasping breath, like a man who has escaped from the close peril of some awful death.

"This is true?"

"True as that we live."

She turned from him, that she might not see his face in that moment of supreme deliverance. There was a long, breathless silence, the silence which is a greater thanksgiving than any words can utter.

He lifted his head at last, and his eyes dwelt on her with a look that repaid her for twenty years of unspoken, unrequited love.

"Her father—*he!* Oh God!"

"Yes, it is strange. And, yet, why do we say so? Life is full of wilder mystery than any fiction fancies. Months ago, in the autumn, you bade me feel a woman's pity for your young, forsaken Tuscan. I sought for her; I wished to know if she were worthy of you. You had told me where you had left her; I went there to find her gone,—lost out of all sight and knowledge. The belief of the people and of the priest was that she had fled with you. I knew the falsehood of that, and I set myself to the discovery, first of her history, then of herself. It took me long, very long; but at last I succeeded. Women rarely fail when they are in earnest. The priest told me, after long conferences with him, that her mother had confided to him a sealed packet, but he was never to open it unless some imminent danger assailed the child; then, and then only, he might read what it held, and act as he might see fit. She had died without confession,—died what he considered impenitent. He was a grand old man in his creeds of duty; he had never violated the sanctity of the seals to sate his curiosity or to lighten his charge of

Castalia. I had less self-restraint. I persuaded him that the moment had arrived. He was very hard to convince; he considered the command of the dead woman sacred. At last, however, I overcame his reluctance. We opened the papers: from them I learned that she was the daughter of Valeria Lulli and of the Duc d'Orvâle."

"She had been his mistress?"

"No, his wife; but she had disbelieved that she was so; hence her concealment of herself and of her offspring. The account of her life is very incoherent; written as women write under wrong and grief. It is plain to see that she was passionate, jealous, doubtless of extraordinary beauty, but of a fervid, uncontrolled temperament,—one to beguile him into hot love, but soon to weary him. There are many such women, and then *you* are blamed for inconstancy! She had left Arles because persecuted by a roué. She went to Florence, and there saw Philippe d'Orvâle. He heard her voice in a mass at Easter, and sought her out. A passion, ardent as his always was, soon sprang up between them. Of course he had no thought of marriage; but she had the same pride that Guido Lulli cherishes so strongly. She would not yield to him; in the end she vanquished him. The marriage was performed privately, and remained secret. Reasons connected with his great House made this imperative for a brief while; but he kept her in the utmost luxury in a palace of his on Como, and intended shortly to announce their union. It is easy to see by her own confession that her jealous love left him little peace, and must have been unendurable to such a temperament as his; but throughout she speaks of his unvarying tenderness, lavish generosity, and sweetness of temper. It is conceivable that he went back to his old freedom when once the restless tyranny of her passion began to gall him; but she never hints that

his kindness or his affection altered. He left her once for
Paris, intending but a short absence. While he was away,
she received anonymous letters, telling her that her marriage had been a false one, that his equerry in a priest's
guise had performed it; that he was faithless to her, and
already loved another. A woman who had read his nature
aright would have known a fraud impossible to Philippe
d'Orvâle; but she was very young, very impulsive,—at
once, as I think, weak and passionate. She flew to Paris;
he had gone to stay with you at Clarencieux. She knew
her cousin was there, and went thither to declare her marriage, or arraign the Duke if he confessed it false. She
was his wife, but she knew so little of D'Orvâle as that!
In the Park, as it chanced, the Duke was that moment
riding with the Countess de la Vivarol and other ladies.
She heard her husband's laughter; she saw the beautiful
women he was with. She knew so little the worth of the
heart she had won, that she believed all the falsehoods
told her in the letters, which were most likely penned by
the libertine whom she had repulsed; or by some forsaken
mistress of her husband's. Her first impulse was to accuse
him before all his friends, the next to flee from him and
from every memory of him, and hide herself and her
shame where none could ever reach her. That she did.
She made her way back into Italy, where she gave birth
to her child. She would not even let him know that she
had borne him one. There is little doubt that the shock
of what she believed his cruelty, had unsettled her reason.
That the Duke sought her far and wide, though unsuc-
cessfully, is shown by the difficulties which she relates
beset her in her avoidance of discovery by him."

He heard in silence, his breathing quick and loud,
his hand on the dead man's.

"Go on; go on!"

"The remainder is soon told. I read this record of a
life thrown away by such blind folly, such mingling of
utter credulity and mad mistrust; her marriage-ring was
enclosed in it, the certificate of the child's· birth, and
other matters. She, of course, wrote her absolute belief
that she was not his wife. I reasoned otherwise. D'Orvâle
might be a voluptuary, but his honour was true as steel.
A false marriage would have been a fraud impossible to
him: he would never have betrayed any one. So—I
sought out the evidence. Most would have gone to him.
That is not my way. I have known the world too well
to call the accused into the place of witness. I sought
Castalia, and I sought evidence of the marriage, ere I
went to her father. I found the priest who had performed the rites, with difficulty; he had joined the Order
of Jesus, and was in Africa. With patience I reached
every link, those who had witnessed it and all. The marriage was perfectly valid, legally recorded, though its
privacy had been kept. It is easy to conceive that, with
his nature, which loved enjoyment and loathed regret,
when he found Valeria irrevocably lost to him, he had
no temptation to re-open a painful thought by relating
his connection with her. Doubtless other loves chased
her memory away, though doubtless that memory always
prompted his extreme tenderness towards Lulli. That the
union was strict to the law, you will see when I show
you the proofs; and in all that you choose to claim for
her, Castalia must be recognised as a daughter of the
house of D'Orvâle."

He heard in perfect stillness, the sudden relief of the
deadly strain which had been on him for the past hours
leaving him giddy and speechless; he doubted his own
hearing: he had touched joy so often only to see it wither
from him, he dreaded this too was a dream. A thousand

thoughts and memories rushed on him: that superb courage which flashed from Castalia's eyes, that imperial grace which had marked her out among the Tuscan contadini, as Perdita was marked out among the peasants of her foster-home, that pride of instinct in her which had repelled insult as worse than death,—they were the heritage in her of the man who lay dead beside him, the heritage of a great dauntless race, that in the annals of centuries had never failed a friend or quailed before a foe. His hand closed tighter on Philippe d'Orvâle's, and his head drooped over the lifeless limbs, the stilled heart that never again would beat with the brave pulse of its gallant life.

"If he were but living——"

In the first moment of a release so sudden that it seemed to break all his strength down beneath his joy, his heart went out to the slaughtered friend whose love had been with him to the last. The dignities, the titles, the possessions that would accrue to her through her heirship with the mighty race she issued from, never passed over his memory; the inheritance that he remembered in her, the inheritance that he thanked God for in one who would bear his name and hold his honour, was the inheritance of her father's nature.

"You noblest among women!" he said, brokenly, as he took the hands of Beatrix Lennox in his own and bent over them as men bend above an empress's. "How can I thank you? What can I render you for the mercy you have brought me, for the torture you have taken from my life? So vast a gift,—so unasked a service! What words can ever tell you my gratitude?"

She smiled, but the smile was very sad.

"You remember, long ago, I told you I would serve you if I could, though it were twenty years later? Well,

I have kept my word; but there is no need of thanks for *that:* it cost me nothing."

"No cost! It is such a debt as leaves me bankrupt to repay it; my life, her life, will never suffice to return it."

Her eyes were very beautiful as they dwelt on him in the dimness of the darkened chamber.

"Chandos, it is paid enough. *You* will know happiness once more. It is your native sunlight; could my lips pray, they should pray that it may shine on you for ever."

And there was that in the words, as they were spoken, which told him the truth at last,—told him of what sort and of what strength this woman's tenderness for him had been.

"Hush!" she said, softly, with that weary smile which had in it more sorrow than tears. "No; do not thank me; do not say more. It only pains me. Ah, Christ! I have done so little good!"

As she spoke, into the shadows of the chamber of death Castalia entered.

She knew no cause for his long absence. She had borne the silence awhile with the absolute submission to him that mingled with the passion of her love; at last the latter conquered; she came to seek him, came to know what this barrier was which had risen up between them with the morning light. She paused as she saw him not alone. Her face was very pale; the suffering and martyrdom that she had witnessed had wrung her heart, and stirred the depths of a nature that had in it the love of liberty, and the tenderness for the people, for which her father had died; but as she waited, beyond the gleam of the funeral-lights, the royalty was on her which had seemed to rest like a crown on her young head when she had lived among the peasants of Tuscany, and had made them speak of her with a hushed awe as a fairy's changeling.

Beatrix Lennox looked on her long in silence, with a

quick deep sigh; there was that in her loveliness which far passed beyond mere beauty, mere youth; and between her face and the kingly majesty which was stretched dead on the bier there was, in that moment, a strange likeness.

The heart of this adventuress, whom the world had long condemned, had thus much of rare nobility and self-forgetfulness in it; it could rejoice in others' joy, rejoice that what it had itself forfeited still lived to gladden others. It was untainted by that which corrodes many whose acts are blameless; it was untainted by the gall of envy.

Beatrix Lennox looked on this life that opened to the fulness of existence while her own was faded, that would lie in the bosom of the man she loved, that would rest in the golden glory of joy whilst she herself had nothing left but regret and remorse and the phantoms of dead years; but there was no bitterness in her; there was only a heartfelt thanksgiving for him.

"She is worthy even of you," she said, softly; then she paused a moment, looking down into the lustrous, meditative, poetic eyes of Castalia with a searching, thoughtful gaze. "You will have a great trust," she said, simply, "and a great treasure; but there is no need to say to *you*, guard both dearer than life."

Then, silently, with one backward farewell glance at the dead man lying there, she passed slowly and musingly from the chamber. Chandos followed her, and took her hands once more within his own.

"Wait. *I* do not judge as the world judges. You have come as the angel of mercy to me; you have released me from a misery passing all I had ever known. You will live in our love and reverence for ever; you will let us both strive to repay you?"

"You have more than repaid me by those words only. I have much still to tell you,—to place with you. But

she will never see my face again. You know what my
life has been!"

He stooped nearer, and, looking upward, she saw a
divine compassion on his face.

"I know that it has had magnanimities many blameless lives have never reached. Hear me. Do you think,
in view of such an act as yours, I could hold a Pharisee's
creed? God is my witness, there is no one whom I
would more fearlessly trust with her than you, none that
I more surely know would reverence her youth and
leave untouched her innocence. Can I say more?"

"More! You have said far above what I merit. But
what you mean cannot be. I am no meet associate for his
daughter, for your wife. She must be above suspicion: she
could not be so were *I* once seen beside her. No, my years
have been too evil to leave me any place with hers; but
they will not be wholly desolate in future, for I shall have
your pity always, and, sometimes, your remembrance."

She touched his hand with her lips ere he could stay
her, and hot tears fell on it as she stooped; then she went
from him,—content, because she had given him happiness; content, because it had been hers to serve him.

He passed back into the chamber where the lights
burned around the solitude of the dead, and his arms
closed on what he cherished with a convulsive pressure
as though she were just rescued from her grave. He
could not speak for many moments, but held her there
as a man holds the dearest treasure of his life; then he
drew her to the bier, where the brave, serene face smiled
on them in eternal rest.

"Your lips were the last to touch his; thank God
that it was so. I have much to tell you; it is best told
here. My love, my love! could you be more sacred to
me, you would be so for his sake!"

That night, in the palace where the dead man lay,—
the palace that, with most of his vast chieftainship, of his
princely appanage, would fall to the only one who owned
his name,—Guido Lulli stood before her in whose eyes
the smile of his lost Valeria looked once more upon him.

"Castalia," he said, softly, "you will be very great
in the world's sight; but you will not forget that your
mother loved me once, when she was a bright and gracious
child, and I had no thought through the length of summer
days and winter nights save to make her pleasure?"

She stooped to him with that grace which, even when
the ban of peasants' scorn and of a foundling's shame had
rested on her, had been so proud, and had so much of
royalty in it.

"Ah! can you think so basely of me as to need to
ask it? My fondest reverence will be ever yours; and as
for greatness, what greatness can there be like——"

"His love?" added the musician, gently, while his
own gaze dwelt also on the man who had come to him
as his saviour in the bleak and burning heat of Spain,
when both were in their youth. "Right. *There* will be
your proudest coronal; and by you, through you, some
portion of my debt will be paid to him."

Chandos silenced him with a gesture.

"Hush! You paid it long ago, Lulli; paid it afresh
to-day; paid it when you gave me a rarer thing than
gold,—fidelity."

"Not so. There are debts that, I have told you, are
too noble to be repaid like counted coin. Mine is one of
them. Let it rest on me ever, ever. It will be my last
thought, and my sweetest in my death-hour."

There was an exceeding pathos in the brief and
simple words; with them he turned and passed from the
chamber. He looked back once, himself unseen, and his

face grew pale with a certain pang. The light that shone on their lives would never come to him; the lotus-lily of which they ate his lips could never touch. There was no bitterness on him, no sin of envy, no thought save a voiceless prayer for them; yet still the pain was there. No joy could ever be his own, no fragrance of Eden reach him. He must dwell for ever an exile from that golden world in which men for awhile forget that no dreams last. Had it been his to give, he would have poured on them the glory of the life of gods; but in their love he saw all his own life had missed, all his own life for ever was denied.

As he went back alone into his desolate home, into the music-room where the things of his heart were, it was deep in shade; only across the keys of the organ at the end a white pure light was streaming from the rays of a lamp that swung above.

A smile came on his lips as he saw it; to him it was as an allegory, Heaven-painted.

"Alone! while I have you?" he murmured.

The artist was true to his genius; he knew it a greater gift than happiness; and as his hands wandered by instinct over the familiar notes, the power of his kingdom came to him, the passion of his mistress was on him, and the grandeur of the melody swelled out to mingle with the night, divine as consolation, supreme as victory.

CHAPTER VIII.
Lex Talionis.

WITH the sunset a storm had broken over Venice, rolling its funeral mass for the souls of those who had died for liberty. At midnight it lulled somewhat; the thunder grew more distant, and died away in low, hoarse anger; sheets of heavy rain succeeded, and through the hot sulphurous air the wind arose in fitful and tempestuous gusts.   In its violence, the Jew kept his patient vigil.

All through the day he had heard the noise of the tumult, the echoes of the firing, the shrieks of women, the clash of swords; he had heard the terror-stricken stillness that fell over the city when a great man was slain; he had heard the murmur of many tongues, that told him many strange, conflicting tales.   And his heart was ill at rest; he feared for his son.   Death had been abroad in the streets; death had smitten the innocent with the guilty: whom might it not have touched?   As soon as darkness gave him the safety and the secrecy that for Agostino's sake he kept, he made his way to the place where his son dwelt.   He heeded neither the fury of the winds nor the beat of the rain; he thought some passing sound, some echo of a voice, some stray word borne to his eager ear, might tell him what he sought.   From sunset to midnight he waited in the shadow of the stone-work, waited and listened.   Darkness and light were alike to him; no sun-rays ever pierced the gloom before his sight, even when the heat of noon told him the golden glow that shone on all the world, denied alone to him and to the Legion of the Blind.

He stood and listened, his long white hair blown back in the wild wind, the rushing storm of driving rain beaten against him unheeded; he waited to hear the one step that should tell him the son he loved still lived: to know that he was near, to be conscious of his presence for one fleeting moment, were enough for the great patient heart of the Hebrew.

For these only he watched now,—watched in vain. No sound repaid him; hours had passed, and there had been nothing. The storm had drenched his garments, and his snowy beard was heavy with water; still he listened,

—listened so eagerly that the caution he had exercised so long to remain unseen was forgotten as he leaned out from the shadow, hearkening in the rush of the rain for the footfall he knew so well. He forgot that the darkness which veiled the world from him could not shroud him from sight; he could not tell that the wavering light of the lamp which swung above from the doorway near fell on his olive brow, upturned as though in the Psalmist's weariness of prayer. He had worn the fetters of his task-master so long; he had so long borne the burden and the weight of his iron silence bound on him; death seemed so long in its coming! It took the young, the beloved, the fair, the child from its mother's bosom, the beauty of youth from the lover's embrace, the glory of manhood from its fruitage of ambition, from its harvest of labour; and it would not come to him, but left him here, poor, old, sightless, solitary, alone in the midst of all the peopled earth.

And yet there was a vague hope in his soul to-night: he felt as though death were not far from him, as though the release of its sweet pity would soon stoop to him, and touch him, and bid his bitterness cease; and ere it came, he longed to hear once more his darling's step,—to feel once more near him the existence born of his dead love,—the heart to which once he had been dear. He had strength in him to be silent unto death, to accept his martyrdom and bear it onward to his grave, untold to any living thing: all he asked was to listen once to a single living echo of his lost son's voice. Through the hush of the midnight the beat of oars trembled; a gondola grated against the stairs. It came,—that sound which thrilled through the rayless darkness which was ever around him, as it never trembled on any ear whose sense was linked with the power of sight,—that sound of Agostino's voice, as it spoke to the boatmen,—that sound which was the sole joy left to the blind. His son came towards him nearer and nearer up the wet stone steps; he leaned forward, knowing not how the light shone down on his face, and an unspoken blessing trembled on his lips in the tongue of the patriarchs of Judea: if he died to-night, he would have prayed with his last breath for the son of the love of his youth.

The footfall paused: it was beside him now, so close that he could hear every breath. A loud, wild cry broke through the night. Agostino staggered back, white-stricken, ghastly as Saul in the cave of Endor. A moment, and he gazed there paralyzed with spectral awe, with superstitious horror; then, unwitting what he did, senseless, and breathless, and prostrate, he fell down at the old man's feet in the supplication of his childhood.

"Father! father! dead or living, for the love of God forgive me!"

The Hebrew stood above in the flickering shadowy light; and on his face there was the strife of a terrible conflict. All his soul yearned to the man flung there in that passionate prayer at his feet: yet for his very sake he must deny him!

"I do not know you," he said, and his voice trembled sorely. "None call *me* father."

There have been heroisms far less noble than this one heroic lie.

Agostino looked up, his face all flushed with warmth, his eyes alight with bewildered, questioning amaze; the voice, once heard, bore back a thousand memories of by-gone years. The words might deny, but the voice blessed him.

"Forgive me!" he implored, scarce conscious of what he said, but remembering alone the sin with which he had wrung the old man's heart so long ago in the days of his boyhood,—the sin which had pursued him ever since.

“Whether you come to me in spirit or in life, come only to me in pardon, by the love you bore me!”

The Hebrew stood mute and motionless, his tall and wasted frame swaying like a reed, his face changing with swift and uncontrollable emotions, under the force of the imploring conjuration. His sightless eyes gazed instinctively down upon his son; but their blindness gave them, to Agostino, a look unearthly and without sense.

“Father! speak, O God!” he cried, “or you will kill me!”

The infinite love restrained in him broke through the rigid fixity of the old man's set features as the sun breaks through the darkness of a winter dawn; his hands were stretched out seeking to touch the beloved head lifted to him; he could hold his silence no more,—no more be as one dead to the son who knew him still.

His answer trembled, tender beyond all words, through the sighing of the wild winds and the rush of the beating rain.

“Agostino! my child! what have *I* to pardon? Rise, rise; guide my hands to you; let my arms feel you ere I die! You have your mother's face, and I cannot behold it; I am blind!”

In the dim light of the chamber within, kneeling at the old man's feet reverently as ever Isaac knelt at the feet of Abraham, Agostino heard his father's history,— heard quivering with torture, his breath caught by sobs, his kiss touching the withered hands that were to him as the hands of a martyr, great tears in his eyes that never left their gaze upon those in whose darkness he could still read love. He heard to the end. Then, when he had heard, he wept convulsively; the torrent of his agony loosened.

"You have borne this martyrdom through him! this curse for his sake?"

"Silence! His name is sacred to me. My son, he had mercy; he spared you."

Agostino sprang to his feet as an arrow springs from the bow.

"Spared *me?* Oh, God, you have thought that?"

The old man bent his head with the patient dignity with which he had ever borne the burden laid upon him.

"He spared you; yes! For it I bless his name. My life mattered nothing."

"Spared me? He cursed me from my youth up!" his voice rang as steel rings: the bondage of half a life was broken at last. "He loosed me from the law's chastisement to break me down into slavery worse than the worst tortures the sternest law ever dealt yet. He let me escape a moment to fetter me for an eternity. He traded in my misery; he traded in my crime. He set me to do the vilest work, and, when I shrank from it, threatened me with my buried sin. He made my life one endless dread; he never let me know one moment's peace, one hour's security. Ah, Heaven! why do I speak of it as past! He does it still. I am his tool, his serf, his hound. Every day I wake, I know that I may rise only to be commanded some fresh infamy to serve him!"

The old man, as he heard, rose also, and stood erect; his sunken eyes filled with the fire of his dead manhood, his mouth set like a vice; years of living vigour, of mighty strength, seemed poured into his veins: his olive face was dark as night.

"What! he was faithless to me! You have suffered?"

"Suffered! It is no word for what I have borne through him. But what is his crime to me, beside his crime to you? I was guilty, I merited my punishment;

but you,—you who endured indignity and torment for my sake and for his, you who had no error, save too firm a loyalty to him, too noble a tenderness to me!"

His voice fell in a deep tearless sob; he had the heart of a woman, and his father's sacrifice was holy in his sight as any martyrdom.

"He has been your tyrant!"

The question was hard as iron.

"*Mine!* what matters that? It is nothing beside *your* captivity!"

"Yes! By it my bonds are loosed; by it my oath is broken. He has had my patience long, my truth long, my servitude long; now he shall have my justice."

His whole height was erect, his blind eyes blazed with fire, his arm was outstretched in imprecation; he stood like one of the prophets of his own Palestine, cursing in the name of Jehovah a hostile host, an ingrate land.

Agostino, looking upward, caught the same fire from him, caught the kindling glow of liberty and of revenge. He had writhed and rebelled under his own bonds, though ever only to sink more hopelessly under the fetters; but before the martyrdom of his father there rose in him that nobler rage for another's wrong which would have made him content to perish himself, if in his fall he could have dragged down his tyrant: it is the emotion which makes tyrannicides.

"Ay!" he cried passionately, "let us be avenged if the power be still with us. Let him shame me, ruin me, kill me; but let me see him struck down ere I die. His guilty secrets have been the curse of both our lives; let them be told against him! *I* was impotent; but you——"

The figure of the aged Hebrew towered in the gloom, and on his face was the stern ruthless justice of the Mosaic law.

"As he dealt with us, so will I deal with him; there is no bond with traitors. An eye for an eye, a tooth for a tooth. It is just. Go! fetch the man he strove hardest to destroy. He is in Venice; bring him here."

The weaker nature of his son trembled as he touched, at last, the liberty, the atonement, the avenging blow for which he had so long thirsted. The slave had been a slave so long, he trembled before the daring that would loose his chains.

"But only to have shared such infamy was so vile! I cannot bear that *he* should know us its accomplices——"

"Silence! What matter? We were beasts of burden; we carried what loads our master laid on us,—dead men or blood-stained weapons. Go; bring him quickly!— quickly! Do you hear?"

An ashen hue stole over the bronze of his face, his lips were pressed in a straight line under the flowing of his beard, his hands moved with a swift impatient movement. Agostino looked up at him in fear.

"Father! wait. You are too weak."

The old man's voice rang, stern and imperious, across his own.

"I shall be strong to do this ere I die. Go to him; tell him I will give him his vengeance. Go to him; I command you—bring him here."

The inflexible command brooked no disobedience; it swayed his listener with the old force of the Jewish parental power. Agostino was once more the youth before his father's might, under his father's hand. He dared dispute no longer.

The old man sat, and waited. Moments seemed hours to him; the flame of his life was burning low, he dreaded lest it should die out ere it should have time to shine upon his vengeance and light the fires that would devour his tyrant's fame and crumble it to ashes in the sight of men. His pulse beat faintly, his heart was oppressed, his limbs felt chill as ice; but he had said that he had strength in him to do this thing ere he passed away among the vanished crowds; and he sat there with his ears straining eagerly, his lips braced, his whole force strung, to keep him in the powers of thought and speech and memory, on which his hold was now fast slackening.

His son knelt near him; he had sent the bidding to the one whom it summoned, and he crouched near like a beaten dog. For the moment, he had panted to break his bonds at any cost; but the vehemence of that impulse had its reaction; he felt sick with shame, he trembled with dread: the whip had done its invariable, inevitable work; it had made the spaniel a coward to the core. Moreover, he loathed his own sins; he held himself viler than the harshest judge would ever have held him, and he feared unspeakably the sight of the man who had cleaved to honour at all cost, the man whom he might have saved, had he but had the courage to risk a personal peril.

Where the Hebrew sat with his head bent forward, his hand clenched on the wood-work near him, his quick hearing caught a distant sound; his lips moved eagerly.

"He comes! Bring him,—bring him quickly! Let me speak while I can!"

Agostino started to his feet, and staggered out, at the imperious command—out into the gloom of the stone passages. From the wild night without, Chandos entered. The storm had risen afresh, the lashing of water and wind had beaten on the black sea-piles, the darkness of the hot tempestuous air was impenetrable, the rains were pouring down in torrents; through the tempest, heedless that his hair was drenched and that the lightning scorched his eyes, he had come, with but one memory on him, with but one hope,—his vengeance.

Passionate as his love was, dear as his heritage, closely as he had cloven to a barren honour through barren years of bitterness, he would have been capable in that instant of throwing honour and heritage and love away, if by them only he could have purchased this one thing. No life so utterly and so surely attains strength, that it may not give way and fall at the last; no life is so absolutely free of baser passions, that when the slaughter-lust is on it, it may not reel headlong into crime.

As he entered, with the glow of passion upon his face, on which the grief that the day had borne and the light of recovered happiness mingled, there was in him the beauty that the Spanish lad had likened in the days of his youth to the golden-haired sovereign of Syria; and as Agostino saw him, involuntarily, unconsciously, he threw himself at the feet of this man, whose wrongs he had buried in silence through the pusillanimity of a selfish terror; he abased himself there as Eastern slaves before their rulers.

"Forgive me, if you can! I can never forgive my-self. I was like one who sees a murder done, and will not raise his voice to stay the lifted blade, lest it be thrust into his own throat instead. I loved you,—honoured you,—though your eyes never fell on me but twice in my boyhood; and yet I never told you where the assassin hid!"

Chandos forced him upward by sheer strength; light flashed from his eyes, his lips parted with fevered eager-ness, his whole frame thrilled with one desire alone.

"If see who you are, I see what you know. If you can give me vengeance, there is no guilt on earth *I* will not pardon you. Vengeance, I say! Give me but JUSTICE, and it will beggar the widest vengeance that men ever took. Your father sent for me: lead on,—quick!"

The softness of his love, the bereavement of the noon, were alike flung off him as though they had no place in his life; the world held nothing for him save this only,—a lifetime of wrong, left unavenged so long.

Agostino looked at him in one fleeting look; then the crouched, shuddering, beaten shame came on him that had moved him when in the oak-forest he had seen the hopeless melancholy of the face that he had once known brilliant as the Spanish sun that had shone on them when they had first met. He had lived in the world, he had made fame, he had carried himself fairly before men; but he had been but a slave, and a slave's weakness and prostration were in his nature for ever.

He gave a heart-sick, shivering sigh.

"Ah, *you* may pardon, but I cannot pardon myself. You have known calamity and desolation; but you have never known the worst pang of all,—to be disgraced in your own eyes!"

Even in that moment the anguish of the accent reached and touched his hearer. He turned and looked an instant on the face that he had once seen in its boyish grace, with the hot amber light of Granada upon it.

"He who feels disgrace so keenly is on the surest road to leave it behind him for ever. Now, lead on,—quick, for the sake of Heaven!"

The wax-like, flexible, impressive nature of the Castilian Jew was awed and stilled by the might of the avenging power he had summoned. He led the way in silence,—led him into the great chamber where the blind man sat, lonely and old and poor, but grand as the sightless seer of Chios.

The light from above beamed on the massive bronze

of his forehead and on the snow-white falling beard. His
eyes strained into the gloom they could not pierce; he
rose at the sound of the footstep, and stood erect as
the Prophet of his own rabbinical tale, when he rose
to bless the Israel whom his taskmaster had bade him curse.

"Come hither," he said, briefly, and his voice gathered
the force of his manhood. "You craved a perilous thing,
and I refused it; the lust is mine now, and I will yield
you what you sought. 'He who rises by the sword shall
perish by the sword:' it is just. You shall deal with him
as by the law of Moses:—'every man shall be put to
death according to his sin.' Come hither and listen while
my lips have still speech."

Where Chandos stood against him, his face was eager
with a fiery hunger, flushed and set with a mighty passion; his breath caught in quick gasps.

"But—your oath?"

The bond was not his, yet he remembered the
sanctity of the vow that had been in his path as a rock.

His slight ironic smile wavered an instant over the
Jew's stern mouth.

"Sir, you are thrice a madman! You guard other
men's honour as well as your own, even to your own
hindrance. Be at rest. My oath is broken justly. It
was sworn for so long as my son was saved by him. He
has cursed my son; I am released. Traitors shall be
slain by their own weapons. I was silent and faithful
whilst I believed silence and fidelity due. He has been
false to me; the bond is rent by his own hand. You said
aright in the night that is past; he whom I served was
your enemy."

The oak-wood of the bench on which his hands were
clenched broke like a reed in Chandos' grasp as he heard.
He had known this iniquity ere yet it had been told; but

its utterance fell on him like the stroke of an iron mace.
His foe's life, had it been by him in that one moment, had
not been worth a moment's purchase; it would have been
broken asunder as the strong rail was snapped in his hands.

"Tell me all," he said, briefly.

"Sir, to tell you all the iniquity that *I* wrought were
to speak for a score of years, and I shall not live as
many minutes," said the Israelite, in his grave, caustic
satire. "'When thou cuttest the harvest in the field,
leave a sheaf for the fatherless,' said the law. Well, we
kept the law so well that we sheared the last wheat-ear
from every land in our reach. 'No man shall take the
millstones to pledge; for he taketh a man's life to pledge,'
the law has written. Well, we obeyed so well that we
took the millstones and ground the life to powder between them. But, of all that we wronged, we wronged
you most. You had had mercy on him when he was a
debtor and wretched; you had given him food, and
shelter, and comfort and friendship, and the smile of
the world; and in payment he wrung your life dry of all
wealth and all peace, as men wring a skin dry of wine."

He paused; life was flickering dully and feebly in
him. Chandos shook with rage where he heard.

"Do you think I have not known *that?* More,—
more! To be told my wrongs is no vengeance."

"Patience. Your vengeance lies in them. Your enemy
never broke the laws of his land; he was too wary in
wisdom: he plundered, but he plundered within the
statutes. The worst felons are those who can never be
brought to the bar. He persuaded you to waste your
substance; he drew it—much of it—into his hands; but
it was always you who signed your own death-warrant.
I have had your signatures by the hundred; the sums
they signed away were cheated from you, because lies

were told you of their use and their purport; but you were very careless in those matters, and he was very able. There is not one of them that is forged; they were all legal, though they were villanies."

"Oh, God; is he never to be reached, then?"

It rang out from him in a loud cry, like the cry of a drowning man from whose hands the last plank slips.

"Patience! Have I not said you shall have your vengeance and mine? You cannot bring him to the felon's dock, but you shall gibbet him in the sight of the nations; you shall rend his robes asunder; you shall tread his crowns beneath his feet. Half—nay, a tithe—of what I can tell would suffice to drive him out in shame and cover his head with ignominy. The breath of his life now is to be untainted before the country that holds him a chief; lay bare his corruption, and ruin will blast him, he will fall, stricken to the roots."

His breath caught, his cheek grew ashen; the strength was dying in him, and the stagnant course of his blood was nigh ceasing for ever; but he had a ruthless will, he forced life back to him, and his words rang clear as a herald's menace.

"Let me say the chief thing first; my breath will fail ere you know one-thousandth part. Briefly, take my signet-ring, here, to one of my people in Paris—Joachim Rosso, a worker in silver,—in the street where you found me. At that sign, bid him give you the sealed papers he keeps for me. He knows nothing of what is in them; but he has guarded them for me many years. He is a good friend and faithful. In them you will find the record of all I have no strength to tell you,—the proofs of the trade that your foe and I drove in men's necessities. This Englishman, my bondmaster, was very keen, very wise; and when he held me by my son's danger and by my

own gratitude, he held me by iron chains; he knew he
could trust me to suffer anything and keep silence.—But"
—his sardonic smile passed over his lips—"he dealt with
a Jew, and the Jew could meet the fox with a fox's
skill. He had heavily weighted me into slavery; and
while I believed him true to the lad, my tongue should
have been rooted out rather than be made to utter one
syllable against him. But a Jew's life is lived only to
cheat, they say; and I outwitted even my tyrant so far.
I kept papers he never knew; I compiled proofs he never
dreamed. Had he been true to me in his dealing with
Agostino, they would have been burnt by Joachim the
day that I died. He broke faith with me; I turn the
blade of his own knife against him; I net him in the
threads of his own subtlety."

There was the sternness of the Leviticus law in the
words as they rolled out from the hollow chest of the
sightless man where he stretched his hands in imprecation.

"As he sowed, so let him reap; as he dealt, so let him
be dealt with; as he filled his unjust ephah with ill-gotten
wheat, so let the bread he has made thereof be like
poison to consume him!"

The fierce unflinching justice thrilled like a curse
through the stillness of the chamber.

Chandos' hand closed on the signet-ring; his face
was very white and through his teeth his breathing came
with a low hissing sound, as though the weight of the
evil of his traitor lay like lead on his chest.

"One word;—my ruin was worked by fraud!"

The Hebrew bent his head, and the red shame that
had before come there in the sight of Chandos flickered
with momentary warmth over the bloodless olive of his
cheek.

"Sir, I duped men without a pang of conscience. I

have said I was very evil. My work throve in my hands so well because I was without one yielding or gentle thing in me. But when we duped *you*, even I shrank. You trusted him so utterly, you were such a madman in your generosity, such a fool in your lack of suspicion, so noble in your utter weakness of carelessness and faith! And I knew that you had served him, fed him, sheltered him,— that you trusted him as a brother. When you were drawn down into our bottomless pit, even *I* abhorred the work!"

"There *was* fraud, then?"

His voice was hoarse; the syllables slowly panted out; till the life of his foe was wholly in his power, he felt as lions feel when cage-bars hold them from their tormentors.

"Fraud?—surely! But I doubt if the law could touch it: it was deftly done. He led you on into a million extravagances; he blinded your sight; he cheated you utterly. You set your name to your friends' bills, and we bought those bills in, and then we wrung the money out of you; you signed what you thought leases and law trifles, and you signed in reality what made you our debtor for enormous sums. You gave him blank cheques; when he filled them up to pay for your pictures, for your horses, for your mistresses' jewels, he drew his own percentage on them all. You gave him fatal power over your properties, and he undermined them. Yet I doubt if, at this distance of time, you could arraign him for fraud. You disputed nothing then; you could scarce dispute now, after the lapse of so many years. It was viler work than murder; he killed you by inches; he drained your blood drop by drop; he made the earth under your feet a hollow crust, and at his signal the crust broke, and you sank into the pit that he had dug. But he kept within the law; he kept within the law!"

There was a world-wide sarcasm in the acrid words;

he had known so many criminals—great men in their nations—whose crimes were never guessed, because "within the law!"

"But what matter! See here." His withered fingers grasped like steel the arm of the man he had aided to rob. "In my papers you will find the whole detail of our business system. You will find the list of the men we helped to ruin. You will see how he stripped bare to the bone the friends whom he fed, and drove, and laughed and jested with. You will see how the chief of his riches was made,—how in real truth he was but a usurer, who churned into wealth the needs of his associates in the world that he fooled. Tell the tale to the world; it will blast him for ever. Show how the man you succoured repaid you. Let them behold the first steps by which their favourite rose to his power; trace the vile subways by which he travelled to dignity. Point to the dead, the exiled, the cursed, whom he dwelt with in friendship while he drove his barter in their shame and their want. Go and unmask him; go and condemn him. You will find proofs in my legacy that will brand him your destroyer and theirs. Go! though he be brought into no felon's dock, you will scourge him, dishonoured for ever, out of the land where he stands now a chief!"

The deep, rich voice of the Hebrew rolled out like an organ-swell; the vitality of manhood was lent for a moment to the wasted powers of age. Faithful through all ordeals to his very grave, he turned in his death-hour to stamp out the traitor whom in that hour he had found false to his bond.

Chandos stood beside him, his lips parted, his eyes filled with fire; his face was dark with the passions of that bloodthirst which had risen in him.

"Dishonour him! dishonour him!" he said, in his ground teeth. "If I slew him, I should be too merciful!"

There was silence for a while in the chamber; they who heard knew the width and the depth of his vast wrong, knew that no chastisement his hand should take could be too deadly. The old man's white head sank, his hands trembled where they were knitted together.

"And forget not that I wronged you equally,—that I forged the steel that pierced and wove the net that bound you! To-night my soul will be required of me; it is dark with evil, as the night is dark with storm. Could it be free of your curse, I could die easier."

Chandos stooped to him; and his voice, though the fire of his hate burned in it, was hushed and gentle with pity.

"My curse! When you succoured what I love! When you render me my vengeance? *No!* equally did you wrong me; you never ate my bread, you never owned my trust. Your martyrdom may surely avail to buy your pardon both from God and man."

The large, slow tears of age welled into the Hebrew's sightless eyes; the hard, brave, ruthless nature was stricken to the core by the mercy it had never yielded; he lifted his hands feebly, and rested them on the bowed head of the man whom he had wronged.

"May the desire of thine eyes be given thee, and thine offspring reign long in the land! May peace rest on thee for ever! for thou art just to the end,—to the end."

Purer blessing was never breathed upon his life than this which his spoiler and his foe now uttered.

Then, as the darkness that had veiled his sight so long was lost in the darkness of death, the old man stretched his arms outward to his son, seeking what his silent unrequited love had found at last only to lose for ever.

"Nearer to my heart! nearer,—nearer. God cherish thee!—God pardon thee! Ah! will any love thee as I

have loved? Death is rest; yet it is bitter. In the grave
I cannot hear thy coming, I cannot hearken for thy step!"

And with his blind eyes seeking thirstily the face so
well beloved, on which they could not look, even to take
one farewell gaze, a deep-drawn sigh heaved the heart
that had been bound under its iron bonds of silence for
so long, the weary limbs stretched outward as a worn way-
farer's stretch upon a bed of rest, and, in a hush of stillness as the tempest lulled, the long life of pain was ended.

CHAPTER IX.
"King over Himself."

THERE was a great banquet in the City of London,—
a banquet held chiefly in honour of the brilliant statesman, the popular favourite, who had quelled the riots of
the North with so fearless a courage, so admirable an
address,—who was the key-stone of his party, the master-
mind of his cabinet, the inspirer of his colleagues, the
triumphant and assured possessor of that virtue of Success which vouches for, and which confers, all other virtues in the world's sight. The gorgeous barbarism, the
heavy splendour, the ill-assorted costly food, the ponder-
ous elephantine festivity, were in his honour; the seas of
wine flowed for his name; the civic dignities were gathered
for his sake; the words he spoke were treasured as though
they were pearls and rubies; the great capital crowned
him, and would have none other than him.

These things wearied other men; this pomp, so coarse
and so senseless and so repeated in their lives, sickened
most whom it caressed as it caressed him; but on Trevenna it never palled. The rich and racy temper in him
never lost its relish for the comedy of life; and the vain-
glorious pleasure of his victories was never sated by the
repetitions that assured him of them. The *Ave Imperator*

was always music on his ear, whatever voices shouted it;
the sense of his own achievement was ever delightful to
his heart, and was never more fully realized than when
there were about him those public celebrations of it,—the
feasting and cheering and toasting and servile prostrating
which to most statesmen are the hardest and most hateful
penalty of power, but in which he took an unflagging
and unaffected pleasure with every fresh assurance of his
celebrity that they brought him. His part in the mighty
farce was played with the elastic vivacity, the genuine
enjoyment, of a jovial humourist; it had no assumption
in it, for it was literally incessant amusement and infinite
jest to him; and the good humour, the mirth, the vitality
with which he came ever among the people, and went
through all the course of public homage and public con-
viviality, were but the cordial expression of the temper
with which he met life.

To-night, at the civic dinner given in his honour, all
eyes turned on him, acclamations had welcomed his entrance, no distinction was held sufficient for such a guest,
and compliment and tribute and reverential admiration
were poured on him in the speeches that toasted his name
and quoted his acts, his fame, his ever-growing strength,
his master-intellect, his place in the councils and in the
love of the nation; and he enjoyed with all a wit's keen
relish the verbiage and the hyperbole and the cant, and
enjoyed but the more for them the ascendency he held,
the fearless footing he had made, the ambitions crowned
to their apex, and the future of ambitions even higher
yet, which had come to the force of his hand, to the com-
pelling of his genius. Of a truth he was a great man,
and he knew it; he had brought to his conquest such
patience and such qualities as only great men possess; he
was a giant whose tread was ever certain, whose eyes

ever saw beyond his fellows, whose armour was ever bright, whose grasp was ever sure. It was natural that on the breathless, pushing, toiling weaknesses of the Lilliputians around him he should look with a Rabelaisan laugh, with a Sullan contemptuousness of unflinching and unsparing victory.

The banquet ended early; for a measure of considerable moment was passing,—a measure framed and carried through two readings by himself, and its third reading was to take place with the present night. The crowded feast had given him all the idolatry and applause of the City of London,—given it with wines, and massive meats, and soups, and sauces, and gold plate, and interminable speeches, as is its custom in that strange antithetical relic of barbarism which must gluttonously feed what it intellectually admires; and from it he went to the arena of his proudest conquest, to the field in which it is so hard to keep a footing when against the wrestler is flung the stone "adventurer,"—to the place where many mediocrities pass muster, but where a combination of qualities the most difficult to gain and the most rarely met in unison can alone achieve and sustain a permanent and high success. If any had asked him to what crown among his many crowns he attached the proudest value, he would have answered, and answered rightly, to the sway that he had mastered over the House of Commons.

As he drove to Westminster, the carriage rolled past the statue of Philip Chandos at which, going and coming from the councils of his country, he oftentimes glanced with the sweetness of his attainments made sweeter by the look he cast at that colossal marble, which he would banter and talk to and jeer at with that dash of buffoonery which mingled with the virile sagacious force of his nature as it has mingled with many a great man's acumen.

"Ah!" he murmured to himself now, with a cigar in his teeth, as he caught sight of it in the gaslight, "the Mad Duke's been shot in a brawl, they say,—in the only end fit for him. *I* will have your Clarencieux, now. Crash shall go the old oaks, and we'll smelt down the last Marquis's coronet into a hunting-cup for *me* to drink out of; my hounds should have their mash in it, only the nation might think me insane. Is there anything you particularly loved there, I wonder? If there were, it should be flung in the fire. The great hall was your beggared successor's special pride. Well, we'll burn it down when I get there,—by accident on purpose! A flue too hot will soon lay its glories in ashes. *Tout vient à point à qui sait attendre.*"

All things had come to his hand, and ripened there to a marvellous harvest; but even the exultation of success and the gravity of power had not changed in him the woman-like avidity of hatred, the grotesque rapacity of spoliation, which he still cherished against the inanimate things of gold and silver and stone and wood which had been the household gods of the race he cursed. It remained the single weakness in a steel-clad life.

As he entered the House, to which he had once come on suffrage, and which he had made the scene of as complete a triumph as the perseverance and the ability of man ever wrung from hostile fortune and hostile faction, all eyes turned eagerly on him. There was the murmur of welcome and impatience; the benches were all full, at midnight, with a crowded and heated audience. His measure had been received with a vehement partisanship, violence in opposition, violence in alliance; and his coming was watched for at once with irritation and anxiety. He made his way to his seat, cool, keen, bright,—as he would have gone alike to be crowned as a king or to be

hanged as a scoundrel. Moments of emergency were the
tonics that he loved best, the wine that gave the fullest
flavour of his life; and none could have arrived to him
that would ever have found him unprepared,—none save
one which to-night waited for him.

Other members had risen as he entered, but. there
were loud imperious cries for his name; the Commons
were in one of their turbulent tempers, when they riot
like ill-broke hounds, and they would have none other
than the man who had learned to play upon their varying
moods as a skilled hand plays on an organ. He had
brought his measure through the tempestuous surf of two
readings; it was now for him to ride it through the last
breakers and pass it into the haven by which it would
become law. It was thought strangely careless that he
should be late on such a night; but this was the temper
of the man,—to be daringly independent at all hazards,
and to take his revenge on a party that had been glad of
him, but that had never fairly relished his alliance, by
caprices which made them wait his pleasure, which kept
them ever uncertain of his intentions, and for which his
popularity gave him full and free immunity.

As he rose to speak, the winged words paused on his
lips, his eyes grew fixed with a set, astonished gaze; he
stood for a moment silent, with his hand lying on the
rail; his glance met that of Chandos.

Among the nobles and the strangers who had come
down to listen to the debate, he saw the form that he had
once seen senseless and strengthless on the wretched
pallet in a Paris garret, where he had watched the throb-
bing of the heart under the naked breast, and had thought
that he would have well loved to still it for ever with an
inch of steel, had not a wider torture been found in letting
it beat on to suffer. The burden of the years seemed

fallen from Chandos, and to him had returned, though saddened and grave with thought, and with a melancholy that would never now wholly pass away, much of the proud, sun-lightened beauty of his early manhood. The vivid sweetness of passion was once more his; the inheritance of his fathers was recovered; the might of avenging justice had been given to his hand; above all, *he was an exile no more.* He looked as he had looked in the days of the past.

The animal thirst to kill, of which he had spoken, had risen; his veins seemed to run fire; there was a wild triumph in his blood even while the heart-sickness at his traitor's baseness was upon him. It was his to avenge, to chastise, to pay back a lifelong wrong, to unmask a lifelong infamy, to hurl his foe from the purples of power and point out in the sight of the people the plague-spot on the breast of the man they caressed. It was his, this vengeance which would cast his traitor down, in the midst of the fulness of life, from the height of his throned successes. It was his at last, this power denied so long, which should pierce the bronze of his enemy's laughing mockery and shatter to dust the adamant of his invulnerable strength. It was his at last, this avenging might which should reach even the brute heart that had seemed of granite, callous to feel, impenetrable to strike. And he felt drunk with it as with alcohol; he felt that its worst work would never plough deep enough, never blast wide enough.

"O God," he thought, "how can vengeance *enough* strike him? None can give me back all that he killed for ever! 'Just to the end.' He shall have justice,—the justice of the old law,—a 'life for a life.'"

And, as their eyes met, the chill of the first fear his life had ever known passed over Trevenna; a vague, shapeless horror seized him; he knew that never would the disinherited have returned to his forsaken land unless the doom of banishment had been taken from him, unless some power of all that he had been dispossessed of had recoiled back into his grasp. For the moment—one brief, fleeting, uncounted second—he stood paralyzed there, the unformed dread, the venomous hatred in him making him forgetful of all, save the eyes that were turned on him, eyes that seemed to quote against him the whole history of his life. He had no conscience, he had no shame, he had never known what fear was, and he had ascended to an eminence from which he would have defied the force of the world to eject him; and yet in that single instant a terror scarce less keen, less ghastly, than that which an assassin would feel at sight of the living form of the prey he had left for dead, came on him as in the lighted assembly, in the midnight silence in which his own words were awaited, he saw the face of Chandos.

It passed away almost as instantaneously as it had moved him; the bold audacity, the dauntless courage, the caustic mirth, the mocking triumph of his temper re-asserted themselves; instantly, ere any others had had space to note the momentary pause, and the momentary paralysis which had arrested the eloquence on his lips and chained his gaze to the features of the man whom he had wronged, he was himself again; he recovered the shaken balance of his priceless coolness; he looked across the long space parting him from his antagonist with a full, firm, laughing insolence in the sunny bravery of his blue eyes; his voice rolled out on the hushing murmurs and the broken whispers of the great gathering, mellow, resonant, far-reaching as a clarion, clear as though each syllable were told out on a silver drum.

The man he hated was before him; the man in whom

he had seen incarnated all the things against which his
life had been arrayed, all the wrongs that he had cherished
till the cockatrice brood had bred a giant's vengeance;
the man whom he had hated but the more, the more he
injured him; the man whom he best loved, of any in the
world, should see the eminence, the power, the sovereignty
which he—the adventurer, the outsider—had aspired to
and won. Chandos was before him, witness of his sway,
spectator of his triumph, hearer of his words. He swore
in his teeth, even in that moment when their glance first
met, that oratory and triumph and sway should never be
so victorious as they should be to-night; that he would
fight as he had never fought, that he would win as he
had never won, that this chamber should ring with acclamations for him as it had never yet rung with them,
favoured and crowned there though he was. The one
whom of all others in the breadth of the empires he would
have chosen as the beholder of his fame fronted him. To
Trevenna the hour was as it was to Sulla when the great
desert King whom he had conquered and weighted with
chains, and brought from the golden suns and royal freedom of his own warm land to the bath of ice of the Tullianum, stood fettered to behold the ovation given to the
welcomed victor of the Jugurthine War.

To Trevenna it was the crown of the edifice that his
own mighty patience and unresting brain had raised out
of the dust and ashes of a banned and nameless life,
when into his own arena, before his own idolaters, the
man in whom the whole passions of that life had seen
their deepest hate embodied came to behold his triumph.
Though he should have died for it with the dawn, he
would have made that night the night of his supreme
success, or perished. There was in him the temper which
in old days made men take oath to their gods to gain

the battle, though they should, as its price, be cast headlong to the foe. In that moment he rose beyond egotism
into something infinitely grander; in that moment, however guilty, he was great.

And he spoke greatly.

The fire of personal hate, the weakness of personal
triumph, did but serve as spur and as stimulant to the
genius in him. To know that the eyes of Chandos looked
on him was to lash his strength into tenfold performance;
to know that Chandos heard his words was to form them
into tenfold eloquence. It was not only to invective, to
rhetoric, that he rose; but the brilliance of thought, the
closeness of argument, the fineness of subtlety, the vastness of memory, were beyond compare. Men who had
held him a master ere this listened breathless, and marvelled that even they never had known what his power
could be. Wit, reason, learning, raillery, wisdom, and
logic were pressed, turn by turn, into his service, and
used with such oratory as had rarely rung through that
chamber. He was what he had never been; he surpassed
all that he had ever achieved; and when his last words
closed, thunder on thunder of applause rolled out as in
the days when Sheridan bewitched or Chatham awed the
listening and enchanted crowds. Once his eyes flashed
on Chandos as the cheers reeled through the body of the
House; no other caught that glance in which the victory
of a lifetime was expressed.

He to whom it was given saw it, and his head sank
slightly; darkness gathered over his face; the thought of
his heart was bitter, less in that moment for himself than
of mankind. He thought, "How great, to be so vile!"

That night was the proudest of John Trevenna's triumphs.

The bill passed, carried by an overwhelming majority,

which secured stability to the Treasury benches and sealed
the trust of the nation in them. If he had been high in
men's fame and favour before, he was unapproached now,
as on their tongues through the whole of the late night
his name and his genius alone were spoken. For it had
been genius to which he had risen, genius that had given
the fire to his words, the persuasion to his speech, the
resistless force to his command, that had borne him
out of himself into that loftier power which makes of men
as they listen the reeds that sway to the wind of the
magical voice,—genius that had wakened in him under
the consciousness of one glance that watched, of one ear
that heard. And for once, in its pride and its dominion,
caution and coolness slightly forsook him; his eyes glittered,
his forehead was flushed, his smile laughed as one warmed
with wine, as he went out to the night.

As the air of the dawn blew on his face, his shoulder
was grasped by a hand that forced him forward. Chandos' words were spoken low on his ear:—

"Out yonder!—come in peace, or I shall forget myself, and deal with you before the men you fool."

Trevenna gave one swift glance upward. Though
bold to the core with a leonine courage, he shrank, and
quailed, and sickened. That one glance told him more
than hours could have spoken. He felt as though a knife
had been plunged and plunged again into his heart, seeking
the life and draining his blood.

"Lead on!" he said, between his teeth; "lead on,
whatever you want. You and I need not waste pretty
words, *beau sire.*"

He felt the hand that was on his shoulder clench closer
and closer till it tightened like an iron clasp. In the
darkness, through the throngs, under the fitful glare of
the gas, the pressure of that hand forced him away out

of the masses and the noise and the tumult of the streets,
down into the quiet of the cloisters, where the grey beauty
of the Abbey rose in the haze of the starless mists of earliest dawn.

Then, where they stood alone under the darkling pile,
that clasp loosed its hold and flung him backward as men
fling snakes off their wrist. Chandos faced him in the
dim grey solitude; the passions that had been held in rein
whilst he watched for his foe broke loose as he stood
alone with the man whose present held so proud an eminence, whose past he had traced into such sinks of villany,
whose favour was so sightless in the nation's sight, whose
guilt had been so vile to net, and pierce, and drain, and
rob, and ruin him.

"You have fooled your world for the last time to-night;
with another day it will know you as you are,—you usurer
who traded in your friends' worst needs!"

The words cut the air like the cords of a scourge lead-
weighted. In that instant it was all he could do not to
stamp out under his feet the life before him, as men tread
out an unclean beast whose breath is poison. Ere the
words were spoken, Trevenna had known that the day of
his retribution had come to him,—a day his acumen had
never foreseen, a day his skill had never forecast. One
glance had told him that his prey had changed to his
accuser, that the man he had exiled and beggared and
reviled had come back to take his vengeance. For a
moment the sickness of the despair that he had often
dealt, and often laughed at, blinded him, and made the
pale shadow of the stormy dawn reel round him: the next,
his blood rose before peril, and his wit grew but keener
in danger. He planted himself firmly, with his arms
folded across his chest.

"We need not waste pretty words, but we need not

use such ugly ones," he said, coolly. "If you called me out to talk libel, why—there are courts in which you'll have to make it good. You always *were* bitter about my success; but you needn't be tragic. You're savage, I suppose, because the Mad Duke's dead, and I shall get my way and buy up Clarencieux for auld lang syne!"

Chandos' hands fell once more on both his shoulders, swaying him back, and holding him motionless there, as they had held the frail form of the musician under the marble Crucifixion at Venice. In the gloom his eyes burned down into his foe's; his face was darkly flushed and mercilessly set, as though it were cast in stone: the muscles swelled like cords upon his arms and throat. He could have strangled this vampire that had drained all the best life of his youth!—the worst chastisement that he could ever wreak was so tardy, so tame, so vain, so ill-proportioned, beside the vastness of his wrongs!

"Speak one more lie, and I shall kill you. Clarencieux is mine; but for your infamy, I had never lost it. Silence! —silence, I tell you, or I shall choke you like a dog! The Jew who was your victim and your tool confessed all to me in his dying hour. Not a thing in your life is hidden from me; not a thread in your network of villany has escaped me. You are free of the law, perhaps,—you were too wise to break it in the letter; but the world shall know you as I know you; the world shall be your judge and my avenger. I will give you justice,—pure justice. I will unmask you as you are, and leave the rest to follow. The men you ruined, the friends you traded in, the usuries that made your wealth, the frauds you worked under a legal shield, the treacherous, shameless, accursed trade you drove in the lives of those who trusted you and fed you and sheltered you,—I shall leave my vengeance to them; they will repay it more utterly than I could now if I laid you dead, like the snake you are!"

Where Trevenna stood, his bright and fearless face grew white as a woman's, a tremor shook him as the wind shakes a leaf, a cold sweat was dank on his forehead: he answered nothing; he was too wise to dream of vain denial, too bold still to betray terror; but he knew that he had fallen into the power of the one living man whose most merciless vengeance would be but sheer and simple justice; he knew that the serpent of his unsparing hate had recoiled and fastened its venomous fangs into his own veins; he knew that the antagonist who stood above him, holding him there in that grasp of steel, would speak no more than he had power to work out to the uttermost letter; he knew that from that hour, at Chandos' will and choice, the magnificent superstructure of his proud ambitions would crumble like a toy of sand, and the bead-roll of his riches and his dignities wither like a scroll in fire under the scorch of shame. The agony and desolation of a lifetime were pressed into that one instant, which seemed eternity.

Yet the courage in him neither cowed nor pleaded.

"It is easy to put lies in dead men's mouths!" he said, with his old insolence; "and Jews have borne false witness since the world began. It will take a little more than a vamped-up slander to unseat *me*, mon beau monsieur!"

Chandos swayed him to and fro as though he were a child. The voice, the glance, the presence of his enemy maddened him; he feared the work of his own passions; he felt drunk with the delirium of hate and wrong.

"Silence!—if you care for your own life,—you traitor, who ate my bread and betrayed me, who took my shelter and robbed me! The commerce you drove in men's miseries, the friends you netted into your bondage, the thefts that made up your wealth, the secrets you stole to trade in, the slaves you ruled with your tyrannies,—I know them; with another day, the world will know them through me. Listen! All the evil you churned into gold with that dead Hebrew for your tool, all the years that you throve on that barter of men's disgrace and men's fears, all the iniquities that went to make up your rise into wealth, all the tortures you dealt on the servant who served you so faithfully, when, to screen your own crime, you sent him out in old age among felons, all the shame and the sin of your past, I know, and can prove to disgrace you for ever. I warn you; I will not have so much likeness with you as to steal on you, even in justice, like a thief in the night; but—as God lives—if the law fail to give me redress, I will so blast your name through all Europe, that the foulest criminal who hides for a murder shall be held to be worthier than you, — you who slew like Iscariot, never knowing Iscariot's remorse. Sum up the lives you destroyed; they will be your accusers, they will be my avengers!"

The breathless magnificence of the fiery wrath was poured out on the hush of the night; the moment in which every joy and power he had possessed had been struck down by his enemy's hand was dealt back at last, as with one blow he shivered to the dust the honours, the dignities, the ambitions, the victorious and secure successes of the career that had so bitterly mocked, so mercilessly cursed, his own.

Trevenna staggered slightly, and an oath of prurient blasphemy was crashed through the locked firmness of his clenched teeth. He saw at a glance how he had been given over to his antagonist's power; he knew without words how out of the multitude of his unmatched successes

one rope-strand had given way and dragged the whole
superb edifice of a life's labours with it. He never denied:
he was too keen to sham a guiltlessness that would have
availed nothing save to render him contemptible; he never
gave a sign of terror: he was too bold not even in that
moment to retain his courage. But he laughed,—a hard
rasped, bitter laugh, that sounded horribly on the silence.
In that instant of supreme peril, of utter desolation, the
keenest pang to him was not even his own extremity, his
own shame, but was the restoration of the disinherited to
the land of his birth and of his love; it was stranger still,
though part and parcel of his nature, that the cynic
humour of his temper found a broad farcical mockery of
himself in the ruin that recoiled on him in the hour of
the most splendid domination his genius had ever yet
attained.

He saw that the man he had wronged knew how he
had wronged him; he saw that enough had been told of
the ruined lives which had been the stones to upbuild the
stately temple of his celebrity and his eminence, to drive
him out for ever a dishonoured outlaw; but he laughed
for all that, and his eyes, glittering like blue steel through
the mists, met those of Chandos without flinching.

"Life's a see-saw; I always said so. Are *you* going
to ride atop again? Scarcely fair; you fooled away such
lordly chances!"

"I fooled away my faith, and gave it to a liar and a
trickster, who took my hand in friendship while he stabbed
me in the back!"

"Damn you! I hated you; I never said I didn't. I
cursed you 'in your uprising and your downlying,' as the
'man after God's own heart' cursed *his* enemies."

"And why? How had I ever wronged you?"

"Did you never guess?"

He spoke with the snarl of a bulldog at bay; an agony was on him as intense as the worst torture he had ever dealt to others; but the firmness of his attitude never changed, and his voice, though bitter as gall, never shook.

Chandos' eyes dwelt on him with the kingly scorn with which the eyes of Viriathus might have looked upon the traitor lieges who sold him for Roman gold to Roman steel.

"You ate my bread, and betrayed me; it was enough to beget your hate."

Wider rebuke no words ever uttered.

Under them, for the instant of their utterance, a red flush burnt in Trevenna's face, a pang of shame smote a shameless heart. The memory of both went backward to that distant time when no gift had been too great for the royal largesse of the one to lavish on the other, whose only coin of requital had been—treachery.

"Well, that *was* enough,—more than enough. We're all cuckoos at soul, and kick out those who feed us. But my hate went further back than that. I hated you when you were a child, and I trampled out your sweetmeats in the street. I hated you when I was an ugly young clown, and you rode with your servants after you and your gold hair a-flying in the wind. I hated you when you were a baby-aristocrat, when you were a boy-patrician. I hated your laugh, and your voice, and your womanish beauty; and I swore to pull you down and get up in your place. I cursed you then, as I curse you now!"

The intense virulence that ran through the words left no doubt of their veracity.

Chandos, where he stood, gazed at him mute with amaze; to his own knowledge, he had never beheld this enemy of his whole life until the days of his young manhood, when with his gold he had released from a debtors'

prison one who had proved the tempter and destroyer
of all he owned on earth. This animosity that stretched
out to the childish years of his bright infancy stole on
him like the cold, clinging, sickly coils of an asp.

"Are you a madman?" he said, under his breath. "In
my childhood!—how could I wrong you then?"

Trevenna looked at him doggedly, with a red sullen
fire in his blue eyes, like the angry flame in a mastiff's
eyeballs. It was deadly as death to him to part with
that one secret,—the secret of his life.

"Answer me! answer! or, by God, I shall do worse
to you! Why was it?"

"Because I was your father's bastard!"

The reply left his lips very slowly; to him it was as the
drawing of a jagged steel out of a deep festering wound.

His listener fell back as though a shot had struck him,
his face death-white, his eyes dilated with abhorrence.

"Great God! *My* father's!——"

Trevenna laughed,—a short contemptuous laugh.

"Ay! why not? You dainty gentlemen never remember your illegitimate sons and brothers that are flung off
to go to hell as they will; but they may crop up awk-
wardly in spite of you. They are unowned mongrels,
banned before they're born; but they've the same blood
in them as you have."

Chandos breathed heavily; a sickening loathing was
upon him.

"It is false! false as your own life!—a fraud vamped
up to cover your own villany. You have no bond of
blood with mine!"

"*But* for that bond of blood, you would have been
free from me. I have as much of your ancestry in me
as you have."

The words were dogged, but they bore truth with

them. Chandos lifted his arm with an involuntary gesture to silence with a blow the lips that claimed kinship with him.

"You hound! you dare to say that Philip Chandos——"

"Was my father just as much as he was yours. Curse him and his memory both! Pshaw! You can strike me if you like; I only say the truth. Look here. I loved my mother; I never loved anything else;—even mongrels love their dams, you know!—and she was one of your father's mistresses. He paid her off when he married a Duke's daughter,—paid handsomely, that I don't deny, but she neither forgot nor forgave, and she trained me to avenge her. She used to take and show me you in all your grace and your luxury, and she would say in my ear, 'There is your father's heir: when you are both men, make him change places with you.' I was taught to hate and destroy you, as other boys are taught their prayers. I did it thoroughly, I fancy. I'd vengeance for a foster-nurse, and sucked hate as Caligula sucked blood: both Caligula and I took to the milk kindly! I had as much of the famous 'Clarencieux race' in me as you had; and you had all the gifts of the gods, while I was a nameless, cross-breed cur, only bred to be kicked to the streets. *You* won the chariot-race, while the people shouted, 'A patrician!'—*I* was sent out to wrestle with the base-born in the Ring of Cynosarges. Well, I swore with Themistocles to drag in the Eupatrid to wrestle with the Bastard, and teach him that the Bastard could throw him. Don't you know *now* why I hated you?"

Chandos stood silent, livid, breathless; this endless hate borne to him from his birth up seemed to press on him with a weight like granite; this kinship claimed to him by the traitor, whose guilt he would have compassed heaven and earth to have exposed and have arraigned, revolted him with a loathing horror.

"Why?—why?" he echoed, mechanically. "No!—you are only viler than I knew before. What wrong had I ever wrought you?"

"How had Abel wronged Cain? By having the favour of earth and heaven!" said Trevenna between his teeth, that were still tight-shut. "I hated you because I was not as you were. Every good you did me, every gift you gave me, every liberality that marked you the noble and I the adventurer,—you the patron and I the debtor, —only made me hate you the more, only made me swear the more to tempt and hunt and drag you down, and see your pride in the dust, and your heritage given to the spoilers, my brilliant, careless, kingly *brother!*"

The word hissed through the stillness of the dawn with the lust of a Cain centred in it. If a word could have slain, that word should have slaughtered.

Chandos shivered as he heard it,—such a shiver as will pass through the bravest blood when the gleam of an assassin's knife flashes out through the gloom. The bond that his vilest foe claimed to him seemed to taint and shame him with its own pollution.

"This cuts you hard? Come! I have some vengeance yet, then. You can't break our kinship! But—you are just; you will be just to me," pursued Trevenna. "I knew that I had the making of a great man in me, and I was born into the world cursed beforehand as a harlot's son whom every fool could jibe at. I knew that I had the brain and the strength and the power to reach the highest ambitions, and I found myself clogged at the starting-point with the ton-weight of bastardy. I was shut out from every fair chance, because my mother had worn no gold toy on her finger: my whole existence was damned, because a bar sinister stretched across it. The blot on my birth, as idiots call it, was the devil that tempted me; and no gifts and no good faith of yours could touch me while you remained what I envied: they only made me hate you the more, because now and then they burned down into what cant will call Conscience. I hated the world; I hated your order; I hated your race and your house, and all things that were yours. I swore that I would win in the teeth of it all; I swore that I would conquer, cost what it should. I was guilty, you'd say; pshaw! what of that? 'He who wins is the saint; be who loses, the sinner.' What did I care for guilt, so long as I once had success? I proved the mettle I was made of; I carved my own fortunes; I trod down my own shame under foot so that none ever guessed it; I vindicated my own rights against all the world. I triumphed: what else mattered to me!"

There was a certain dauntless grandeur in the words, despite all the shameless hardihood, the brutalized idolatry of self, that ran in them; his means had been vile, but his indomitable resolve had its element of greatness, and the hour of his direst extremity could not make this man a coward. There was that in the words which, foul as they were to himself, touched Chandos to the same passionate regret for this vileness of nature that ran side by side with this splendour of courage, as had moved him when he listened to the genius of the traitor whose secret villanies he came to unmask and avenge.

"Oh, Christ!" he cried, involuntarily, "with so much greatness, how could you sink into such utter shame? Why have hated and tortured me? Why not have trusted me?"

For the moment, over Trevenna's face a softer, better look passed, though it died instantly. This man, whom he had wrought worse work on than murderers do, knew the depths of his iniquity, and yet had a noble regret for him!

"*Why!* Don't you know what hate is, that you ask?" he said, savagely. "Oh, I don't lie to you now, because you have got me at last in your power! I would not recall one thing in the past if I could. You suffered: I would suffer a hell myself to know that. You have your Clarencieux back! Well, that is more bitter to me than the shame that you threaten. But you will never have back the years that I ruined!"

Chandos moved to him with a sudden impulse, as a lion moves to spring.

"Are you devil incarnate? God! Can you face me now and think without one pang of remorse of all you robbed from me for ever? My wealth, my treasures, my lands, were as nothing; it was the years that you killed, the youth that you murdered, the faith that you withered, that you can never restore! I would forgive you the gold that you stole, and the riches you scattered; but the life that you slew in me,—never!"

He turned away; he was sick at heart, and he could not bear to look on the face of this man who had betrayed him as Judas betrayed, and now claimed the kinship of blood.

Trevenna placed himself in his path.

"One word. You will take your vengeance?"

"I will have justice. You know its measure!"

"Very well! I thank you for your warning. I shall be dead before the sun rises. I do not wait for disgrace while the world holds an ounce of lead in it."

It was no empty menace, no stage-trick of artifice, no piece of melodrame: it was a set and firm resolve. He who had counted no cost all his life through to attain triumph, would not have counted a death-pang to escape defeat.

Chandos' face was dark and weary beyond words, as the paleness of the early dawn shone on it.

"You will end a traitor's life by a suicide's death!
So be it: so died Iscariot."

Trevenna said nothing either in prayer or plea; he stood
with a bold, dogged determination on the features that had
a few moments ago flushed with victorious pride and
lightened with a glow of intellect. He was made of too
tough a courage, too bright a temper, to know a coward's
fear of death; and death to him meant only annihila-
tion, and conveyed no thought of a possible "hereafter."
Yet, as he felt the course of the brave blood through his
veins, the strength of the virile life in his limbs, as he
felt the might and the force of his brain, and the power
of his genius to achieve, an anguish passing any physical pain or poltroon's terror came upon him.

"To kill all *that*, while fools live on, and beget fools
by the million!" he said, ferociously, in his ground teeth.

It was the man's involuntary homage to his own intellect, his irrepressible longing to save, not his body
from its dissolution, but his mind from its extinction. It
was a suffering that had its dignity; it was a regret far
higher and far nobler than a mere regret for the loss of
life.

Chandos stood silent, his face white and set. He thought
how mercilessly his foe had done his best to stamp out
all intellect and peace and power from his own existence,
—how brutally he had doomed him to perish like a dog
in the years of his youth, in the brilliance of his gladness. Trevenna would have but the fate himself that he
had dealt with an unsparing hand. It was no more than
justice, tardy and insufficient justice, take it at its widest.
He lifted his eyes, and turned them full upon his betrayer.

"Did you ever remember that with *me?*"

The one reproach struck a throb that was near akin

to shame from the mailed callousness of Trevenna's conscience; but his gaze did not flinch.

"No," he said, sullenly, "I never did. I would have
killed you a thousand times, if you could have died a
thousand deaths. *You* are right enough; I don't deny it.
You only take blood for blood."

"I do not take even that. I but give you to the
world's chastisement, that the world may know what it
harbours."

"Call it what name you like! Words matter nothing.
You will have your vengeance,—a swift one, but a sure.
See, here, Ernest Chandos. You know what I am, what
I have been. You have seen how I could keep hold of
one purpose through a lifetime; you have seen what eminence and what power I have gained in the teeth of all
arrayed against me. And you know, as we stand here
to-night, that I will never live for one taste of Defeat. I
don't complain; I don't plead,—not I! You are acting
fairly enough. Only put no disguise on it. Let us understand one another. You will take your vengeance, of
course, since you have got one; but you may be sure as
we both live to-night that you shall only find my dead
body to give to the public to kick and to strip. That's
all. It is good Hebrew law,—a life for a life. You've
fair title to follow it. Only, know what I mean to do; I
shall die in an hour."

There was no quiver in his voice; there was no tone
of entreaty: he spoke resolutely, coolly; but to the uttermost iota he meant what he said, and his own death was
as sure as though he had plunged a knife in his entrails.
Chandos shuddered as he heard. All his life through,
the web of Trevenna's subtlety had encompassed him,
and it netted him now. He had a justice to do, in which
the rights of the world met the rights of his own venge-

ance; and by it he would drive out this man, who claimed the same blood as his own, to a suicide's grave, by it he was made to stand and to feel as a murderer! He knew that the hour which should find his traitor self-slaughtered would be but late and meet chastisement of a lifetime's triumphant guilt; and the burden of that slaughter was flung on his hands, so that, giving to justice its course and its due, he was weighted with the life that through justice would fall.

"So be it!" he said, in his throat; "if you die for your crimes, what is that to me? Murderers die for theirs; your brute hatred has been viler than any murderer's single stroke."

"Perhaps so! Well, you can hang me, when I am dead, as high as Haman; but you shall never pillory me *alive.* You give me my death-warrant, and I dare say it's just enough; only remember it's the blood of the man that lies yonder you shed, and *but* for that blood you had never had my hate or my envy. You are just; you'll be just even to me, and put so much down to the credit side when you tell the world of my wickedness. Farewell! If you are to reign again at Clarencieux, tell your heir, when you have one, that the Bastard of your House beat you hollow till he was betrayed by a Jew's fluke, and that even when he was beaten he showed himself still of your cursed race, and died—game to the last."

There was not a touch of entreaty or of shrinking in the firm, contemptuous words; he laughed shortly, as he ended them, and turned away. The caustic mirth, the ironic audacity of his temper, found a terrible satire in his own fall, and triumphed still in the thought of how long and how proudly he had vanquished the race against which he had pitted himself.

Chandos stood motionless; his forehead was wet with

dew; he breathed heavily in the grey twilight, out of whose mists the beauty of the great pile where his father's ashes lay rose dim and shadowy, and mighty as the dead it guarded.

"Just to the end."

The dying words of the Hebrew's blessing came back upon his memory. Which was justice?—to yield up the traitor to the death he merited and the obloquy he had earned, or to remember the birth and the breeding that from its first hour had stained and warped the strong tree which without their fatal bias might have grown up straight and goodly and rich in fruit? Vengeance lay in the hollow of his hand, to slay with or to spare. With the dawn this man would perish,—perish justly in late-dealt retribution for a long career of guilt, of treachery, of base and pitiless hate. He merited a felon's death; let him drift on to a suicide's!

Trevenna stood a moment, in his eyes the red, angry fire of a chained hound still burning, but on his close-braced lips no tremor,—all the courage, all the insolence, all the resolve that were in him summoned to meet the awful chastisement that had suddenly fallen upon him in the plenitude of his power and his pride.

"*Beau sire,*" he said, with that pride of intellect which in its arrogance was far above vanity or egotism, "there is not one of your haughty line who will beat the mongrel for power! You and your people were born crowned; but I have won *my* diadem out of the mud of the sewers and in the face of the whole world set against me. You have nothing so grand in all your princely escutcheon as that. Pshaw! if a dying Hebrew had not turned virtuous and played king's evidence, I'd have had my grave by Philip Chandos yonder, and been even with him to my death.

You have a fine vengeance at last. Few men kill as much brain as you'll kill in *me!*"

He motioned his right hand towards the Abbey, and turned away,—to die before the dawn. The action was slight, and had no supplication in it; but it was very eloquent, — eloquent as were the words in their contemptuous self-vindication, their insolence of self-homage.

Chandos involuntarily made a gesture to arrest him. "Wait!"

The word had the command of a monarch in it. His head sank on his hands, his whole frame quivered; one who had brotherhood with him went out to lie dead with the breaking of day.

"Oh God!" he moaned, in a mortal suffering. "I cannot send you to your death; and yet——"

And yet — his whole soul clung to the justice that would strike the traitor down in his crime: half a lifetime of torture claimed its meet requital. To spare this man passed his strength.

Trevenna mutely watched him without a sign of supplication, but with an acrid, ruthless hate, — the hate of a Cain who saw his brother rise from the murderous blow that had struck him to the earth, and deal back into his own heart the fratricidal stroke.

Chandos stood with his head dropped on his chest, his breathing loud and fast; to let go his vengeance was harder than to part with his own life. The wrongs of years that seemed endless in their desolation bound him to it with bands of iron. Yet he knew that, if he took it, his foe would die ere the sun rose,—die in his guilt, cursing God and men, as he had once bidden his own existence end.

There was a long, unbroken silence.

A justice higher, purer, loftier than the justice of revenge stirred in him; a light like the coming of the day came on his face. He remained true to the vow of the days of his youth, and, though men had abandoned him, he forsook not them nor their God. He was king over himself,—sovereign over his passions. He lifted his eyes and looked at his betrayer; there was that in the gaze of which Shakespeare thought when he wrote, "This look of thine will hurl my soul from heaven!" It spoke wider than words; it pierced more deeply than a death-thrust.

"I give you your life," he said briefly; "learn remorse in it if you can! Go,—and show to others hereafter the mercy you need now."

The words fell gravely on the stillness. Over his enemy's brow a red flush of shame leaped suddenly, his firm limbs trembled, he shook for a moment like a reed under the condemnation which alone bade him go and sin no more. Of mercy he had never thought; as he had never known it, so he had never hoped it. It pierced and beat him down as no revenge could ever have power to do; under it he suffered what he had never suffered. While their lives should last, he knew that bond of pardon would be held unbroken: and for once he was vile and loathsome in his own sight.

"*Damn you!*" he said, fiercely, while his white lips trembled, "you are greater than I at the last! For the first time in my life I wish to God I had not harmed you!"

In the savage words, as they choked in their utterance, was the only pang of remorse that John Trevenna had ever known.

———————

In the vast shadowy space of the porphyry chamber Chandos stood, with the lustre of starlight sleeping at his feet, and the glories of his race made his once more. In the silence, that was only broken by the dreamy distant sound of many waters, he looked upon his birthright,—looked as the long-banished alone look on the land for whose beauty they have been an-hungered through a deadly travail, for whose mere fragrance they have been athirst through the scorch and solitude of desert wastes.

Every sigh of forest leafage came to him like a familiar voice; every breath of woodland air touched his forehead like a caress of one beloved; the odour of the grasses, as the deer trod them out, was sweet to him as joy; the free fresh wind seemed bearing back his youth; the desire of his eyes was given back to him, the passion of his heart was granted him. He gazed, and felt as though no gaze were long enough, on all for which his sight had ached in blindness through so many years of absence; and, where he stood, with the life that he loved folded in his arms and gathered to his heart, his head was bowed, his lips trembled on hers, his strength broke down; the sentence of severance fell off him for evermore.

Through the hush of the night a murmur like the sough of the sea swelled through the silence,—the murmur of a great multitude whose joy lay deep as tears. It was the welcome of a people.

The sound rose, hushed by the death which had given them back their lord, through the stillness of the night, through the endless aisles of forest, reaching the halls of the great race whose sovereignty had returned and whose name was once more in the land.

Where he stood, they saw him; his eyes rested on them in the soft shadows of the night, and his hands were stretched to them in silence,—a silence that spoke beyond words, and fell in turn on them, upon the vast throngs that looked upward to his face, unseen so long, upon the strong men who wept as children, upon the aged who were content to lay them down and die because the one they loved had come to them from his exile; and that hour repaid him for his agony.

He had dealt with his enemy, and reached a mercy that the world would never honour, laid down a vengeance that the world would never know. No homage would ever greet his sacrifice; when death should come to him he must fall beneath the stroke with that victory untold, that foe unarraigned. He would see his traitor triumph, and lift up no voice to accuse him; he would behold men worship their false god, and hold back his hand from the righteous blow. But through bitterness he had cleaved to truth, through desolation he had followed justice, and while men forsook him he had remained constant to them, constant to himself. He had followed the words of the Greek poet; he had been "faithful to the dreams of his youth," and peace was with him at the end.

In the hush of the night, with the sanctity of a people's love upon him, the bitterness of the past died; the crucifixion of his passions lost its anguish; the serenity of a pardon hard to yield, yet godlike when attained, came to him with the self-conquest he had reached, and the promise of the future rose before him,—

Even as the bow which God hath bent in heaven.

THE END.